THORN IN HIS SIDE

HELEN JULIET

Thorn in His Side
Copyright © 2020 by Helen Juliet

DARIUS

It had been a while since Darius Legrand had begun his day contemplating murder. However, extraordinary circumstances called for extraordinary measures.

He let out a guttural bellow as he kicked at his old four-poster bed frame, thrusting his large arms into the blazer that he'd snatched from his wardrobe. He hadn't been expecting company, but as usual his father had appeared unannounced specifically to trip him up. Darius wasn't going to give him the satisfaction of seeing Darius in a tatty rugby jumper, that was for sure. But that had meant changing into a shirt and jacket at the very least. The jeans would have to stay. He didn't have enough time.

Getting dressed was a pain in the arse Darius preferred to tackle only once a day. Even though he'd managed to avoid looking in any mirrors, he was still left with the familiar bitter taste in his mouth and pounding headache that came from being reminded of his body. All in all, his temper was raging by the time he won the battle with the jacket.

"How long's he been waiting?" he asked as he stormed back out from his bedroom.

"About ten minutes now, sir," said Bartholomew dryly, raising a single eyebrow. "You know, it's not too early for whisky."

Bartholomew, Darius's butler and sadly the closest thing he had to a friend these days, was probably right. Under the circumstances, whisky wouldn't be out of the question, even though it was before noon. But Darius's last shred of sense told him to save drinking until after their meeting.

It would undoubtedly be needed more urgently then.

Darius paced like a caged animal across the living room of his personal quarters in the castle's west wing. "Did Victor *seriously* send you with that message?" Darius snarled, fighting with a tie he'd slung around his neck. He knew his father got his kicks from belittling his only son, and sending such news through a servant would be exactly his kind of twisted humour. But this was low, even for him.

"Word for word," said Bartholomew. He was a neat and tidy gentleman in his late fifties. Having served Darius's family for most of his life, he didn't appear to be ruffled by Victor Legrand's fuckery. Then again, he wasn't the one whose whole life had just apparently been turned upside down. "I left out some of the more sinister chuckles. Would you like to hear the missive once more with its original smugness and malice?"

"No, thank you," Darius growled.

He gave up on the blasted tie and flung it away. It caught an empty vase that had been collecting dust on top of one of the cabinets, not having contained flowers for some years now. The tie sent it toppling down to smash explosively on the stone floor.

Darius and Bartholomew both flinched at the noise, frozen for a moment in the silence that followed.

Balling his fists and screwing up his eyes, Darius counted

back from five. "I'm sorry, Bartholomew," he ground out between his teeth.

"It's no bother, sir," Bartholomew said gently. "I'll clean it up. I was only going to preoccupy myself with a game of patience whilst you were in your meeting. You head downstairs, now. Your father is waiting in the drawing room for you."

"He's waiting in *my* office?" Darius repeated incredulously as he opened his eyes. Bartholomew arched his eyebrow again, as if to say 'what else did you expect?' At least he was there and not loitering in Darius's beloved library. Whatever damage or mischief he might get up to in the drawing room-turned-office was minimal compared to the library. Darius had to give thanks for small mercies, he supposed.

He breathed in and out through his nose a couple of times, composing himself. His father's announcement wasn't wholly unexpected. He'd been threatening this for weeks, but honestly, Darius had thought he'd been joking. Obviously not. He would have at least expected further discussion on the subject, not to have it dropped on him like a grenade.

That just showed how dim-witted he was, though, didn't it? He should have anticipated that his father was going to spring this on him without his consent.

"I guess I'd better go get this over with," Darius muttered, his mood thunderous.

Bartholomew nodded. "I think that would be best, sir. I'll have a glass of whisky breathing for you upon your return."

Darius nodded. "Help yourself, too."

Bartholomew tilted his head. "Oh, I intended to, sir."

There was no sense in dawdling any further. Being kept waiting would only rile his father up more. He'd clicked his fingers, and therefore Darius was expected to jump to attention. So Darius marched out of the west wing and into the belly of the castle.

The jacket didn't quite fit properly as Darius hadn't bothered buying a new one in the past few years. The material strained over the muscle he'd kept building up since his early retirement from the army. He tugged irritably at it as he hurried down the stairs, his jaw clenched and his skin hot.

As much as Darius loathed rushing to do his father's bidding, he knew from past experiences there would be consequences if he didn't. It didn't make it much easier to swallow the fact that he knew he wasn't in control of his own life, though. With every step, he seethed more, resenting the hand he'd been dealt. In thirty-seven years, he'd grown used to his father's meddling ways, but this went beyond the pale.

And it wasn't just Darius who Victor was manipulating and coercing this time.

Fury boiled through Darius's veins. He tried unsuccessfully to stifle his temper as he marched through the deserted halls. Nobody could make him rage quite like his sole surviving parent. Instead he cracked his neck and rolled his bulky shoulders, doing his best to dispel the tension that was trying valiantly to turn his whole body into granite.

He was vaguely aware of scuttling feet and slamming doors as he made his way through the dark and droughty castle. Ordinarily, he didn't see the point of lighting the whole place when he only kept to his rooms. As he marched down the corridors, however, he was reminded of how lifeless it all felt in these forgotten quarters, how unloved. He wasn't the only one who lived here, after all.

Most of the time, he was ashamed to say he forgot he had staff aside from Bartholomew and a few of the other senior managers. Nothing irked him more than being fawned over. But the truth of the matter was that a place this large couldn't run unless there was a team dedicated to its upkeep. Even then, he knew Thorncliff Castle was struggling. Darius could never seem to find the energy to invest in the property like he knew he should, though.

Another door squeaked, and he heard whispers as he swept past the long-abandoned nursery. He'd rather his family's drama wasn't aired in front of his employees, but this couldn't wait, and gossip travelled like wildfire around here regardless.

Better to get this whole messy business dealt with sooner rather than later. Darius steeled himself, then pushed through the heavy double doors. "Father," he barked.

As expected, Victor Legrand was standing in the drawing room, inspecting one of the bookshelves as if it had personally insulted him. He ran a finger along the spine of one of the sun-faded books, wrinkling his nose.

It was easier to think of him as 'Victor'. After all, Darius hadn't known a paternal act of love from him in almost forty years. The two men were as different as chalk and cheese. While Darius was broad and muscular, with dark wiry hair covering most of his body, Victor was slim and delicate, his thick hair white for decades. To an outsider looking on, it would perhaps seem obvious that Darius could overpower his father in the blink of an eye.

Therefore, they might think it strange that instead Darius flinched as Victor's icy gaze swept towards him. They would have no idea of the power Victor could wield despite his small stature. "Calm yourself," Victor said, sounding almost bored at Darius's entrance and clear outrage.

Darius was aware that he still clung to some of his ingrained childhood fear of the old man, but the fact remained that he was beyond furious, and the anger quickly gave him back his conviction.

"You can't *seriously* be expecting me to go through with

this ridiculous scheme?" he demanded, advancing closer. He knew better than to get too near, lest his father felt disrespected. But he wasn't going to lurk by the doorway like a nervous schoolboy, either.

This old family estate had been forced upon him by his father when Darius had been compelled to retire from the army. Consequently, Victor still felt perfectly entitled to act like its lord. He did so just then, by walking around Darius's grand oak desk and dropping into the creaking leather chair. He laced his long fingers together, fixing Darius with a glacial stare.

"I warned you that I might have to take drastic measures. Bellamy's business was in dire straits *before* he lost an entire shipment at sea. He is beyond bankrupt."

Christopher Bellamy ran some sort of transportation company through the nearby Dover port, shipping cargo for Victor overseas to the rest of Europe and beyond. Darius vaguely recalled his father griping about extremely disappointing sales figures over the last few quarters. It didn't matter, though, not at this precise moment. Darius had far greater concerns.

He could feel his hands curling into claws as he shook his head, trembling from head to toe. "So your solution is to *marry off his son to me?*"

The smile that crawled over Victor's mouth was revolting. Malice and pleasure danced behind his pale blue eyes. "I warned him that I held all the power over him. He should never have made such poor decisions with *my* cargo."

Darius knew he wasn't particularly intelligent, especially when compared to his father, but he wasn't stupid, either. This was far more than a business decision. He didn't know all the details, but somewhere along the line, Christopher Bellamy had personally slighted Victor Legrand. If there was one thing Darius knew about his father, it was that he never left a grudge unpunished.

But this?

Goddamn it. Surely Bellamy's son hadn't done anything to warrant being married off like livestock. As he was the heir to the Bellamy shipping company, though, Victor probably saw that his marriage to Darius would make it so the business was now entirely Victor's to salvage however he saw fit to recuperate his losses.

It came as no surprise that Victor would get a kick from derailing Darius's life. Darius had never been under the illusion that he would be able to marry in peace, let alone to a man of his choosing. But it seemed particularly cruel to inflict him on a young innocent like Bellamy's son. Not that Darius had even met him yet. Christ, was this guy even gay? What was his *name?*

"There must be some other way?" grunted Darius, clenching his fists into balls.

He regarded his father with bated breath, feeling like he was ready to spring into battle at any given moment. But truthfully, he knew there was nothing he could really do. If Victor had made up his mind, particularly in a cruel twist of other people's lives such as this, there was no going back. He always had something despicable in his back pocket to make sure all his little pawns behaved on the chessboard.

Sure enough, the old man leaned forwards, resting his elbows on the desk and lacing his fingers together. "Oh, I'm sorry," Victor said smoothly. "Is there another suitor you have waiting in the wings that I was unaware of? Has *anyone* ever shown the slightest interest in marrying you?"

Even though Darius should have known better than to let the barb sting, he still winced. He did his best not to think of the hole in his heart his one and only love had left because he was long gone. Victor had never even been aware of him, but somehow it was worse that he thought Darius was that unloveable when he'd come so close to actually being happy.

"I am simply asking if there's an alternative way other than something so draconian as an arranged marriage in this day and age," Darius snapped. "It's the twenty-first century. May I suggest something as outrageous as a bank loan?"

Slowly, Victor rose to his feet, placing his spindly hands flat down on the wooden desktop. "Are you disobeying me, boy?" Darius worked very hard not to wince at the moniker. As much as he knew his father would never treat him like a man, the jibe still hurt. "This is *my* little kingdom. Bellamy knew the consequences of failing me. I am simply trying to recoup my assets."

"By punishing his son?" Darius demanded. He daren't add 'and me'. Victor would only see his suffering as an incentive to double down.

Even so, that filthy, stomach-turning smile oiled its way back onto Victor's face. "What's wrong, son?" he asked smoothly, his eyebrow twitching. "I thought you'd like a pretty young boy in your bed."

Revulsion flashed through Darius, forcing him to fight back a wave of nausea. So this was his father's joke, a lifetime in the making. He'd called him a pervert for almost twenty-five years. Now he was proving his point.

It was on the tip of his tongue to demand how old Bellamy's son was, but he knew his father would never technically do anything illegal, so the poor guy had to be at least eighteen. Darius prayed that if they were forced to go through with this, he was at least a little older than that.

Surely Bellamy could fight this? This wasn't the Middle Ages or some Elizabethan court. There was that bit in wedding ceremonies where the officiant asked if anyone objected to the union, and that included the people getting married. They still had free will, didn't they?

But before Darius could get carried away, he made himself look at Victor's expression, really absorbing every line of his handsome, wicked face.

Victor had leverage. Something to make sure Darius, Bellamy, and his son would do what he wanted. Whatever it was, Darius knew Bellamy was aware that this sham wedding would be better than the alternative. Darius's stomach dropped. He could protest all he wanted that he was unwilling to be shackled to a man he'd never met for the rest of his life, but he was being childish.

In his heart of hearts, he was already accepting that for now, it was best just to go along with the whole diabolical scheme. Because it wasn't just the Bellamys who Victor would have something to coerce compliance with. If Darius didn't behave, there would be another shoe waiting somewhere to drop, and who knew who would get hurt from that.

No. If Victor had decided that this marriage was going to solve his problems, not to mention make Darius suffer, then he was going to see it through to the bitter end.

But that didn't mean Darius had to like it.

"Okay," he snarled, glaring daggers at Victor. "Marry me off to Bellamy's son. I'm not convinced it'll do you any good other than make a bunch of people miserable, but if that's what you want, go ahead."

Victor chuckled softly. It was always his most terrifying sound. "Miserable?" He walked around the desk, tracing a single finger along the wood as he went. "Oh, my dear boy. This will simply *tickle* me. It's all for the good of the empire, you see?"

Empire. That was what other people might call family, but not Victor Legrand. He was so desperate to believe that his legacy would live on for generations, his name repeated with a sense of reverence reserved only for royalty, that Darius was astonished he wasn't being married off to a poor girl who would be coerced into bearing several of his children, all in the name of the 'empire'.

Maybe that would come later, when Victor got bored with this particular game.

"And if I refuse?"

Darius knew it was dangerous to ask. But this wasn't merely some business arrangement. This was two people being forced into something that should be treated with utter reverence.

To his surprise, his father simply shrugged. "I suppose Bellamy and his son would be driven into desolation. Thrown penniless onto the streets. What would you care, though, hmm? You've never met them."

He was right. Darius wouldn't know them from Adam. But that wasn't his way. *No man left behind.*

It was senseless to point out that his father was behaving like some Charles Dickens villain. Victor would only take that as a compliment. Playing games with other people's lives, especially those he saw as beneath him (which, really, was everyone) was his greatest pleasure in life. No, this wasn't fair. But fighting Victor would most likely only make things worse for Bellamy's son.

Darius had a lifetime of experience to fall back on when it came to his father's cruelty. Bellamy's son knew nothing of the sort, he was sure.

"Fine," snarled Darius, already turning and heading out of the room. He might have heard several pairs of feet scrambling away, but by the time he wrenched the door open again, the corridor was deserted. He paused and curled a lip at his father. "But you won't win, whatever it is you're planning."

Victor laughed as if his son had just made a charming joke. "Oh, dear boy. But I already have."

Darius didn't want to believe that. However, as he stormed off down the hallway, he couldn't convince himself that it wasn't really true.

2

JOSHUA

THIS WASN'T HOW JOSHUA BELLAMY HAD EVER IMAGINED HIS wedding day.

He couldn't say he was one of those people who had sat around fantasising about marrying the man of his dreams, but dear *lord*. He'd always assumed that if he did get hitched, it would at least be to someone he loved. Liked. Fuck, right now, he'd even accept someone he *knew*.

First impressions of Darius Legrand hadn't been kind. He was a large man, in a way that suggested he was made of muscle rather than a slovenly pig, at least. But still, he was twice Joshua's size width-wise and at least a foot taller.

It was difficult not to feel intimidated.

Darius had scowled as Joshua had been ushered into a sort of office. The wallpaper looked to be about three decades old and was peeling, and the carpet smelled faintly of mildew.

So romantic.

Really, the décor wasn't important. Joshua knew he was focusing on these details to distract himself from the larger issue at hand.

He was fucking terrified.

He trembled as he was told where to stand by a kindly-seeming middle-aged lady who offered him a sympathetic smile. She was Black with a lovely cloud of natural curls and was wearing a trouser suit and blouse that suggested she was staff. There was something motherly about her that calmed Joshua a little.

But everything else in him was screaming that he should run away from this grizzly brute standing beside him. His black suit strained against his impressive form and was so dusty and frayed that Joshua wondered when it had last seen the light of day. His beard was scraggly, and the dark hair falling around his ears wasn't much better. However, as Joshua took his place in that dingy office, Darius flicked his gaze towards Joshua, catching his eyes.

And...*oh*...what eyes. They were an astonishing shade of blue, like a bright sky over fresh snow. But Joshua firmly ignored the primal surge of lust that flared through him in that brief moment their gazes locked.

Because the rest of Darius Legrand was goddamned barbaric.

Although Joshua had to admit he didn't feel much of a catch himself in his dad's hand-me-down suit. They hadn't been able to afford to buy Joshua anything of his own for the occasion, so he was lucky his dad's old suit fitted him at all. But it didn't give a great first impression of him to the man he was having to marry. Darius was probably extremely pissed off that he was being shackled to a pathetic little thing like Joshua. At least he was gay, apparently. But aside from that, Joshua was pretty sure their similarities ended.

Aside from the friendly woman, there were three men in the small room with him and Darius. Joshua's father, Christopher. Mr Victor Legrand, who ran the business that owned Dad's former shipping company. And finally, a snooty-looking registrar who tutted and glanced at his watch, suggesting he had places to be other than here.

Joshua felt a surge of irritation that this man could treat the unravelling of Joshua's whole life as a tedious inconvenience. But his anger quickly faded into sombre acceptance. He'd raged for days when Legrand's lawyers had come to the small home Joshua and his dad shared, informing them of this ridiculous marriage that would apparently cancel out the company's debt and catastrophic losses.

Not that anything could bring back the crew of the sunken ship.

A lump rose in Joshua's throat. It had been made abundantly clear that if he didn't go through with this, he and his dad would be made homeless. His dad was already only hanging on by a thread, devastated by the tragedy. Despite owning the business, Joshua had never comprehended why his dad had always been so strapped for cash. He guessed it didn't matter now. Joshua wouldn't see him thrown onto the streets at any time, but especially not in winter. However, it wasn't just their family Joshua had to consider.

He didn't understand the nitty-gritty, but the lawyer had made it clear that without this union, there would be nothing to salvage from the doomed shipping company his dad had run his whole life.

Including the pensions and life insurance policies from all the crew that had been lost at sea.

Joshua tried not to think of the grief the dozen families must be feeling right now. The accident had only been a few weeks ago.

Just before Christmas.

The least Joshua could do was ensure that they all weren't ruined either. Most of them were migrants as well, who might face deportation without the proper support. So Joshua would swallow his pride and his fear and do his duty as a son. Marrying the younger Legrand was the only power Joshua had left to him.

Not that Darius was exactly 'young'. Joshua snuck another peek at him as the registrar droned on, his heart flipping with a strange mix of emotion. He was mid-to-late thirties, which logically Joshua knew wasn't 'old' per se, but it was a hell of a lot older than his own twenty-one years. He felt like such a baby as he fumbled over vows he'd thought he wouldn't be saying for years.

Hell, one of the reasons he'd never thought much about getting married or saying any vows was because he'd never even had a *boyfriend* yet. How many experiences was he being robbed of with this gut-wrenching deal? He'd never dated… never even been touched by another man. He was as much of a virgin as could be.

Shame flared through him and he did his best not to blush. This probably wasn't the best time to think of such thoughts. But what would Darius expect of him? They were getting married, after all. There were certain things people expected when that happened. But Joshua had no idea if he would be able to go through with it if – or when – the time came, regardless of the brief flare of lust he'd felt. There was a vast difference between that and actually having sex with someone.

Nausea washed through Joshua again and he tried not to swoon in his panic. The last thing he wanted to do was faint and worry his dad any more than he already was. From the corner of his eye, Joshua could see the poor man was trying his best not to cry unhappy tears. He was small, like Joshua, with thinning hair and a small pot belly, looking frailer than his years in his neat but old shirt and trousers. Joshua was wearing his only suit, after all.

15

As furious and devastated Joshua was at the stripping of his freedom, he knew his dad was sick to his stomach with guilt over it. So Joshua had done his best to put on a brave face, telling his dad it wasn't really that bad. He *was* going to get to live in a castle.

A damp, chilly castle. Good lord, Joshua had been in more inviting car parks in his time. As he and his dad had been escorted through the corridors, it had been nothing but gloom and disrepair. Joshua had glanced at his phone a couple of times before the pitiful excuse for a ceremony had begun, and neither times had he seen even one bar of signal. Maybe once he connected to the Wi-Fi, he'd be okay. But what the hell was he going to do out here in the middle of nowhere?

They were somewhere in the Kent Downs, miles away from any real civilisation. There was a small village – also called Thorncliff – that they'd passed through on the drive here, but it wasn't much more than a post office and a few cottages. A far cry from Folkstone, where Joshua had spent his whole life. God, he thought he'd been lonely there.

What was life going to be like here? This wasn't supposed to happen. He wasn't supposed to be there. In fact, he wished he was pretty much anywhere else in the whole world.

He was pulled from his reverie as the impatient registrar said his name. "I-I do," Joshua spluttered, his throat dry. "I mean, yes. I mean…uh, what do I mean?"

The registrar huffed and arched an eyebrow. "We're not quite there yet, Mr Bellamy. Repeat after me."

Out of the corner of his eye, he thought he saw Darius's mouth quirk in a hint of a smile, just for a split second, but then the stony gaze was back. Great, they hadn't even spoken one word to each other, and he already thought Joshua was a joke.

But then they were facing one another, holding cheap

silver rings in their hands, ready to put them on each other's fingers. Joshua looked up to stare for longer than just a second into the depths of Darius's bright blue eyes. They burned with such intensity that Joshua had to drop his gaze and focus on their touching hands instead. It felt like such a wicked mockery of an intimate moment, supposed to be shared by two people who were madly in love.

Not two strangers who clearly had nothing in common.

Joshua took a slow, deep breath. Thousands – probably *millions* – of people had done this in the past. They still did it all around the world, in fact. After resolving himself to the situation, Joshua had made himself feel a little better by researching online. In many cultures where arranged marriages were still practiced, the families generally took great care over the matches, and the couple in question often ended up having long, happy marriages.

He was almost certain that wasn't the case here, but the thought still gave him some comfort. He wasn't alone in this situation, no matter how much he felt it.

All too soon, everything that needed to be said was said, and Joshua found himself signing papers alongside Darius. Then the registrar was packing everything into a leather briefcase, muttering to himself as he swept from the room.

"Excellent," said the elder Mr Legrand. He grinned coldly at Joshua as he wrapped a slender hand over Joshua's dad's shoulder and visibly squeezed. "Now that's all taken care of, Bellamy and I have much business to discuss. I'll walk you out, Christopher."

What? *Already?* "But-!" stammered Joshua.

"Oh, um, sir," piped up the kindly plump woman, raising a hand. "Camille and I have prepared a light supper in the dining room to celebrate. I-"

"No one asked you to do that," said Mr Legrand

dismissively, already walking Joshua's dad out of the small study.

"Dad?" he cried out, trying not to feel like a small child about to burst into tears.

"It's okay, Joshua," he replied, already in the corridor and out of sight. "I'll speak to you soon."

And then he was gone. Joshua hadn't even had the chance to say goodbye.

He choked back the sob that threatened to escape from his throat, gritting his teeth and looking at the stone floor.

"Well, then," said the woman awkwardly. "Shall we, uh…"

"We'll find our way," Darius said. His voice was a low grumble that vibrated through Joshua's already trembling body. "Thank you, Mrs Weatherby," he added, like he wasn't used to speaking to her. "That was kind of you."

Mrs Weatherby looked between them, as if unsure if she should leave them alone. Joshua had to admit he felt the same. But then she nodded and bustled out of the door. Joshua was almost too afraid to breathe too loudly.

Darius grunted and extended his hand, indicating Joshua should exit the room, too. Back out in the hall, there was no sign of anyone, let alone his dad. Joshua tried to push down a pang of resentment and regret. This was it, was it? How he was going to be treated now he was the property of the Legrand estate.

A heavy silence stretched between them as they walked along the cold stone floor. Couldn't they afford carpets or rugs even? Joshua was going to freeze to death that night, he was sure.

Oh…*god*. There was a thought. Where was he expected to sleep? Again, fear rose in him as he scrambled for a way to ask. He didn't really know *anything* about how their lives were going to operate here.

But no words would come. It was as if they were all

locked away and couldn't escape past the lump in his throat. He shoved his hands into his pockets in an attempt to stop them from shaking.

"What do you do?" Darius blurted out as they made their way down the corridor. Joshua glanced over to see him staring at the floor, his big hands clasped firmly behind his back.

Joshua swallowed, trying not to feel embarrassed. He was strangely grateful for the conversation opener, but he didn't relish the only answer he could give. "I, uh, I work at a pub. Worked, I mean. I was a barman." That was sure to impress Darius and win him over. Joshua mentally rolled his eyes.

The trouble was Joshua had still been trying to figure out what the hell he wanted to do with his life. He wasn't one of those who'd gone off to university with a specific career plan in mind. His dad had never put any pressure on him to take over his business once he retired despite what Victor Legrand might think about Joshua being some sort of heir. His dad had always said Joshua would forge his own path. He'd thought he'd had time. Plenty of time, in fact. Never in his wildest dreams would he have seen himself here, in this draughty castle, married off to a stranger.

He wasn't sure he'd marry anyone.

Joshua had been an awkward child, gangly and shy. Neither he nor his dad had known what to do after his mother's sudden death, so they'd been left struggling it out together, just the two of them. He made himself easy to be overlooked, and Joshua liked it that way.

By the time Joshua hit his mid-teens, and puberty changed him from an ugly duckling to a glorious swan, though, it was painfully obvious that people had tried to treat him differently because of his looks. Much harder to stay out of the spotlight when everyone assumed you were a model or wanted to turn you into one.

It wasn't vanity. In fact, Joshua wished he wasn't as beautiful as he knew he was. Personally, he fiercely believed that beauty came in all shapes and sizes. But like it or not, people seemed to generally agree that he'd been blessed, and wanted to give him special treatment because of it. However, any door that opened because of something so random and unearned as good genes wasn't a door Joshua was interested in walking through. So he made it his mission to be as unnoticeable as possible, taking up the least space. He'd rather have nothing than opportunities he hadn't fairly earned.

Not that guys didn't try it on with him all the time. But the leering and cliched come-ons had been exhausting. So Joshua had never been tempted to date, choosing to satisfy his desires privately. Marriage had been as unexpected as a trip to the moon.

Despite all that, though, he couldn't be resentful of his beauty. He knew from pouring over old photos that his looks came from his mum, and he loved that. Like he always had something of her with him, no matter what, taking care of him like a guardian angel.

Perhaps she would keep him safe in his new life in the middle of nowhere with this scary brute. What did he think of Joshua's looks?

If he were to glance at Joshua for more than a second, Joshua might be able to make a guess. But it was like he couldn't even stand to look at his new husband. Joshua couldn't blame him. As far as he understood it from his dad, Darius had been given about as much choice in this arrangement as Joshua had. But for some stupid reason, Joshua felt like he wouldn't mind if Darius thought he was pretty. It might make this whole business slightly more bearable.

He inwardly scolded himself. If Darius was only

interested in being nice to Joshua because he thought he was gorgeous, then he was no better than any of the other guys Joshua had rejected over the years. It wouldn't ultimately improve anything.

Perhaps it would be better if Darius was repulsed by Joshua and only liked big, tough, muscly guys like himself? It would probably be safer that way. After all, Darius looked like he hadn't had a haircut in months, and his expression so far had been a permanent scowl. Joshua wouldn't want him anywhere near him, he was sure.

Darius had merely nodded at Joshua's reply about being a barman. But for some reason, Joshua wanted to keep talking. If there was any luck in this world (which he was sure there wasn't), he and Darius could at least be civil to one another. Maybe even friendly.

"H-how about you? What do you do?"

Darius seemed surprised by the question, raising his eyebrows and glancing down at Joshua as they approached a room that finally had some lights on. "Imports and exports," Darius said, already looking away, of course. But the second they'd held each other's gazes had sent the tiniest spark through Joshua. At least Darius was acknowledging him, however briefly. "I was in the army, but..."

They reached a door on the ground floor, and Joshua realised it was a dining room, the one Mrs Weatherby had mentioned. But unlike the other rooms, which were lifeless, this one had been rejuvenated.

It wasn't a large room compared to what Joshua had seen of the rest of the castle, but it was still probably large enough to fit the whole ground floor of Joshua's terraced house back in Folkstone. A crystal chandelier blazed over a long table that had a pristine white cloth laid over it. Delicious-looking finger food had been piled up on silver platters, and an ornate ice bucket held a popped bottle of real French

Champagne, not that fizzy wine Joshua had served down the Rose and Crown.

The spark of excitement was so unexpected Joshua almost didn't know what to do with it. He turned without thinking to beam at Darius. Even on this complicated and confusing day, maybe they could share a nice moment, and their marriage wouldn't get off to such a terrible start after all.

But the second Joshua clapped eyes on his new husband, his stomach dropped. Darius's face was one of horror and panic. He backed up, hitting the edge of the wooden door, his leather shoes thudding heavily on the stone slabs as he retreated from the room.

"I-I'm sorry," he uttered. His blue eyes were wide as a flash of anger crossed his face, overriding the panic. "Please excuse – I can't – please enjoy." He gave an awkward half bow, then fled into the darkness of the hallway, pulling the door to behind him.

Joshua stared at the wood for several seconds, his eyes filling with tears in the silence that followed. So, Darius was so repulsed by him he couldn't even bear the thought of feigning a smile and toasting their marriage, not even for ten minutes. Joshua sniffed and let the tears fall before hastily scrubbing his face. Well, it was *his* wedding day too, and if nothing else, he was going to celebrate the fact that he hadn't passed out and had been able to do the right thing for his dad and his late-employees' families.

With a determined huff, Joshua marched over to the table, poured himself a long glass of bubbly, then walked over to one of the tall, arched windows that looked out over the castle's grounds.

The sun was setting on a grey, rainy day in January. The trees were bare, and the ground was muddy, and other than the castle's stables, there wasn't another building in sight as the vista stretched out towards the white cliffs of Dover. It was lonely and bleak, but Joshua took a shaky breath and forced himself to acknowledge that there a raw and harsh kind of beauty to the landscape.

So he sat on the windowsill, unbuttoning the old suit jacket, slipping off his shoes, and curling his feet under him to watch the sun continue to set. Coldness from the glass and stone seeped through his clothes, but he stayed there on the sill, sipping his Champagne, letting the alcohol thrum through his veins.

This was it. The wedding was done. The business, his dad, and the families they supported were saved, and now he was on his own. So he had better make what he could of it because there was no one coming to save him.

No matter how much he wished they would.

3

DARIUS

Darius was so fucked.

He sighed angrily and flung the book he'd been trying to read onto his desk, nudging the mouse and bringing his computer back to life where it had fallen asleep. With a vigorous snarl, he regarded the spreadsheet that had just reappeared. He couldn't care less most of the time about adding figures up for the company his father had forced onto him, but especially not right now.

Darius was too busy trying desperately not to think about the other thing his father had forced onto him.

In the few days between learning of the arranged marriage and meeting Joshua for that miserable excuse for a ceremony, Darius had pictured him a hundred different ways. An internet search surprisingly hadn't yielded any information, let alone a picture, so Darius had been left to his own imagination. He'd wondered if he was going to be married off to a sullen brat, a sweet but unfortunately shaped lad, a lazy layabout, or any number of undesirable matches.

It hadn't occurred to him that Joshua Bellamy might be heart-shatteringly beautiful.

THORN IN HIS SIDE

Darius had used every ounce of strength not to let his jaw drop like some kind of hungry dog when Joshua had walked into the study several days ago. Darius hadn't had any trouble discerning that Joshua, even in the ill-fitting grey suit, was perfectly proportioned, small and slender, with high cheekbones, soft blond hair parted to the side, and delicate-looking hands.

But his lips. Those eyes. Darius groaned just thinking about them, shifting in his creaking leather chair and pulling at the crotch of his trousers before they got too tight. Joshua's mouth was light pink, bow shaped, and made for kissing. His eyes were round and brown, like the bark of an oak tree after the rain.

He was unlike no man Darius had ever met before, and yet he wanted him immediately.

So of course, he couldn't have him.

The very idea was utterly unthinkable. The poor chap was barely in his twenties and had spent the entire marriage proceedings trembling like a leaf. Darius had been struck with the wild and preposterous idea that he'd wanted to wrap his arm around the young man's shoulders to try and reassure him that everything was going to be okay.

But it went without saying that he hadn't. He was letting his protective instincts get the better of him, but ultimately, that would have been the worst thing he could have done.

Joshua was here against his will. Darius's father had forced him and his father into a devil's bargain. It would be wholly unforgivable for Darius to give in, even for a second, to his attraction for the man he'd been forced to marry. He would never take advantage like that. Over his dead body.

Which is why he'd baulked at the prospect of sharing a romantic moment in the dining room. Mrs Weatherby and the castle's cook, Camille, had outdone themselves as usual, making a genuine and sweet moment for Darius and Joshua to share on what was otherwise a miserable and awkward day. But when Darius had seen the cosy, brightly lit room and the treats for them to enjoy, he'd been overcome with the urge to bolt. He couldn't share something like that with Joshua. It wasn't fair. There was a power imbalance in their relationship, and Darius wasn't going to abuse that. Unlike his father would.

This was a business arrangement. Darius didn't want to be cruel, but he needed to stay far, far away from these feelings that were writhing inside him whenever he pictured Joshua's happy face at the simple wedding breakfast.

Besides, it wasn't affection. It was lust, probably mixed in with a misplaced notion of protectiveness from Darius's caveman brain. Joshua wasn't even his type. Darius liked burly men, someone you could really fuck. Someone like…

No.

Darius grimaced and reached for the tumbler of whisky he was nursing. The light through the windows had fallen while he'd been distracting himself with his ridiculous book about the adventures of eighteenth-century naval officers. So he sat in the drawing room, in the dark, studiously *not* remembering Richard's face. The deep rumble of his laugh, the way he'd gnashed his teeth when he'd come, the stink of him when he pushed Darius to keep up with him running drills.

The way he'd winked at Darius, their secret sign, seconds before he'd died.

The memory was a ghost now, but every now and again it flared up, as if Darius was right there in the thick of it, smelling the burning metal and hearing the screams. He closed his eyes, knowing that would do nothing to dull the images once they'd decided to make an unscheduled appearance, but Darius had to at least try and protect himself.

He rubbed his shoulder through his jumper, not really feeling the pressure but knowing the increased blood circulation would do his muscles good. The stiffness never really went away. He should probably do some physio exercises, but that would involve thinking about his body, possibly even looking at it. The mere suggestion made him glug another mouthful of whisky. Best to just keep ignoring it. A hot bath was the only thing he could stand to help him, and he didn't feel so exposed under the water. He promised himself one later.

What was done was done. Darius had just been sitting in the right place at the right time that day. Still, the guilt was always there for those he'd left behind against his will, simply by surviving.

To hell with it. Darius knocked the rest of the drink down his throat, making it burn all the way to his stomach, then poured another measure from the crystal decanter. Now was not the time for wallowing in years-old hurt. He had enough bullshit in the present to keep him more than occupied.

He rubbed his eyes and glanced at the soulless columns of numbers glowing from his computer screen, but not seeing them at all.

What the hell was he going to do?

So far, he'd gone out of his way to avoid Joshua. He'd instructed his housekeeper, Mrs Weatherby, to make sure he was looked after and comfortable in his own bedroom. Darius had been slightly worried that Joshua might have protested that arrangement, expecting to share a bed with Darius. But his rooms were his sanctuary, the only part of the castle he'd made clear Joshua was not free to roam. Darius needed his space, or he would lose his mind.

Thankfully, Joshua had appeared fine with them each having bedrooms on either side of the castle to each other. At least, he hadn't complained as far as Darius was aware. But

Joshua *was* living here now, and Darius was finding himself increasingly agitated at the constant worry of running into each other at unexpected times.

Inappropriate feelings aside, he just didn't know what to talk to him about. Awkward chit-chat about the weather seemed dreadfully insulting when Joshua had been pulled from his home and his life as a punishment for his father's misfortune. All in all, it left Darius completely tongue-tied whenever he saw his beautiful new living companion.

It was best to just give each other room to adapt to this bizarre new situation.

Or so he thought.

A knock on his door startled him and made him blink out of the stupor he'd fallen into. Irrational anger flared through him at being disturbed, but this wasn't his father barging in on him any damn time he pleased. At least, he didn't think so. It was almost certainly Mrs Weatherby coming to ask a perfectly reasonable question or Bartholomew checking that he wasn't throwing darts at photos of his father against centuries-old walls.

Again.

Darius cleared his throat and took another sip of whisky. "Come in." He flicked on a lamp so whoever it was could see him and vice versa.

He was surprised when the door creaked open and Joshua timidly poked his head around the edge. "Um, hi. I hope I'm not disturbing you too much? I just, uh, wanted to ask you a couple of things."

Darius was tempted to tell him he could ask Mrs Weatherby anything he wanted to know, but that was just fucking rude. The poor man had put up with a lot of nonsense over the past week. The least Darius could do was hear him out.

He waved a couple of fingers, encouraging Joshua to

come fully into the drawing room. He'd only brought one suitcase of possessions with him as far as Darius was aware, so it wasn't surprising to see him in his usual attire of blue denim jeans and long-sleeved T-shirt. However, for the first time, Darius noticed that he was also wearing fluffy knitted cream booties that appeared to be his slippers, and Darius's ridiculous heart flipped over. So what if that was cute? What practical use did 'cute' ever have? He needed to get control of himself.

When Joshua didn't speak, Darius raised his eyebrows and shook his head as if to say 'what is it?' He didn't trust himself to actually talk in that moment, in case his voice did something stupid. The whisky was warming his veins nicely, but he would never forgive himself if he said something inappropriate about his attraction towards Joshua and made him feel uncomfortable.

"Oh, right, yes," said Joshua breathlessly. "I was wondering…well, I asked some of the staff already, but they seemed to think there wasn't any Wi-Fi. I-I asked them for the password, but they said to ask you."

Shit. Darius hadn't thought of that. Urgh, of course not, because he was so wrapped up in his own head to think of other people's needs. He grunted and sipped his whisky, not looking Joshua in the eye.

"No. No Wi-Fi. I have a connection set up here for work." He waved absently at his desk, glad the silly adventure book had landed with the cover down. For some reason, he didn't want Joshua to judge him for his reading choices. "I'll talk to Bartholomew about getting people in to fix it up somewhere else. Anywhere you like."

Joshua shifted uncomfortably on his feet. "You mean you'd have to have cables and stuff put in? That's – don't worry about it. Then. That's okay."

Darius frowned at him. "Do you want internet or not?"

Joshua hugged himself and cleared his throat before dropping him arms again. "I mean...yes, I'd love it. But only if it's not too much-"

"It's done," Darius said, waving a hand dismissively. Goddamn it. Joshua needed to get better at asking for what he needed. It was hardly an outrageous request.

Joshua nodded and rubbed his palms together. "Okay. Uh, thank you."

"Anything else?"

Darius was anxious to get rid of him. The longer they spent talking, the more chance he had of saying something stupid. Even in scruffy jeans and a jumper, Joshua still looked like some kind of angel. The picture of innocence waiting for someone like Darius to ruin him. The thought of Joshua losing that sweet light that shone from him was devastating. Darius wasn't going to tarnish him any more than he had been by this heinous arrangement.

Joshua looked wretched as he wrung his hands and rocked on his feet. "I'm not sure about food. I'm used to, uh, sorting myself out."

"Camille will be happy to accommodate you in any way," Darius assured him. But Joshua licked his lips, and his brown eyes were glossy. Almost like he was on the verge of tears.

"That's...lovely. Thank you. But, uh, there's eggs and bacon and toast and something that might be *kippers* every morning. Just for me. I'm happy to make my own toast or pour some cereal or have nothing at all. I'm worried it's a terrible waste, but I don't want to hurt the cook's feelings."

Well, that was almost inevitable with Camille, but Darius kept that little joke to himself. "I'll make arrangements," he said, pretending to click things with his mouse as he moved it around the desk. It was easier than looking at Joshua and would hopefully give him the hint to leave.

Except...Joshua didn't leave. He cleared his throat again,

and when Darius looked back up, the pools in Joshua's eyes had filled and were threatening to overflow. His lip trembled, and he clenched his fists by his sides.

Oh, Christ almighty, what the *hell* was wrong?

"Joshua?"

"I'm sorry," he blurted out. Twin tears fell as Joshua blinked, running down his cheeks.

Every inch of Darius bristled. Seeing Joshua upset was completely unacceptable. It made Darius want to tear the castle walls down. He managed to rein in his temper and compose himself. "You've nothing to be sorry for," he said immediately, not caring what Joshua thought he'd done wrong. He couldn't have done anything that bad, Darius was sure.

But Joshua took a shaky breath, fixing his gaze first on something apparently fascinating on the drawing room ceiling, then somewhere around Darius's feet. "I know...I know we're married now. And I feel I've been completely failing at anything close to resembling husbandly duties."

Darius stared at him blankly. Not that Joshua would see. He was fixated on the back of the silly adventure book that was perched on the edge of Darius's messy desk, as if it held the answers to the universe.

Darius looked at his whisky, equally hoping it could give him some help, then back at Joshua. Fuck. He was about to say that Joshua hadn't failed at all, but then what did Darius know? He'd shut him out for the better part of a week. The entire time he'd been at Thorncliff, in fact.

And, really, what the hell did *Darius* know about being a husband? He'd never allowed anyone to call him *boyfriend* before, not even...not even Richard. And they had been so important to one another.

"What do you mean?" Darius asked. Was Joshua thinking Darius expected him to run around and wash his underwear? That was a ridiculous thought if Darius had ever had one.

But Joshua pursed his mouth in a horrid, wobbly line. His beautiful brown eyes were still wet and those traitorous twin tracks shimmered down both his cheeks. "I-I understand there are certain rules to this arrangement. Your father sent me a letter." At the mention of Victor, Darius immediately bristled and wanted to roar, but he quashed any of those reactions. They weren't for Joshua. They were for his father.

He didn't say anything, waiting for Joshua to continue.

"T-that I shouldn't leave the grounds. That I can't take employment. And, uh…" He really did screw up his face then, another pair of tears tracking down his cheeks. Darius was confused about what those things had to do with being a husband, but then Joshua continued. "I understand…I *understand* if you expect to consummate the marriage. I've been thinking about it, and that's okay."

Darius felt the whole world tilt underneath him.

Wishing he hadn't had two glasses of whisky, he gripped the edge of his desk and gritted his teeth, trying to make his heart calm down after it had exploded like a pneumatic drill. *What* had Joshua just asked him? What *exactly* had his father implied in this letter of his?

No, no, *no*. None of that mattered. Victor could play mind games all he wanted, but he wasn't actually here, was he? This was Darius's bloody home. His rules. *His* marriage.

"Is that what you want?" he asked, the words coming out like rock passing through a blender. But he had to know where this request was coming from.

Joshua's lip trembled, but he stuck his jaw out stubbornly. "I'll do whatever it takes to look after my family. After the families we employ…that I have to protect after the accident. Tell me what you want."

Darius's whole insides flipped over in revulsion, and all

that whisky threatened to come spewing out. Jesus *fucking* Christ. He knew Joshua was talking about some letter Victor had sent him, but was this Darius's fault? Had he, despite his best intentions, somehow implied that this was what he wanted?

That sex was what Joshua owed him?

"Get out," he growled. His vision was spinning. Was this who he'd become? Some desperate, pathetic, unlovable thing that latched on to the first innocent, vulnerable man who came his way?

"W-what?" Joshua said.

"Get out," Darius repeated, worried the desk might crack from how hard he was digging his fingers into it.

Joshua's heavy, panicked breathing had filled the room. Darius's vision swam, but he was pretty sure Joshua had gone pale as he blinked and shook his head. "Out. Okay. Uh, thank you. Thank you very much. Um. Bye."

He practically sprinted for the door, letting it slam shut behind him. Darius sunk as low as he could into his cold, scratchy leather chair, clutching his crystal tumbler of whisky to his chest. It was okay. That was awful, but technically, nothing *bad* had happened. It didn't matter what Victor had implied in the letter he'd sent to Joshua. Darius would never in a million years take advantage of Joshua in that way. He hated that Joshua had even for a second thought he might.

He wasn't that monster. And no matter what his so-called father did, he wasn't going to become one.

4

JOSHUA

GET OUT.

Joshua took a deep breath of fresh air, his feet crunching on the gravelled path as he walked farther from the castle's side entrance. He knew he should have been relieved at Darius's rejection. After all, it wasn't like Joshua was thrilled at the idea of offering himself up like that. But Darius had been *so* revolted. He obviously thought Joshua was completely beneath contempt.

As hard as he tried, Joshua couldn't help but feel deeply hurt by that.

Was he a hypocrite? He didn't want to be treated differently because he was pretty, but was he now upset because Darius hadn't fallen for his looks like so many others had? Why did he care what Darius thought of him sexually? If Darius didn't want to bed him, that was a *good* thing. Because Joshua definitely didn't want to talk himself into shagging that brute.

So why was he still in such a funk about it? And why did a small part of Joshua keep remembering the initial, fleeting spark of lust he'd felt at the wedding ceremony?

Get out.

It had been a couple of days since that awful moment, during which those two words hadn't stopped ringing around Joshua's head, even though he hadn't seen Darius at all. Shame filled Joshua every time he pictured Darius's disgust. Maybe he was just having a normal human reaction to being shouted at? Nobody liked that, did they?

It was probably for the best that they hadn't run into each other in that time. But it begged the question of how Darius would react when they finally did meet again. Would he still be angry or have forgotten all about it? With no one else to bounce his thoughts off, Joshua was going a little out of his mind with all these questions.

Because he couldn't talk to Darius about that altercation, *obviously.* But Victor had been very clear in his letter that Darius would expect to be 'taken care of in a husbandly fashion', and basically if Joshua hadn't let him fuck him yet, he'd better hop to it.

Or suffer the consequences.

Joshua wasn't even sure what the hell that meant. Was Victor still threatening his dad? Their employees' family benefits? Or was it something more intimate?

Was he threatening Joshua himself?

He wasn't sure with what. He'd had everything taken away from him, including access to the outside world via the internet. What more could Victor do to him? It was like he was in prison. How would he even know if he and Darius had gone to bed or not? Joshua needed to stop worrying so much.

That letter had been the only outside contact Joshua had experienced since the wedding, as Bartholomew the butler had informed Joshua that laying the internet cables was proving to be an extremely arduous task. Joshua had guiltily said they didn't have to, but Bartholomew had simply inclined his head and promised it would be done.

Eventually.

Victor's letter certainly hadn't brought Joshua any comfort. Victor had made it very plain that he was in charge and pulling all the strings around here. Like the ominous grey clouds currently hovering overhead as he walked, Joshua was just waiting for the storm to begin on both counts.

He shoved his hands further into his coat pockets as he wandered around the cold and windy castle grounds. It would be too generous to call them gardens, as from what Joshua could tell, everything had been left to grow wild or shrivel away from neglect. Darius obviously had about as much time for this house as he did Joshua.

He sighed, his breath coming out as a steam cloud. Why did Victor Legrand hate him so much? Because this was way more than just making a business arrangement to recuperate costs.

This was a punishment.

Why else would Joshua be forbidden from working or seeing anyone or having any kind of life? Bank robbers got kinder sentences than this. Maybe there was someone around here who Joshua could ask?

So far, he'd spoken most with Mrs Weatherby, who was in charge of the staff and ran the house. It seemed to Joshua that she needed about ten more pairs of hands than she currently had, but she was always in a cheerful mood when he saw her. However, she was always busy bustling from here to there, either with arms full of linen to wash or socks to darn. It didn't give the impression that she had a lot of time to sit down for a cup of tea and a chat.

She wasn't there to be Joshua's friend, either, so he tried not to bother her. Other than that, he'd spoken briefly to

Bartholomew, the butler, who was a very proper sort of gentleman with a curly salt-and-pepper moustache. He'd heard rather than spoken to Camille, the hot-tempered French cook, who shouted a lot in her native tongue and probably thought Joshua was an uncultured swine for just wanting cornflakes or beans on toast half the time.

And that was it. Joshua's whole world now. No more customers at the pub or checkout ladies to say hello to or even strangers on the internet to talk shit about movies or politics. He'd thought his world had been small before when he'd purposefully pulled back from dating and social media. Now it was almost non-existent.

He was genuinely worried the boredom might kill him.

In one little silver lining, Joshua had found an old television in what looked like a children's nursery from many years ago. There were lots of classic toys in wooden crates, a rocking horse, and a playpen. Joshua wondered with a pang who they might have belonged to. Such a desolate place wasn't fit for children, in his opinion. Maybe they had been Darius's? It was strange to think of him ever being that small.

He'd had to familiarise himself with the VCR to make the collection of tapes play, something that had strangely brought him a sense of joy and feeling of accomplishment. The quality was pretty poor compared to live streaming or even DVDs. But he wasn't so lonely with shelves full of movies from the eighties and nineties to keep him occupied.

Thunder rumbled overhead where Joshua was walking. The rain had let up for a few hours, giving him the opportunity to dash out and stretch his legs in the fresh air for a while. But another storm was evidently brewing from the ominous iron-grey clouds in the distant horizon rolling closer. Joshua figured he still had some time, though. He couldn't bear the thought of going back inside just yet, so he found an old wooden bench to sit on and looked at his surroundings.

Once upon a time, this must have been a fancy garden, the kind Joshua had seen on the telly. Years ago, the little winding paths had probably led through beautiful flower beds and sculpted bushes. Joshua leaned forward, inspecting some of the dead-looking branches. The thorns made him wonder if these had once been blooming roses.

A wild thought overcame him.

Could he save the gardens?

He wasn't sure why he would think that. He'd never done a day of gardening in his life. All he and his dad had to work with at home was a small patio out back and a couple of potted plants that were hardy enough to cope with very little love and care. But then Joshua remembered when he'd been little, and they'd planted cress at school for a project. He'd been obsessed with watering the small box of dirt every day. Then, for a while, he'd kept a small herb garden in the kitchen as well, even though he couldn't recall his dad ever cooking with them. He'd loved the act of caring in itself without the plants needing to be useful for anything.

He got down on his hands and knees, and touched the dull-looking mud, wet from the torrents of recent rain.

If he attempted this, he'd need some resources. He was desperately hoping that Darius would keep his promise and install internet access for him soon. But in the meantime, perhaps there were some gardening books lying around he could read.

Several feelings bubbled through him, and for the first time in days, he felt himself smiling. Hope and purposefulness made his tummy swoop. Having never considered it before in his life, suddenly gardening sounded like the perfect thing to occupy his time. Joshua could see himself working hard, really creating something, nurturing things into life.

That sounded amazing to him.

Brushing his hands, he stood as thunder rumbled again. He squinted up at the clouds that suddenly seemed a lot closer. They had a funny purple tinge to them, and the wind was picking up something fierce. In the distance, he could just make out trees that were thrashing like they were fighting for their lives.

Joshua didn't let the ominous sight dampen his brand-new enthusiasm, however. With a fresh spring in his step, he began making his way back to the main entrance of the castle. They were still in the grips of a typical miserable English winter. Would that be a bad time to start planting or not? Would he need to clear all those dead-looking rose bushes, or was there something still left there to salvage?

It felt like weeks since Joshua had been filled with so many interesting and exciting thoughts. Probably more than that. Months? Years? When was the last time he'd allowed himself to follow an interest? Could gardening become a passion?

There was only one way to find out.

By the time he reached the castle doors, the dark clouds had already caught up with Joshua, and the wind was whipping up a storm. However, it wasn't rain that hit Joshua in the face as he pushed against the doors, but snow. Great. He was pretty sure snow was the opposite of what you wanted if you were thinking about planting flowers. He shook his head and scrubbed his feet on the bristly mat. It was okay. It wasn't like he was going to run out there this minute and start pruning roses. He needed time to do some research and plan.

For the first time since he'd arrived at Thorncliff, he envisaged a pleasant evening in front of a fire, surrounded by books, possibly with a nice bottle of wine. Maybe he'd be brave and go talk to Camille and see if she'd make one of his favourite meals. Something hot and filling, preferably covered in cheese.

But he wasn't sure he was ready to stop walking yet. His legs felt good for getting some proper exercise for the first time in the couple of weeks since he'd arrived here. So he hung up his coat and scarf, then carried on through the depths of the castle, deliberately looking for rooms he hadn't explored before. If he got lost, he had all evening to keep walking and find his way back to his rooms.

This was exciting. He'd grown up in a small terraced house that had absolutely no secret hiding places or interesting nooks and crannies. The most adventurous thing Joshua had ever done was sneak out of the bathroom window and down the drainpipe at night so he could go stargazing in the back garden. Thorncliff had so many more tantalising secrets to offer.

Joshua was so wrapped up in his exploring he completely forgot that there were places he wasn't supposed to go.

He was too busy finally noticing that a lot of the castle was actually very beautiful if you turned the bloody lights on, which he was currently doing. He'd been too afraid to before, but with his new-found optimism, he figured what was the worst that could happen? He could turn them off again.

Because with the lights on, Joshua was finally able to appreciate all the stunning paintings that were hanging from the walls, as well as the ceramic vases, suits of armour, and coats of arms. It was like he was living in a museum of treasures. He needed to open his eyes and enjoy the rich history around him more. Did all these artefacts belong to Darius's family?

Distracted and disorientated, Joshua kept aimlessly pushing through doors, wandering along corridors, and climbing staircases. This was his *home.* It might have taken a couple of weeks for the feeling to start sinking in, but he needed to see it for the blessing it was. Yes, he was kind of lonely, but hopefully, that might not last forever. In the meantime, he had so much to explore and learn.

He opened another door.

Entering the new room just as Darius did from a different door. If Joshua had to guess, he'd come from a bathroom because all he was wearing was a pair of trousers, and his locks of wavy, dark hair were dripping wet as he dried them with a towel.

It was as if time stopped.

Joshua froze as he took in Darius's expansive body. Yes, he was just as muscular as Joshua had expected, and the thick, dark hair that usually peeked out from cuffs and collars of Darius's shirts was dusted over his whole body.

Or it would have been.

The right side of Darius's chest was covered in twisting scars that spread over his shoulder and down his arm to his elbow. The flesh resembled tree roots, angry and red looking. But Joshua's immediate reaction wasn't revulsion like he thought it might have been. It was a deep pang of sympathy that cut through him like a knife. What the hell had Darius been through?

Unfortunately, Joshua wasn't going to find out. In the second or two it had taken him to absorb the sight of a half-naked Darius, Darius dropped his arm and the towel he'd been drying his hair with, seeing Joshua was there.

Guilt flooded Joshua even before Darius could react. He felt like he'd intruded on something incredibly private. His suspicions were confirmed as Darius threw the towel so it slapped wetly against the wall, his fists balling and his face distorting with a vicious snarl.

"What are you doing here?" he roared, storming towards Joshua.

"I'm sorry!" Joshua spluttered, stumbling backwards with his hands raised. "I didn't know where I was. I never meant to intrude!"

Darius stopped his thunderous advancement, but he was still vibrating with fury, his chest rising and falling as he breathed heavily through the gritted teeth he was baring. "Get the *fuck* out! It's bad enough I have to put up with my home being invaded, but you won't even listen to basic instructions. These rooms are *MINE!"*

He lashed out with his hand, sending a photo frame crashing against a wall, its glass shattering. He didn't seem to care about his bare feet as he stepped forward again towards Joshua.

"I didn't want this," he bellowed. "I didn't *ask* for this. You have no right!"

Joshua couldn't stop the tears from falling as he gasped and tried to fumble his way back out of the room. But he tripped and fell on his backside, leaving him staring up in horror at Darius's enormous, raging form.

"I'm sorry," Joshua whispered again.

He wished with everything he had that he hadn't opened that fucking door. Even though Darius was screaming and acting like he might hit him, Joshua's only thought was terrible guilt that he had violated Darius's privacy. It was painfully obvious he was ashamed of his scars and didn't want Joshua to see them.

"You have NO idea," Darius snarled, pacing like a caged animal as he clenched and unclenched his fists. "None. You *silly* child. You *boy!"*

Those words finally cut through Joshua's remorse, sending a flash of anger through him. He scrambled back up to his feet, balling his own fists and standing on his tiptoes, like a chihuahua facing up to a tiger. "I said I was sorry," he snapped, blinking away more tears. "But I didn't ask for this! This is my home now, too!"

Darius scoffed. "It's not your fucking home. How stupid are you? This is our *prison*."

Yes, Joshua figured he was stupid. How could he have possibly thought he had a chance of being happy here? That he and Darius might get along. Darius was a monster, just like his father was for inflicting this whole sham marriage on them both. But at least Victor had never screamed at him or made him feel physically threatened.

Fuck this shit.

Joshua didn't bother replying to the brute he'd been shackled to in matrimony. Instead, he turned and ran.

And ran.

He pushed his way blindly through doors, trying to see through his tears of rage. If Darius wanted him to get out, that was exactly what he would do.

Eventually, he was able to get his bearings and flee back towards the main entrance. He wasn't even sure what he had on him. His phone was so useless he'd stopped putting it in his pocket, but he was pretty sure he had his wallet.

As he shoved his arms back into his coat, he decided that would have to do.

Luckily he'd kept his boots on, so he just grabbed his scarf from where it had been left hanging by the side door, and pushed his way back outside. To think he'd been so happy when he'd last passed through here, thinking of something so benign as a rose garden. Darius was right. He was just a silly child, trying to cover up his real problems with trivial little pastimes.

Still sobbing, he jogged down the steps out into the freezing evening. Night had fallen and the snowstorm had fully come over them, meaning Joshua's feet were already running through half an inch of snow. He wasn't sure where he was heading except towards the nearby trees. The village was beyond the forest, away from the cliffs behind the castle. Perhaps if he could make it to even just a small scrap of civilisation, he could find a business and borrow a phone.

He desperately needed to hear his dad's voice.

The wind was howling over his messy cries, following him as he ploughed through the treeline. To start with, he was able to follow a dirt track, and he prayed it might lead him to the village. But once he was inside the forest, the light plummeted, and he quickly became disorientated. Thanks to the canopy, the snow wasn't falling as thickly, but the wind was still cutting viciously through him, and overhead thunder and lightning raged.

"Keep going," he uttered to himself through chattering teeth, hugging his coat tighter to his chest. Anything had to be better than going back to that godawful place.

He wasn't going to be *anyone's* prisoner any longer.

He couldn't make himself stop crying as he forged through the increasingly tangled trees, the branches cruelly snagging at his coat and jeans. He wished he'd grabbed some gloves. His hands felt like icicles.

Angrily he scrubbed his equally cold face, trying to stop the tears from falling. So what if Darius hated him? Joshua hated Darius too for treating him the way he had. Not just for the shouting but also for ignoring him and making an impossible situation so much more unbearable.

Pitifully, though, deep down, Joshua knew he'd just wanted a small hint that Darius *didn't* hate him. That they were comrades in this situation they'd been forced into. Joshua hadn't expected them to become best friends, but fucking hell, he hadn't wanted them to be enemies either.

It was too late for that now.

He gasped in several breaths of cold, damp air as he stopped to try and get his bearings. The snow was getting through the tree branches now, filling the dark night with strange shapes. It was like being caught in a snow globe, and Joshua was struggling to see anything at all. Not to mention the fact that he was so cold now it was becoming painful. His head ached, his lungs burned, and his fingers and toes were losing sensation.

Real fear was starting to creep through Joshua. This wasn't like getting lost in the castle. He wouldn't eventually find his way back if he gave it enough time.

Enough time stumbling helplessly around here would give him hypothermia. He was already feeling weak and tired.

He rubbed his face and tried to steel himself as he wrapped his scarf over his head, trying to retain some body heat. What should he do? As much as he didn't want to go back to the castle, that had to be closer than the village. But could he even find his way there?

A sob escaped his throat as his feet propelled him forward. Moving at least kept him a fraction warmer than standing still. But his limbs were getting so cold they were becoming numb, and within seconds, he tripped over a tree branch, only stopping himself from crashing to the ground by shooting his hand out to brace himself on the closest tree. Unfortunately, the bark also sliced through his hand, giving him several shallow cuts that stung, even though there was little feeling left in his hand.

"Fuck!" Joshua bellowed, cradling his hand to his chest as he continued stumbling onwards. Was he even going in the right direction?

It was as if every time he felt like he couldn't feel any more alone in this life, the universe proved to him how wrong he was. There was every chance he could die out in this storm without a soul for miles. Certainly no one near who cared about him.

No one who would mind if he lived or died.

"I'm sorry, Dad," Joshua choked out as he careened off another tree. He'd just wanted to hear his voice over the phone. Now he was never going to hear it again.

Suddenly, Joshua's foot slid out from under him as the ground abruptly changed texture. It almost felt like he was standing on wooden boards. But why would anyone put those in the middle of a forest?

It was so dark and the snow so thick, Joshua couldn't even see the trees anymore.

Or the *absence* of trees.

One second, he was tripping and sliding over the slick wooden boards. The next, he was flailing through the air as the ground fell away from him altogether. As he hit the freezing water, all the air rushed from his lungs. Joshua thought his heart might stop from the cold. He couldn't tell which way was up as he thrashed, already desperate to take a breath.

But it was hopeless. However he'd managed to fall into the water, he'd done so where it was deep enough that he couldn't find the bottom to at least push himself back to the surface. And even if he made it out, he'd be so cold now it wouldn't take long to pass out.

He was going to die.

5

DARIUS

For a big man, Darius wasn't aware he could possibly feel so small.

After Joshua had left, it must have taken him at least a couple of minutes to come out of his rage haze. It was as if he'd suddenly surfaced from underwater as he blinked and looked around what he considered the living room of his quarters. He stared at the glass that was shattered on the floor, briefly wondering how it had got there as he brushed a couple of chunks from the soles of his feet, glad he wasn't bleeding much.

Then it all came flooding back.

He looked down at his naked chest as shame swept through him. *Fuck.* This was exactly the kind of shit that had made him leave the army. It was as if he'd had no control over his emotions, adrenaline rushing through his system like he was right there, back in Afghanistan. There was no excuse for it, especially not with innocent Joshua. Darius wasn't a mindless beast.

But there was nothing he hated more than anyone seeing his scars. The ever-present reminder of how he'd failed and what he'd lost. Why should he get to still be here when others weren't?

When Richard wasn't?

Screwing up his eyes, Darius forced himself to take several breaths, then went to get fully dressed. He didn't want to tackle the broken glass until he had shoes on. Guilt followed him as he put his clothes on. What the hell must Joshua think of him, yelling like that? Joshua hadn't don't anything so terrible, not really. Yet Darius had lost his fucking mind at him.

His shoes safely on, he felt another pang as he lifted up the photo frame. It was one of his favourite pictures of his late mother. She'd passed away while he'd been in his teens, so almost twenty years ago now. The photo was a hard copy. There wasn't another floating around in cyberspace. He kept meaning to get it scanned but had never got around to it. At least it seemed unscathed from his inexcusable outburst.

He touched the image of her smiling face, her light hair braided over her shoulder like she always wore it. She'd been so young and full of life then, before the cancer had taken hold. Before Darius's life had changed forever.

He cleared his throat and set the glassless frame upright again before making short work of yet more mess he'd made in his quarters. He'd be so ashamed if Bartholomew saw what he'd done, but he would be even more ashamed if anyone were to find out how he'd treated his supposed husband.

He had to make things right with Joshua. Right now.

Yes, Darius had made it clear he shouldn't wander uninvited into Darius's rooms. But Joshua was also right. This was his home too, now, and Darius needed to stop acting like a junkyard dog protecting his territory. He'd been so thrown by their last encounter and Joshua's questions about them having sex, Darius hadn't actually considered that things could get any worse. But evidently, they had.

Belatedly, he covered his mouth and realised that part of his outburst might have been linked to that exchange. *Fuck.* Darius had been so preoccupied with keeping any of his temporary lustful thoughts to himself and recoiling from the idea that Joshua felt they were bound by duty to have sex, he'd undoubtedly reacted even more poorly to Joshua seeing his scarred and twisted body.

"Fuck," Darius growled to the empty room, thoroughly ashamed of himself. In trying to keep a lid on this completely inappropriate attraction, he'd inflamed the situation.

His throat thickened, wishing he'd put a shirt on, wishing he'd still been in the bath, wishing he'd been anywhere else aside from half-naked at the moment Joshua had accidentally walked in on him.

He'd wasted enough time just standing around and picking up glass. He needed to go look for Joshua.

Sheepishly, Darius bothered running a comb through his hair for once. If he was going to face Joshua again, he could at least try and not look like he'd been dragged through a hedge backwards. After he'd double-checked for any last shards of glass, he ventured out into the castle.

It was as if Joshua had left a trail of breadcrumbs for him to follow. Darius couldn't remember the last time he'd seen so many of the lights on. He decided not to turn them off as he passed. Thinking of Joshua in the dark didn't sit well with him. Perhaps it was time to illuminate the castle more often?

He expected to be led to Joshua's bedroom and other quarters. Darius hadn't visited Joshua while he'd been there, but he knew which area he'd been allocated. However, before he could get too far, his path was blocked.

Mrs Weatherby drew herself up to her full five feet and three inches, jamming her hands onto her ample hips. Her light brown cheeks were usually a little rosy, but in that moment she was flushed and blotchy, her expression a furious scowl.

"Enough!"

Darius winced. "Sorry, Mrs Weatherby," he said sincerely, although he wasn't sure what she was specifically referring to.

However, he could probably take a wild guess.

She was in her fifties, but her fingers were already starting to go a little crooked from arthritis. It was especially obvious as she thrust out a hand and pointed in the direction of Joshua's quarters. "That poor boy is alone and afraid! And what have you done? Acted like it's his fault. Left him all alone. He's the victim here! I thought that's why you joined the army, to look after people?"

Darius sighed glumly. "You're right."

"I bloody know I'm right," scoffed Mrs Weatherby. She crossed her arms and raised her eyebrows at him. "So get your head out of your arse and start acting like a civilised human being. I know you can, so get on with it."

Darius nodded, eager to prove that was exactly what he'd just been doing. "I was on my way to find him. I...I know I've behaved poorly."

Mrs Weatherby huffed and fixed him with a pointed stare. "You mean that charming display in your quarters just now? Your old mum would be *so* disappointed, Mr Legrand."

It didn't surprise him all that much that someone had heard his and Joshua's fight. These walls had ears. But Mrs Weatherby was a sly one. She would never mention his mum unless she had to. She knew her imagined disapproval would crush him, just like it did then. It was only ever her last resort, telling Darius what he already knew.

That he'd really fucked up.

She was totally right, though. If that was what it took to

make Darius behave, then he deserved that low blow. His mum would absolutely be mortified by him right now. Joshua didn't deserve to be treated so shamefully.

It was time for Darius to set things right. Not just after the argument but also to stop acting like Joshua was an intruder in his life.

Whether he liked it or not, Joshua was a *part* of Darius's life now. It was up to Darius how that played out. He wasn't used to having people close to him, though, and honestly, he feared what might happen to anyone in his life when his father next decided to be cruel. But his and Joshua's marriage was a direct result of Victor's last scheme, and it was *Darius* who had been cruel the past couple of weeks.

He needed to stop being afraid of what might happen to Joshua if the two of them became friends, and start worrying about what was already happening thanks to Darius's neglect.

Joshua had looked so scared as he'd fled. He was probably still scared right now. Darius needed to find him and make things right.

A voice in the back of his head reminded him of his dreaded secret attraction. But in light of his unforgivable loss of temper, his stupid crush paled in comparison. He was sure his feelings towards Joshua in that regard would fade after this. Joshua probably hated him, rightly so. There would be no danger of inappropriateness, surely?

Darius could deal with that once he'd apologised. His priority now was finding Joshua. There were a lot of places to hide around here.

"Do you know where he is?" Darius asked, feeling contrite, but the words still came out as a grunt. He really needed to work on that if he was going to be talking to people more. He'd only been out of the army for a few years. How had he become such a Neanderthal?

Mrs Weatherby shrugged and looked a little mollified. "Well, he's not in his rooms. I can tell you that much. The lights were all off when I popped my head in to see if he wanted any dinner."

Damn. Darius nodded and chewed his lip, deciding to keep following Joshua's lightbulb breadcrumb trail. "Oh, thank you," he remembered to call over his shoulder before he'd stomped off too far.

"You're welcome," Mrs Weatherby replied, sounding faintly amused.

Darius found himself by the side door that led out into what had once been the castle gardens, but there was still no sign of his wayward husband. "Joshua?" he cried out. Curiosity compelled him to open one of the doors. But as he'd suspected, it was filthy weather. A gale was blowing, and snow flung through the air. As Darius grimaced, thunder rumbled overhead. He was about to close the door when something caught his eye.

Was that a footprint?

It was difficult to tell, as the snow was still falling, but Darius was almost certain that he was looking at a faint outline of a shoe tread on the stone step.

Jerking the door, he looked back inside at the coat stand. Joshua's shabby blue jacket was no longer there, and neither was his scarf.

"Fuck!" Darius yelled, already throwing on his own long coat and shoving his feet into his boots. Why would Joshua go out into the cold and dark like that?

Because Darius had literally screamed at him to get out.

Bitter shame swelled in Darius, but he ignored it for now. His priority was finding Joshua. How long had he been outside in the storm? At least the snow might make him easier to track.

Darius slammed the door behind him as he ran towards

the stables. The lead stable hand, Paulo, looked startled at Darius's sudden appearance but wasted no time in helping him gear up his trusty Clydesdale horse, Hephaestus.

"Are you sure you want to go out in this, sir?" Paulo asked in concern as Darius steered the horse towards the stable doors.

Darius shook his head grimly. "I haven't got a choice. Could I ask you to wait for our return? Heph will likely be cold."

Paulo nodded. "Of course, sir," he said emphatically. "Good luck."

Even though Paulo didn't know why Darius was venturing out into the storm, Darius still appreciated the sentiment.

"Come *on*, Heph," Darius growled as the damn horse whinnied and sulked about having to go out into the snow. Darius tapped his flanks with his heels. "It's important, Heph. *Please.*" Heph brayed loudly, clearly explaining that he would cooperate, as it was obviously an emergency, but he didn't have to be *happy* about it.

Within minutes, they were galloping into the night. Joshua's tracks were harder to locate this way, meaning Darius had to stop and start a few times, searching for any traces of footprints or kicked-up snow and mud. But once they were on their way, Hephaestus made the journey much faster.

Darius's throat thickened as they entered the forest. Joshua was so *small.* He hardly had any meat on his bones. He'd feel the cold far more keenly than Darius ever would. Was he wearing a hat? How much heat had he already lost?

Pushing through the dense foliage, Darius was beginning to appreciate pretty damn fast how upset he would be if anything happened to Joshua because of him. If anything happened at *all,* but especially if it was because of him. He was innocent, and Victor might have pushed them into this marriage, but it was Darius who had scared Joshua into the middle of the woods in a snowstorm.

Mrs Weatherby was right. When he'd joined the armed forces, all Darius had wanted to do was protect people, and here he was endangering the man he'd literally taken vows to love and cherish.

He was pretty certain he and Joshua couldn't love each other. They were worlds apart, and Joshua deserved someone so much better than a grizzled, bad-tempered oaf like Darius. But by god, Darius was going to make sure no harm came to him, that was for sure.

Fear was gnawing at him, though. There was still no sign of Joshua himself despite the trail of muddy footprints and broken tree branches Darius and Hephaestus had been following. Darius bellowed out his name again, straining for any response over the howling wind. But there was nothing.

"No, no, no," he growled to himself, tugging at Heph's reins as they forced their way further into the woods. Where the hell had Joshua been going? Had he even had a destination in mind? Maybe he'd been hoping to find the village, but that was east, and they were heading farther north.

Unfortunately, because they were crashing through the undergrowth, that meant they were making a fair bit of noise over the howling winds themselves. So when Darius thought he'd heard a voice cry out in the distance, he was too slow at stopping Heph to hear any more.

He cursed under his breath and held his horse still, straining for anything further. He and Hephaestus were panting heavily, their breaths clouding up the air already thick with fat, wet snowflakes, and the wind howled like a wounded beast. Darius wasn't sure what he was hoping to pick up over all that.

Just as he realised he should shout out Joshua's name again, he definitely *did* hear another noise. But it took him a second to register what it could possibly be.

A splash?

"The lake!"

Darius flung himself off Hephaestus. He might be faster on horseback in the long run, but in this dense foliage, he would be just as quick on foot, and he'd have the advantage of being able to hear more. He was almost certain he was heading in the right direction. It was pretty much impossible to get his bearings in such nasty weather, but he'd caught a glimpse of the moon's position through a break in the clouds, suggesting the lake was up ahead to the left.

"Joshua!" he yelled as the dock came into sight. *Shit.* With dread, Darius dashed over to the wooden boards, seeing quite clearly where a pair of shoes had slipped, leaving skid marks in the slimy dirt. The lake's surface was full of ripples and waves thanks to the snowstorm, but with no other sign of Joshua nearby, Darius realised with dread what had almost certainly happened.

What he had to do.

In a flash, he ripped off his long coat and yanked his boots from his feet. There was no sense in drenching everything. Wasting no more time, he sat on the end of the small dock, hissing as he dropped his feet into the turbulent, icy waters. He had no idea how deep the lake was at this point or how long Joshua might have been under. Taking a deep breath, Darius shoved himself off the edge of the dock and plummeted into the black depths, praying he wasn't too late.

6

JOSHUA

JOSHUA WASN'T GIVING UP. NO WAY. HE HAD TOO MUCH LIFE left to live. This wasn't the end. It couldn't be.

That just wouldn't be fair.

But life wasn't fair. No matter how much he thrashed and fumbled in the depths of the freezing cold water, he couldn't find any purchase. How deep was this lake? Which way was up? It didn't matter. His clothes were dragging him down like stones around his ankles.

No! He couldn't just give up! But his lungs and eyes were burning, and he could feel his strength slipping away. He still reached and kicked, praying for a miracle.

A hand closed around his wrist.

Terror surged through Joshua, making him scream out his last precious scraps of air. But then he was being pulled, and his head broke the surface of the water. Coughing and spluttering, he gasped for air, still thrashing as he tried to right himself.

"I've got you. I've *got* you." The voice was hoarse and low. Joshua jerked as two large hands seized him by the shoulders.

Suddenly, he found himself staring up at a soaking wet Darius.

"W-wha-?" Joshua stammered as Darius trod water, still clinging to Joshua's shoulders. Fucking hell, he was so confused, and he'd never known cold like this. It was as if it was slicing directly into his bones. His head throbbed, and his lungs still burned as Darius hauled him back to where he'd fallen. Joshua could now tell it was a dock, and he'd slipped right off it.

Idiot.

In a flash, Darius dragged himself out of the freezing lake, the water streaming off him in rivers as Joshua clung to the side of the dock with a numb hand. Then Darius reached down and pulled Joshua out after him.

Joshua wasn't sure if it was better out of the water or worse.

"F-f-*fuck*," he stammered, shaking so badly he felt like he was going to rattle apart. Snow was flinging through the air around them, the gale still howling like a wounded beast. Joshua was dimly aware of Darius walking away from him and thrusting his big feet into even bigger dry boots. Then he picked up a coat from where it had been hanging from a tree branch and slung it over Joshua's shoulders. Joshua groaned at the immediate relief it gave him, not resisting when Darius hugged him against his massive form, rubbing Joshua's back vigorously.

"We need to get you back to Thorncliff, right now," Darius barked. Joshua wanted to agree, but it was like his tongue wouldn't work. So he didn't even think to protest when Darius swept him up in his arms like a bloody ragdoll, carrying him through the trees.

Was he going to carry Joshua all the way home? That seemed like too much. Joshua pawed at Darius's chest, trying to tell him to put him down, that he could walk. But all of a sudden, there was a horse. Where did the horse come from?

Joshua clutched the massive coat around him as Darius lifted him and sat him sideways on the saddle. Then Darius used the stirrup to push up as well, slinging his meaty leg over the horse's back. He pulled Joshua against him, cradling him with a solid arm. The other hand grabbed the reins and steered the braying horse, turning it around. Then they were galloping through the trees.

Joshua had never ridden on a horse, let alone side-saddle. It was a jarring, somewhat overwhelming experience. But all the while, Darius clutched Joshua to his chest, making him feel secure.

The wind whipped mercilessly around Joshua's ears, and his hands felt like they might never move from the tight grip they had on Darius's coat. In fact, they didn't feel anything anymore. They were so numb. His head rolled as he was abruptly overcome with exhaustion, thumping into Darius's chest.

"NO!" Darius yelled, scaring the shit out of Joshua and waking him right back up again. "Stay with me, Joshua. Don't fall asleep!"

Joshua wanted to ask why. Sleep felt like a really good idea. But thanks to Darius's shout, adrenaline was pumping through him again, making his heart race. So he nodded against Darius's chest, showing that he understood.

Breaking through the tree line felt almost as much of a relief as when Joshua had finally re-emerged from the lake. The snow and wind were worse here, but it felt like he could breathe again. He gasped, filling his lungs with cold air.

The castle was in sight.

Sleep was trying to claim Joshua again, so he began counting, telling himself they would reach the main entrance before he got to one hundred.

At seventy-three, Darius pulled the horse to a stop, making the animal rear up and whinny. A man Joshua hadn't seen before appeared from the stables outside of the dining room Joshua had spent his first night looking out of.

"Is he all right?" the man asked, confidently petting the horse's nose. He must work in the stable, Joshua realised, which was probably why he hadn't seen him until now.

While he was mulling over benign thoughts, his brain too tired to cope with much else, Darius swung down from the horse. "Shh, Hephaestus," he murmured, rubbing the horse's nose, then resting his forehead against it. "You did magnificently. Paulo, make sure to take extra good care of him tonight. He's been through a lot." Darius looked up at Joshua. "I'll deal with everything else. It's fine."

"Of course, sir," said the stable hand, although he didn't seem convinced that everything was fine, and Joshua had to agree with him.

He was freezing to death.

Teeth chattering, he tried to slide off the saddle, but then Darius was there, pulling him back into his arms and carrying him across the grounds and into the castle. Joshua moaned at the sudden warmth as they crossed the threshold back inside. Until that moment, he would have put money on the castle only ever feeling like a tomb. He'd been going to bed with three hot water bottles every night since he'd arrived. But now it felt toasty, welcoming.

It felt like home.

He clung to Darius as they barrelled up the stairs and along bright corridors. Were those lights still lit from when Joshua had turned them on hours ago? How long had that been, really? It could have been days for all Joshua was aware.

His senses were slowly coming back to him, enough to realise that they were headed towards Darius's private quarters, where Joshua wasn't supposed to go. But now,

Darius didn't hesitate as he shoved his way through the various doors, bringing Joshua into a darkened bathroom. Carefully, Darius rested Joshua on his feet again, checking he was okay to stand before letting him go. Then he flicked on a couple of lamps and flung open a cupboard. He pulled out several large bath towels and draped one hurriedly around Joshua's shoulders over Darius's voluminous coat, then Darius rubbed at his own drenched clothes and hugged the towel around him.

Joshua watched, shivering, as Darius filled the freestanding copper bath, his boots sliding occasionally on the tiled floor as he moved. He poured some kind of oil in too, making the air thick with the scent of lavender as soapy bubbles crept over the surface of the steaming water. Darius's shoulders were hunched under the towel, his face glowering as he watched the bath fill.

Joshua's teeth chattered as he stood there feeling foolish. He'd caused such a bloody fuss. It was almost too much to remain in Darius's presence. He was so embarrassed. But it was as if he was unable to make his frozen feet move. There wasn't much else for him to do but study his rescuer's profile in the dimly lit room.

Darius didn't have to come after him like that. In fact, it would have solved a lot of his problems if Joshua had been lost in the snow.

So why had he followed?

Joshua didn't realise how tightly he was hugging himself until Darius turned suddenly and discarded the towel and coat around Joshua's shoulders before prying his stiff fingers from his arms. Methodically, Darius proceeded to peel Joshua's icy, sodden clothes from his body, yanked off his ruined shoes, and dumped them all in a pile. When he got to the underwear, he didn't hesitate, pulling down Joshua's briefs as if it were perfectly normal to be seeing him naked.

Joshua barely had time to let out a little gasp of surprise before Darius scooped him up in his muscular arms and carefully deposited him in the now full bath. The water was almost too hot, making Joshua hiss, but it was also glorious after the snow and bitter wind. Within seconds, Joshua sighed, submerging all the way up to his chin. He was glad of the suds that were now hiding his modesty.

Darius turned off the two taps, the metal squealing loudly. But then the bathroom was oddly quiet. Joshua was almost afraid to move and disturb the water. He watched as Darius slumped to the floor, his back against the bath as he dropped his head in his hands, his elbows resting on his raised knees.

The lavender in the steamy air was opening up Joshua's lungs and making him feel wide awake, his skin prickling with anticipation of what might happen next. Guilt was eating him alive, and it wasn't long before words blurted from his mouth.

"I'm sorry."

He bit his lip, studying the back of Darius's head for a reaction.

Darius huffed and dropped his hands between his knees, his head still bowed. The silence stretched on, making Joshua think that maybe Darius wasn't going to reply.

He did eventually, though.

"You're not a prisoner here," he said heavily, not lifting his gaze from the chipped tiled floor. "I didn't mean…I know this isn't what either of us want. But I never should have shouted or said those awful things. I hate that I made you scared."

Joshua swallowed. That was possibly the most kind words he'd heard Darius string together yet. He couldn't help but feel warmed by them.

"I shouldn't have run out into the middle of nowhere in a

61

storm like a child having a tantrum," Joshua said through clenched teeth. At least they'd stopped clacking. "It was stupid. I don't know what I was thinking."

"That you wanted to get away from me," Darius growled. "I don't blame you."

For some reason, that stung. Yes, Joshua had lashed out and tried to take back some control. But Darius hadn't caused the situation they were in. They were both victims here when it came down to it.

Joshua lifted his right hand from the water, the droplets noisy as he tried his best to shake it dry. Then he reached over and squeezed Darius's shoulder through the towel. "I was scared," he admitted, doing his best not to let his voice tremble. "You really shouted at me. But...I was wrong to barge in on you like that. I understand why you were upset."

To his surprise, Darius's large, calloused hand suddenly came up and covered Joshua's, giving it a good squeeze. It was freezing, reminding Joshua that Darius had been in the lake, too. Darius dropped his hand almost as quickly as he had lifted it, leaving Joshua slightly breathless at the ghost of the sensation.

"Nothing excuses that sort of temper," Darius said, sounding so bitter it made Joshua's heart ache. "I don't want you to be afraid of me. I'd hate that."

Joshua licked his lips, not sure if he should remove his hand or not. Rather than linger awkwardly, he gave Darius what he hoped was a reassuring squeeze on his shoulder, then slipped his arm back under the warm water. He wasn't used to offering anyone comfort other than his dad – not even a friend, as Joshua had purposefully shied away from them for most of his life. So to offer sympathy to another man in such an intimate moment made him feel slightly light-headed.

"I don't think I am afraid of you," he said slowly. "Unless you shout and throw things. So maybe, um…"

"Do less of that?" Darius suggested.

Was Joshua hearing things, or had there been a hint of mirth in those words?

He swallowed and frowned at the back of Darius's head, trying not to let his heart race too much. But that was all he wanted. Some kindness and camaraderie. Hell, even sharing these few words were going such a long way to give Joshua some faith that he hadn't been married off to a total monster.

"We're in this together," Joshua said firmly. "We just have to be better toward each other, that's all."

"I'll be better," said Darius. It sounded like a promise.

"Thank you," Joshua said, looking down at the water. It was amazing how quickly it had gone from scalding to tepid in response to Joshua's freezing body. Darius might have been twice his size, but he still needed to warm up as well.

For one, utterly mystifying second, it was on the tip of Joshua's tongue to suggest Darius get into the bath *with* him. He'd probably fit, but the idea of them sharing a space *naked* together was completely ridiculous, not to mention beyond embarrassing. So Joshua did not suggest that. But he was still worried about his rescuer.

"You need to get out of those clothes," Joshua croaked. His eyes widened, realising what he'd just implied. "You'll catch your death!" he added with a squeak, sloshing the bathwater as he sat up a little straighter. "I mean, uh…"

Darius glanced over his shoulder and nodded. "Stay there." He rose to his feet and walked through the door into the only adjacent room, which Joshua was pretty sure had to be his bedroom. He hadn't exactly been making a map when they'd made their way here.

When he heard rustling and drawers being opened and closed, Joshua decided he probably had a minute or two. So he drained a few inches of now lukewarm water, then ran the hot tap again to top it up. He also poured in another slosh of the lavender oil, encouraging more bubbles to cover his naked body. Darius had already seen him, but there was a difference between a quick glance and lying there exposed.

Just as Joshua was turning the squeaky tap back off, Darius returned, wearing jogging bottoms, a hoodie, different boots, and a dressing gown. He wasn't clean, but he at least looked warm. He had a relatively large and flat cushion in his hand that he dropped on the floor, where he proceeded to sit himself down cross-legged, facing Joshua.

Joshua gulped.

Especially glad of the extra bubbles now, he clung to the edge of the copper tub and peeked at Darius over the rim. For a moment, they just stared at each other.

"Tell me how to be a better husband," Darius blurted. Then he shifted uncomfortably, looking down at the dirty clothes on the bathroom floor.

Something funny twisted inside Joshua at the use of the word 'husband'. It was almost as if that word finally meant something between them.

But that was silly. Darius was just asking how they could improve this highly unusual arrangement between them.

Joshua cleared his throat and licked his lips, a faint taste of lavender from the water on them. "I don't know," he said softly. "I've never even had a boyfriend before."

"But you're-" Darius began, his eyes flashing up and boring directly into Joshua's. Then they softened. Darius swallowed and seemed to consider what he wanted to say. "That surprises me."

Joshua tried not to blush in embarrassment. He might as well have had a sign over his neck, saying 'I'm a big, fat virgin!' But Darius didn't appear to be mocking him, so Joshua just shrugged.

"I don't know how to be in a relationship. I don't know how to live with a partner."

Darius tilted his head, the waves of dark, wiry hair glinting in the lamplight. "Tell me what you *do* know, maybe?" Joshua was surprised by how kind the words were. Darius wasn't ordering Joshua. He was asking him. Nicely. "What are you thinking, I mean?" Darius looked sheepish. "I'm aware I haven't asked you that at all since you got here. I'm sorry."

Joshua's chest twisted, but not in an unpleasant way. For Darius to apologise for his neglect was somehow more meaningful than him apologising for yelling and smashing things. That bad behaviour was much easier to recognise than the more subtle silent treatment.

Joshua almost told Darius that it was okay, but it hadn't been. "Thank you," he said instead, offering him a tentative smile. "I appreciate that."

Then he bit his lip and leaned his chin on the bath, wracking his brain. What *was* he thinking? What did he want?

"It would be nice to see you a bit more often," Joshua said, deciding to just go for honesty. He'd almost died. This wasn't the time for beating around the bush. "I know you might not like me, but-"

He was going to say that they were stuck in this together. However, Darius interrupted before he could finish.

"*I like you,*" he rasped, looking back down at the tiled floor. He traced a pattern along the cracks with one of his blunt fingers. "You're kind and thoughtful."

Joshua opened and closed his mouth, staring at Darius as he kept his head bowed, his dark waves hiding his face. Joshua hadn't been expecting that at all. How did Darius know that he was those things? Had he seen him being kind and thoughtful when Joshua wasn't looking?

Well, he wasn't about to look a gift compliment in the mouth. "Uh, thank you."

"I'll stop hiding away in my tower like Nosferatu." To Joshua's surprise, when Darius lifted his head, there was a twitch of a smile playing on his lips.

Joshua couldn't help but bark a laugh in response, the sudden noise echoing loudly in the quiet bathroom. He splashed the bathwater as he clapped his hands over his mouth, but he'd been so relieved to see any hint of warmth from Darius it had been too much of a shock *not* to laugh. And now Darius was really smiling at him, showing teeth and everything. It was strange in a sort of wonderful way.

"Okay," Joshua said breathlessly once the water had calmed again. "Let's try getting to know each other, maybe?"

Darius nodded. "Deal." He pulled a thread on his dressing gown. "Is there anything else you want that I can do? I'll put a rush on the internet connection. I'm sorry it hasn't already been done."

Warmth blossomed in Joshua's chest. He knew broadband wasn't a classic romantic gesture, but to him, it felt extremely touching in that moment.

Not that any of this was romance. But perhaps he and Darius were starting to become friends? Or, at least, not enemies?

"That would be brilliant, thank you," Joshua said sincerely. Then he remembered *why* he'd wanted internet earlier, not just to connect with his dad and the outside world again. "Actually, I was hoping I might…I mean, if you don't mind…it's just no one is taking care of it right now…"

"Spit it out," Darius said firmly, his eyebrows raised.

A shiver of lust ran through Joshua's whole body, taking him completely by surprise. Wow. Apparently, Joshua liked it when Darius took control. That was…new.

Darius shook his head. "You have every right to ask for

what you want. Unless you're being rude, you can ask me anything. This is your home. I think we both need to stop acting like you're a guest, or worse, an intruder."

Joshua took a moment to swallow and consider what Darius was saying. "Okay," he said slowly. "I want to try and replant the garden. To save it. But that would take supplies." Money, was what he really meant, something he technically had none of now. It was all in Darius's family's name.

A curious expression came over Darius's face as he looked at Joshua. Joshua was tempted to squirm under the scrutiny and slip further under the suds. But having just been told to be more assertive, he refused to let himself fidget.

Darius swallowed, his mouth twitching in one corner as he regarded Joshua. "The gardens here belonged to my mother before she became too sick to tend them. No one has cared for them since." Darius blinked and shook himself as if coming out of a reverie. "You can have whatever you need. I'll set you up a credit card. Once the internet is up and running, you should be able to order anything to be delivered here."

Joshua felt his mouth open and close, completely taken aback by Darius's openness. He almost protested that if the grounds had been special to his mum, who was obviously no longer with them, then a professional should take care of them.

But what the hell else was Joshua going to do around here if he didn't take on a project? Besides, knowing that they'd once been the pride and joy of Darius's mum made him want to bring them back to their former glory even more.

He was going to do this for both of them. And their mums.

"I lost my mum when I was little," Joshua blurted out, not sure if he was doing the right thing. Darius's eyes widened, and for a moment, they held each other's gazes.

"I'm sorry," Darius murmured eventually.

Joshua nodded. If he was horribly honest with himself, he barely remembered her anymore. He hated that. But he did know one thing.

"She liked roses. Dad's company was always struggling. I don't really understand how, seeing as he was the boss and all. However, we were always pretty poor. But every year, Dad would get her a single rose on her birthday, and she'd keep it thriving for weeks. Then she'd press the heads into a book with a little note of what was going on that year. Like, if she got a new job, or when I was born."

That book was currently under his pillow in his bedroom here at the castle. Dad had given it to him after Mum had died, and little Joshua had cried himself to sleep, hugging it for weeks.

Darius smiled at him again, but this time it wasn't toothy and filled with laughter. It was something else.

Something deeper.

"Then I think the rose bushes should be the first thing you revive," he said, his rumbly voice even lower than usual as he blinked slightly shiny eyes.

Joshua's heart ached. "I think so, too."

It was baby steps. Barely any progress at all. But to Joshua, it felt monumental, like they'd made leaps and bounds.

Maybe this marriage wasn't going to be a total disaster after all?

7

DARIUS

DARIUS HAD COMPLETELY FORGOTTEN WHAT IT FELT LIKE having someone with expectations of him that weren't total failure. It was strange. He had to remind himself what it was like to be needed.

Wanted.

The incident at the lake had been a nasty wake-up call for how easy it was to be a selfish son of a bitch. It had nearly cost Joshua his life. Regardless of Darius's feelings towards him, no one should be put in danger because the other person was a stupid, stubborn dickhead. But the truth was that Darius was starting to care quite a bit about his new living companion.

His *husband*. The word was becoming slightly less alien to him, and he was trying not to be so weird around Joshua. It had been completely unacceptable to ignore him the way Darius had, and Darius's reasoning seemed so pathetic now. That night, sitting on the cold bathroom floor, finally looking into Joshua's eyes for the first time, and truly listening to him, had changed everything.

Joshua was lost. It was up to Darius to keep him safe, and not just from physical danger.

But from being alone.

How was it possible that Joshua had never had a boyfriend before? Darius couldn't even fathom it. He'd seen Joshua's surprise when Darius had called him kind and thoughtful, but he knew it to be true. That, combined with his looks, should surely have made him the catch of his home town.

Well, those men had obviously been fools. And it wasn't any of Darius's business anyway, especially now he was doing better at wrestling with his morals.

Joshua being beautiful wasn't his problem. It was Darius's. After such a fright, Darius realised it was actually pretty simple to keep his thoughts respectable and his hands to himself. Responsibility was something that always succeeded in kicking his arse into gear, so once he saw the wrangling of his feelings as a kind of order to himself to protect a junior officer, it was almost easy.

Besides, Darius was now getting a completely different kind of joy from Joshua's company, something quite new and unexpected for him.

Joshua was thriving, and seeing him bloom made Darius happier than he could have ever imagined.

It was the simple things, like realising he was confident enough to ask Camille for the food he preferred now, including pastries. Darius wasn't sure who was made happier by that development. Camille, for discovering she had a new, willing taste-tester; Joshua, who learned that macarons were now his favourite treat and got them freshly baked most days; or Darius, who simply appreciated the results of Joshua eating better.

It wasn't like Joshua had been underfed before, but he'd definitely been on the skinny side. Now in the couple of weeks since the lake incident, his cheeks were glowing and looking less hollow, and he had a very slight but totally adorable round tummy.

Not that Darius was looking. Too much. Maybe a little. He was only human, after all.

Whether either of them had wanted it to, their relationship had changed fundamentally that night. They hadn't so much crossed barriers as smashed them to pieces. It was inevitable that Darius's feelings for Joshua would become more complicated, purely from the fact that he was no longer doing everything he could to steer clear of the poor man.

Initially, even after their conversation in the bathroom, Darius had wondered if *Joshua* might treat him differently, in a bad way. Darius would have earned it after the way he'd lost his temper, but it was more than that he'd been worried about.

Joshua had seen his scars.

Once the shock of that night had worn off, Darius began to look for signs that Joshua was repulsed by him. He'd got a full view of Darius's worst failures in all their glory. But if anything, Joshua had been more upset over the intrusion than Darius had been, apologising many times until Darius had firmly assured him that everything was okay.

Emotionally, it had taken some time for Darius to detach himself and understand that he hadn't been attacked or violated. Of course Joshua hadn't tried to hurt him on purpose. But it hadn't escaped Darius's attention that Joshua had never once mentioned his scars since. He'd apologised for coming in unannounced to a place he'd been told was off limits, but he'd not even hinted that there had been anything unusual about Darius's appearance.

He must have noticed. How could he fail to? The career-ending attack had left Darius hideous, of that he was fully aware. Yet Joshua didn't bat an eyelid or remark on a thing. He must have had questions, but so far, Darius hadn't even caught him glancing at his chest. It gave Darius a strange sense of peace, like he'd been holding his breath and hadn't even realised it.

He appreciated Joshua not making a big deal over the most painful moment of his whole life, as bizarre as that might seem to some people. His CO had tried to get Darius to open up and talk about that day, but he'd always refused. What good would hashing it over do? What was done was done.

Except, in a strange way, now that Joshua knew, it was as if some pressure had been taken off Darius. They didn't need to talk about it, but knowing that Joshua was aware of his darkest secret and hadn't rejected him made Darius feel less of a monster. Perhaps that was why he was able to see Joshua as less of a beautiful ornament and more of a person with feelings.

Maybe fate had meant for them to run into each other in that moment, so they could both start to see the other as more human?

So no, Darius refused to feel guilty or ashamed for appreciating that Joshua looked happier and healthier since his arrival at Thorncliff. In fact, he was proud of himself for managing to stutter out such a thought to him over dinner one day.

Because that was something else that they'd been trying their best to do: share meals. It certainly made the grouchy Camille happier that her food was no longer going to waste, but Darius had also discovered that it wasn't *so* terrifying to sit down for at least a few minutes with his new husband a couple of times a day. Even if they'd just spent the past fortnight clumsily discussing the weather and Joshua's gardening research.

Darius was definitely less lonely. He got the feeling from Joshua's shy smiles that he was too.

It was therefore tempting to start to relax, to feel like maybe this marriage – this whole situation – wasn't going to be such a disaster after all.

But Darius had known his father his whole life.

It had taken him a couple of days, but after his and Joshua's scare had worn off and they were attempting to feel out a new kind of relationship of living together, it had suddenly occurred to Darius that he'd almost missed one of Victor's schemes.

Initially, he'd assumed that his perverted insistence that Joshua and Darius sleep together had been with the intention of putting Joshua in an unbearable position of having to offer himself up to Darius in an almost transactional way. Which had probably been a part of it. But then it had occurred to Darius that Victor had more than likely been intentionally trying to force Darius to reveal his scars.

Suddenly, it all made sense. Why would Victor willingly agree to set his son – who he'd spent a lifetime hating – up with a gorgeous partner? A *man,* no less. Victor had called Darius a pervert ever since he'd found gay porn magazines under his bed as a teenager. But when Darius realised Victor had the perfect opportunity to ridicule Darius for the rest of his life, the pieces all came together. Victor could put someone in place to be repulsed by Darius's twisted form every single day. And who better to do Victor's bidding (albeit unwillingly) than perfect, beautiful, innocent Joshua?

For an awful few hours, Darius had wondered if Joshua might have been in on the plot. After all, Joshua had come and raised the issue of them sleeping together of his own volition.

But it was clear to see that Joshua wasn't malicious. He was gentle and loyal. If Victor had made him feel like his father or any of their employees' families would be at risk if he didn't offer himself up, then it was no surprise to Darius that he'd do it.

So Darius had quashed those fears and tried to focus on enjoying his time with Joshua as they tentatively tried to get to know one another. Darius was ashamed to say he was still skittish at spending time one-on-one, afraid that he'd run out of conversation and Joshua would realise how thick he was. But so far, they'd survived several dinners together, one random meeting in the hallways, and a walk through the castle's grounds.

The spontaneous stroll had been the most illuminating for Darius as he'd had the chance to see Joshua's face light up as he talked about ideas he had for the gardens. It was clear he didn't know the names of a lot of things, and he was fumbling his way through vague concepts, but he was just so enthusiastic about tidying up the place and showing it love that none of the technical jargon mattered.

What mattered was that caring for something was making Joshua bloom as much as being cared for was, and that warmed Darius's heart in strange ways.

Life breathed life. And emptiness only created more sorrow and loneliness. Now Darius had stopped skulking in his rooms, he was seeing that more of the staff were out and about, making themselves busy in a way that Darius couldn't remember since his mother had been alive and he'd lived here with her. Joshua had received his first delivery of gardening equipment and had begun digging up the dead plants and freshening up the soil as much as he could in mid-February. There weren't even any flowers yet, but there was already more wildlife populating the grounds, Darius was certain.

It didn't hurt that Joshua would come in from a day's work, smelling like warm earth and musky from manual labour, his dirt-streaked face beaming as he talked about what he'd achieved. As the days passed by, Darius found himself keeping an eye out of the window for when Joshua would start packing up his tools. Darius would then just happen to wander down to the front entrance, passing by at a convenient time for Joshua to tell him excitedly about what bulbs he was planting or how tricky a particular tree stump was being to uproot.

Darius didn't have much to add to those conversations, but his heart sang, knowing that Joshua was no longer feeling like a prisoner in this castle.

At least, so Darius hoped.

There was still a lot of Darius that was holding back and being cautious. He mustn't mistake Joshua's tentative happiness and purposefulness as any invitation for Darius's inappropriate feelings. Joshua had still been pulled into this marriage and this castle against his will. He'd almost got himself killed trying to find his way back to civilisation.

But there were rules they had to stick to, even if they were archaic and preposterous.

Victor always had to be obeyed. Darius knew that from painful experience.

Darius's father had apparently been very clear about that in this letter Joshua had received but Darius had only heard of. He suspected Joshua was embarrassed by it. But Darius wouldn't have minded clarification on that by reading it with his own eyes.

According to the rules, Joshua was to remain at the castle – for how long Darius wasn't sure and didn't feel he could find out yet without poking the wasps' nest. Joshua seemed okay with not earning as he was still keeping himself busy and Darius's credit card was buying him anything he needed.

It felt strange to be spending money again. After all,

Darius didn't really earn a salary from his joke of a job that Victor had forced upon him.

But that didn't mean Darius was poor. Far from it.

When his mother had passed, she had been in possession of a large fortune from her own independently wealthy family. Although she never spoke ill of her husband, Darius was certain that in her final days she'd begun to suspect that he was no good. So that substantial inheritance had been iron clad in Darius's name. It was one of his only true accomplishments in life that he'd so far managed to keep his father's greasy paws off it.

But Darius had also been loathed to squander any of that money on anything even remotely connected to Victor. Since Thorncliff had been forced on him by his father, Darius had been reluctant to spend even a penny on renovations. He would rather live in a crumbling mausoleum than waste his dear mother's money on Victor's 'empire'.

But that was before Joshua had arrived and reminded Darius that he was hiding in the dark to spite himself.

Not to mention the couple of dozen staff who also lived and worked at the castle. By simply flicking on some lights, Joshua had woken Darius up to how selfish he'd been by imposing his miserly ways on them.

His mother wouldn't want that. In fact, Darius was surprised that Mrs Weatherby hadn't scolded him for being a grumpy old bastard and letting his mum down like that. Why keep the place miserable when a little investment could make it grand again?

So Darius had trusted Joshua with a credit card and told him to get whatever he needed for his garden project, forcing himself not to fear that his mother's fortune was being wasted. After all, it was vast. Joshua would have to buy a fuckton of roses to even make a dent in it. Darius had nothing to worry about.

Especially when Joshua was clearly so happy, and Darius knew his mum would be happy too if she could only see him.

It hadn't taken Darius long to figure out that he would do almost anything to protect that sweet happiness. Which was why when Darius heard that his father had shown up unannounced yet again, his reaction hadn't been his usual mix of furious incredulity. It was a calm, cold rage that he almost relished.

Almost.

"Oh, marvellous," Darius said with a sigh.

Bartholomew gave Darius a knowing look as he delivered the message that Victor was once again waiting for Darius in the drawing room.

"Remind me again why this place doesn't have a moat and drawbridge?" Darius muttered, quickly running over several scenarios in his mind as to what his father could want.

Bartholomew raised his eyebrows. "Then it would be too easy to have unfortunate accidents, sir," he replied dryly.

Darius wasn't convinced they'd be all that 'unfortunate'.

He stomped all the way to the drawing room, his head held high.

"There is this amazing invention called the telephone," Darius griped as he threw the door open, making it bounce off the wall. He was disgruntled that his good mood from talking with Joshua about rhododendrons earlier had been extinguished so fast. "It would be nice to know you were coming."

So Darius could raise the metaphorical drawbridge. For the first time in years, it felt like he had something worth protecting from his father's meddling. Probably exactly why Victor was visiting for the second time in a month.

"Telephone reception? Out here?" Victor scoffed. "Besides, this is my house. I can visit when I like."

Darius marched into the room and sat down at his desk

before his father could beat him to it like last time. "No, it's *my* house. You gave it to me. And it's not a house. It's a bloody castle."

Because that was what Victor did. He bought things so he could control them, not out of any sense of love or generosity. Darius had felt owned his entire life, which was why he had escaped to the army the first chance he'd got. It was somewhat ironic that the only time Darius had felt truly free had been when he'd been in one of the most regulated and disciplined professions in the world.

Unsurprisingly, Victor ignored Darius's clapback. Instead, he rested his hands on the desk, looming over his son. "Your reports are late," he said, his voice silky.

Darius narrowed his eyes at him. Technically, yes, they were a little bit late. But he knew full well they weren't really needed for at least another week. He'd been busy living life for once.

"And you came all the way down here to tell me that?" Darius quipped. "I'm honoured. You'll have them by Friday."

For a few moments, Victor didn't move. He just continued to study Darius. Darius refused to squirm under his gaze. He wasn't going to be bullied by his old man in his own home. Not today.

He should have known better.

"How is Joshua getting along?"

Inside, Darius froze, but he did all he could not to show it externally. "Okay, I guess," he said with a shrug. "Kind of annoying, but I'm getting used to it." It felt awful to lie like that, but there was no doubt in his mind that if he gave any hint as to the joy his new husband was bringing him, Joshua would be in serious trouble.

Victor wrinkled his nose in disdain. "He almost reminded me of Athena. So eager to please. Do you remember her? That mutt you had?"

Anger sparked, but Darius kept control of it. Of course he remembered his childhood golden Labrador, and Victor bloody well knew it. But rather than reply, he just stared at his father.

"I see," said Victor with a chuckle as if Darius had replied. "Well, I trust this particular puppy is pleasing his master in *all* regards?"

There was no missing the sexual innuendo as he leered at Darius over the wooden desk. It took a great deal of self-control for Darius not to sweep everything off it and lunge for the disgusting old man. He was obviously testing to see if Darius knew about the stupid rules he'd given Joshua.

Although rage and revulsion flared in Darius, he maintained his control. Losing his shit would be exactly what his father wanted. He could sidestep the true nature of his question about the rules easy enough. But Darius couldn't quite resist the urge to take a jibe at his father and play him at his own game.

"I would have thought discussing that sort of thing would turn your stomach," he said as calmly as he could, his eyebrow twitching. "Bellamy is a spectacular fuck. Is that what you want to hear? I pounded his sweet little arse until he cried."

For a split second, Victor looked like he wanted to gag. Darius immediately felt guilty about saying such disrespectful things about the man who was slowly becoming his friend despite the odds, but he had to shut his father down from whatever sick game he was currently working on. If that meant playing dirty, so be it. What Joshua would never know, wouldn't hurt him.

Victor wiped his mouth and stood up straight, looking slightly pale. "There's no need to be vulgar, boy," he hissed. Right. Because Darius's father *never* went for the low blows. "I expect those reports by Friday. Friday *morning*." He turned and headed for the door. But at its threshold, he paused and curled his lip in an imitation of a smile over his shoulder. "Say 'hello' to Joshua for me, won't you?"

And with that, he was gone.

Darius shuddered, nausea rolling through him as he rubbed his forehead. He didn't like the way Victor had enquired after Joshua at *all*, but he could see from his view through the window that Victor was leaving the premises and therefore couldn't do Joshua any harm.

For now.

"Fucking *hell*." It was only four o'clock, but Darius reached for his whisky decanter and poured himself a measure with a shaking hand.

Yes, he'd managed to get a few punches in, but he was under no illusion that he'd pay for them later, probably when he'd least expect it. He was pretty sure he could take anything Victor threw at him.

But Joshua?

Darius scrubbed his face as dread sunk into the pit of his stomach. No, thinking about it, this was *good*. This was the wake-up call he needed right now. He'd been letting himself get complacent.

It was okay to be nice to Joshua. He'd specifically asked that Darius not ignore him, so he wouldn't do that. Darius would continue to support him with his gardening and working on his conversation skills.

But he needed to put his heart back in a steel box.

It was one thing vowing to never give in to his carnal temptations, no matter what. But Darius was growing too fond of Joshua, allowing sentiment to creep in.

That was a very bad idea. That was how people got hurt.

That was how *Joshua* could get hurt, for real. And Darius had vowed to do anything to stop that from happening.

It didn't matter that Victor was an old man. He had his

ways, and sometimes nasty 'accidents' happened when he was nowhere to be seen.

Gritting his teeth, Darius snarled and rubbed his eyes. He was being selfish. He couldn't drag Joshua into Victor's ugly web because Darius got careless. It had been close, but there wasn't anything they couldn't come back from. They could still be civil. After all, Joshua had no idea of the depths of Darius's affections.

And he never would.

It wasn't like Darius was in love or anything so ridiculous. Darius could just nip his feelings in the bud but still be friendly. Dial back the dinnertime chitchat and garden strolls.

No matter how much it pained him to do so.

From now on, pursuing anything more than a civil friendship with Joshua was Off Limits, with capital letters. It might be difficult, but compared to other trials he'd been through, it would be fine, Darius was sure.

At least, that was what he told himself as he sipped his whisky, the light slowly falling around him until he was left once more sitting all alone in the dark.

8

JOSHUA

"WHAT THE HELL AM I DOING WRONG?"

Joshua dropped his head with a thump against the kitchen table, not caring that there were several members of staff buzzing around who could see him. So long as he wasn't getting in their way as they rushed around preparing the evening meal, he was happy to embarrass himself. They probably couldn't care less, as busy as they were. After all, it wasn't just Joshua and Darius living at Thorncliff. They fed and watered almost thirty members of staff, breakfast, lunch, and dinner.

Joshua was easy enough to see through as he moped and stuffed his face with macarons.

"What you are doing wrong," said Camille, pointing a wooden spoon at him, dripping with wet chocolate cake mixture, "is you are stuffing ze macaron all in at once. Like – how you say – ze pig? Take *one* bite. *Enjoy* ze flavours!"

Joshua raised his head and scowled at the head cook. Camille was tall and blond, with pixie-cropped hair and broad, muscular shoulders, probably from years of whisking.

Or hand-to-hand combat. Joshua would honestly bet on either.

As if to prove her wrong, he picked up a salted caramel macaron and shoved it all into his gob, chewing the slightly tacky sweet noisily. "I *mean* with Darius. We were getting on great! It felt like we were finally making friends. Is it wrong of me to want to be friends with my *husband?* Then, three days ago, *snap"* -he clicked his fingers- "he goes back to being all broody and monosyllabic."

Angrily, he rubbed the crumbs from his mouth and took a glug of the *Chateauneuf-du-Pape* red wine that Camille enjoyed plying him with. After three glasses, it had loosened his tongue enough to talk about Darius with the two people he'd got to know best in the castle. Which probably wasn't wise, because those people also happened to be Darius's cook and his house keeper. His butler was also sitting nearby, drinking tea.

Speaking of which, Bartholomew raised his eyebrows over his cup as he took a sip. "If I'm not very much mistaken, that would be around the time Mr Legrand senior visited."

Joshua picked a pistachio macaron off the plate and swung his legs on the high stool he was sat on as Camille shouted at someone in French, apparently extremely distressed about what they were doing to some broccoli.

"Probably," Joshua admitted, although he wasn't sure. He might have been aware that Victor had dropped by the castle, but he couldn't think he'd seen him with his own eyes. Come to mention it, there might have been a car parked out front a couple of days ago, though. "Am I allowed to say that Victor seems like a proper wanker?"

Camille snorted as she turned away. Mrs Weatherby pursed her lips, then sipped her own tea. Bartholomew, however, regarded Joshua with a firm stare. "As staff of this illustrious house," he began sombrely, "it is *not* our place to question our employers."

Joshua fidgeted awkwardly in his seat. He knew he shouldn't have said anything.

Except Bartholomew's mouth twitched. "So it's a good job that Master *Darius* runs Thorncliff, and therefore we can call that old windbag Victor anything we like."

The guy chopping up the broccoli almost dropped his knife. Bartholomew smirked and sipped more tea.

Joshua rubbed his nose and chewed on the second bite of his pistachio macaron (having followed Camille's advice and eaten this one in two halves). "So...he *is* a wanker?"

"Victor isn't very kind, no," Mrs Weatherby conceded. She seemed like she might not be as comfortable as Bartholomew with speaking openly out of turn regarding Victor Legrand. "So I shouldn't be too worried that Darius is in a poor mood after he's seen him." She reached over and patted Joshua's hand with a warm smile. "But he's been *so* much happier since you've been here. Hasn't he, Camille?"

Camille shrugged and thrust the used wooden spoon covered in cake mixture at Joshua. "Eat zis, skinny boy." She bobbed her head back and forth. "I guess you make *Monsieur* Darius less of a *trou du cul.* Therefore, we like you."

Joshua licked the spoon, knowing he shouldn't really but feeling delightfully naughty for enjoying the raw batter anyway. "I honestly can't decide if he's likable or not. I *mean"* -he took another swig of wine- "I *do* like him. But I'm really not sure if I should after all he's put me through. You know?"

To his horror, tears threatened to pool in his eyes. This was what he got for letting Camille top up his wine glass so freely. But bloody *hell* he was getting whiplash from this treatment of Darius's. So hot and cold it was unreal.

But this time, it was worse. Joshua had really been enjoying their slow but steady progress towards friendship.

He had no idea what could have changed between them to make Darius become so distant and cold again, but Joshua was convinced it had to be himself at fault. So therefore, fairly or not, he had become wracked with guilt, hence sneaking into the kitchen for a blowout on wine and pastries.

It was slightly scary how much he wanted Darius to just be a little kind to him. That was all he was asking.

Mrs Weatherby sighed. "Yes, I do know what you mean."

"If I may, sir," said Bartholomew, carefully placing his delicate cup and saucer down.

"Of course," Joshua prompted, sniffing and thankfully managing to blink back his tears.

Bartholomew nodded. "Master Darius has been through some trying times. A difficult childhood."

"Growing up rich in a *castle?*" Joshua blurted out before he could think.

Bartholomew narrowed his eyes, his salt-and-pepper moustache turning downwards. "Life can be cruel to everyone, Mr Bellamy. Including the 'rich and privileged', as you would put it."

Joshua rubbed the back of his neck, feeling sheepish. "Yeah, totally," he agreed, glad Darius hadn't heard his thoughtless, slightly drunken comment. "He, um, mentioned his mum. I'm so sorry. I know what it's like to lose your mum."

It was as if the kitchen was put on pause. It felt like – just for a second – all hands faltered and the clatter stopped. Then it began again as if nothing had happened, the whole room taking a collective breath and moving forward by unspoken consent.

"Oh, Maree," said Mrs Weatherby, picking up her teacup with slightly trembling hands. "What a sweet girl. I remember her well."

Camille mumbled something angrily in French, and Bartholomew cleared his throat.

Joshua restrained himself for three whole seconds, but he was dying to know more about Darius, and it appeared the man himself had gone back on his word and clammed up again. "Was it unexpected? With his mum, I mean. Darius said she'd looked after the gardens before she got too ill."

Mrs Weatherby shook her head. "No. It was cancer, poor dear. It was quite slow and sad, truth be told. Darius was a *rock*. He came here to support her when..." She trailed off, her mouth becoming a hard line.

"When Victor realised his wife was no longer young, beautiful, and *healthy*, so he lost interest," said Camille bitterly, topping up Joshua's wine glass with a loud *glug glug glug*.

"No?" Joshua uttered in disbelief. Surely no one could be that cruel. Well...he *had* met Victor Legrand and experienced his own twisted kind of cruelty from the man, so maybe he shouldn't have been so shocked.

Bartholomew poured himself another cup from the pot, since it was clear that Camille didn't attend to anything so boring as tea. "Maree was an angel," he said faintly. "I think it's fair to say, though, that Victor is not a natural caregiver, no. He fled from her illness. Whereas Darius chose to be home-schooled by a tutor, and spent Maree's last couple of years by her side, here." He cleared his throat and blinked several times. "Her death hit him very hard."

"He signed up to the military to shoot people in the head," Camille announced, slapping globs of cake batter into tins. *"Bang! Bang! Bang!* And this is healthy, *non?"*

"It was a *little* more complicated than that, Camille," Bartholomew said patiently with an arched eyebrow.

Joshua sipped more red wine, even though he knew he probably shouldn't. Half a dozen macarons didn't make a

THORN IN HIS SIDE

dinner. But he was worried sick that he was doing something wrong with Darius, and the liquid courage was helping him to ask questions and gain more insight.

He was trying to keep his distance and not get clingy. After all, he was busy now with the gardens, and he had made sort of friends with the staff, so he wasn't as lonely anymore and in desperate need of Darius's attention. So *why* did he still crave it so badly? Any glimpse he could get into what was going on behind those blue eyes was a blessing. Darius was a mystery Joshua wanted to solve in a way he'd never experienced in his whole life.

He tried reminding himself that might just be because he'd never, *ever* let himself get this close to anyone before. So his current melancholy was probably just a reaction to a little bit of intimacy, then having boundaries thrown up in his face. But still, Joshua had to know.

Because he ached. He ached in places he hadn't known existed. The more he drank, the more he was able to admit to himself that this wasn't a reaction to any random man who happened to be in the vicinity, and therefore Joshua was getting attached like some kind of Stockholm Syndrome. This was specific.

He bloody *loved* the way Darius thought he was being so stealthy, wandering past when Joshua came in from the gardens, then acting all surprised and asking about Joshua's day. Because he then listened to every fucking word Joshua said about seeds and mud and pesticides and worms like it was poetry.

Or the way he *had* been doing that, until three days ago.

Joshua also loved the dinners they'd had, even though half of them had been spent in terrible, laughable silence as they both visibly scrambled around for something to say. He loved that he didn't have to make up his hot water bottles for bed now because someone had turned on the heating in the castle. That same person had also started turning on more of the lights.

Joshua grinned around the rim of his wine glass. Despite knowing that Darius was being an arse right now, he'd been acting *lovely* since that night of the lake incident.

The night Joshua had seen him half-naked.

He'd been extremely good at not objectifying his new almost-friend, but the wine was throwing away those inhibitions and allowing Joshua to remember Darius in all his delicious glory. Of all the things, it was the dark body hair that Joshua couldn't get out of his mind. The way it swirled, how he imagined it would feel under his hands.

Against his tongue.

Fuck. What would it *finally* feel like to touch another man? To kiss him? Joshua had been dreaming of such a moment for so many years, and it was as if Darius was now unlocking a secret part of him.

A part of him that wasn't afraid to have another man's hands running over his body. Over his cock. Kissing him, tasting him.

Worshipping him.

Would sex be as good as he'd so desperately imagined?

Would Darius ever be interested in helping him find out? In his drunken fluster, Joshua even dared to imagine that Darius wouldn't be disappointed in Joshua's inexperience.

Joshua coughed and remembered he wasn't alone. He was hopeless, ridiculous. Darius was obviously not attracted to a silly, delicate little thing like him. He'd probably be mortified at the way Joshua's fantasies were getting out of hand. But it was only when he lost himself in wine that he really acknowledged the facts.

He wanted Darius. Badly.

Why was it he had to stay away from Darius, again?

"So Darius and his dad don't get on," he blurted out in a

gross understatement, more trying to remind himself of the conversation thread than anything else.

Mrs Weatherby tutted and patted her voluminous hair. "It's not like Mr Victor gave poor Darius much choice in the matter," she grumbled.

Bartholomew tapped the tabletop at which they were sitting. "If I may, sir?"

"Of course," Joshua murmured, taking another drink of wine. He wanted to know everything.

Bartholomew sipped his tea in a mirrored gesture. "I can only speculate so much, Mr Bellamy. Do you understand?"

Joshua nodded. He really wanted some chips or something else salty, but he was more invested in getting more tidbits about Darius and didn't want to jeopardise its continuation. So he drank another mouthful of wine and chewed on a raspberry macaron.

"There are some men who are not meant to be fathers," said Bartholomew. "I would say that perhaps Victor Legrand was one of those men. Even just *one* son was too much for him. Everything was always an inconvenience when it came to Darius." Bartholomew's jaw ticked. "Then Maree became ill, and everything became an inconvenience about *anything*. Who was to blame Darius and Maree for becoming inseparable?"

"Victor?" asked Camille in mock surprise, slamming the oven door shut on her cake tins.

Bartholomew ignored her.

"It was clear Maree wasn't going to live long, but she shielded that from Darius," Bartholomew continued. "She brought him a present."

Mrs Weatherby sniffed quite loudly, getting up and busying herself with washing up her teacup.

Joshua was almost too afraid to ask. "What present? Do I want to know?"

"Probably not," grumbled Mrs Weatherby.

Camille rolled her eyes. "It's *fine*," she said impatiently at Bartholomew. "Skinny boy, lick ze spoon. Tell me what you zink?"

She brandished yet another spoon at him. "It's yummy?" Joshua said, licking the batter and possibly getting a little on his nose.

"Yes," Camille snapped, "but can you taste ze ginger?" She dissolved into grumbling French, snatched the spoon back, then licked it herself. "Yes, you can. You may have zis back."

"The present," Joshua implored, rubbing his nose, then fixing Bartholomew with a wide-eyed stare. "What was it?"

Bartholomew sighed. "A puppy."

Horror washed through Joshua. "No, I take it back. I don't want to know."

"Mon dieu." Camille clicked her jaw. *"Oui,* it was not nice, but not so very bad."

"Athena showed up with a broken leg!" Mrs Weatherby cried, her eyes glossy. "No one knew how! It *had* to have been deliberate!"

Joshua's stomach rolled, and he was suddenly afraid that all his wine and macarons would make a reappearance. "Victor broke a puppy's leg?" he said incredulously, fighting back a sob. "Of all the heartless, *despicable-*"

"You all right there, Bart?" A young workman in grubby overalls sauntered into the kitchen, dropping his equally dirty toolbox onto the kitchen table with a loud bang. Joshua gasped and flinched, his tears springing free thanks to his sudden movement.

"Martin!" Camille yelled savagely, waving her hands and snarling. "Out, out, *out!* What have I told you about zis muck and grease? Out!"

The man, Martin, didn't seem all that bothered by the cook's commands. Instead, he looked Joshua up and down, his gaze lingering on Joshua's fluffy bootie slippers, clearly unimpressed. "Sorry," he said dryly. "I didn't realise we were having a party."

Joshua squirmed uncomfortably at his scrutiny. This guy clearly didn't think much of Joshua, but all Joshua really cared about was that he left so he could find out about the puppy.

Bartholomew sighed impatiently. "Any progress on the internet situation, Martin?"

Martin sniffed and wiped his nose on the back of his hand. "Nah, this place is a nightmare. I can't even piggyback off the line Legrand already has installed. It's fucked."

Joshua's heart dropped. No internet, *still?* This was getting ridiculous. He was currently corresponding by physical post with a local gardening company he'd found in a two-decade-old copy of the Yellow Pages that was thankfully still in business. But he'd hadn't been able to talk to his dad or anyone else in a month, and he was losing his mind. When they'd been getting on, Joshua had thought of asking Darius to borrow his computer for a while, but now he didn't have the confidence.

And it looked like there wouldn't be any other access for a while to come.

"Perhaps someone else can do zis?" Camille asked, batting her eyelashes innocently. "Someone – hmm – better?"

Martin scowled and snatched up his toolbox again, having left a grimy smudge on the kitchen table. Mrs Weatherby immediately leaped forward and cleaned it away with some kitchen roll.

"I'll *sort it,*" Martin griped, first glaring at Camille, then Bartholomew, then landing his disgruntled gaze back on Joshua. Martin managed half a smile, but it didn't reach his eyes. "Enjoy your party, *sir.*"

Joshua watched him leave, wondering if he'd see him

again. Then he shook himself. What was a bit of rudeness? Everyone else at Thorncliff had been lovely. Joshua didn't need everyone to like him.

"Sorry about that." Bartholomew narrowed his eyes at the door that Martin had left swinging on his departure. "He normally at least makes an attempt at civility."

It's okay," said Joshua breathlessly. "I don't mind. But, um, you were telling me about Darius's puppy, when he was a teenager. Was she okay?"

"Not really," said Mrs Weatherby, clearly still upset as she dropped back onto her high stool at the kitchen table and copied Joshua by stress-eating an entire macaron in one go.

Camille narrowed her eyes. "A broken *leg*. Not dead! *Monsieur* Darius sent the dog to live wiz anozer family."

"And it broke his heart!" Mrs Weatherby argued determinedly around the macaron in her mouth.

"It did," Bartholomew agreed with a nod. "No one ever knew how poor Athena was hurt, but it was suspicious. Darius announced he didn't want her anymore, that she was 'boring'." Bartholomew nudged his teacup left, then right on its saucer. "He spent *weeks* looking for the best new home to send her to, never letting her out of her sight until she left."

Joshua looked between the three of them, tears pooling in his eyes. He knew he was drunk, but he couldn't bear what they were saying. "Victor broke a puppy's leg because it was giving Darius some comfort while his mum was dying?"

The only reason the kitchen didn't fall into audible silence this time was because Camille slapped a blender on, turning away while she blew her nose. Mrs Weatherby found some tea towels that urgently needed folding, and Bartholomew shook the teapot upside down trying, to get a final drop from it.

That would be a 'yes', then.

Joshua's stomach twisted in a knot. What an unspeakable

thing to do to an innocent animal, never mind a grieving child. Suddenly, his irritation at Darius's withdrawnness seemed utterly petty and selfish.

"Ze puppy was *fine*," Camille insisted once she'd turned the blender off and spun back around. "Happy ever after!"

"I think," Bartholomew said delicately and fixing Joshua with a very firm stare, "what we're trying to say is that when Master Darius becomes quiet, there is often a storm raging beneath the stillness. Unless he is behaving inappropriately-"

"Like that night when you almost drowned!" Mrs Weatherby called from down the end of the kitchen, angrily shoving tea towels into a basket.

"-then don't necessarily assume the worst," Bartholomew continued. "It's not your job to fix or interpret him. But I'd urge you not to always assume you've done something wrong. It could be another totally unrelated thing going on in his head."

"So you *ask* that stubborn mule," Camille said with a crooked smile. "You say, 'Is it me? Because I zink it is you being a *fils de pute*."

Joshua offered her a tiny smile. He was still feeling devastated over a puppy he'd never met, and he swallowed some more wine, hoping it would help. But at least there might be a small silver lining if they were trying to assure him that he might not be the reason for Darius's sullen mood or that he might not even be angry with Joshua.

Maybe there was a chance things were still okay between them, after all?

Suddenly, Joshua was determined to do a nice thing for Darius. From the sounds of it, he'd been through so much at the hands of his father and with the death of his mother. Not to mention those mysterious scars that he was so protective over. In that moment, Joshua was overcome with the urge to *do* something.

He grabbed the bottle of *Chateauneuf-du-Pape* Camille had poured his last glass from. This one was almost full, as Camille had previously been finishing off another bottle. "Thank you, really, you've all been brilliant," Joshua said, trying not to slur. He did pretty well. He also stood up straight and didn't teeter. But he'd had an *insane* idea, and he needed some liquid courage for him to see it through. "I really appreciate it. Camille, may I take this?"

"*Oui*," she said without missing a beat as she turned around and slammed down a bowl of *cassoulet* that had appeared from nowhere. "So long as you take zis to eat, too. You little drunken sailor." She cackled, then advanced at a young cook who was apparently murdering some courgette.

Awkwardly Joshua balanced the wine bottle and glass, as well as the bowl of casserole, as he got to his feet. "Thanks. Bye. Thanks."

He felt Bartholomew watching him as he managed to make his way towards the kitchen door. Joshua nodded at Mrs Weatherby and her towels as he bumped his way out. He was eager to get up to his room and back to the local papers he'd been collecting, so desperate for reading material he'd even been devouring the ad pages.

He was pretty sure he had a plan.

It was probably a dumb plan, but the more wine Joshua drank, the more confident he got that this was the *best plan ever.*

All he could say when he awoke in the morning, full of doubt, long after he'd slipped his letter in the outgoing post and the van had collected it, was that Darius had given him that credit card and a cheque book to go with it. Could he *really* be mad when Joshua used it?

He really hoped not.

9

DARIUS

Darius was so fucking tired of this limbo.

He felt like he'd been suspended in its grip for most of his life, but at least most of the time he was only vaguely aware of it. Right now, it was like a pulsing, living thing, pressing in all around him.

He couldn't behave the way he wanted to around Joshua for fear that his father might hurt him, *literally*. But being standoffish was clearly upsetting Joshua again, which Darius had vowed not to do.

It was so tempting to give in and be friendly once more. Darius had so been enjoying their time together those couple of weeks until Darius had shut back down. Joshua's hurt and disappointment the last several days were palatable, not to mention right in front of Darius's face. Even though he was fully aware of the lengths Victor could go to even while his father wasn't physically in the castle, Darius so desperately wanted to shrug off his sinister questions about Joshua's health and pretend they were nothing.

Then he would remember Athena, sober up, and close himself off again.

It wasn't like he was being *rude* to Joshua, he was sure. They still talked a little about the gardens and the weather (which was improving the closer they crawled towards spring) and what terrible eighties animated movie Joshua had discovered that day for the first time on the VCR he'd claimed for his own. Or rather – Joshua talked and Darius listened, his heart aching with pitiful longing.

However, Darius was holding firm to his promise not to get too invested, and that meant not asking *too* many questions or appearing like he might care *too* much. He couldn't let Joshua become attached. He couldn't allow that happy, beaming face to rely on Darius, because thanks to his father, Darius knew all too well that way led to disaster.

So now this was his limbo. But holding back from Joshua was becoming more of a torture day by day.

He shifted awkwardly in the back of the car he was being driven in, watching the scenery out of the window at they neared Thorncliff. He'd been forced into Canterbury to meet with some of his father's suppliers. Darius knew his company position was just a token one, and his father liked to torture him with meaningless responsibility. So he soothed himself that this nonsense meeting had at least been in the nearest town rather than say London or Paris.

He couldn't wait to get home.

Urgh, *no!* He gripped his knees and tried to centre himself. That kind of thinking wasn't helpful. Joshua wasn't eagerly waiting for him so they could both have dinner together. Darius kept telling himself that he hadn't left the networking drinks early in the hopes of that. Because there couldn't be anything between them. He was only punishing himself by even thinking otherwise.

Fucking hell. He was going to get blindingly drunk once he'd shut himself in for the night.

"Here we are, sir," said his driver, Asher. Darius hadn't realised they'd pulled up the driveway. He'd been so wrapped up in his thoughts. But Asher had got him back safe and sound.

Normally, Darius would pass the journey catching up with Asher, who, like a lot of the staff, had been with the family for many years. Darius felt bad that he'd barely grunted a handful of words to him on this occasion, so was already reaching for his wallet to give him a tip on top of his regular salary. Luckily, Asher had been listening to a podcast about the football team he was mad on and didn't seem to mind Darius's rudeness. Still, now that Darius was more aware of how his sullenness affected his staff, he was determined not to go back to his old grumpy ways. It was bad enough that he was forcing himself to close off from Joshua. He wasn't going to do that with the people at Thorncliff, too.

"Sorry about that," Darius said, shaking his head and offering out some notes between the front seats.

Asher frowned and turned down his Maidstone United podcast. "Don't worry about that, sir," he said, holding up his hand and looking concerned. "You've obviously got a lot on your mind. I don't need you to entertain me while I drive. It's my job to get you from A to B."

It was Darius's turn to frown. "Still," he said quietly. "I'd feel better if you took it."

Asher sighed and relented. "I'll take my little boys out with it, sir. Thank you." He smiled as he pocketed the cash. "Is work troubling you?"

Darius looked up at Thorncliff through the car window. "Something like that," he mumbled.

He didn't want to get out of the car.

How long could this charade realistically go on for? He and Joshua were supposed to be *married*. Was Darius expected to keep Joshua at arm's length for the rest of their lives?

Knowing his father, probably yes.

Now Darius had worked out that as far as Victor was concerned, Joshua's sole purpose on this planet was to torment Darius, Darius couldn't see their relationship ending in anything other than tragedy. Victor wouldn't settle for anything else. Joshua was bright, young, and beautiful. Darius was getting over the hill, battle-scarred physically and emotionally, and had such bleak prospects for the future he had very little in the way of happiness to offer anyone.

But did that mean that Darius and Joshua just put up with this half-lived life until the day Victor died?

There had to be another way. No matter what Victor had intended, their differences wouldn't matter if they actually liked each other. It was tempting to believe they could be friends. Maybe more.

But with Victor in the picture, Darius didn't realistically see how. Not without Joshua getting his leg broken.

Or worse.

"Thank you," he grunted at Asher, exiting the car. "Get home safe," he added before he closed the door. Asher nodded and gave Darius a smile and salute.

Heart heavy, Darius plodded up the steps to the main entrance. Absently he noticed that the evenings were getting longer and it really wasn't as cold as it had been as he pushed open the door. It was funny, but he swore the castle was *smelling* different these days. He stood and inhaled deeply, allowing himself just a second to relish in a brief moment of happiness for something so silly as the faint smell of hot food and a few more minutes of sunshine each day.

Until the clattering of footsteps tore him from his reverie and he snapped his eyes back open.

Joshua skidded to a halt in front of him in his knitted

slipper booties, his hands clutched in front of his chest and his brown eyes wide. "You're home!" he announced like it was a surprise. But clearly it wasn't, because it looked as if he had sprinted there to meet Darius at the door. He did his best not to let his heart get carried away with that ridiculous fantasy he'd been having in the car of Joshua eagerly waiting for him to get home from work. But it was difficult not to when Joshua was looking all excited and anxious at him.

Darius swallowed and shifted from foot to foot. "Shouldn't I be?"

Joshua quickly shook his head and ran his fingers through his blond hair, taking a few shallow breaths. "No, no. That's great! I was sort of waiting…I mean…" He cleared his throat and inhaled deeply. "Could you come with me? I have a surprise."

Unfortunately, Darius's initial gut reaction wasn't to be touched or excited but suspicious. However, this was Joshua. If he said he had a surprise, that was going to be a nice thing, right?

Except Darius was trying to *not* encourage any 'nice' things between the two of them. Just civil. Joshua was Off Limits. If Victor found out…

What? If Victor found out that Darius's heart was fluttering in the entrance foyer just because he could tell Joshua was excited that he had a surprise for Darius? How was Victor going to know that?

Darius wasn't a fool. He hoped he could trust most people in the castle, but the truth was that people were coming and going all the time. Just because Darius was trying to be friendly with the members of staff he'd known for years and at least learn the names of the newer ones didn't mean anything. Anyone of them could have a hidden agenda and be reporting back to Victor.

They had to be safe. Logically, Darius knew it wasn't like

his father was in his prime now. Was he going to swoop in and smash Joshua's legs with a cricket bat? No. But could he pay someone to push Joshua down the stairs?

Absolutely.

But then Darius had a sudden, illuminating thought. It felt like the dusty curtains had been yanked open on a summer's day, letting the light in. There was no guarantee that wasn't Victor's plan *already.* He knew Darius would care if Joshua got hurt, regardless of how close they were, just like he knew Darius would have never let him languish on the streets if he refused to marry him. Victor was fully aware that his son had a soft heart and would be devastated by anyone's suffering, let alone the man he'd taken vows to protect.

So that was what Darius needed to do.

Pulling away *wasn't* the answer. Keeping Joshua *close* was what he needed to do, to deter anyone from trying anything sinister.

It was like Darius could breathe fully again for the first time in a week since his father had last darkened his doorstep. He was aware that all these thoughts had raced through his head in the few seconds that Joshua had been staring anxiously at him, his hands clasped together and his eyes getting wider.

"Sorry," Darius blurted, unable to stop the smile from spreading over his face.

This didn't mean anything more than friendship would ever happen between them. Darius was still aware that Joshua was in a vulnerable position, having been forced into this marriage and would never think of Darius in a sexual way. But his heart was aching in the best kind of way to think they might be able to resume their friendship again. If Joshua had been thoughtful enough to organise a surprise for him, surely there had to be a small hope of that?

"Sorry for not saying anything, I mean," Darius explained. "I was just, well, surprised at getting a surprise." He laughed bashfully, hanging his coat up and rubbing the back of his neck. "You didn't have to do anything for me. I know I've been grumpy this week. I'm really sorry. My dad visited, and he just drives me crazy."

Part of Darius wanted to own his poor behaviour and explain his actions, not blame Victor. But that was too complicated. Besides, the relief on Joshua's face told him he'd made the right decision, and it wasn't a total lie.

"Oh, I see," Joshua said, beaming up at Darius. "I did wonder. I mean, not that it's any of my business, but, uh…" He bit his lip, and the mere sight of the action sent lust rushing straight to Darius's cock.

Behave!

Darius cleared his throat, aware that they were still awkwardly standing in the hallway. "It *is* your business when I promised not to shut you out like that again," Darius murmured. "I'm sorry."

He expected Joshua to smile at him some more. Maybe show a little added relief. But if anything, guilt flashed across his face, and he started hopping from foot to foot, seemingly torn between ecstatic and nervous as hell.

"I've definitely fucked up," Joshua blurted, nodding frantically. "But it might be okay anyway…I don't know. Oh, *God.* I was drunk, and it felt like a fantastic idea at the time. But now I think I might have gone *completely* overboard and made a huge mistake. Especially because I *did* make a mistake, as in an error. I didn't order what I meant to order, and because it was via post, there was no way to check or cancel it. And now, fuck, I hope. I mean-"

"Joshua, *breathe,*" Darius instructed, holding up his hand. "You said you got me a surprise?" he prompted. Joshua nodded. Darius thought about that a second, trying not to feel overwhelmed. "I can't remember the last time someone organised a surprise for me. Thank you."

Joshua raised his eyebrows. "You don't even know what it is yet."

Darius quirked a smile at him, warmth blossoming in his chest. "I'm not sure I need to," he said sincerely. "The act itself is touching. But I'm still excited."

Joshua pressed his hands to his chest, staring at Darius as he inhaled slowly. "Shall I just show you? Then we can decide how much of a disaster this is?"

Darius chuckled, hoping to put them both at ease by lightening the mood. "Sure. Lead the way."

It seemed to work, as Joshua's face lit up with that smile Darius had been hoping for. Then Joshua reached out...and took Darius's hand.

Immediately, Darius's heart leaped into his chest. He was amazed that his feet continued to work as Joshua began pulling him through the castle to wherever they were going. His entire focus was on the point at which Joshua's warm, soft hand was meeting with Darius's stiff, calloused one. He should pull away. He shouldn't encourage this...

But apparently Darius was a weak man, and he couldn't make himself let go.

It didn't take them long to get to Darius's quarters, where Joshua stopped just outside the living room, looking up at Darius and chewing his lip. "I hope you don't mind I put it in here."

Darius shook his head. Ever since their awful fright, he had made it clear that Joshua could come here now so long as he knocked. Seeing as he'd known Darius was out for the day, he didn't mind if he had come and left something there. In fact, after the way Darius had been behaving this past week, he was positively thrilled that Joshua had felt confident enough to come here.

Maybe there *was* hope that Darius hadn't totally fucked things up between them.

"Of course not," Darius said warmly. "This is your home, remember. Nothing is off limits."

"Okay, good," said Joshua, hugging himself and nodding, like he was trying to reassure himself. "You promise you won't be cross, then?"

Darius wanted to laugh at the idea he could ever be cross with Joshua, although he *was* getting a little nervous. What the hell had Joshua got him?

Outwardly, though, he smiled in what he hoped was a comforting way. "I promise."

Joshua licked his lips before taking a deep breath and pushing the door open to the living room. He braced himself as he held it open, clearly inviting Darius to go in first.

He did, immediately noticing the large crate in the middle of the room that usually wasn't there. As Darius walked forward, it squeaked.

He stopped.

"Like I said," Joshua explained meekly from behind him. "I was drunk."

Curious, Darius stepped closer. The crate was open at the top, and it was definitely squeaking and shuffling. Not really wanting to make a guess, Darius just took the last few steps to its edge and peered inside.

Where a small cloud was currently running back and forth, yapping bravely, its tail wagging non-stop. Two coal-black eyes suddenly turned up and stared back at Darius.

It was a puppy.

A fucking puppy.

"I thought he was a completely different breed," Joshua's distressed voice was saying as Darius kept staring at the white cloud. It had started barking again, dashing from one side of the crate to the other, never taking its eyes off Darius.

"You should have a big dog, right? Because you're a big guy. I thought it was that big grey kind. I don't know why. But it's something called a *Bichon Frise*, which is small and fluffy and silly, and if you hate him, I'll make all the arrangements to send him back to the shelter. I'll get you a proper dog or none at all. I don't know why I thought..."

He trailed off what he was saying, probably because Darius had unceremoniously dropped on his arse, sitting cross-legged next to the crate so he could reach inside and gently scoop out the yappy little cloud to cradle him against his chest.

He was worried his heart might genuinely detonate through his ribcage, so he hugged the puppy to him, as if that might stop any explosions. "You got me a puppy?" he asked thickly.

This was the last straw in Darius's defences. He might have decided mere moments before that the best way to keep Joshua safe was to have him close by, but all the rest of Darius's emotional walls crumbled in that moment.

Joshua had bought him a *puppy*.

A part of Darius was immediately afraid for the little pup after what had happened with Athena. But all those protective instincts he'd been feeling as he vowed to keep Joshua safe just doubled. When Athena had been hurt, Darius had been small and powerless himself.

But not anymore.

Yes, Victor was a merciless bastard who had his fingers in many pies and knew all the strings to pull to get what he wanted. But Darius was a fucking war veteran three times his size. It was about time he stood up and protected what was his.

As of that moment, that included the little puppy as much as it did his husband.

What Victor *wanted* was to trap Darius in the limbo that

had been tormenting him, that holding pattern. The truth was, if Victor really wanted to hurt Joshua, he probably would. But his real power was in the psychology, and in that moment, it all fell apart like wet *papier-mâché*.

Joshua had got Darius a puppy as a complete surprise. The kindness of that gesture felt like an impenetrable fortress around both Darius and Joshua that even Victor Legrand couldn't penetrate.

The little guy was wriggling in Darius's hands, his curly white fur soft against Darius's palms. He reached up and licked the tip of Darius's nose with a shrill yap. He'd grow out of that particular noise, Darius was sure, but for now, it was adorable. *Yap! Yap! Yap!*

It was as if the puppy was saying 'I'm here! Do you love me? Are you my new daddy?'

Joshua had sunk down next to Darius, but Darius had only been dimly aware of that fact until Joshua spoke. "So… you don't want to send him back?"

"He looks like a cloud," Darius said, aware he probably sounded fucking stupid, but he didn't know what else to say as the little guy did his best to growl fiercely before attacking Darius's shirt cuff. His bum waggled as he hopped back and forth in Darius's hands, trying so hard to be tough.

Joshua reached over and gently petted the top of his fluffy head. "He won't get very big. It's a small breed. Are you sure you like him?"

"He's a little thunder cloud," Darius said again as the puppy growled.

It made Darius think of that terrible night where he'd rescued Joshua from the snowstorm. He'd always named his pets after Greek gods, and if this little cloud growled like thunder, there was really only one name he could give him.

"Zeus," he announced, finding the idea of a small, fluffy little pup being named after the god of all gods kind of hilarious. But this cloud was full of thunder, Darius could tell.

Joshua's sniff suddenly yanked Darius back to reality. He jerked his head over to see Joshua wipe his eyes. "Sorry," he whispered. "I thought I'd messed up and we'd have to send him back to the adoption place. He's so small."

"He's *perfect*," Darius insisted. God, he'd forgotten what it was like to have a dog. But it was as if a piece of his heart he hadn't known was missing was suddenly full again.

Oh...*fuck* this. Fuck it all! Let Victor do his worst. He'd already stripped everything away from Joshua. Ironically, by marrying them, the law specifically *said* that Joshua was Darius's to protect. That was probably a caveman way to think about it, but Darius was bristling with protectiveness in that moment. Nothing was going to harm Joshua or Zeus with Darius around.

So why was Darius still fighting his feelings?

Enough. He liked Joshua so very much, and Joshua had just surprised him with a goddamned *puppy.* That had to mean he liked him in some way, right? Life was too short. Darius knew that. What was the point if they didn't live it?

What was the most impressive, outrageous thing he could think of to make up for the way he'd been behaving and to show Joshua how much he really cared for him? He was still pretty certain that Joshua wouldn't be interested in anything sexual with him. But that was okay. Darius just wanted to have a friendship. A *real* one.

"Would you like to go to the opera?" Darius blurted out, fixing his gaze on Joshua. Joshua blinked and gaped back in confusion for a moment.

"The...opera?"

Darius swallowed, figuring he should explain, just a little. "I saw in Canterbury that Carmen is playing. I love it. It's an opera. I thought...well...would you like to go with me?" He shifted awkwardly with Zeus in his hands, wondering if he'd just put his foot in it. "I love my surprise. I'd like to do something in return for you."

Joshua's pretty brown eyes widened ever so slightly. "Like…a date?" he whispered.

Fear lanced through Darius's chest, but he refused to let it take hold. "Yes," he agreed gently, but not wanting to scare Joshua off. "A sort-of date. A…getting to know each other, friendship date. If you'd like? No pressure for anything else," he added, making sure he was crystal clear.

With all of Victor's mind games hanging over them, he knew they were in murky waters. Victor expected Darius to be tormented by Joshua's company, stuck in this indecisive limbo. He also wanted Joshua to feel pressured into having sex to humiliate Darius even further and no doubt make Joshua feel cheap. Darius absolutely didn't want Joshua to think he was expecting sex from this.

Joshua chewed his lip. "I don't know anything about opera," he said quietly. But before Darius could backtrack and say that was okay and to forget about it, Joshua beamed that beautiful smile at Darius. "But I'd like to learn."

Darius used one hand to reach out and squeeze Joshua's arm, the other still cradling Zeus to his chest. "I'd love to teach you what I know," he said. Then he laughed. "I really don't know anything. I just went with my mother to see this one. You'll know one of the songs from it, I bet. It's pretty famous." He tried to sing it, but it was so bad Joshua just ended up giggling at him.

Darius wanted to bottle that giggle for a rainy day. It was gorgeous.

"So, that's a yes? To the…um…friendship date?" Darius had never been on a date. He'd done loads of stuff with Richard, but it had all just been hanging out, playing video games, watching movies, fucking. Never something formal that they'd planned. Darius felt like a nervous teenager, which was so ridiculous that he wanted to laugh.

Joshua petted Zeus's fur again, grinning as he bit his lip. "That's a yes to the friendship date," he said.

That was it, then. No going back now.

10

JOSHUA

Something broke slightly in Joshua at the sight of huge, scary Darius cradling and cooing over a small, fluffy puppy.

He was pretty sure he was glad to have it broken.

Darius's face was completely different as he marvelled at 'the cloud', as he'd called him. Zeus. Joshua was almost certain that he'd never seen anything that looked less like a Zeus in his life.

It was perfect.

Joshua knew what he was doing. He was focusing on the puppy and how thrilled he was at Darius's completely wonderful reaction to him. Because if Joshua didn't do that, he might spiral and start thinking about what they'd just agreed.

To go on a date.

Friendship or romantic, Joshua had never been on a date before. As much as he tried to keep focusing on the wriggling puppy, his insides bubbled and fizzed with excitement. Because Darius didn't want to go on just any old date. He wanted to take Joshua to the *opera*. That seemed bloody fancy.

Joshua suddenly realised he had a problem.

Worry immediately dampened his enthusiasm and writhed in his belly. He chewed his lip, trying to think of a solution.

He almost jumped out of his skin when Darius touched his knee, just for a second. "We don't have to go out if you don't want to," he said in his low, rumbly voice. "To the opera or anywhere. You're not obliged."

Joshua blinked. "Oh," he said softly. "Don't you want to?" He gestured to Zeus. "I didn't get him so you'd get me anything. I just thought he would make you happy." He didn't want to mention the story he'd heard about Athena. He felt like that might make Darius sad in what was supposed to be a joyous moment.

But maybe it was still joyous because Darius smiled, that shadow that had been hanging over him the last week finally gone.

"He's made me incredibly happy," Darius said, causing some of the tension in Joshua's chest to ease. He tentatively smiled back. "I wanted to make you happy too, but not everyone likes the opera. And..." Darius scrubbed his face, a dark look passing over it. "And you shouldn't feel obliged to spend time with me if you don't want to."

"I'd *love* to!" Joshua blurted out before he could second-guess himself. "I...I've really enjoyed getting to know you. And the opera sounds super fun. I like trying new things. But I realised I'd probably have to wear something posh, like a suit. I don't have anything good enough."

His cheeks were flaming by the time he finished babbling, so he dropped his gaze to the floor, embarrassed. All he had was his dad's old suit. Darius wouldn't want to be seen in public with him in that.

But to his surprise, Darius touched his knee again to get his attention. "In case you didn't notice at the wedding, I don't have anything posh either." He smiled at Joshua. "I'll call a tailor in. He can fit us both with suits. Then I'll book opera tickets for some time next week."

Joshua went from being embarrassed to kind of overwhelmed. Darius would do all that for him? Well, it sounded like Darius was getting a suit anyway. It made sense to get one for Joshua at the same time. But still, he couldn't help but be a little touched.

"Thank you," said Joshua.

The last few weeks had been tough. Going from being miserable and lonely to almost dying to becoming friends, to getting ignored again – it had been a tumultuous time between the two of them. Joshua just wanted to revel in the fact that Darius had been so quick to reciprocate Joshua's gift with something so amazing.

However, he had already thought of another problem. Fuck, Darius was really going to think he was coming up with excuses and didn't want to go when he really did. Even if it was just as friends, he didn't want to miss an opportunity to share something like this with Darius.

But he was pretty sure he had to mention it.

"Your dad said I shouldn't leave the grounds."

Darius raised his eyebrows at the reminder. Joshua knew he wanted to see the infamous rules letter Victor had sent Joshua with his own eyes, but the truth was, Joshua was embarrassed. Having strict instructions laid out for him just reinforced how much he was a prisoner here. By not showing Darius, it was like the commands didn't really exist. But they did. And after hearing that Victor had been willing to break a puppy's leg, Joshua was more certain that he'd find ways to impose his outrageous demands.

Darius nodded thoughtfully. "Yes, he did say that," he said

darkly. "And trust me when I say we don't want to piss him off. I'd rather not frighten you, but if we don't obey his rules, he could react quite seriously."

Joshua gulped and looked down at Zeus. He'd realised (once he'd sobered up) that by adopting Darius another puppy, he was giving Victor another opportunity to hurt his son and putting an innocent animal at risk. But from somewhere deep inside him, a spark of fury ignited in Joshua.

"What can he do?" he demanded. "If he tries anything illegal, we could just call the police. That's what they're *for*." He was aware he sounded naive and childish, but fuck Victor for treating them like this. He wasn't above the law.

But Darius tilted his head, giving Joshua a strange look. Almost like he was impressed at Joshua's defiance against his father. "He has ways around the law. *But*," he added determinedly, frowning his thick, dark eyebrows, "that just means we need to find ways around his rules, too." He fixed Joshua with a firm stare. "If we're smart and don't shout about going out for an evening, I won't let you out of my sight and make sure you're safe. Do you trust me?"

Joshua shivered as he looked into Darius's sky-blue eyes. He *loved* the idea of Darius not taking his eyes off him. He wanted to be that important to Darius, to occupy his time and thoughts, like Joshua really mattered to him. "Yes," he whispered. "I trust you."

And he meant it. Darius had already proved that he would go to extreme lengths to keep Joshua safe. His protectiveness made Joshua's insides squirm and his cock throb.

They shared a look for a moment, the seconds trickling along as Joshua felt his skin prickle and his breaths shorten. Why was Darius looking at him so intently?

Was he leaning closer?

Suddenly, Darius cleared his throat and scooped up Zeus again, looking at the puppy rather than Joshua. "Right, well then. Brilliant."

Joshua bit his lip and nodded. He mustn't get carried away. There hadn't been a 'moment' just then between them. He was imagining things. Darius had specifically said this evening out was just a friendship thing. He wasn't wooing Joshua or anything so ridiculous.

It was harsh, but Joshua made himself remember how Darius had recoiled at the thought of them having sex. Clearly, Darius didn't find him attractive in that way. That was fine. Joshua had never wanted different treatment for his looks, so he should be grateful that Darius wasn't giving it to him. They were just making the best out of this arranged marriage by getting to know one another and sharing an evening as friends.

Joshua needed to be content with that and push this developing crush away again. It was just lust. Purely physical. Which was stupid anyway because Joshua shouldn't be attracted to Darius's size and strength when those were the very things he feared the most about him.

"Okay," said Joshua awkwardly. "I'll, um, leave you guys to make friends." He gestured towards Darius and Zeus, then stood up. He knew Darius had said he wasn't forbidden from being in his quarters anymore, but Joshua still kind of felt like he was intruding. "I'll just…" He indicated the door and turned to leave.

But a hand snagged his own, making him gasp and look back down. Darius gave his fingers a quick squeeze before letting them go again. It reminded Joshua of his daring only a few minutes ago when he'd taken Darius's hand to lead him up here. It was like he'd been in a trance, but that brief touch Darius had just given him made every detail flood back.

It was like Joshua's hand belonged in Darius's big, strong one.

But that was ridiculous.

"Thank you, Joshua," Darius said, looking him square in the eyes. "I'm not sure what I did to deserve such kindness, but…" He cleared his throat and looked away. "Thank you."

Joshua nodded. "You're welcome," he whispered.

Then he left before he could do anything stupid. He'd almost cried when Darius had said he wanted to keep the puppy. Joshua had already got attached in the few hours Zeus been at the castle and hadn't wanted to send him away again. But witnessing just *how much* Darius seemed to immediately love the puppy was too much. Then the invite to the opera…

If Darius was just someone Joshua had met down the pub, he'd be tempted to think that something more than friendship was blossoming between them. But this whole situation had been artificially created, and Joshua couldn't tell what was 'real' or what was just them making the best of being forced to live together.

Because Joshua so desperately *wanted* to be excited about their upcoming date. He just wasn't sure if he should or how hurt his heart would get if he did.

It was a long time before Joshua managed to get to sleep that night.

OVER THE NEXT couple of days, Joshua distracted himself by working extra hard in the gardens, even when it was raining. The more he thought about going to the opera, the more he convinced himself it was going to be a disaster.

Victor was going to find out and break Zeus's leg. Or Joshua wasn't going to understand the show and then Darius would hate him. Or Joshua was going to look ridiculous despite getting a new suit, and Darius would be ashamed by him.

Joshua huffed and rubbed his face, knowing it would smear dirt on his skin but not caring. Maybe he wanted to be ugly for once. He was supposed to be getting a suit fitting later, but he was on the verge of telling the tailor not to bother.

It felt like he was at a tug of war inside himself. His simple gut reaction to the impending night out was to be happy and excited. But then other thoughts were complicating matters, confusing Joshua to the point where *he* was now the one shutting off and being quiet. He shouldn't be looking forward to this or enjoying himself, because if he did, he was being a massive hypocrite.

The cold hard truth was that Joshua wouldn't be in this arranged marriage situation if he wasn't beautiful. He'd been sold off, valued for the way he was born. Which wasn't *handsome.* It had been specifically because he was pretty and delicate. Beautiful.

Because beauty equalled femininity, and femininity equalled weakness.

Joshua angrily threw his trowel down and let out a frustrated cry. He hated that kind of talk. It was one of the other reasons he'd not bothered with dating apps. So many men talked like that, acting like there was only one way to be a 'real man' and like any hint of femininity was a failure.

Why shouldn't some men be beautiful and soft? Why shouldn't some women be handsome and strong? There were lots of ways to be a man or a woman or something in between. Joshua wasn't going to change who he was, even if he'd wanted to.

He *liked* the way he looked, he honestly did, and not just

because he was the spitting image of his mum, and that gave him comfort. He just liked what he saw in the mirror. But he hated everything else that came with it. He'd always been walked over and taken advantage of, forcing him to withdraw from the world and hide.

Which was exactly what he was doing now. Darius was obviously redoubling his efforts to make conversation and be friendly, especially now that he had the excuse of the puppy to come visit Joshua outside. They also had something else to talk about over meals.

But if Joshua wasn't beautiful, Darius wouldn't need to be thinking of these excuses. It was all built on something forced and unnatural. So what did it make Joshua if he allowed himself to enjoy this attention? Was it Stockholm Syndrome or something worse? Was he cheapening himself by accepting this devotion? Should he be fighting it tooth and nail to prove that he was worth more than something beautiful to be used in a transaction?

He rubbed his face again, fighting his tears and not caring about the mud. The thought he mostly kept coming back to was did it make him a bad person for wanting Darius's praise and attention? Was he degrading himself by being desperate for any hint that Darius *did* find him attractive?

Because Joshua really wanted Darius to be attracted to him. Oh, *lord*, he did.

The nights were getting out of control. It was like every time Joshua closed his eyes and tried to sleep images of Darius's smile filled his mind. Not only that but also his gentle laugh, the careful way in which he handled Zeus, and the earnest hope in his eyes when he'd asked Joshua to go out with him.

Not to mention the image of his body, half-naked and dripping wet, that was burned into the back of Joshua's retina, no matter how hard he tried to be honourable and decent. But when he remembered the way those firm muscles rippled, the dark hair just waiting to be caressed, that skin begging to be kissed, it was like Joshua's hand was wrapped around his cock before he'd even realised it.

Darius might not have orchestrated this marriage, but he was still Joshua's captor. Joshua shouldn't be fantasising about the man who was keeping him imprisoned. What the hell was wrong with him? Didn't he have any self-respect? Apparently not, because no matter how hard he tried, he just wanted Darius to desire him in the same carnal way Joshua was lusting after him.

But to make Joshua's stupid, humiliating crush worse, there was that voice reminding him that even in his wildest dreams, the idea that Darius could fancy him back was just plain ridiculous. Lots of men preferred their boyfriends to be big and burly. 'Proper men'. Not guys who looked like boys. Darius had obviously taken a lot of time to buff himself up, so chances were a hunk was what he'd be looking for in a partner.

No matter how many puppies Joshua bought or gardens he planted, he wasn't going to change who he was at his core. And the truth was he might never be the kind of husband that Darius would have picked for himself. Not to mention his humiliating inexperience. Darius had probably bedded dozens of men in his time, and Joshua had never even been kissed. He was pathetic.

So now the date was beginning to feel like rubbing salt in the wound, just tormenting Joshua with something he couldn't have. Getting a suit especially fitted for the occasion made him feel like he was dressing up and playing make-believe.

This was ridiculous. Joshua was just chewing his thoughts around and around, coming up with new problems and not getting anywhere, least of all with these stubborn rose bushes. He'd been pricked with the thorns so many times that afternoon he was starting to believe that the bushes didn't want to be saved. The first drop of rain on the back of his neck was enough to make him call it quits for the afternoon.

He shoved his tools into the workbag he'd been using, disappointed that he'd not found at least a little joy and peace from his new favourite pastime. Until this point, gardening had done a very good job at soothing Joshua's frantic thoughts. But today was evidently not his day. The suit fitting was highlighting everything that was pulling him back and forth about the date. Because really, if it was all that bad, he should just cancel it. But the thought of missing out on spending time together and letting Darius down made him want to cry.

Enough. He was done sitting out here with his thoughts. If he was going to commit to going out, he needed a suit, and if he was going to get a fitting, he needed to have a shower. But as he stood, he had the sudden urge not to go back into the castle. He didn't exactly want to run again – that had ended very badly last time. But he needed...*something.*

On a whim, he spun around and headed towards the stables. He wasn't sure why. He'd never been inside. The closest he'd got had been the night of the lake incident. But that was where his feet were taking him, so he decided to just see what might happen.

Inside there were a couple of staff members milling around, doing chores, including Paulo, the man who'd taken Darius's horse that night and promised to take good care of him. Paulo spied Joshua and gave him a wave.

Suddenly, Joshua wasn't sure if he was supposed to be in there or not. "Sorry," he mumbled, shuffling backwards.

But Paulo shook his head and rested the broom he'd been

using against the wall. "Not at all, Mr Bellamy. How can I help you?"

Joshua bit his lip and gripped the strap of his bag. "I thought I could say hello to, um, Darius's horse." As if summoned, an enormous brown head poked its way out of one of the stalls. He had a striking white stripe down his nose, which Joshua now recalled Darius stroking and petting. He'd been so determined that his horse be taken care of properly after he'd helped Darius to rescue Joshua. Joshua's heart contracted just thinking about it.

Beneath all the gruffness, scowls, and unruly hair was a man who was gentle to beasts large and small, for no other reason than to be kind.

Goddamn it. How was Joshua *not* supposed to find that attractive?

Paulo grinned and patted the horse's nose. "Look, Hephaestus, you have a visitor." He fished into his pocket and pulled out a packet of sugar-free mints, offering them to Joshua. For a ridiculous second, Joshua wondered if Paulo was expecting Joshua and the horse to kiss. "Would you like to give him one?"

A kiss? Joshua raised his eyebrows, thinking logically. "A mint?"

Paulo nodded. "Horses love them. He'll nibble it right off your palm if you hold it flat."

Fear bubbled in Joshua's belly that he was going to get bitten. But he'd told Darius that he liked trying new experiences, and he meant it. He'd spent far too long hiding in the shadows. "Um, sure," he said, putting down his gardening tools and walking towards Paulo. "What did you say his name was?"

"Hephaestus," Paulo repeated. "It's the name of a Greek god who was a blacksmith. Mr Legrand always names his pets after Greek gods, apparently."

Joshua accepted the packet of mints Paulo offered him, his mouth tweaking with a smile. "Yeah. He's called his new puppy Zeus. I thought that was funny."

"I heard about that." When Joshua looked up, Paulo's expression was wry and knowing. But instead of commenting further, he pointed at the sweets. "Put one in the middle of your palm, then bend out your fingers back as far as they'll go to make your hand flat."

"You're sure he won't nip me?" Joshua asked uncertainly. Hephaestus was snorting and bobbing his head up and down. This close, he really was huge. Joshua couldn't believe he'd ridden on his back.

Paulo chuckled. "Completely sure. Give it a go."

Joshua and Hephaestus eyed each other up. Joshua knew it was probably his imagination, but he felt like Hephaestus narrowed his big black eyes as if saying 'Come on! Be brave!'

He had a point. Wasn't that what Joshua was trying to do here in his new life? Be brave, hide less?

He could feed a bloody horse a bloody treat.

So he took a breath and did what Paulo had told him, straining his fingers back to make his hand as level as possible. With the flat, round mint in the centre of his palm, he held it out to Hephaestus.

The horse snorted, the top of his mouth lifting to show big teeth and pink gums. But then his lips were nuzzling against Joshua's hand, scooping up the mint with his tongue. The tickling sensation made Joshua giggle, and he marvelled as Hephaestus crunched that mint right up.

"He likes you," Paulo said approvingly.

Joshua grinned and offered up another mint, filled with pride and accomplishment. "I think he just likes my sweet treats, but that's okay."

As Hephaestus munched on the second mint, Joshua remembered what Darius had done and carefully stroked the horse's nose, following the direction of his hair. Hephaestus snorted and grumbled again, scuffing his hooves noisily. Joshua felt like he was telling him that the petting was acceptable and Joshua may continue if he wished.

Joshua laughed softly, getting more confident with his strokes. "I think you're a brat," he murmured affectionately.

"You'd be right," Paulo said with a wink. "But I have a feeling he'd be happy to see you any time you wanted to come visit. Feel free, whenever you like."

Joshua knew it was a small victory, but after his dark mood earlier, it felt huge to him. He'd faced up to the enormous horse and not been scared. Maybe he could face this suit fitting after all?

Once he'd thanked Paulo, he grabbed his tools to store safely away, then jogged through the drizzle back to the castle and up to his rooms. He wanted to have a thorough shower before the tailor arrived. Joshua wasn't sure if he was supposed to wear anything special, but seeing as he didn't already have a suit that fit him properly, he wore his favourite jeans and T-shirt instead, as well as his comfy bootie slippers. He almost didn't but changed his mind at the last minute. If this guy thought the knitted slippers were girly, that was his fault. Joshua thought they were *cute*, and cute was for any gender.

Suddenly, the door to his quarters slammed open, commanding all of Joshua's attention.

The tailor was a beanpole of a man in his forties with a pencil moustache and sparkling eyes. Unsurprisingly, he was wearing a perfectly fitted suit, dark blue and pinstripe. He was ten minutes late but waltzed into Joshua's lounge like he owned the place. When he saw Joshua standing gawkily in the middle of the room, twisting his hands together, the tailor stopped in his tracks. He looked Joshua up and down.

"Well, smack my arse and call me Daisy," he said in a

nasal, cockney accent. He sashayed over to Joshua with one hand in the air like he was leading a parade. Joshua tried not to let his mouth hang open like a goldfish. "You are fucking *gorgeous*, my sweet. Oh, we're going to have some fun here. You have no idea how often I'm expected to turn a sow's ear into a silk purse, but *you*, darling, are already one hundred per cent silk."

He stalked around Joshua, his eyes still sweeping up and down. Joshua licked his lips. "Um, thanks," he said breathlessly. "I just want to look respectable. Like a man."

The tailor narrowed his eyes, meeting Joshua's gaze for the first time. This close, Joshua could see he was wearing smudged black liner. It looked so cool.

"Are you a man or not?" the tailor asked, then blinked. "I don't mean that in a dickhead way. I'm asking if you identify as male."

Joshua resisted the urge to step back. This guy was pretty intense. "Um, yes," he said.

The tailor waved his still-raised hand and continued with his inspection. "Then whatever suit we put you in *will* be manly. And fit you like a French letter. Speaking of which, you should see what I'm putting that incredibly fuckable husband of yours in." He groaned. "Well, I guess you will see it, won't you? You lucky bastard. Right, arms up!"

Before he could get into a fluster over what he'd said about Darius, Joshua did as he was told. He let the tailor – who eventually introduced himself as Strutton, which Joshua didn't know was his first or last name – measure every inch of him, swiftly and efficiently. Then Strutton hummed and swore a fair bit, scrolling through pages on his tablet too fast for Joshua to keep up with, making notes, and drawing things with a stylus pen.

"Okay, babe. What about this?"

He flipped the pad around and showed Joshua a rough

mock-up of himself. Obviously Strutton had snapped a photo without him realising, then put his head on a model wearing a royal blue suit with a white shirt, red polka-dot tie, and tan shoes.

Joshua's immediate response was to step back and shake his head in horror. He couldn't possibly wear something like that. It was far too loud and bright. But then he stopped and really looked at the image, feeling Strutton's eyes fixed patiently on him.

Yes, it was loud. But it was also kind of beautiful, and the cut of the suit was classic. Strutton had added a few little extra details to his quick mock-up, like a red pocket handkerchief peeking out of the jacket's breast pocket and a smart silver tie clip.

"Uh," said Joshua. *Be brave!* he told himself. He'd fed a horse. He could do this too. "Do you think it'll suit me?"

Strutton rolled his eyes. "No, I picked it because I wanted you to look like a dog's dinner. *Cupcake,* I think you'll be the belle of the ball! I've been doing this shit for twenty-five years. I'd stake my life on you looking absolutely stunning." He placed a solid hand on Joshua's shoulder and batted his eyelashes at him. "Do you trust me, sweet pea?"

Joshua wasn't sure. He'd only just met the guy. But – hang on. The point was that he *didn't* know, but he should take the leap of faith anyway. He was trying new things, embracing his different life, trying to shake off that old shyness.

Why *shouldn't* he enjoy his good looks? He had Darius to protect him from any unwanted attention from other guys, after all. Why shouldn't he be his best? And not to try and impress Darius, because Joshua's feelings for him were still too thorny and complicated.

But why couldn't he look good for himself? Embrace his beauty rather than keep hiding from it. He couldn't control what other people did or thought, but he was totally in command of how he felt like when he looked in the mirror.

For once, he wanted to see what it would be like to dress to impress.

"Yes," Joshua said firmly. "I do trust you."

Strutton winked at him. "Then let's fit this bitch."

11

JOSHUA

THREE DAYS LATER, JOSHUA FOUND HIMSELF TURNING FROM side to side as he looked in the mirror, lost for words. It turned out Strutton was just altering suits, not making them from scratch, which explained how he was able to turn them around in time for the opera. But Joshua had never expected to feel like this when he put on the finished product.

"Oh, don't you look *handsome*," Mrs Weatherby gushed as she fussed with Joshua's tie. Darius had even arranged for a hairdresser to come and see them both at the castle. It was Joshua's first trim in a few months, and he had to say he appreciated it. But the suit…

He knew it was going to be bright, but actually wearing it was a totally different experience. Joshua was just concentrating on breathing in and out as he studied his reflection.

He was pretty sure he loved it so much his heart wanted to burst.

But he'd spent so long trying *not* to be noticed by anyone he wasn't sure how to react. Like he couldn't trust his instincts. A voice in his head was already whispering that a simple black suit would have been so much simpler and allowed him to blend.

But blend with whom? There would be no hiding when he went down to meet Darius shortly.

His heart skipped a beat. He hadn't really seen Darius all day. But despite Joshua being a bundle of nerves and too quiet for the last several days, Darius had kept up his side of things. He'd started asking how the garden was doing again, like he'd been doing before Victor's visit. And now they had the added bonus of Zeus, who not only gave them something to talk about but obviously gave Darius an excuse to walk around the gardens Joshua had been throwing his heart and soul into.

Joshua was grateful that so far Darius hadn't appeared annoyed that he'd withdrawn into himself, flipping their previous roles and leaving Darius to do all the talking. But despite Joshua's insistence that he was going to be braver, he was still apprehensive about spending an intense period of time together tonight. He couldn't not be. This evening was going to be so many firsts for him that it was natural to worry about fucking up, wasn't it?

He breathed slowly and deeply, brushing his hand down the front of the royal blue suit, adjusting his cufflinks. He wasn't sure where they'd come from – they had arrived separately with no note. But they were silver roses, and Joshua loved them.

He took a small step back and regarded his whole reflection with scrutiny.

Did he think he looked handsome?

Yes.

And beautiful.

He was himself, and for once, that didn't feel like something to be hidden away.

"Thank you, Mrs Weatherby." He smiled at her as she

reached out and fussed over one more crease. "Do you think Darius is ready yet?"

She nodded, her eyes shiny as she clasped her hands in front of her chest. "I believe he'll be waiting for you by now. Why don't you head down and let him see you?"

Joshua smiled at her. That was sweet, but he knew they were just going out as friends. He didn't need Darius to approve of his new look so long as Joshua himself liked it.

Which he decided he very much did. No more second-guessing.

He headed downstairs to the main foyer by himself. The castle felt oddly hushed, but perhaps that was Joshua's imagination. Or his nerves.

Okay, maybe he did care just a *little* what Darius thought of how he looked.

Nerves fluttered in his belly as he took the steps one at a time, focusing very hard on not tripping down them. That was not the kind of entrance he was hoping to make. He looked over the bannister down onto the entrance hall, looking for Darius.

He was almost all the way to the bottom stair when Darius finally came into view. He'd had his back to Joshua, but probably upon hearing his footsteps, Darius turned.

Joshua froze and gasped.

Holy. Fucking. *Shit.*

He was pretty sure he stopped breathing altogether.

Darius was wearing an exquisite dark blue suit with an open-collared purply-blue shirt. His shoes were shined. His beard was trimmed.

And his hair was cut.

Short back and sides with a smart longer finish on the top, clearly styled with products to give it some bounce and shine. It was as if Joshua was truly seeing his face for the first time ever.

And that face was smiling bashfully.

"Oh, Joshua," he said softly. He began walking closer, his blue eyes blazing in the sparkling chandelier light from above. "You look beautiful."

For at least a good three seconds, Joshua was pretty sure he was never going to talk again. All the blood in his body had rushed between his legs, and he was doing his best not to tremble.

He was so screwed. Darius was *drop-dead gorgeous*. How the hell was Joshua supposed to not fall madly in love with this new polished version of him? He felt like he could cope with the kindness and generosity and the rash acts of wild protectiveness. But a clean-cut Darius smiling at Joshua like he'd just hung the moon?

That was too much.

And *shit*. Joshua was doing exactly what he blamed other people for doing to him. Judging by appearances. But honestly, all that nobility went flying unashamedly out the window because Joshua was only fucking human, and Darius was so incredibly hot it was like Joshua had lost all capacity to think with anything other than his cock.

Using his last ounce of sense, Joshua reassured himself that he already liked a lot about Darius's personality, so it was okay to pant after him like a dog in heat.

"T-thank you," Joshua eventually managed to stutter. "You too. Very beautiful."

He expected Darius to correct him as soon as he'd realised his mistake. He should have called him handsome, not beautiful. But Darius just chuckled and held out his arm for Joshua to take. "The car is waiting for us. Shall we?"

Joshua didn't trust himself to speak. He just nodded and slipped his hand around Darius's thick arm encased in a million-thread-count cotton. He almost didn't spot the way Darius's Adam's apple bobbed as he swallowed, his mouth a tight smile. Joshua relaxed fractionally. If Darius was nervous too, that made him feel better.

The car journey to Canterbury was painfully long, but luckily their driver, Asher, had some pop music playing quietly over the sound system, so Joshua didn't feel quite so uncomfortable sitting next to Darius for an hour barely capable of thinking of anything to say. Darius managed to get a little conversation out of him as he talked about Zeus, the gardens, and Camille's latest outburst over someone ordering the wrong kind of quail eggs. Joshua smiled and nodded as best he could, but he felt too queasy to say much in return.

There was no denying the desire that was rolling through him. He'd never wanted to throw himself at a man more in his entire life. But Darius didn't want that, did he?

You look beautiful.

GET OUT!

Which words were true? Was he attracted to Joshua or not? God, he wished he had a crystal ball so he could read Darius's mind or look into the future.

The theatre was bustling by the time Asher pulled up to let them out. Joshua noticed that as soon as they left the car, Asher changed from the pop music to a football match, and Joshua wondered if Darius had asked him to play the other station for Joshua's benefit. He'd mentioned once or twice over dinner that he liked pop and dance music best. Had Darius remembered that?

The theatre was a modern building, all geometric shapes, lit up with dazzling purple spotlights. The audience for the performance that evening was walking in clumps up the stairs. Women wore long dresses in a variety of colours, a lot of them sparkling with diamantés and sequins, whilst the men wore dark-coloured suits.

None of them was in anything like Joshua's royal blue,

and uneasiness crept up his neck, frightened people would be judging him.

But why? If they didn't like his outfit, that was very much their problem, and the few people who did look his way seemed to smile or nod in approval. Joshua breathed out and tried to relax. He could do this. There was no reason to hide. Still, he was a little nervous at heading into the unknown situation of the opera itself. He was still convinced he was going to do something 'wrong' and embarrass Darius, although he had no idea how.

In a mad urge, Joshua almost reached out and took Darius's hand to hold for reassurance. But that would be inappropriate, right? He bit his lip instead, taking in the thrumming atmosphere as they made their way to a private box.

Which...wow. A private box, all to themselves, with their own waiter to get them drinks and snacks? Joshua had long suspected that Darius *had* money. He was just reluctant to spend it on himself or his home.

But apparently, he was willing to spend it on Joshua.

His tummy flipped as he took his seat, peering over the edge down at the people in the seats below. He was so confused. He wanted to believe that Darius might actually like him, but he'd said that this night was just as friends, and anyone looking on could see they didn't make sense as a couple. Joshua might be feeling more confident after his little makeover, but they were so fundamentally different. Little and large, masc and fem, older and younger. Everything about them was opposite.

So why, when Darius rubbed his back and smiled at him, did Joshua feel a sense of calm?

He bit his lip, his gaze roaming over all the people below, wondering if any of them were having as much of an internal crisis as he was this evening.

"Do you like it?" He turned to see Darius watching him anxiously, his large hands now clasped between his knees.

Joshua almost burst a blood vessel in his effort not to look beyond those hands where the bulge between Darius's legs was pretty easy to see. Those trousers were *tight*, tempting Joshua with sights he should definitely not be seeing.

He cleared his throat and looked back over the auditorium. "It's amazing," he said honestly. "The setting, the company, everything. All amazing. Thank you."

Darius squeezed Joshua's knee, but unlike the night when Zeus had arrived, this time he didn't let go. "You're welcome."

For a moment, they stared at one another. Joshua's heart was hammering in his chest. But then the orchestra started up, and the lights dimmed. Darius's hand slipped away, and they both turned to watch as the opera began.

It was all in French, but that didn't really matter. Joshua soon found himself enthralled in the tale of the beautiful Spanish Gypsy. Every now and again, Darius would lean over and murmur what was going on, sending shivers down Joshua's spine. The plot was irrelevant. The music was transporting him away, and Darius's warm body was so close in the next seat it was driving Joshua wild. They sipped Champagne and watched on as Carmen was fought over by her lovers, eventually falling foul to one of them at the close of the production.

As the whole auditorium burst into rapturous applause and the actors took their bows, Joshua didn't even think. He stood up immediately. Joshua sniffed and swallowed around the lump in his throat. He'd never experienced anything like that before. It was as if the music had filled him up and made him glow. He felt almost breathless from it.

The house lights came up, and Darius placed a hand on the small of his back. Joshua jumped slightly. When he turned to face him, Darius was looking down at Joshua fondly.

Joshua worried he'd been too enthusiastic and made a spectacle of himself. But Darius grinned at him. "It was good, wasn't it?"

"Brilliant," Joshua gushed. "Was it like you remembered?"

Darius licked his lips and looked Joshua up and down. "Better," he murmured.

Joshua's heart skipped a beat. *He's talking about the opera!* "Oh, good, good," he babbled. "That's nice. Great, I mean. I'm glad you weren't disappointed."

Darius tilted his head and gave the smallest of sighs. "Definitely not. I'm so glad I got to share this with you." He glanced around at the emptying auditorium. "Are you ready to go?"

No.

Joshua didn't want this evening to end.

Darius had chosen to share something so magical with Joshua, and he didn't know how to convey what it had meant to him. But instead, he nodded mutely, allowing Darius to lead him through the theatre and back out into the chilly night air.

His hand was on Joshua's back again, and as a sudden wind cut through them, Joshua gasped and inadvertently stepped closer to Darius's side.

Darius slipped his hand around Joshua's waist, keeping him there as they walked towards the car.

What the hell? What the hell? What the HELL? Joshua thought his brain might short-circuit as Darius hugged him close. This wasn't like the night of the lake, where their embracing had been for survival. Even if it had been prompted from the wind, it wasn't as if Joshua was at risk of getting hypothermia this time. Why was Darius holding him so close?

So tenderly?

Joshua's legs felt like they might buckle, but he made it all the way to the car without doing or saying anything embarrassing, even if his brain was still in overdrive from Darius's touch. Joshua felt like he was lucky he didn't have a raging boner or that his heart hadn't stopped.

It was pretty close on both counts, though.

Darius released him to open the car door. Joshua wasn't sure if he was relieved or disappointed to break their contact, but he did have to say he was glad of the warmth as he got inside. He was feeling a little light-headed, and not just from the Champagne. As the car pulled off, he helped himself to the complimentary bottle of water, glugging half of it down in one go.

"So," said Darius tentatively. Joshua looked over to see his wry smile. "Would you say you like the opera now?"

Joshua took a breath and wiped his mouth in case any water droplets lingered. Then he carefully screwed the cap back on, considering what he wanted to say.

"I think I liked *that* opera," he replied slowly, nodding to himself as he focused on the back of the seat in front of him. "I'd definitely be up for seeing another one. I loved that I didn't understand every word. Or any words, to be honest." He laughed and felt ridiculously relieved when Darius laughed too. "But I felt it. In here." He rubbed his chest. "It was very moving." He chewed his lip and decided to be honest. "But it upset me that she died in the end. That didn't seem fair. Those blokes both chased after her. She should have just been able to say she wasn't interested without them losing their minds."

"She was cursed by her beauty," Darius mused.

Joshua hummed. "I think they were just wankers, personally."

Darius really laughed at that. A loud bark that made

Asher look back sharply in the rear-view mirror to check everything was okay. Which it was. It was wonderful. Joshua loved making Darius let go like that.

He tried his best not to think of other ways he'd love to help Darius let go.

Unlike the drive up to Canterbury, which had been stiff and awkward, the drive back passed in a blur as Joshua and Darius discussed the many finer points of the show, from the songs to the costumes to the lighting. Joshua felt like his mind was tingling as much as his skin was every time Darius brushed his hand against his arm or his leg whenever they agreed on something. The water might have helped Joshua rehydrate, but he was still feeling dizzy.

What was happening between the two of them?

As they finally pulled up at the front entrance of Thorncliff, much like leaving the theatre box, Joshua didn't really want to get out of the car. He was worried if they left this bubble, it would break whatever spell was happening, and Joshua didn't want the magic to end. For the first time in weeks, he *wasn't* feeling confused or lost or out of place.

He felt like he was exactly where he was supposed to be.

But Darius did exit the car, and walked around to open Joshua's door when his dithering meant that he didn't move in time. Joshua smiled bashfully up at him. "Thank you," he said breathlessly.

It was late. The lights throughout the castle were lowered as they made their way inside. Darius asked if Joshua wanted anything to eat, but he declined. He was suddenly too nervous to even think about food.

There was a kind of tension between them as Darius began walking Joshua up the stairs, like electricity crackling in the air before a big storm. Joshua's heart was racing. They were approaching the point at which he would turn right for his quarters and Darius left for his.

What was going to happen when they reached the juncture? Well, he was about to find out.

Joshua was sure he gulped audibly as Darius paused, turning to face him. For several moments, they just stared at one another. Then Darius licked his lips…and took Joshua's hand gently in his own.

"Thank you for a wonderful night," he murmured. His blue eyes were wide as he swallowed, his Adam's apple bobbing enticingly. Joshua had definitely stopped breathing. Which probably caused a lack of blood to Joshua's brain, the only explanation for what he did next.

Because he was so sure *something* was going to happen. But then Darius frowned, gave him a tight smile, then let his hand go, turning to walk away.

No! Joshua was done with this limbo. Done not knowing how Darius really felt. Done second-guessing everything he was feeling and everything that transpired between them.

Enough. He had to know.

Now.

So he shot up on his tiptoes, grabbed either side of Darius's face…

…and kissed him square on the mouth.

DARIUS

IT ALL HAPPENED SO FAST. DARIUS KNEW HE WAS WALKING A tightrope, trying to be respectful while he was aching all over to stay with Joshua. Just because he'd decided to give a big 'fuck off' to his father's threats didn't mean Darius was insensible to the situation between them. Joshua was young, beautiful, full of potential.

Darius was...not.

Darius really would be a monster if he pressured Joshua into anything. Even after such a perfect night. It might have had a kind of stilted start, but the way Joshua had loved the show – the same one Darius had fallen in love with as a teenager – had melted Darius's heart even more than it already was.

Even better, though, was the journey back when Joshua had been brave enough to criticise the opera's plot, even though he'd enjoyed it. Even though he knew it had special memories from when Darius had seen it with his mother. Darius felt like that showed how far Joshua had come on in recent weeks. He'd never have said boo to a goose when he'd first arrived for the wedding. But tonight, he had been confident in poking holes in the plot and defending the character of Carmen.

Darius liked that far more than if Joshua had just agreed with everything he'd said. In fact, he kind of loved it. So much so that he'd been aware he was giving Joshua little touches as they talked in the back of the car, but Joshua seemed to lean into them, and he beamed so sweetly as he talked with enthusiasm about the opera. Darius couldn't help himself when the touches had been quite innocent and, as far as he could tell, welcomed.

But up in the hallway, he'd tried to do the right thing.

He'd tried to leave.

So naturally, he'd ended up with his hand tangled in Joshua's hair, kissing him desperately, pressing his other hand against Joshua's back so their bellies and cocks were rubbing together.

No!

He was supposed to be protecting Joshua! Not seducing him!

Darius wrenched himself back with a cry. Joshua's brown eyes flew open as he covered his mouth with his hands. "I'm sorry!" Joshua whispered, tears pooling in his eyes. "I'm sorry. I'm *so* sorry!"

Darius looked at him in total confusion, already fearing he'd made a mistake. "Why would you be sorry?" he eventually uttered in bewilderment.

Joshua hugged himself whilst blinking furiously. "I shouldn't have kissed you. We had a nice night, and I spoiled it. I'll go."

He went to spin around, but Darius grabbed his arm, applying just enough pressure to urge him to stop.

God, if there was any justice in the world, he had to stop. Darius had definitely made a mistake. If Joshua wanted to kiss him, why would he stop that? Out of some misplaced idea of nobility? Darius was a fucking idiot. He was already wishing he could kiss Joshua again.

But was it too late?

"Don't go," Darius rasped. They stared at each other, breathing hard. "I – it – we *did* have a lovely night. Incredible, in fact."

Joshua bit his lip. "I know you don't fancy me," he said. "I know you're just being kind. I'm sorry I jumped you like that."

Darius shook his head, all the words rattling too fast through his mind. Breaking off the kiss had seemed like the right thing to do, but he was already bitterly regretting it. He couldn't let Joshua leave, especially not if he thought that Darius didn't care about him. "In the bath!" he spluttered, trying to form the best linear thoughts he could. "I asked you what you *did* know. But…do you know that? What you think you know?"

Joshua blinked in confusion. Darius didn't blame him. "Know…?"

"That I don't fancy you?" he murmured, tugging on Joshua's arm, urging them closer again. If there was a chance that Joshua felt the same way as him, he was going to be selfish and find out. Mercifully, Joshua turned back to face him. "That I don't *need* you," Darius continued. "That I haven't been fighting this since the moment I met you."

Joshua's mouth popped open, and his eyes grew wide. "This?" he asked weakly.

"Us," Darius uttered.

But then he swallowed and cleared his throat, dropping Joshua's arm and stepping away. "I know my father had urged you to, uh, consummate things. I don't want that."

"You don't?" Joshua asked.

Darius shook his head. "No."

"Oh." Joshua inhaled and stepped back. "Okay. Like I said. Goodnight."

"What?" Darius asked, aware he'd barked pretty loudly. "You don't me to want us to fuck because my father ordered us to?"

Joshua raised his eyebrows. "Huh?"

Darius balled up his fists and made himself count backwards from five in his head. He was scared and confused and vulnerable, not to mention he felt like his heart was going to explode. Joshua deserved his patience, so for the first time in a long time, he didn't just give in to that short fuse. He forced himself to take a breath and speak *clearly*.

"Joshua," he said, hearing his voice crack but continuing anyway. "I don't want to say anything inappropriate. You were brought to this marriage and this castle against your will. But...but I think you're rather lovely. Very, *very* lovely, in fact. Inside and out. Heart and soul. If you wanted to kiss me again, that's what *I* want. But only if it's also what *you* want. Only if you're not doing so under *any* obligation or idea that you owe me and *definitely* not anything to do with my father." Darius was feeling sick from just mentioning Victor in the same breath as talking to Joshua about kissing. "But because it's what we both want. Because-"

Wumph. Joshua's mouth collided with him like a freight train. He threw his arms around Darius's neck, their chests banging against each other as lips and tongues smooshed sloppily together. It was mismatched and uncoordinated, and Darius was so giddy with joy he thought he might fall over. Instead, he scooped his hands under Joshua's arse and hauled him into his arms, letting him wrap his legs around Darius's waist as they kissed and kissed some more.

He was afraid, though. There was a part of him that still wasn't sure this was a good idea because of the risk to Joshua's safety from Victor. But that voice was being drowned out easily by the other voices that were cheering in jubilation. Joshua had kissed him *twice* now. There was only so much Darius could fight his heart.

And his cock. God, it was hard in these damn tight trousers. He'd need release, and soon.

But that was moving things way too fast. If this was some casual hook-up, he'd be happy to suggest they jump right into bed. But Joshua was too important for that. Darius wanted to treat him respectfully.

Even if his dick was throbbing and Darius's lizard brain was already thinking of all the different ways they could be naked and fucking.

It was more than that, though. Joshua felt so right in Darius's arms, and his skin tasted so perfect. Darius felt like he'd been waiting an eternity to experience this after so long imagining it all. He wasn't sure he had the strength to step away from Joshua now.

However, Darius did draw back, but only fractionally. Their foreheads were still pressed together as they panted. "Do you want to come to my room with me?" he murmured, caressing the side of Joshua's beautiful face.

They were so close it was impossible to miss the way Joshua's eyes widened in panic.

"Or not," Darius added quickly.

"No, I..." Joshua bit his lip and closed his eyes. "I don't want to stop kissing."

Darius exhaled in relief. "Me neither. We can just do that, if you like. Nothing more. I just don't want this night to end." But Joshua still looked anxious, so Darius leaned back a little and raised his eyebrows. "Or nothing. Or just talking?" He was pretty shit at talking usually and felt like he'd done an awful lot of it that evening already, but he'd do whatever it took to make Joshua happy.

It was easy to think he'd made a big mistake in encouraging this kiss.

Joshua swallowed and blinked, his eyes getting glassy. "Sorry," he whispered.

Darius shook his head and let Joshua back down to the floor. "Why would you be sorry?" he asked for the second time in so many minutes. What had gone awry? Joshua had been the one to initiate the kisses. Why was he getting upset now?

Joshua scrubbed his face and damp eyes, taking in a couple of breaths. "I'm all over the place. I don't know what I'm doing, swinging from one extreme to the other."

Darius rubbed his arm. The suit he was wearing was impossibly gorgeous. It had been difficult to watch the opera when all Darius had really wanted to do was stare at his date all night.

Because it *had* been a date. There was no denying that now. But clearly Joshua was uncomfortable about something, and Darius didn't have the words to ask what exactly was bothering him. "Have I, um, done something wrong?"

"No, no," said Joshua quickly with a gasp. He sniffed and blinked a couple of times, but his face had gone all red, and he was trembling. "I suppose...I guess..."

He paused and bit his lip again, stirring all kinds of lustful and protective thoughts in Darius. He wanted to hold Joshua safely in his arms while they made love all bloody night.

But Joshua needed to say what was on his mind. Darius felt it best to wait and give him the time he needed to find the right words. So he rubbed his arm and tried not to imagine Joshua saying anything bad. Like he *did* feel pressured and found Darius completely hideous.

The words he eventually spoke were not those. In fact, they were kind of the opposite.

"I'm not really convinced that someone as gorgeous as you would be interested in a meek little thing like me," Joshua said in a rush, all the words blending together. Then he screwed his eyes up, apparently holding his breath. "I don't know what kind of men you like, but I know I'm not exactly 'manly'."

Darius opened and closed his mouth a couple of times, thoroughly confused. "You...you're not convinced that I'm attracted to you?" Joshua had to be pulling his leg. He'd spelled out that he'd been attracted to him from the moment they'd clapped eyes on each other. But Joshua shook his head, his eyes still firmly closed. Darius huffed and touched his index finger and thumb gently to Joshua's chin. He tilted his face up a fraction and stroked his jaw. "Joshua," he asked, "please, could you look at me?"

Joshua licked his lips and shuddered, but he did peek out through his golden eyelashes up at Darius.

Darius smiled down at him. "Thank you. Joshua, I think you're the most beautiful man I've ever seen. Far too perfect for a gnarled old brute like me. I should be asking *you* what the hell you see in *me*."

That made Joshua scowl. He tugged his chin from Darius's fingers, then placed his hand tentatively on Darius's chest.

Above the scarred flesh over his thumping heart.

Shit. How had Darius not thought about the fact that he might have to expose himself? Well, if Joshua was feeling timid, maybe they wouldn't even take their clothes off. He'd offered that they could just talk or kiss, after all. Darius could always keep his shirt on. He refused to let panic ruin the moment.

"You're so big and strong and, uh..." Joshua's cheeks were flaming, but he pushed on with a quick breath. "So muscular and manly. And, um, I love the new hair."

Darius waited, but no mention of his burns came. His

142

heartbeat had still increased, though, and his body was pounding with adrenaline from the fear they were about to address his ruined body.

But the way Joshua described him didn't make his scars sound as horrible as they were at all. In fact, he was planting slightly, his pupils dilated as he gently caressed the fabric of Darius's new suit.

Darius wasn't sure how to react. He'd not even been with a man since the accident…since Richard. He'd braced himself for repulsion, and instead, Joshua was clearly reacting with lust.

So what was the problem if they both wanted each other? Was he still missing something?

"Uh, thanks," he grunted. But then he couldn't find the right words to ask what was stopping them. He'd offered that they could go their separate ways or just kiss or – bloody hell – he'd honestly be okay with cuddling on top of the sheets right now. "Can I do anything to help?" he asked eventually.

Joshua seemed to snap from a reverie. "No," he said softly. "It's me. I'm the problem."

"I doubt that," Darius grumbled. "I'm the prickly old bastard here. You've been very patient."

But Joshua shook his head, still looking distressed. "I should go," he whispered.

"Please don't," Darius said urgently, gripping Joshua's arm. He then swallowed and loosened his grip. "I mean you can, if you want. But I don't understand the problem. If you told me, maybe-"

"I'm a *virgin*," Joshua blurted out, tears springing from his eyes before he covered them with his hands and turned away from Darius. "I've never even *kissed* a man before!"

Something hot and powerful surged through Darius. *That* was Joshua's problem?

Not to be flippant, but Darius didn't see how that was a problem in the slightest.

Gently, he placed his hand on Joshua's shaking back, encouraging him to turn around and face him again. But Joshua stayed where he was, snuffling against his hands.

"That was your first kiss?" Darius asked faintly.

Joshua nodded, head still in his hands.

Darius exhaled loudly. "Fuck me, I'd never have known. That was amazing."

Slowly Joshua lowered his hands and peered at Darius over his shoulder. His brown eyes shimmered with glassy tears. "Are you just being nice?"

Darius shook his head. "I mean, I'd like to think I'm not the kind of arsehole who'd criticise you for bad technique on your first go, even it was a bit crap. But no, I'd never have known. I liked it."

Joshua swallowed and gradually turned back to face Darius. "Really?"

Trying not to get too visibly excited, Darius cupped the side of Joshua's face, sensing progress. "Really. Hence being pretty keen to do it again."

A smile twitched at the corner of Joshua's mouth. "I'm keen, too," he admitted. Was it Darius's imagination, or was there a playful sparkle in his wet eyes as he spoke?

Darius took a moment to breathe. "No expectations," he murmured, rubbing his thumb against Joshua's cheekbone. "No doing anything at all if you don't want. But I'd like to hold you for a while, in bed. You could stay the night, if you wanted. Just cuddling." Darius tried not to get his hopes up, but he hadn't shared a bed with anyone since Richard, and that had usually been awkward bunking situations.

The idea of falling asleep with Joshua in his arms was almost too much.

But if Joshua said no, that would be okay. It had to be. Darius didn't want him to feel in any way pressured.

Joshua frowned, appearing to mull something over. "So… you *don't* want to have sex?"

Darius couldn't help it. He barked out the laugh before he could stop himself and had to clamp his mouth shut again at Joshua's startled look. "Petal, I'm *desperate* to have sex with you. If that's what you want, and when the time's right. I've waited this long. I'll wait as long as you need. I'm not going anywhere."

Joshua blinked. It finally looked like he'd stopped shedding tears, and his mouth quirked with real warmth and humour. "Petal?"

Darius was positive he felt himself blush. "Sorry, that's a bit naff, isn't it?" He wasn't sure where the word had come from. It was quite a northern term of endearment. But in that split second, it had felt right.

"No, I…I really like it," said Joshua breathlessly. He inhaled deeply, running his hands up and down Darius's arms. It made Darius want to shiver, but he did his best to stay as still as he could so as not to spook Joshua. "I also think I'd like to cuddle. I've never shared a bed with anyone."

He blushed again, but Darius rubbed his cheek and kissed his forehead. He had nothing to be ashamed of. "I'm going to say something terrible," he uttered gruffly, "because I hope it might help you feel better."

Joshua cleared his throat. "Okay?" he said uncertainly.

Darius pressed their temples together, not sure he could say what he was thinking if he looked Joshua in the eye.

"It is *such* a turn-on knowing that no one else has kissed you or slept with you or fucked you, Joshua Bellamy. I get to be the first one."

Maybe the only one, a voice whispered at the back of his head.

Darius ignored it. Who knew if this marriage would last? This whole situation had been artificially created and was quite bizarre. But right now, Joshua was completely his, like pure snow.

The caveman in Darius fucking *loved* that.

Joshua's breath became shallow, and he trembled in Darius's arms. For a second, Darius wondered if he'd gone too far.

Then Joshua pulled away a few inches and cradled the side of Darius's face in his small, soft hand. "Y-yeah," he stammered. "That does make me feel better."

Darius exhaled and grinned down at him. He was raging with lust, but his heart was also full of something gentler, more authentic.

Deep affection.

"What do you want, then?" Darius asked, running his hand down Joshua's spine.

Joshua nodded, looking into Darius's eyes. "Take me to bed," he said in a rush.

Darius forced himself not to get too excited. He was genuinely all right with just some cuddling. "We'll take it slowly," he promised.

But a mischievous look crossed over Joshua's face. "Well," he said, looking Darius up and down with eyes that were suddenly full of sin. "We don't have to go *that* slowly."

JOSHUA

So this was kissing?

Joshua could get used to this.

Fuck, his cock throbbed in his trousers as Darius leaned down and met his mouth, pressing their bodies together, rubbing his hands up and down his back. Joshua felt like he was on fire, his skin tingling and quivering all over.

Particularly between his legs.

He hadn't been aware he could get this hard. He felt like he'd spent half his teenage years wanking, so it wasn't like he was totally innocent in that regard. But apparently, it was *wildly* different when it was someone else's hands on you, someone else's lips.

As Darius picked Joshua up again, he suspected that he wouldn't be feeling this way about any random bloke he hooked up with at the pub or off Grindr. This was because of *Darius*. It was Darius's warm breath and strong arms and spicy musk. And, oh, *god,* Darius's thick, hard cock poking Joshua in the belly as they made their way towards Darius's quarters.

More lips. More tongue. Fingers digging into his skin. Joshua had never felt so *alive.*

Darius was desperate to take him to bed but had made it clear he wouldn't do anything Joshua wasn't comfortable with. That was hot as fuck. But Joshua had to admit, in that moment, he couldn't really think of much he wouldn't be willing to do if Darius asked.

He was ashamed of the wobble he'd had. He'd almost ruined everything with his insecurities. But he genuinely had believed that Darius might not be interested in him as more than a friend, and if by some miracle he was, he'd definitely be put off by the fact that Joshua was a virgin. He felt so awkward and inexperienced.

During the past anxiety-ridden year, it had never once occurred to him that a man might find that a turn-on. Certainly not to the extent Darius clearly did. It made Joshua even harder as he recalled the way Darius had growled in his ear, clearly possessive and excited by being Joshua's only partner.

That kind of encouragement was incredibly confidence building. Joshua had gone from feeling like a failure to a precious jewel in the blink of an eye. Which was lucky because *things* were clearly happening between him and Darius that night. Joshua felt dizzy with anticipation. He'd never been seduced before. He had to say he was really enjoying the hell out of it so far.

He moaned and rutted against Darius's body, amazed at how easily Darius held Joshua up. That power was intoxicating, but even more so was the delicate way Darius's large, calloused hands held Joshua, making him feel protected and safe.

How many men how Darius fucked? How many men had he made come over the years? Joshua assumed he was a top, just from his take-charge sort of attitude. Joshua always kind of presumed he'd bottom when he finally had sex, naturally assuming he'd want someone else to be in control of the situation for him. He couldn't help but hope that would make them a perfect match.

He was getting way ahead of himself. They weren't going to have sex right now. But Joshua had to shudder and moan, wondering if they'd at least make out, and he might get to see Darius's cock.

He'd watched so much porn over the years he was amazed he hadn't gone blind. But would he finally get to see another man's penis in real life? Maybe even *touch* it? He salivated at the thought.

Darius chuckled against his lips. "I like your moans," he whispered. "Shows you're having fun."

Joshua was. He *really* was. It was amazing how being horny could wipe away all his previous fears so fast.

He wasn't going to let himself worry or second-guess what was happening, not for the rest of the night. They'd already talked enough in the corridor. He was going to relax and enjoy whatever was about to happen between him and Darius.

He was going to trust him.

They pushed their way through the doors that led to Darius's living room. Zeus was passed out on his back in his plush basket, little fluffy legs in the air, snoring and dead to the world. Joshua smiled, still not quite believing that his gamble had paid off.

But then his attention was quickly drawn back to Darius, who had his fingers in Joshua's hair, tugging as he kissed and nipped at his neck. Joshua squeezed his legs around Darius's waist, encouraging him as they spilled through the next door.

Into Darius's bedroom.

Joshua hadn't looked that closely at it last time. He'd been too frozen getting into the bathroom, then too sleepy when Darius had escorted him back to his own rooms.

But now, he got a second or two to take a look.

It was like something out of a Netflix adaptation of a fantasy novel. A wooden, circular chandelier hung above a four-poster bed that was covered in faux-fur throws. A couple of fur-like rugs were laid on the stone floor, and there was an actual bloody fireplace, its flames burning low, obviously having been lit by the staff in anticipation of Darius's return from the opera. Photo frames dominated the room, although at a quick glance Joshua couldn't tell who they were of. There were framed maps on the walls and an antique globe standing on one of the small tables. Also certificates, and maybe awards, were dotted about.

Joshua couldn't absorb any more. All he got was a quick glance as Darius placed him back on his feet before he took hold of either side of Joshua's face and kissed him reverently.

"I know I shouted at you once when you came in here," Darius's voice rumbled as he kissed down Joshua's throat, then stopped to meet his gaze as he cradled his back. "That haunts me. I feel like shit every time I think of it. So I want to make sure you feel safe now. I want you here, but is there anything I can do to help you feel that way?" He looked squarely in Joshua's eyes.

Joshua gulped. "You act like you don't have any feelings," he marvelled. "That you're thoughtless. But all you care about is *my* feelings. I hated that night, but I'm okay now. I'm *great*. I want to ask if you're okay."

Darius blinked, his blue eyes such a contrast to his thick, dark eyelashes. "Me?"

Joshua nodded, suddenly fearful again. But the whole theme of this week had been for him to be brave. So he rallied his courage. "Yes, you," he whispered. Then he laid his hand on Darius's chest, feeling the irregular skin under the cotton of his shirt. He stared at the back of his hand instead of Darius's face, hoping he wasn't making a terrible mistake. But Darius was the one who had wanted them here, in his bedroom, getting naked.

Joshua needed to check in that he was truly all right, like he had done with him.

Joshua had never imagined anyone making being a virgin sound so unbelievably sexy. Darius had given him that gift, so Joshua wanted to try and give him something in return. He just wasn't sure he knew how to do it without being clumsy or saying the wrong thing and destroying the mood.

"I snuck up on you last time. When you were undressed. I invaded. That wasn't right."

He breathed in and out several times, feeling Darius's strong grasp on him not faltering. So he inhaled and was honest, just like Darius had been about finding him being a virgin hot as fuck.

"I liked what I saw, though," he whispered. "I'm worried you don't think I did. But you're gorgeous. All of you."

He bit his lip and waited, hardly daring to move. But Darius didn't shove him away. He breathed heavily as well, his gaze fixed downwards. "I don't like people seeing that," he said eventually.

Joshua nodded, not disappointed. In fact, he was glad Darius was talking to him. He'd half expected him to scream at him to get out again. "I'm sorry," he said again, rubbing his fingers gently against Darius's shirt. "I'd never want to hurt you. Whatever happens next, I totally understand if you want to keep your shirt on. But there's nothing about you that I don't want to see. I like it all because it's you."

"You can't possibly mean that," Darius snarled.

Joshua gritted his teeth and kept still. He didn't appreciate being talked to like that, but he sensed Darius was a wounded animal, lashing out when he was scared. Joshua didn't know much about much, but he wasn't here to be Darius's punching bag.

Sure enough, a few seconds later, he felt Darius deflate ever so slightly. "I'm sorry," he mumbled.

"Thank you," Joshua whispered back.

He heard Darius swallow over the gentle crackling of the fire in the hearth. Then he lifted his hand and stroked the back of Joshua's hair. "I don't deserve your patience," he said in a rumble. "Or your kindness."

"Yes, you do," Joshua insisted. He lifted his gaze and locked eyes with Darius. "Because *you're* patient and kind."

There was a long pause. Darius held his gaze for a few seconds, then looked away into the fireplace. "I was in an attack. It ended my military career. People died. People I cared about."

Joshua tried to blink back the tears that sprung into his eyes. Darius didn't need him blubbering. It was incredible he'd even opened up that much to Joshua. "I'm so glad you're still here," he whispered. Darius screwed up his mouth, then opened it. But before he could protest, something angry rose in Joshua. "I don't know if enough people have told you that," he said defiantly, trying to stand up a little taller. "I'm glad you survived. I'm *so* sorry for what happened, but you're important, and I really like you. Those scars show what you went through to get here, Darius Legrand."

Darius inhaled sharply, like he'd been slapped at the word 'scars'. He bit his lip, his jaw ticking, but he was breathing and looked like he was thinking. "You don't know what I went through," he said. However, it wasn't an accusation.

"No, I don't," Joshua agreed. "But that doesn't mean I'm repulsed by it."

Joshua didn't want to feel triumphant. It wasn't that kind of situation. But he was sort of relieved when Darius winced, telling Joshua he'd been right. Darius thought that Joshua was disgusted by his scars, which was completely not true.

But Joshua had no experience with men. How did he reassure Darius that he was sexy without sounding patronising? How did he bring the magic back after having to address the elephant in the room?

He thought of telling Darius that he would ignore the burned area. Reminding him that he'd said that he could leave his shirt on if that might make him happy. But if there was one thing Joshua had learned over the past few weeks – especially the last few days – it was that hiding got you nowhere.

"Can you feel anything?" Joshua asked, deliberately running his hand gently and slowly over Darius's scarred area, tracing his rigid flesh through his shirt. He was ready to stop in a flash, but Darius frowned and breathed quickly in and out.

"In some places."

Joshua almost squealed in delight. He'd been so terrified that Darius would reject him for being 'only a virgin'. But he'd treated him with such reverence, such desire, that it made it easier now for Joshua to be more confident than he felt, doing his best to be brave. He and Darius had been through too much to let it all fall apart now. So to get a direct answer was as exciting as it was a relief.

"Can I see?" Joshua asked, hoping he wasn't pushing too fast.

Darius met eyes with him again, tilting his head. He knitted his brow. "Okay," he said simply.

He stepped back from Joshua, swiftly removing his dinner jacket and dropping it to the floor. He opened his shirt cuffs, then began working slowly down the buttons. But he paused halfway.

"It's okay," Joshua said quickly. "You don't have to do anything you're not comfortable with."

Darius huffed out a laugh. "I thought that was going to be my line."

Joshua stepped forward and placed his hands over Darius's. "It can be both of ours."

Darius gave a light chuckle again. Then he did something wholly unexpected. He squeezed Joshua's hands before switching them around with his own and pressing them against the next shirt button. "You do it," Darius murmured.

Joshua raised his eyebrows, but one look shared with Darius told him that he was serious. So Joshua willed his fingers not to shake despite all the nerves and adrenaline flying around his system, and he popped the next button through the small hole.

Then the next and the next until he was pulling the shirt out of the trousers, revealing all of Darius's magnificent hairy chest. Looking at Darius first to check it was okay, he then reached up and slid the material over his shoulders, exposing everything Darius was ashamed of, and Joshua was determined to prove was just a different part of the same gorgeous body.

Darius's chest rose as he held his breath. Joshua knew he was waiting for his reaction, but Joshua wasn't going to rush, as nervous as he felt. He wanted Darius to feel just as confident as he'd made Joshua. So Joshua looked at the scarred flesh in the firelight, noticing several welts amongst the burns that looked more like straight lines. Whatever had happened to Darius had been complicated and painful and had probably taken him a long time to recover from physically.

Mentally, Joshua suspected he was still working through a lot of things.

If he didn't like anyone looking at his scar tissue, then had he been trying to persevere alone?

Well, not anymore. He had a husband now.

First, Joshua gently ran his palms over Darius's unmarred side, the skin hot and responsive under his hands. *Fuck,* how many times had he imagined the way the coarse body hair would feel against his fingertips? But it was soft and springy, not rough. Darius shuddered, giving Joshua a thrill. *He* was making this gorgeous man respond like that.

Then he let his hand wander, touching the other side of Darius's chest where the skin was twisted. Like Joshua had suspected, he wasn't repulsed by it in the slightest. It was just a rippled texture, smooth with none of the thick, swirling hair on the other side. But he could tell by the way Darius was watching him and not flinching or shivering that he could no longer feel the pressure of Joshua's fingers.

He didn't let that deter him, though. He let Darius look at him as his own gaze followed the trail his hands were making over Darius's chest and around his shoulder, investigating the ridges of his flesh.

Suddenly, as Joshua's fingers ran along Darius's ribs, Darius inhaled and bit his lip, grinning. Joshua looked up at him, keeping his hands still, meeting his gaze. "Did that tickle?" he asked hopefully.

Darius nodded. "A little," he rasped.

Joshua looked back down and gently caressed the spot that looked much like the rest of the scar tissue to him, but Darius groaned, clearly affected. Joshua wanted to cry, his emotions a mess. He felt joyous that Darius was experiencing a positive moment with something that had been causing him so much distress. Sad that Darius had been hating himself for so long. Excited that he, Joshua Bellamy, was making another man moan with his touch. Anxious that he was suddenly going to step over a line and make Darius's temper erupt again.

But something told him Darius was working hard to not give in to his temper like that anymore. Besides, fortune favoured the bold, didn't it?

So Joshua rallied his courage, leaned in, and kissed the sensitive spot he had found.

Darius let out a vulnerable gasp and cupped the back of Joshua's head as he kissed there again. He wanted to find all the special parts Darius might like being touched, so he continued to trail his lips and fingers over more of the scar tissue until he jerked and gasped again.

"Joshua," he murmured, letting him kiss just under his shoulder, then pulled him up so their mouths could meet again. There was such passion behind this kiss. Joshua's heart ached.

Darius's hands began to work, undoing and removing Joshua's suit jacket, then his tie, before Darius's blunt fingers found the silver rose cufflinks and fondled them. "Do you like them?" he mumbled against Joshua's mouth.

Joshua smiled and took a moment to gaze into Darius's eyes. "I'd hoped they were from you."

Darius blushed. "Petals for my petal," he said with a grin, sounding quite embarrassed by his corniness, but Joshua didn't care. He loved it.

Carefully they removed them together and placed them on one of Darius's chest of drawers. Then Joshua vowed he wasn't going to get nervous and freak out as Darius began unbuttoning his shirt. He'd seen him completely naked, after all.

But that had been in a totally different scenario, one that was practical and almost clinical.

Nothing like the quivering sensation Joshua was having now, knowing that another man was slowly, sensually undressing him for both their pleasure. Darius had assured him that being a virgin was a surprising – and more than welcomed – bonus.

But how was Joshua's soft, small body going to measure up?

Before he could let his doubts creep in too far, Darius separated the shirt all the way, then laid his large, rough hand against Joshua's slightly rounded belly. He sucked it in, but Darius chuckled, low and carnal. "Don't you dare try and hide this," he rumbled, catching Joshua's earlobe between his teeth and tugging. "It's my favourite. Did you know you look so much healthier now than when you arrived?"

Joshua felt himself blush furiously. Darius *liked* that he'd put on a few pounds from all of Camille's macarons? Would tonight's surprises never cease?

So Joshua stood naturally, allowing Darius's hands to roam over his skin. Delicious sparks flew over his body, making him sigh contentedly. He barely even noticed as his shirt fluttered to the floor to join Darius's.

Then Joshua yawned, and he could have *kicked* himself.

"I'm not tired," he yelped, meeting Darius's gaze. "Honestly."

Darius smiled fondly and brushed back a lock of Joshua's hair before hugging them together. It felt so weird to have someone else's belly touching his own, but weird in a good way.

"Well, I'm fucking knackered," Darius said with a laugh. "It's been an eventful day. You still want to cuddle up with me tonight?" He waggled his dark eyebrows, making Joshua giggle.

"Um, sure," he said shyly. He rested his head on Darius's arm, specifically choosing the marked one, and kept looking up at his lover. "Maybe…maybe we could take the trousers off?"

Darius nodded, leaning down to place a sweet kiss on Joshua's lips. "I'm sure I have a T-shirt you could borrow-" he began, but Joshua shook his head.

"Underwear is good if it's good with you?"

Darius didn't reply verbally. Instead, he quickly slipped out of his trousers, shoes, and socks. He wore boxer briefs that didn't leave much to the imagination. He wasn't fully erect, but Joshua could clearly see the hard outline of his thick cock, a beautiful bulge curled up neatly in its pouch. It made his mouth water.

But he didn't feel able to reach out and touch it yet, simply standing still as Darius took charge and began unbuckling Joshua's belt. This was what he'd been craving, this kind of caring, gentle authority from Darius. He revelled as Darius stripped him down to just his briefs as well.

"Come here," Darius murmured. He took Joshua by the hand, leading him towards the bed. He then pulled back the covers, slipped inside, and wrapped his arms around Joshua as they quickly found the best way to lie together under the duvet.

Joshua could have whimpered. It felt like heaven. Darius's body was hot and large, feeling like it was all around Joshua as they nestled against the fat pillows and soft sheets. Joshua lay with his back to Darius's chest. The only sounds filling the room were their steady breaths and the crackling of the fire.

"I'm not tired," Joshua mumbled again.

Darius chuckled and kissed the back of his neck. "Goodnight," he murmured.

Joshua tried to fight it, but his eyelids were drooping. Maybe it couldn't hurt to close them for a minute? But he was afraid of what might happen once this bubble burst. Would the magic still be there when he next woke up?

He guessed he'd soon find out, as he was already tumbling into darkness, sleep claiming him completely.

———————

Joshua woke in the large, unfamiliar bed to feel the thunder rumbling through the depths of the house. It seemed another storm was raging overhead. However, that wasn't the only noise that had disturbed him, apparently. Across the wide mattress, Darius whined and grunted, twitching and flinching. They must have rolled apart in their sleep. *"No,"* he growled, his brow furrowed as his teeth clicked.

Joshua edged over, the cool bedsheets sliding against his warm skin. "Darius?" he said tentatively. He rested his hand on Darius's broad chest, feeling the ticklish hair under his palm. Darius's flesh was clammy, and he didn't appear any closer to waking. "Darius, it's okay. I'm here." It felt stupid to suggest that he would be safer for Joshua's presence, but he didn't know what else to say to try and pull him from what had to be a nightmare.

Suddenly Darius turned, slinging his meaty arm over Joshua. He dragged Joshua to him, pressing his muscular, scarred chest to Joshua's back. Burying his face against Joshua's neck, he flattened his large, calloused hand over Joshua's soft tummy and flung a hairy, solid leg over both of Joshua's.

"Mine," he said, the word calmly uttered on a warm puff of air into Joshua's hair. Immediately Darius's breathing became even, his body once more heavy with deep sleep.

Joshua hardly dared to move.

After what seemed like an age, he inhaled carefully, feeling like his heart was beating so loud it was competing with the thunder outside. There was so much of Darius's naked flesh pressed against him, and it felt *incredible*. But not nearly as good as the single muttered word that probably didn't mean anything in the throes of a bad dream.

Mine.

Joshua couldn't help it, though. He clung to it like a life raft. Was he really Darius's? As much as his own feelings had become complicated for the not-so-brutish brute, Joshua still struggled to believe something could really work between them. The marriage might have brought them together, but they were from different worlds.

However, as the rain splattered on the window panes, and the long night stretched out before him, Joshua let himself dream, just a little.

Wouldn't it be amazing to belong to someone like Darius?

No, not 'someone'.

Darius.

They still had a lot to work through. But as Joshua finally drifted back off to sleep, secure in the arms of his lover, he couldn't stop his heart from hoping.

Because he didn't want to stop himself. If Darius ever wanted Joshua to be his, he knew now that was what he would be.

14

DARIUS

For a moment, Darius couldn't quite figure out where he was or what was going on. There was another body entangled in his limbs, soft puffs of air hitting his neck and making his hair move. Then everything came flooding back.

Darius inhaled deeply, filling his lungs with the warm, woodsy smell that was Joshua. A lump threatened to rise in his throat. Joshua was really in his bed, almost naked. They'd crossed that line, and Darius had no regrets.

Well, nothing to regret in terms of him and Joshua. If they truly felt that way about one another, then it would be stupid to hold back from their attraction.

But there were other factors to consider.

Darius didn't want thoughts of his father intruding on the first moment of domestic bliss he could remember feeling in a long time. And truth be told, it had never had the chance to be like this with Richard, god rest his soul. But Darius had to be sensible.

Victor was a real threat.

As much as Darius had been overjoyed with the arrival of

Zeus into his life, he wasn't an idiot. Having the puppy made Darius vulnerable. He remembered all too clearly what had happened with Athena when he'd been a teenager. The truth was that throughout his life, anything he'd loved, his father had tried to destroy.

And the one time his father hadn't been able to destroy that love, fate and a surface-to-air missile had done the job for him.

So any worries Darius had felt upon accepting the new puppy into his life were currently increasing a hundredfold as he wrapped Joshua up tighter in his arms. Was this wise? Or was he being a selfish prick and knowingly putting Joshua in harm's way?

Darius honestly couldn't say. This was a unique situation. Victor had never married him off before. Would his father care now he'd got what he'd wanted in the control of Christopher Bellamy's company? Or did he still want what he *always* wanted?

To make his son suffer.

Darius figured he probably knew the answer to that.

But what could he do? The cat was out of the bag. He and Joshua had kissed and *so* much more.

Darius refused to let himself get too smug, but he'd never known one of his father's schemes to backfire so badly. If his intention had been to use the bankruptcy of Bellamy's company to humiliate Darius, it couldn't have had a more opposite outcome. He was almost certain Victor had intended for lovely Joshua to make Darius feel wretched when Joshua inevitably saw and fled from Darius's scarred and twisted body.

Trust Joshua to see the beauty in Darius and find a way to turn his worst shame into a moment of delicate, cherishable intimacy between them. Darius knew he was supposed to

THORN IN HIS SIDE

massage his scars and do physiotherapy, but he'd never really seen the point in trying to fix the mess he'd been left with. Now, maybe he did.

Darius had been vaguely aware that there were spots amidst the scars where he could still feel touch, but to have Joshua find them was almost like discovering entirely new body parts. Darius bit his lip, gently rubbing one of them as he lay in bed, his thoughts swirling. Joshua had been so nervous and worried over his virginity. He had no idea how sexy his burst of confidence to treat Darius like that had been.

Darius nuzzled his face against Joshua's soft hair, smelling the fruity products he'd used the night before. Darius would never have believed that he'd be lying here with his scars on display. But Joshua hadn't treated him like a grotesque monster. The memory of the way he'd touched and kissed them made Darius shiver. He'd thought it impossible that anyone could be accepting of his body since the attack.

But he'd never met anyone like Joshua before.

Darius's heart skipped as his lover stirred in his arms. Darius didn't want Joshua to think he'd been staring at him whilst he'd slept, but he wasn't going to pretend to be asleep, either. So Darius kissed his temple and rubbed their stubbly cheeks together.

"Good morning, petal," he said, grinning at his own ridiculousness. When it had first escaped his mouth, he'd been mortified by the cheesy pet name. But now it was sticking, and Darius had to say he kind of loved it.

Joshua grumbled adorably and yawned. "Morning," he said as he rubbed his eyes.

Darius chuckled, glancing at the sunshine spilling around the curtains. "This is you 'not tired', is it?"

"Shut up," Joshua mumbled playfully, turning in Darius's arms and poking his chest. But then it was like the air pressure changed around them as they both seemed to realise the same thing at the same time.

They were pretty much naked, and their bodies had clearly reacted to that fact whilst they'd been cuddling during the night. It was difficult to miss the stiffness between both their legs.

Darius held his breath. As much as he wanted to devour Joshua, he'd meant what he said about respecting his needs and taking things slowly. So he didn't move.

But Joshua did.

He dropped his gaze, looking at Darius's chest. Darius almost flinched, wanting to turn away. But the truth was there wasn't anywhere to hide. More importantly, after the way Joshua had treated him last night, for the first time since the attack, Darius felt like maybe it wouldn't be a disaster to have someone looking at him while he was vulnerable.

Someone he cared for, anyway.

"Are you all right?" Joshua asked, throwing Darius off guard. That wasn't what he'd been expecting Joshua to say.

He blinked a few times. "Yeah," he said. "I think so?"

Joshua bit his lip, touching Darius's collarbone and watching as he traced it with his fingers. Darius shivered at the touch. "You were having nightmares."

Oh. Had he been? Probably, but that didn't surprise him. He'd never shared a bed with anyone since the attack. Often, he'd wake up in drenched, tangled sheets.

Screaming.

"I hope I didn't scare you."

Joshua shook his head. Then he rested his head against Darius's shoulder, wrapping his arm around his chest. "You just sounded distressed, is all."

Darius's heart constricted. It wasn't like his horniness had gone away, but there was a heaviness around them now. In a sudden burst of madness, he decided to just lay it out in the open. "I was shot down. In Afghanistan. In a helicopter. My CO dragged me from the wreckage. I was on fire." Darius ground his teeth in bitterness. "Others weren't so lucky. I...I said that I lost people close to me. There was one in particular. Someone very dear to me."

Joshua looked at him with wet eyes. "I shouldn't have asked. I'm sorry."

But Darius shook his head. "No," he murmured. "It's kind of nice to talk about it. Not nice..." He trailed off, feeling shitty. How could he mention Richard's death to his new lover and feel *good* about it?

"Healthy?" Joshua suggested. He trailed his fingertips along Darius's jaw. "I want to be here for you, Darius. I...I'm your husband. I want to take care of you. Like the vows said."

Darius almost bit out that they both knew those vows were fucking bullshit, concocted for his father's amusement.

But they didn't have to be, did they?

Why couldn't he and Joshua pledge to look after one another? Darius had known since the lake that he was prepared to go to all kinds of lengths to protect Joshua. Was it really so crazy to think that Joshua might want to do the same for him?

Because he didn't deserve it, that voice in the back of his head hissed. *Because he was here and Richard wasn't, and that was good enough. He should be grateful for that, not be wanting anything else.*

It wasn't good enough, though, was it? Darius challenged the voice back. Because he was just drifting through half a life in the shadows. Existing, not really living. Until Joshua.

Darius hugged him tightly. "I want to take care of you, too. Thank you."

Joshua petted his hair for a bit, playing with the shorter

locks that Darius was still getting used to. "Thank you for sharing with me. I'm here for the dark, not just the light."

Darius inhaled deeply. Joshua was warm with sleep, but he still had that woodsy, earthy scent about him that was uniquely his. As far as he could see, Joshua was all light. But he agreed. He wanted to be with Joshua for the ugly as well as the pretty.

Speaking of pretty...

It seemed they could only be distracted from their carnal instincts for so long. Joshua was running his hands over Darius's back and kissing his neck. More than that, though, he was rutting his cock against Darius's leg, clearly hard.

Darius's emotions were running high, so it felt comically easy to switch from grief to lust. But they said that was often the case, didn't they? Whoever 'they' were. That adrenaline and life and death could easily get your blood pumping and make you gagging for it. It was a way of reminding yourself that you were still alive.

Darius had spent so long feeling guilty for living. Joshua had been surprisingly fierce the night before when he'd firmly told Darius that he deserved to still be in the world. That Joshua was happy he was. For the first time in a long time, it gave Darius something to cling on to as well.

He *was* happy to be in the here and now, if only because it meant he got to share this moment with Joshua.

So he wouldn't waste it.

He ran his hand up Joshua's side and down his spine, feeling all of his gloriously naked skin. His cock wasn't huge, but it was definitely protruding against his briefs and nudging Darius's leg.

That caveman was back, making Darius's heart pound and his mind blur with a red lust haze. He ran his hand over Joshua's crotch. "So, no one else had touched you like this before?"

Joshua whimpered and thrust his length against Darius's palm, shaking his head into the crook of Darius's neck. "N-no."

"Do you like it?" Darius asked. Joshua gave another little squeak and nodded frantically, digging his fingers into Darius's back. Pride purred in Darius's chest. He wanted to be the one to make Joshua feel this good – the *only* one. "What do you want?" he whispered in Joshua's ear, and nipped at the lobe with his teeth.

Joshua groaned for a second before kissing Darius's lips urgently. "I want to see...can I see...?" He screwed up his face and huffed. "Your *cock,*" he spat out, blushing beautifully again.

The purring in Darius's chest got louder. He might hate a lot of his body, but his cock had never failed him. He took Joshua's hand in his own, caressing the palm with his thumb. Then he lowered it beneath the sheets and placed it on his straining erection in his briefs. "You want to see this?" he growled playfully as Joshua gasped.

"Uh-huh," he uttered, curling his hand around the pulsing length. Darius groaned and quivered. How long had it been since he'd felt another man's touch there?

For a second, guilt and sorrow threatened to flare up. But that was ridiculous. Richard would be happy that Darius had met someone, and Darius damn well knew it. So from that moment on, he vowed only to think of Joshua.

It wasn't difficult. Joshua was gorgeous and *so* getting off right now for the first time ever with another man.

Darius was ridiculously proud to be that man.

He wanted to tell Joshua that he had to remove Darius's underwear. Darius got the feeling he liked being bossed around a little. But Joshua was also brand new to this, and after the serious conversations they'd been having, Darius just wanted to keep things fun and sexy right now. So he slipped his own fingers under his waistband and kicked the briefs off in a matter of seconds, leaving his leaking cock proud and exposed, the bedsheets pushed down past their knees.

Joshua let out another beautiful cry, tentatively sliding his fingers along the shaft, running his thumb over the slit.

Darius hissed, making Joshua's head snap up in concern. "Is that okay?" he asked anxiously.

Darius resisted the urge to laugh. "It's amazing. Keep going. Everything you're doing feels fantastic."

Joshua gave him a giddy little giggle and kissed his lips. "Can I suck it?"

At that, Darius couldn't contain himself. He burst out laughing and kissed Joshua passionately through his grin. "Abso-fucking-lutely," he rasped. "Fill your boots, have a play." He rubbed his thumb over Joshua's lower lip. "Anything you do with this pretty mouth is going to feel fucking brilliant, I promise."

That sparkle was back in Joshua's brown eyes. "Okay," he said breathlessly. He took a second to think, then he began making his way down Darius's body, pushing the duvet all away from them as he did. The fire had long gone out, but the room still held some warmth. Besides, Darius was generating enough of his own heat just watching Joshua approach his throbbing, sticky cock with his sweet mouth.

He seemed to study it, gently running his fingers along the shaft again, driving Darius crazy. Darius sucked in air through his teeth, not wanting to stop Joshua as he leaned in and ghosted hot breath over the sensitive skin.

Then he kissed and licked the tip.

Darius groaned and dropped his head onto the pillow with a thud, unable to keep watching as Joshua slid his lips over the end of the shaft. He was overcome with sensation.

Joshua might have been tentative and clumsy, but Darius wasn't lying. Everything he was doing was completely amazing. Eventually, Darius had to crane his neck and watch again as Joshua bobbed his head, sucking messily. This was too good to miss.

"Yes, beautiful," he murmured, carding his fingers through Joshua's soft hair. "Like that." Joshua looked up through his golden lashes as he slurped around Darius's cock, squeezing the base. He looked delighted at the praise. "You can touch my balls, too. I like that."

He got a thrill from teaching Joshua the basics of giving head. In a way, it was better than a confident, experienced mouth. Joshua was humming and eager, each movement new and exciting for him.

It was pretty exciting for Darius too. He could feel his climax building. Normally he knew it would take more to make him come, but he'd been on edge for weeks now, thinking Joshua was off limits, yet so tortuously close. To have him here, now, sucking enthusiastically on Darius's dick, was enough to have him panting and writhing in minutes.

"Joshua," he grunted, tugging his hair slightly to make him look up again. "I'm close. You don't have to swallow."

Joshua popped off, his lips red and shiny. "Can I, though?"

What a question. Darius just nodded, not trusting himself to speak, so Joshua slipped his pretty mouth right back over the shaft again, sucking and licking.

It didn't take long after that. Darius allowed himself to let go.

He bellowed and arched his back as his orgasm ripped through him. For a few moments, he couldn't see, even after he opened his eyes, struggling to find purchase in reality again. But then Joshua was gasping too, coughing as he wiped the cum that had spilled over his chin. He blinked, like he couldn't quite believe what had just happened. Then he was scrambling up Darius's body and flopping next to him.

"Was that okay?" Joshua asked hoarsely. Darius was surprised to realise that he seemed genuinely concerned.

He caressed the side of Joshua's face. "That was perfect," he assured him, shaking his head. "I told you, anything you want to do with that mouth will be brilliant."

Joshua chuckled shyly. "Thanks," he said, wiping his mouth again.

Darius kissed him, tasting his own musk. "It's okay if you don't get it all," he rasped against Joshua's ear. "I'll find the rest."

Joshua blushed so sweetly Darius guessed he'd never heard dirty talk before. Even though he was spent, that still made Darius's balls tingle.

He was going to be the first man to make Joshua come.

"Can I?" he asked, rubbing Joshua's still semi-hard cock through his underwear.

Joshua didn't ask what. He just fluttered his eyes closed and nodded. "Yes," he whispered.

Darius kissed him some more, nipping at his lower lip and jaw. "I can take these off?" He pinged the band of Joshua's briefs against his hip. Joshua giggled.

"Please."

That was good enough for Darius.

He yanked the briefs down over his ankles, freeing Joshua's cock, finally. It was mouth-watering.

Joshua was obviously close, but Darius didn't want to rush this first time for him. So he kept his movements steady, teasing Joshua back to full hardness with his hand. Joshua whimpered into Darius's mouth as they kissed, their breaths quick and hot, their noses rubbing together.

Darius's chest ached with a sense of completion. Joshua felt so right pressed naked against him like this, trusting Darius with his intimate pleasure. It was like Darius hadn't even known how big the chasm was in his life, but with Joshua here, like this, he now felt whole again.

He'd do anything to protect that feeling. To protect Joshua.

"Good, so good," Joshua gasped. His fingers dug into Darius's arms, and he pressed his forehead against Darius's shoulder. "Darius!"

"It's okay. I've got you." Darius quickened his pace as Joshua thrust against his palm, kissing him sloppily. "You're all right. Let go."

Darius knew this moment wasn't about him, not really. But he'd never talked to anyone in bed like that before. More often than not, it was macho bullshit and dirty talk that was more insulting than sexy. He and Richard had always taken the piss out of each other. Darius would never have imagined how good it felt to coax and urge with such tenderness.

Urgh. He was tempted to be annoyed that he'd promised himself not to think of Richard, and yet here he was making comparisons again. But how could he not? Joshua was unique. Darius was only trying to make sense of this incredible but wholly unconventional attraction. This frighteningly fierce protectiveness that was thrumming through his whole body. He wanted *everything* for Joshua.

Wait. Was this-?

His slightly scary thought was blown out of the water as Joshua suddenly yelled out, his cock spurting thick, white ropes of cum over them both. Joshua screwed up his face and tried to catch his breath, his fingers digging almost painfully into Darius's arms. He wondered if Joshua's fingernails might leave scratches.

Darius found he really liked the idea of being marked by

171

Joshua, which was insane if he stepped back and thought about it. He'd spent the last few years tormented by the scars on his body. Yet here he was, hoping Joshua might blemish him further?

How could a few touches and kisses over Darius's burns make such a difference in less than twelve hours?

Darius would have to think on that some more. It was too much to contemplate now, especially with Joshua gulping down air and quivering in the wake of his orgasm. Darius hummed and kissed along Joshua's cheek and jaw, letting him breathe freely as he recovered. "Was that good?" he murmured against Joshua's throat, kissing his fluttering pulse point.

Joshua slapped his hand over his eyes as he took an extra big breath. "I feel like I waited forever for that, and yet somehow, it was better than I'd ever imagined."

Darius knew it was probably vain the way he puffed up with pride, but he didn't care. He loved hearing that he'd made Joshua happy.

He loved so many things about Joshua.

Which brought him back to his interrupted question.

But even now, as he held a trembling, giddy Joshua in his arms, he couldn't even think the words. Because this couldn't be love, could it? They were too different. The arranged marriage had brought them together, but Darius still found it too difficult to believe that Joshua could be happy with a gnarled old grump like him. He deserved so much better.

But here they were, and Darius couldn't fight what he wanted. He'd denied himself so much for so long. Who knew what the future might bring? All they had was now.

So he held his lover, cherishing him in their afterglow, murmuring sweet nothings about how beautiful he was, hoping his first time had been truly special. Because if nothing else, Darius could take comfort from the fact that he'd shared this with Joshua. He would always have that – they both would.

For now, Darius couldn't ask for anything more.

15

JOSHUA

JOSHUA FELT LIKE HE WAS IN A DREAM.

He lay in Darius's arms, panting. His damp skin was cooling as he slowly came down from his orgasm. He'd *never* come like that before. Even wanking off to his wildest, most debaucherous fantasies hadn't given him such a high.

Was it too much to hope this was the start of something real between him and Darius? Joshua couldn't help but feel like it had been building since the lake incident. It was like something seismic shifted between them that night, leading them along a path that had eventually, maybe inevitably, brought them here.

Had Darius just used him for sex, though? that familiar voice whispered at the back of his mind. The one that had protected him since puberty, fending off sex pests and charming assholes all his life. But now Joshua wasn't sure it was being helpful. Darius had said many times that he really liked Joshua for more than just his beauty. Besides, he was a man of so few words, Joshua couldn't help but take the ones he did utter at face value.

But he was still unsure as to where that left them.

"Um," he said shyly. He wondered if he could pull up the covers, but their bodies were sticky from his mess, so that probably wasn't a good idea. "What happens now?"

Darius brushed Joshua's hair back, a simple gesture that made Joshua's stomach flip-flop. "A shower, I was thinking," Darius said in his low rumble with a chuckle. "Then maybe breakfast?"

Joshua swallowed, nerves fluttering in his belly. "Oh. I meant, uh…"

Darius gently touched Joshua's chin with his finger, encouraging him to look up and meet his gaze. "What, petal?"

Fucking hell. That one word did the most ridiculous things to Joshua. He wanted to blush and laugh and maybe even cry. It was enough to help him be bold and voice his real question. "I mean between us. Is this…I mean, do you…uh…" He took breath and gave Darius a nervous laugh. "Are we dating now? Would you want to have sex again?"

Darius grinned. "'Dating' seems kind of a strange word, *husband*. But it's probably the best one. I'd love that, if you do?"

Joshua exhaled in relief, his smile so big it was probably goofy. "Yes. Yes, please."

Darius ran his hand along Joshua's spine, making him shiver.

Joshua loved how rough those fingers were. He was getting a couple of little bumps himself from working with the gardening tools. It was cool to think that maybe he and Darius had something in common after all.

"How about we change a couple of things?" Darius suggested with his eyebrows raised.

"Like what?" Joshua asked.

Darius toyed with a lock of Joshua's hair. "Do you want to try sleeping in here?" he asked in a rush. "I can't say how I'll be with the nightmares. I haven't shared a bed with anyone since the attack. So I understand if that's too much to handle, or if it's just too fast in general, but-"

Joshua surprised himself by placing a finger against Darius's lips. "I'd love to." He almost made a quip about being way past 'too fast', but he could tell that Darius's nightmares were connected to his scars and the helicopter attack, so he decided that sincerity was the way forward. Besides, his heart *leaped* at the invitation.

But it was nothing compared to the way it melted at the slow smile that crept over Darius's face. When Joshua first met him, he'd never have thought someone who could scowl so fiercely was also capable of such warmth.

"Are you sure?" Darius asked.

Joshua gave a one-armed shrug and played with some of Darius's chest hairs, swirling them with his fingers. "We *are* married," he said, not sure if he was going to say the wrong thing and break the spell. But then he needed to stop worrying about that with every single thing that came out of his mouth.

Besides, Darius had just said he very much enjoyed what Joshua had done with his mouth. Remembering that made him flush with pride and feel bolder.

He smiled up at Darius and stopped hiding his gaze. "I really hoped that we'd learn to be friends. I like this better."

Darius chuckled, the sound a low rumble that Joshua felt through his chest. He pulled Joshua into a sticky hug, kissing his forehead. "I do, too," he assured him. "It...it would make me very happy to have you feel at home here, in these rooms. It's like you and Zeus have breathed life into them for the first time maybe ever."

Joshua gasped. "Zeus!" he cried. "Can I go see if he's awake?"

Darius beamed at him fondly. "Of course. Bring him in here if you like?"

Joshua sat up, ready to go. But then he realised he had mess on his chest, and suddenly felt awkward.

Darius leaned forward, kissing his neck from behind. "Why don't you have a quick clean in the bathroom, and I'll get you a T-shirt?" Joshua could almost have laughed. A T-shirt of Darius's would easily come to Joshua's thighs, he was sure, so it would hide his meat and two veg.

"Thanks." Joshua looked over his shoulder, and was rewarded with a sweet peck on the lips. His heart skipped a beat at the easy, casual intimacy.

He'd always imagined that having a boyfriend would be sexy. But he wasn't prepared for how safe Darius was making him feel, like he was now protected because this was where he *belonged.* What would it feel like to always know if he leaned over, he'd get a kiss? Or if he wanted a cuddle, Darius would be there with his big, secure arms. More than that, if he was sad or scared, or even happy, he'd have someone to tell.

But…what if it didn't work out?

Joshua gave Darius a nervous little smile, then scuttled into the bathroom quickly, trying not to expose himself so much whilst being naked. With the door closed, he stood at the wash basin and looked at himself in the reflection of the mirror.

What if it didn't matter that their chemistry was incredible right now and that they'd had an amazing time in bed? If they were a normal couple, they'd try dating and take years to really get to know each other, seeing how they fit in each other's lives. Then maybe get engaged.

Normal couples didn't get married *first.*

What could the chances be that Joshua had been married off to the guy that he actually *wanted* to spend the rest of his life with? That was such a long shot. What if Darius's ugly temper came back? What if he withdrew and got sullen and

177

wouldn't come out of it? What if he got fed up with Joshua and stopped seeing his youth and naivety as charming, but instead started to be annoyed by it?

They couldn't just break up. They'd have to get divorced, if Victor would even let them.

And then there were Victor's rules.

Just because Joshua was a happy prisoner now didn't make him any less trapped. He hadn't even been able to contact his father since he'd been here. Victor's assurances in his letter that he was fine only went so far. Joshua couldn't leave the castle and go into town on his own. Sure, they'd snuck out to the opera last night, but what would Victor say when he found out? Would there be repercussions?

Joshua turned on the squeaky hot tap, flicking his hand under the stream, waiting for the sweet spot where it would heat up enough to splash water on himself, but not get too scalding. He sighed. Had he made a big mistake in kissing Darius? Would it have been better if they had just continued ticking along as friends? He rubbed water over his chest as he chewed over his thoughts.

He heard a soft rapping of knuckles through the door. "Everything okay in there?"

Joshua startled and turned off the tap, grabbing a towel to wipe his chest. Then he slung it around his hips to protect his modesty before opening the door. "Of course," he said.

But Darius frowned at him. He'd changed into jogging bottoms and a T-shirt, and had something in his hand that looked like a T-shirt for Joshua. "What?" Darius asked.

Joshua's skin prickled. Shit, he hadn't been talking out loud to himself, had he? He was sure he hadn't, but over his lonely years, he'd developed a bit of a habit. "Nothing," he said as sincerely as he could.

Darius narrowed his eyes and tilted his head. Then he reached out his free hand, offering it to Joshua.

Considering the thoughts he'd just been having, Joshua should have hesitated. But his traitorous heart ached, and he took the hand immediately. Darius pulled him closer and studied him.

"I may be shit at talking, but your face doesn't say 'nothing'. If you regret what we did last night and just now, we can reset. Pretend it never happened."

"But it *did*," said Joshua, biting his lip and willing himself not to cry. For fuck's sake, he'd just had sex for the first time, why was he ruining it?

Because it wasn't just sex. It was Darius, and apparently, he did actually care about Darius – about *them* – a lot. It couldn't be undone. Joshua didn't *want* to undo it.

"I don't regret it," he mumbled with a sniff. "But I'm worried. What if it all goes wrong? We're *married* and we can't get out of it. What if you start to hate me and I'm not allowed to leave?"

He didn't realise any tears had spilled until Darius brushed his thumb over his cheeks. "Shh," he said gently, then guided Joshua back to the bed where he tugged him down onto the mattress. Darius enveloped him so they were cuddling chest to chest, with Joshua wrapped up in Darius's big, thick limbs.

"You think I'm *not* worried you're going to get fed up with me?" he asked, rubbing Joshua's back. "We could drive ourselves crazy worrying about the future. I know we're bound in the marriage, but let's just take it one step at a time, hmm?"

Joshua sniffed and rubbed his face, unable to meet Darius's eyes. "Yeah?" he asked.

Darius kissed his temple. Joshua couldn't help it, he leaned into the touch. "Yes, petal."

Joshua laughed wetly and scrubbed his eyes. "Sorry. I didn't mean to spoil it."

"You haven't spoiled anything," Darius said gruffly. "In fact, I think you might do me good. Get me talking more about stuff in my head." He cleared his throat and caressed the back of Joshua's head. "I don't know what might happen between us. But I know I like you, Joshua. I want this. You make me happy."

Finally, Joshua moved and looked Darius in the eyes. "You make me happy, too." He was startled by how much he meant that.

Darius sighed, a big, content sound. "Why don't you go find Zeus, and I'll call down and get us breakfast in bed."

It was stupid, but Joshua's heart skipped a beat at such a simple suggestion. "Really?"

Darius nodded then kissed his lips. Joshua inwardly tutted at himself. What the hell had he been so afraid of? Why was he fretting over the future when right now was *amazing?*

Darius grinned mischievously. "Shall I tell Camille you'll have cornflakes?" he asked, waggling his eyebrows.

Joshua slapped him playfully. After all the fuss he'd made over wanting simple breakfasts, he did feel a bit stupid asking for a full English now. But...

"Tell her I worked up an appetite," Joshua said, blushing at his own boldness.

"Oh, really," Darius growled, nipping at Joshua's neck and running his palm over Joshua's ribs. Joshua gasped. He couldn't be feeling horny already... could he?

He figured he was about to find out, as he and Darius were kissing messily again, and Darius's hand was tugging at Joshua's precariously tied towel.

Breakfast could wait. Joshua had some more exploring to do.

16

JOSHUA

THE NEXT FEW DAYS WENT BY SURPRISINGLY UNEVENTFULLY. Even though Joshua's whole world had changed, in a lot of ways, it hadn't altered anything at all.

He was still Joshua Bellamy. He'd just had a new experience now. A wonderful one that was lifting his spirits and keeping him buoyant, but other than that, his life wasn't all that different.

The days were getting longer and warmer as spring approached, and Joshua could see some real difference in the gardens he'd been labouring over already. Most of the flowers wouldn't bloom until April, but the soil was looking fresh and healthy after all the digging Joshua had been doing. He'd also planted a hell of a lot of shrubs, giving the garden plots between the winding paths shape again and bringing greenness to the grounds. When he breathed deeply, Joshua could smell the leaves in the air, making him smile.

For the first time ever, he was truly making a mark on the world. The work he was doing at Thorncliff was proof that he'd been there and not just drifting through like he had the rest of his life. Not only that, he felt like he was finally discovering who he really *was*. All his years at school hadn't shown him any kind of calling. But one moment of inspiration from seeing a withered rosebush had changed all of that.

Those bushes were Joshua's pride and joy, even if they hadn't bloomed yet. He called them the 'family roses' in his mind, thinking of his and Darius's mums as he tended to them. He still had his precious scrapbook hidden away in his room, but he'd made an effort to dig out some old photos he had saved on his phone. It was kind of heart-breaking that he had to remind himself what his own mum looked like, but that was only human, he was sure. She'd been gone a long time. But even if her face was fading from his memory slightly, Joshua's love for her was as bright as ever. He talked to her quietly as he worked in his gardens, telling her all his news. It was their special time.

"And this is Zeus," he told her that afternoon, scrambling to pick the puppy up before he got absolutely filthy (again). "He likes digging holes and eating worms, don't you, naughty boy?" Zeus yapped and licked Joshua's nose, his little bum wagging furiously as his tail threatened to fall off it was moving so fast. Joshua smiled at him, his heart bursting with love. "He's part of the family now, isn't he, Maree?"

Joshua also imagined over the last couple of days that by restoring the roses, he was getting to meet Darius's mum, Maree. Darius had a photo of her in his living room that Joshua had seen, but they hadn't talked about her yet. He imagined her death was just as painful for Darius as talking about his helicopter attack, and he'd done so well opening up about that. Joshua trusted that he'd talk about his mum when he felt ready.

Joshua realised that Maree's photo had been the one that had got smashed the night of the lake incident. He was very glad to see the glass had been replaced and the photo was all right. He memorised her smiling face, and practiced introducing himself to her as he clipped at branches in the bright and breezy afternoon. He hoped that she'd approve of him for her son.

Joshua received another letter from Victor. As scared as he was to open it, when he finally did, it simply informed him that his father's business was recovering and that he was also well. Joshua would rather have spoken to his dad in person, but phone reception was still abysmal at the castle.

Unbelievably, there was still no general internet or Wi-Fi either. Apparently, that guy Martin said they were having extreme difficulty in laying the cables because Thorncliff was a listed building and therefore they couldn't alter certain things. Joshua couldn't help but think Martin blamed Joshua for this impossible task he'd been given, as Joshua had caught him looking daggers at him again on his last visit. But this was Joshua's home now, and he refused to feel guilty for his pretty basic request to have access to the outside world.

Darius had gladly allowed Joshua time on his computer, the only machine that was online, promising to tell Joshua the second his dad emailed back. But so far, there had been nothing. Joshua just had to trust Victor was telling the truth when he said his dad was doing well. It worried Joshua that his dad hadn't even sent a letter, but there was every chance that he was over his head with salvaging the business. He never did know when to ask for help. *Stubborn mule*, thought Joshua fondly.

In his letter, Victor even said that he hoped Joshua was settled into castle life now. Joshua didn't entirely trust that wasn't a veiled threat from Victor that he *should* be settled because he wasn't escaping any time soon. But seeing as he genuinely was settled now, he didn't worry about it. He didn't even mention the letter to Darius, as he knew he would only worry at any mention of his father.

And then there was Darius himself.

Oh, Darius.

Joshua hadn't been sure what it would mean to start sleeping in Darius's bedroom instead of his own, but he soon found out. It was Heaven on Earth. And not just for reasons that Joshua might have expected.

It started with his phone charger. He always plugged it in overnight, so it made sense that first night when he'd planned to go to bed there that he'd brought it with him.

The second night it had been his toothbrush and some comfy clothes for the morning.

By the fifth night, Darius had just given up and allocated Joshua a drawer to put his underwear in, and hung Joshua's dressing gown on the back of his door on top of his own one. Every morning, Joshua would wake up and see a little more of himself in his husband's quarters, and he'd never felt more at home anywhere.

Then there were the nights.

To begin with, Darius kept telling Joshua that he was okay to go slow and that he shouldn't feel pressured into anything. So for the first night, Joshua had held himself back, incredibly worried about pushing Darius and his issues with his scars but also not wanting to come across as some kind of gigantic needy slut.

He must have been vibrating or something, though, because after an hour of them trying to get to sleep, Darius had asked if he was okay, and slipped his arm around Joshua.

Joshua had spun around and kissed him like it was a matter of life or death, much to Darius's apparent delight, and shared hand jobs had followed shortly afterwards.

From then on, Darius had changed his tune, encouraging Joshua to ask for whatever he wanted. He probably hadn't expected Joshua to be absolutely gagging for it non-stop, but every time Joshua had hinted he was interested in getting off,

Darius had jumped at it. They'd shared blow jobs and hand jobs and lay with Darius on top, both jerking off into Darius's large, skilled hand, their cocks rubbing blissfully together.

Every time they got off, Joshua had braced himself for Darius to ask about anal. Even though it scared Joshua a little, he told himself he was ready. All the porn he'd watched had looked incredible, and he was more than overdue the chance to experience it for himself. But so far, Darius hadn't even hinted at it. Not that Joshua was disappointed in anything they'd done together. But it was like he was waiting to graduate.

Then, on their sixth night, when they'd got into a comfortable routine of having dinner together and watching TV on Darius's laptop before going to bed, they hadn't been kissing more than a few minutes under the covers in the dark when Darius's hand started to wander.

He caressed Joshua's backside through his briefs, then slipped his fingers under the waistband, touching the dip just above where Joshua's arse crack started.

Joshua popped off Darius's lips with a gasp. "Do you want to fuck me?" he asked anxiously. He'd been washing himself thoroughly down there the last couple of evenings, just in case. Darius must have wondered what the hell he'd been up to in the bathroom, but Joshua wanted everything to be as perfect as it could be for Darius.

But Darius blinked in the faint moonlight shining around the curtains and stared at him for a second. "We *have* been fucking, beautiful," he said with a smile, caressing the side of Joshua's neck.

"You know what I mean," Joshua mumbled as embarrassment crept up on him. "Sorry, was that too eager?"

Darius huffed and kissed Joshua firmly on his lips. "*Stop* saying sorry for anything you want. Especially with sex. I

HELEN JULIET

fucking love how eager you are, okay? But that's a big deal, and...well, not to be blunt, but I'm big, too."

They both glanced down to where Darius was pretty hard in his underwear. Joshua didn't think he was *that* huge, but he was aware his only comparison was porn star cocks. Besides, the most he'd ever stuck up his own arse was his finger. As good as that felt, he was fully aware that Darius's cock was about four times the size of that.

"I thought we could have a little play, though," Darius continued before Joshua could get further wrapped up in his own thoughts. He had to remind himself several times a day still of just how *scorching* Darius had sounded when he'd told Joshua how much he loved that he was a virgin.

I'm giving Darius a gift, Joshua told himself silently, his little mantra to reverse all those years of being ashamed of his virginity. There was a lot to undo there, but the chant helped.

"Play?" Joshua repeated faintly. Darius was kissing his throat and rubbing their cocks together through their underwear.

"Uh-huh," Darius growled, nipping at Joshua's collarbone where he already had a love bite. Joshua had spent about half an hour staring at it in the mirror that morning, amazed at how turned on it made him. That mark made him *Darius's.* He loved it.

"Anything," Joshua breathed. He meant it. There hadn't been a single moment during sex so far where he'd panicked or felt out of his depth.

Darius hummed and leaned back. They were side by side. As much as Joshua loved it when Darius was on top of him, pinning him down, it did leave him a little breathless. Like this, it was less intimidating.

"Is anal something you want?" Darius asked bluntly.

Joshua was a bit taken aback. He'd assumed that was what *every* gay man wanted, wasn't it?

"Of course," he said, confused.

But Darius shook his head. "You don't have to. It's not a rule or anything. We can keep frotting and sucking each other off."

Fucking hell, there went those alarm bells in Joshua's head. Did wanting to get fucked make him a slut? He bit his lip, not sure what to say.

But then Darius did his trick of gently touching Joshua's chin and lifting it, encouraging them to meet each other's gazes. For someone who struggled with talking, Darius certainly knew how to get Joshua chatting when all he felt like doing was clamming up.

"I want it so badly," Joshua blurted out, his eyes stinging. He begged himself not to cry. "I've been fantasising about it. But if you're not interested-"

"Oh, I'm interested," Darius said quickly, his cobalt-blue eyes wide as he nodded. "You know what I'm like. I just have to check that you don't feel you have to."

Joshua puffed out his cheeks. "I can't stop thinking about sex," he bemoaned, voicing his worries for the first time out loud. "I'm obsessed! I'm worried you're going to think I'm a freak!"

A smile played on Darius's mouth. "Beautiful, you're *twenty-one*. I was an army cadet fucking my way through half of Aldershot at your age. I even tried sex with a few women I was so horny. You're not a freak." He leaned in and bit Joshua's earlobe almost too hard, making him gasp and sending a jolt of electricity right to his cock. "But you *are* a little slut for me, and I love it more than I can say. So I'm not going to say anything. I'm going to show you. I'm going to eat you out and finger your pretty virgin hole. Then I'm going to fuck between your legs and wank you off. Does that sound nice?"

Joshua had to breathe in and out a couple of times before he could trust himself to speak. There was a very real chance he was going to come right there and then in his briefs without either of them touching his dick.

"Y-yes," Joshua stammered, trying to take deep enough breaths to stop him from getting light-headed.

Darius growled and kissed Joshua's mouth. "Lie on your front."

Joshua did as he was told, his heart hammering as Darius straddled his legs and kissed his way down Joshua's spine. Then he shifted further down, removing Joshua's underwear. He took both of Joshua's cheeks in his hands and massaged them, nuzzling his soft beard against the skin as he kissed the round flesh.

Then he pulled the cheeks apart and blew softly against Joshua's exposed entrance.

Joshua jerked a little and gasped, clinging onto the pillow where his head was resting. His vision swam so much he worried for a second he might pass out.

But then Darius's lips and tongue touched Joshua's hole, and he was perfectly awake again, struggling not to scream, swear, or cry. Then he realised he didn't have to.

He was free to do all three.

"Jesus *fucking* Christ!" he wailed, digging his toes into the mattress. "Yes, Darius, like that. Like *that.*"

Darius was kissing him, still pulling Joshua's arse apart, his face buried between the cheeks as he licked and sucked and probed. Joshua hadn't spent much time stroking himself around that tight ring of muscle, more interested in the sensation of being fingered. He was glad now, though, because the shock meant he was enjoying this experience *so* much more.

Darius was evidently enjoying himself, too, taking his time as he loosened Joshua's hole bit by bit. Then suddenly he slipped his hands under Joshua's thighs and pulled his backside into the air so he was on his knees, but his face still smushed into the pillow.

The sound of Darius spitting made Joshua flinch, but then he felt a wet finger circling his entrance before pushing inside. The intrusion was still a bit of a shock, and Joshua coughed and spluttered. But then Darius was kissing the base of Joshua's spine as he pulsed the finger in and out. "You're doing *so* well, beautiful. Just relax. That's it."

Joshua closed his eyes and tried to do what Darius asked. He wanted this so badly, but Darius's cock was way bigger than his finger, and even just that was bigger than one of Joshua's-

His thoughts stalled as Darius spat again. All of a sudden there were two fingers, and the only thing Joshua could feel was the burn. He whimpered and wondered if this was what he wanted after all? "Shh, it's okay. It'll ease," Darius murmured, kissing behind Joshua's ear and nuzzling his hair with his nose. "Unless you want me to stop?"

Joshua shook his head. If Darius said it would get better, he trusted him. It had to, right? Otherwise, why would so many people have sex this way? So he lay there and did his best to embrace the sensation, and he did have to admit it did get better. But then Darius removed his fingers and began using his tongue again, and Joshua moaned in deep pleasure.

"Fuck, *yes,*" he howled into the pillow. "I love it, Darius. Feels so good." He rutted against the air, desperate for any friction. His cock was hard and leaking, but he couldn't find relief. Not yet, anyway.

Darius gave his hole one last kiss and pulled back, letting his cheeks go, then rubbing up and down Joshua's thighs. "You need to keep your knees together for me, okay, petal?"

Joshua nodded, his legs trembling. He was glad he wasn't up on his hands as well. Otherwise, he wasn't sure he would have been able to hold his weight. Darius nudged his legs so they were flush, dropped his own underwear to the floor. Then he spat again.

The next thing Joshua felt was Darius's hard, weeping dick rubbing against his hole before it moved down and pushed between his thighs, brushing against Joshua's heavy, tingling balls.

"Oh, *fuck,*" Joshua cried out at the unexpected sensation. He liked it, but he was becoming desperate for real release.

Luckily, Darius was there to take care of him, like always. He gripped Joshua's hip with one hand, then reached around with the other, curling it over Joshua's cock and stroking him firmly.

"*Shit! Fuck! Yes!*" Joshua bellowed, thrusting against Darius's palm. Oh, he'd needed that touch desperately, but combined with feeling Darius's large dick rubbing against his surprisingly sensitive thighs and sack, he was all over the place. "Close," he uttered, screwing up his face and turning it into the pillow.

"Me too," Darius grunted, digging his fingers into Joshua's hip as he thrust faster. "Don't hold it. Come when you want."

Darius's hand was almost too rough as he jerked Joshua off, but it was exactly what he wanted. It was sensation from all around, the *slap slap slap* of their skin filling the darkened bedroom over the sounds of their pants and grunts. Joshua couldn't hold it any longer.

"*Darius!*" he managed to yell before he was coming all over the bedsheets and Darius's hand. He sucked in air, quivering in the aftermaths of his orgasm. But he still had his thighs clamped together because Darius wasn't done yet, and there was no way Joshua was letting him down.

Thankfully, though, within a few more thrusts, Darius

gripped both of Joshua's hips and slammed his hips against Joshua's arse, coming explosively between his legs. After a few seconds of trembling and panting, they both collapsed side by side on top of the mattress. Joshua sluggishly turned so they were facing, and placed a tired kiss on Darius's lips.

"That was very nice," he said breathlessly, using Darius's ridiculously understated word from earlier.

Sure enough, Darius laughed and hugged Joshua to him. They were lying in the wet patch, but luckily, Darius's bed was massive so they could sleep on the other side. It just meant more closer spooning, but Joshua didn't mind that.

Everything was perfect. How could he have been so worried? Fate might have brought them together, but he'd obviously been wrong with his panic on the first morning after sex. Things just kept getting better and better, and he didn't see how anything could really fuck up. Not if they cared for each other this much.

His heart ached in places he hadn't known existed – the good kind of ache. He was compelled by this feeling that he was tethered to Darius by an invisible cord that was always straining to pull them back together again.

He felt it so strongly Joshua had to wonder if this was what falling in love felt like. Was he getting way ahead of himself? Probably. All he knew as he fell asleep in Darius's arms that night was that he was more at peace than he'd ever been in his entire life. The feeling returning that he was exactly where he was supposed to be.

It was so strong, he couldn't imagine there was anything that could possibly break it.

17

DARIUS

"Zeus," Darius growled, lengthening the word in a stern warning. Or at least, that was his intention. Zeus just wagged his tail furiously and shook the leather shoe clamped between his jaws. "Zeus, no!" Darius snapped, holding up a finger and scowling. "You have about a hundred actual toys. Put Daddy's shoe down, now!"

Zeus gave a squeaky bark before launching himself forward, dashing between Darius's legs and scrambling on his small but surprisingly fast legs out of the door and down the hallway, the shoe most definitely still between his teeth.

"Zeus!" Darius wailed in frustration, spinning around and taking chase. As much as he didn't want his loafer destroyed, part of him did delight in their game. He'd forgotten that half the fun of having a dog was the chaos they caused. Which was why he found himself laughing as he ran after the naughty pup down the stairs and out into the grounds.

Joshua had probably left the door open when he'd been coming and going whilst working. Darius didn't mind, seeing as it was a cool but gloriously sunny day. However, that did mean that Zeus made a beeline for the nearest patch of soil and leaped on it, then dug with his front paws like he was going all the way down to Australia.

Darius laughed and jogged over, leaning down to tug at the shoe. Zeus growled, but Darius frowned, adopting the pack leader voice his mother had taught him with Athena.

"Leave," he said firmly, tugging the shoe again, showing Zeus who was boss. Zeus narrowed his eyes and growled around the leather. But Darius raised his eyebrows, not letting himself be fooled by those puppy dog eyes. "I said *leave*, Zeus."

With a grumble, Zeus opened his mouth to let Darius have his prize. Then he began pawing sulkily at the dirt, like he hadn't even *wanted* the stupid shoe anyway. Darius chuckled and inspected the loafer for teeth marks. Once he'd wiped away the slobber with the sleeve of his rugby shirt, the damage didn't seem too bad.

Darius shielded his eyes with his free hand, blotting out the sun as he scanned the grounds for Joshua's small form. Sure enough, he was working quite far out today, stabbing at the ground with some kind of pronged tool. Darius sighed as he smiled.

If he was brutally honest, it was frightening how much his heart fluttered at just the sight of his new lover. Darius had never felt this kind of all-consuming attraction. It wasn't just physical, although having Joshua in his bed had proved so much better than he'd ever imagined. Darius had struggled not to laugh when Joshua had worried that him wanting sex all the time was a *bad* thing. Didn't he realise how insatiable Darius was for him? How incredible everything they were doing together was?

And they still had so many things to try.

Darius had taken to his teaching role in the bedroom as eagerly as Joshua had to sex itself. It gave Darius a sense of achievement and completion that he hadn't known he'd yearned for. Every single thing Joshua tried for the first time was Darius's responsibility to make sure he enjoyed it or that he wasn't hurt. The thrill of that duty tapped into something Darius hadn't even realised was inside him but gave him such pleasure.

His favourite part of being a captain in the army had been the soldiers he'd mentored and looked after. How he was feeling with Joshua was kind of like that, but the care he'd given a hundred people was now all poured intimately into just one.

It was a lot to process, but Darius loved it.

It had crossed his mind once or twice that it could wear off as Joshua became more experienced, but Darius sincerely hoped not. Besides, that was the future and exactly the kind of thing Darius had told Joshua not to worry about himself. All that mattered was the here and now, and at present, everything was wonderful.

Darius didn't just mean the sex, either. It was startling how much joy he was getting from snuggling up and watching a TV show with Joshua every evening. The simple act of eating dinner together and talking about the little things that had happened during their days. It was mostly trivial chat about worms and seeds and the boring people Darius had to deal with. But it felt important because every shared story was a moment they got to know each other better.

Darius knew he should get back to work, but instead, he found himself strolling down the winding paths towards where Joshua was on his hands and knees, hard at work. It was proof that Darius was becoming a victim of his own stupid heart because his first thought wasn't how fuckable Joshua looked in that position. It was concern for his back and wondering if Joshua had made time for a lunch break.

Fuck. Darius really was smitten. So far, that wasn't

presenting a problem, but he would be a fool to think he could feel so strongly about something – about his *husband* – and not have to fear the consequences. He had to tread carefully, for both their sakes.

But it was difficult to remember his father's potential threats when everything seemed so easy when it was just him and Joshua.

As Darius approached, he was surprised when the wind picked up and he caught the distinctive sound of Joshua's voice. Who could he be talking to? The phone reception was utterly bollocks out here, something Darius was looking into now he had more than himself to think about. But short of putting a pylon in the ground closer to the property, he wasn't sure what he could do.

Joshua was definitely talking to someone, however. Darius swung his head back and forth as he got closer, but there wasn't anyone else around.

"-he said about moving some clothes into his wardrobe." Joshua's words carried over the wind. Darius stopped several feet away. Was Joshua talking about him? Because Darius had suggested that earlier today. "I was worrying it was too fast to do something like that, but the whole idea of 'too fast' is kind of strange for us. We're already married." He chuckled as he thrust the gardening fork in his hand into the earth, churning it up. "I know, I know. You and Dad moved in after three weeks, and Grandma almost had a heart attack. I guess we both jumped in with both feet, huh?"

A lump rose in Darius's throat. *Holy shit.* Joshua was talking with his mum. Talking about Darius with such warmth and affection. Darius's throat clamped with emotion.

But then Joshua kept talking, really knocking the stuffing completely out of Darius.

"I know he's a big softie at heart, Maree. How did I ever

think he was scary?" Joshua laughed. "Yeah, yeah. I know, I'm useless."

Darius covered his mouth as his eyes stung. Joshua was talking to *his* mother, too? Darius had been suffering from the occasional bout of melancholy, lamenting that his mother would never get to meet him. Yet here he was, chatting away with her as if they were all having tea together.

It was too much. Joshua was beyond precious, and Darius was so overcome with affection and protectiveness, making him want to fight the whole world to keep him safe. Adrenaline flooded his system, and he was still emotional, making him feel fractious and trembly.

Darius definitely shouldn't have been eavesdropping on such a private moment. It didn't matter that his heart warmed at hearing Joshua saying he was already committing to their relationship so quickly. Darius wasn't supposed to hear that. So he hastily turned on his heels and went to march straight back to the castle.

Except that was the exact moment Zeus decided to come sprinting past, his muzzle covered in dirt as he hurtled towards Joshua, barking his head off in excitement that he'd found where he'd been hiding.

Joshua jumped first at the sudden noise, then again as he caught sight of Darius. Darius waved, striding confidently towards him, hoping to make it look like he hadn't been standing there long. He definitely wasn't going to mention that he'd heard anything Joshua had said or even that he was aware that he'd been talking to both their late mothers.

"Hi!" Darius cried out cheerfully, blinking any tears away from his eyes and clearing his throat. After a brief second of looking startled, Joshua waved back as well. Good. Hopefully, he wouldn't think Darius had heard anything after all.

"Hello," Joshua replied from where he was sitting, smiling

sweetly and squinting up against the sunshine. "It's nice to see you out here."

Darius showed him his slightly mauled shoe. "I had to rescue this from a certain naughty puppy," he explained.

Joshua gasped and looked down at the mucky pup. "No, surely not!" he teased.

Whilst he was facing the dog, Darius crouched down. Then when Joshua turned back around, Darius smiled and leaned in for a kiss. It was stupid, but the novelty still hadn't worn off that Joshua leaned in too without hesitation, their lips meeting for a chaste kiss. "Hello, petal," Darius murmured.

Joshua beamed, his wind-swept cheeks healthy with a rosy glow. "This is a nice surprise," he said shyly, glancing around the patch of garden he was currently engrossed with. "Did you have a break from work?"

Darius pretended to scowl at Zeus, who was sat looking quite innocent, aside from all the black dirt around his white mouth. "More like I was *forced* to take a break. But then I wanted to make the most of it. How's it going today?"

Not caring if his jeans got muddy, Darius sat and let Joshua explain how he was hoping to make a border of pansies around a centre of higher-growing lupines. "Then," Joshua said, flushed and grinning as he pointed to another area, "I think this would be the perfect spot for a pond. But I need to research that some more and think about whether I'd want fish. Because then I'd risk herons coming and eating them, which I'd *hate*, but heron proofing is ugly. *But* I like the idea of fish. So maybe if I make a big enough pond I could get massive fish, like koi carp, so the herons couldn't pick them up, and – what?"

He stopped and frowned at Darius, his hand shielding his eyes from the sun again.

"What?" Darius repeated with a chuckle. "I was enjoying listening to your ideas!"

Joshua narrowed his eyes at him, but his smile was playful. "You were laughing at me. I know I was rambling," he grumbled. "I'm just so excited."

"I know," Darius assured him gently, rubbing his arm through his gardening jumper. "That's why I was smiling. I love seeing you so happy."

Joshua smiled bashfully. "Yeah."

Darius shrugged, not even really thinking properly as the words formed in his mouth. "Yeah. I love y-"

You. *I love you.* He'd so nearly said it easily because in that moment, it was painfully obvious how true it was. But an urgent cry broke through the peaceful afternoon, making them both snap their heads towards the castle. Darius wasn't sure if he was relieved or devastated. He hadn't meant to say anything. But as he turned to see his housekeeper approaching, he was pretty sure disappointment curled around his heart.

It was okay. There would be another chance.

"Joshua!" Mrs Weatherby yelled. She was running down the path, one hand pressing down on her ample bosom, the other in the air, waving a letter. "This just came for you by urgent courier!"

Darius glanced at Joshua just as he looked back at him. Joshua looked as confused as Darius felt. But Darius had spent his entire life on alert, always waiting for the other shoe to drop. In some ways, he wasn't surprised at all that bad tidings were almost certainly on their way.

And he bet anything that somehow, his father was behind it.

"For me?" Joshua asked, standing and pulling off his gardening gloves. Darius mirrored him, getting to his feet as Mrs Weatherby arrived in front of them, huffing and puffing.

Joshua's eyes suddenly widened. "From who? Is it my dad?" He looked at Darius. "I've been so anxious about not hearing back from him."

"I know," Darius said, rubbing his arm. Privately, he'd been very suspicious that Victor was stopping Christopher from writing back to Joshua. Hopefully, this letter would be from him and would set Joshua's mind at ease.

"I've got no idea who it's from, darling," Mrs Weatherby said, thrusting the letter out for him to take. Then she bent over and leaned on her knees as she breathed heavily. "But the man said it was urgent."

Joshua bit his lip and slid his finger along the seal of the envelope, tearing it open and yanking out the single sheaf of paper. Within a second, his face drained of all its previous rosiness.

"What?" Darius demanded, immediately by his side with his hand on his back. All his hackles rose, as he anticipated some new low from his father. But when Joshua lifted his eyes, his lip wobbling, it wasn't Victor's name he spoke.

"This says my dad was in a terrible accident. *That's* why he hasn't contacted me." Tears pooled in Joshua's eyes as the letter trembled in his hands. "Something with a machine at one of the warehouses. Oh god, it sounds *bad.*" His eyes frantically scanned the letter as Darius's heart dropped. "This is from one of his doctors. Apparently, they've been trying to contact me. Shit!" Tears spilled down his face as Mrs Weatherby gasped and reached over to squeeze his shoulder.

"I'm so sorry," she said, shaking her head.

"You need to go to him," Darius said, feeling sick. He knew *exactly* how one catastrophic moment could change your life forever. He would never wish that on anyone, but of course, it happened every day.

"But I can't leave the castle grounds," Joshua whispered, looking up at Darius with big, wet eyes.

Joshua had been separated from his father when he needed his son the most, all because Victor liked to play games. Joshua should *never* have been cut off from his only family like that. Well, not anymore. Damn the consequences. Darius would deal with any fallout.

Darius shook his head. "This is an emergency. Mrs Weatherby, could you have Asher bring the car to the front as soon as possible?" She stood upright and took a deep breath, nodding. "Joshua, let's get you inside and cleaned up right now. There isn't a moment to waste."

Joshua didn't move, though. "I can't leave the castle," he whispered fearfully. "I *can't*. Your dad…"

He trailed off, both of them knowing what he meant.

Damn Victor to hell, Darius thought viciously. He clenched his jaw and squeezed the shoe still in his hand. It seemed so ridiculous now in such a serious situation. He had to think this through and be smart.

His knee-jerk reaction was to go with Joshua to protect him from anything. But a medical emergency went beyond Victor's inane rules. He *had* to be made to see sense.

He took Joshua by the shoulder with his free hand. "You go. Asher will take you wherever it is you need to see your father. In the meantime, I'll reach out to Victor and explain what's happened. He *has* to make an exception for this. I'll make him understand."

The truth was Darius was long overdue a confrontation with his father. If Victor wanted to drop everything and come to Thorncliff to yell at Darius, so be it. But Joshua shouldn't be a prisoner here, and maybe this was what was needed to fight for some leniency in Victor's outrageous demands.

Joshua bit his lip and nodded. "Okay," he whispered, his beautiful brown eyes pooling with tears. "The letter says I need to go home first, to get Dad some of his things. Oh, god. Darius. My *dad…*"

He broke down into sobs, and Darius hugged him tightly. Over his head, he nodded at Mrs Weatherby. She nodded back and took off towards the castle to arrange the car. Joshua needed a moment, and Darius wanted to give it to him.

By their feet, Zeus whimpered and pawed at their legs, distressed by Joshua's crying. "It's okay. Good boy," Joshua mumbled wetly.

Darius cradled his face and kissed his damp cheeks, tasting the salt from his tears. "It *will* be okay. Does the letter tell you your dad's prognosis?"

Joshua sniffed and nodded. "Serious, but stable," he said with a hiccup. "I just feel so guilty that he's been hurt in a hospital room and I've been here, having fun!"

He broke into a fresh wave of sobs, and Darius hugged him tightly again, rubbing his back. "You didn't *know.* And that's my father's fault, not yours, a fact I'll be reminding him of if he has a problem with you leaving the castle grounds. All that matters is that he's stable and you can go to him now. Come on, darling."

He urged Joshua to walk with him back to the side door. Zeus hopped anxiously by their feet. "What if I need to stay overnight?" Joshua asked.

"We'll pack you a bag," Darius said firmly. "And I'll be here in case my father wants to discuss the situation further." *When*, he added mentally. Victor would undoubtedly be furious when Darius emailed him to inform him what had transpired, but so be it. Darius was Joshua's husband, and he was here to fight this battle on his behalf. For once, his dad would just have to lump it.

That voice in the back of Darius's mind piped up, reminding him that Victor loathed being contradicted. Logic wouldn't play into it. But Darius hoped that if he remained at Thorncliff and invited Victor to come and use Darius as his punching bag, he wouldn't punish Joshua.

He had to hope because Darius wasn't going to deny Joshua access to his father in an emergency, simply because Victor had made up a preposterous and arbitrary rule.

They were getting close to the side door. By their feet, Zeus whimpered as he struggled to keep up with their pace. Darius didn't want to waste any more time, though. He hoped with everything he had that Joshua's father was going to be okay. He'd already been through so much with the loss of his mother, a pain Darius knew all too well.

"If you really, *really* need me, though, just email," Darius insisted. Victor could go fuck himself. "I'll be right there. But I want to be here to smooth things over."

"Thank you." Joshua nodded. They crossed the threshold back into the castle. Darius felt a pang as he watched Joshua pull his muddy boots off and yank his knitted bootie slippers back on.

Oh, who the hell was Darius kidding? *Of course* he loved his precious, adorable but *fierce* husband. There was no one else like him, and he'd completely stolen Darius's heart.

Especially when he looked back up and held both of Darius's hands between their chests. "But I'm coming back," Joshua promised, his brown eyes shining earnestly. "This is my home now. I'll see what the hell is going on with my dad and make sure he's all right, but I'll come home."

The lump threatened to rise in Darius's throat again. Christopher's health was the priority, no question. But Darius couldn't help but take a moment to be selfish and wrap himself up in the warmth those words gave him.

Joshua felt this was home? That was funny because Darius hadn't ever really felt that about Thorncliff until Joshua had come along and filled it with his light.

Darius nodded. "If you need to bring your father here, then that's what we'll do. I don't care what my father has to say about it. Whatever is necessary." He cupped the side of Joshua's face. "Now, come on. We need to hurry."

Darius was careful to be nothing but confident and supportive in his words and actions. But deep down, fear was bubbling.

Joshua had just promised that he would come back. But Darius had loved precisely two people in this world, and they had both been forced to leave him forever. Logic couldn't compete with the dread of circumstances outside of Darius's control.

What if he was about to lose Joshua too?

Darius couldn't know for sure what would happen when Joshua returned to his hometown. He'd tried to flee once and almost died. Despite just saying that his home was here, with Darius, would he really want to return once he'd regained his freedom?

Then so be it. Because that was true love, Darius knew. He would rather Joshua be free and happy than a prisoner.

Even if that meant Darius lost him.

It might not come to that. Joshua might stay and nurse his father for a while, then come back to Thorncliff as per the conditions of their marriage. Or simply because he wanted to. Darius had to hope that was the case, but it was out of his hands. Fate would either bring his love home to him or not.

But it was with a heavy heart full of trepidation that Darius stood on his front step later, Zeus in his arms, watching until Joshua's car disappeared out of sight.

Would he see him again?

Only time would tell.

18

JOSHUA

By the time the car reached the town Joshua had lived since birth, the letter had been scrunched up so much by his twisting hands it was amazing it hadn't ripped apart. He knew every word by heart now, but that hadn't made the tortuously long journey any easier.

Apparently, his dad had been mauled by some sort of machinery. *Mauled.* That word had stood out horribly for Joshua, making it sound like his dad had been attacked by some sort of wild beast.

As soon as they escaped from the black hole of Thorncliff, Joshua had frantically called the big hospital over in Ashford, as Folkstone only had limited services and no A&E. But Ashford had no record of a Christopher Bellamy being admitted, and neither did the smaller Folkstone hospital. After hanging up with the apologetic receptionist, Joshua frowned at his phone for a minute. He must have been injured whilst out at work, in that case. Who knew where that could be? Dover? Hastings? All the way down in Eastbourne or Brighton?

Joshua didn't have any messages. None that mattered, anyway. There were a few from the people he used to work with down the pub – the closest thing Joshua had to friends who he'd left behind – but none from any health care professionals trying to reach him. That surprised him, considering the letter said that Joshua was listed as his dad's next of kin and they'd been trying to reach him for days. Maybe the black hole of Thorncliff had swallowed them up? But then why had the messages from his former colleagues got through?

Joshua bit his lip and looked at the contact details from this Dr Smith who had written the letter. He realised that there was no contact information on the footer or the header. It was just a regular slip of paper, with no indication of which hospital it had been sent from. But at least there was a mobile number from the doctor. They'd just apologised and said that it had taken them some time for his dad to regain consciousness for long enough to give them an address to reach out to Joshua.

Joshua closed his eyes and let that give him comfort. Asher was almost at his house now. Just a few more minutes. But it was important that Joshua held on to the fact that his dad had been conscious at all, and Joshua would soon be able to see him.

So he didn't give up. He needed to know where to tell Asher to drive next, after all. So he then tried the mobile numbers for both Dr Smith and his dad, but frustratingly, neither got an answer. He'd just have to try again. But for now, he pressed his nose up against the glass and gasped as Asher turned down the last road.

Joshua was home.

He wished it wasn't empty. He wished he was returning under better circumstances.

He wished Darius was there by his side.

Joshua's heart squeezed painfully at the thought of leaving Darius. He completely understood why it was sensible for him to stay at home and talk to his dad, but then Joshua's anger flared at Victor's fucking stupid rules. Why shouldn't Joshua rush to see his injured father? And why shouldn't his bloody husband be able to travel with him? Joshua would give anything to be holding Darius's hand right now.

But if there was one thing that Joshua had learned about himself from his time in his new home with his new husband, it was that he was a lot tougher than he'd ever thought. Darius had helped him to start believing in himself. So although he was scared and fighting the urge to throw up with worry, he knew he could get through this.

Whatever 'this' was.

He'd undone his seat belt before the car had even pulled up alongside the pavement. Theirs was one in a long line of terraced houses without a driveway, so that was the closest they were going to get anyway. Joshua slung his backpack over his shoulder and leaped from the car, armed with his front door key, the letter scrunched up in his other hand.

"Thank you," he cried to Asher as he slammed the door shut behind him, then bolted from the car and down the garden path. He jammed the key into the lock...realising immediately that it wasn't double-locked.

Holy shit. Had his dad been discharged in the time it had taken for Joshua to get the letter? Was he already at home and on the mend? Hope leaped in his chest as he flung the door open.

"Dad!" he yelled as he let himself into the narrow hallway. It was strange. He'd only been gone a couple of months, and nothing looked to have changed, but to Joshua, it felt completely alien. Like he'd been a different person when he'd lived here. "Dad! Are you home?"

"Joshua?"

Relief flooded Joshua so quickly his knees tried to give way. Joshua grabbed the end of the bannister where – as usual – his dad's rain mac was hanging. He sucked in a breath, aware that he'd left the front door open and Asher was outside with the car still running, but he didn't care about any of that as he ran into the living room…

…and saw his dad looking perfectly fine aside from the bandaged foot propped up on the sofa.

For the second time in a minute, all the blood rushed from Joshua's head. This time, his legs did give way, but luckily there was an armchair waiting to catch him as he collapsed. For a few seconds, he and his dad just stared at each other.

"You're all right?" Joshua croaked eventually.

Was it his imagination, or did his dad flinch?

"Well…" he said slowly. "I'm not as bad as I perhaps made it out to be."

Joshua didn't understand. Then his gaze snapped down to the crumpled letter in his hand.

"Did *you* send this?" he asked incredulously.

His dad suddenly looked incredibly tired. Worse than that, his eyes were glassy, like he might cry. His dad *never* cried. Not even at Joshua's sham wedding when he'd been devastated. What the hell was going on here?

He cleared his throat. "Do I hear a car running outside?" he asked.

Joshua blinked. "Uh, yeah. Asher drove me."

His dad nodded. "Maybe you can tell them to leave. I hope you'll stay the night at least now that I've got you back?"

Joshua still wasn't sure what was happening, but the truth was the road was too narrow for a car to hang around. Between the lines of parked cars on either side, there was only room for one vehicle to drive up or down. Asher was blocking the way.

Without knowing why on earth his dad would have made his injuries sound a hundred times worse than they really were, or more to the point, pretended to be a *doctor* when he wrote that letter, Joshua didn't know how long he was going to be here. But also, despite whatever fishy business was going on, he *was* glad to see his dad for the first time in forever.

In a daze, Joshua wandered out to let Asher know he could return to Thorncliff. Joshua got a pang that he wasn't going with him, but seeing as his dad wasn't severely maimed, he told himself that he could probably go back home to Darius in no time.

Darius...who *had* been brutally burned and impaled when his helicopter had been blown from the sky. Darius, who had lost a friend that day, a friend who Joshua strongly suspected to have been his lover. Darius, who had been left scarred physically and mentally by his attack.

During the few seconds it took Joshua to storm back up to his dad's house, he was furious enough that he slammed the door shut, making the walls rattle. He dropped his backpack in the hall, shoved his keys into his pocket, then marched back into the living room, brandishing the letter that had made him worried sick.

"Would you care to explain *why* you felt the need to lie and manipulate me like that?" he snarled. He couldn't believe his dad would do this.

His dad held up his hands, looking imploringly at Joshua. "I can explain," he said. "Please. I didn't know what else to do. I was so worried about you."

Some of Joshua's anger simmered down. His dad looked so old and frail, even though he was only in his fifties. Stress seemed to have aged him a decade in these past months. Joshua sighed and pointed at the bandaged ankle.

"So are you at least a *little* bit hurt?" he said, the accusation clear.

His dad huffed and looked miserably at his foot. "It's just a sprain. I tripped over a forklift truck arm. That was it. But…well, I thought it best to exaggerate a real problem than try and make something completely up."

Joshua dropped into the armchair again. The living room was pretty small and still decorated from the nineties with lots of mismatching dark wood furniture and odd throw cushions. Joshua's school photos hung on the walls, and his dad's West Ham football memorabilia everywhere.

"Why did you make up such a horrible story, Dad?" Joshua tried not to let his voice rise, but he was fuming. "Darius was in a *real* accident. It derailed his life. That's not something to joke about."

At the mention of Darius's name, his dad's face darkened. "Him. That's why."

Joshua was so surprised he sat back in the chair and blinked for a moment. "No, Dad," he said after he'd regained his wits. "I know we haven't been able to talk, and you must have been worried sick, but Darius is…he's wonderful." Joshua tried not to blush when he thought just how wonderful. "He's kind, and he's taking such good care of me. We're friends now." He wanted to explain that they were more than friends, actually, but it was all so new and fragile, he wasn't sure how.

A chill ran down Joshua's spine as he watched his dad sigh heavily and shake his head. Then he reached into his trouser pocket and pulled out his ancient mobile phone.

"Josh," he said. He was the only person who called him that anymore. "Someone sent me a voicemail two days ago."

"Who?" asked Joshua, immediately suspicious. "Victor?"

His dad shrugged as he punched at the buttons. "No. It's an unknown number. I don't recognise the voice. But…I think you should listen for yourself, okay?"

Joshua frowned, not sure what his dad was talking about. Suddenly a man's voice filled the room. Joshua didn't think he recognised it, but maybe he did? He wasn't sure. He was too busy focusing on the words.

"Mr Bellamy," it began. The words were rushed, and it sounded as if the speaker might have been walking or even running. "You deserve to know the truth. Both you *and* your son. Legrand isn't what he seems. He's just like his father. They're in on it together. I know something has changed between him and your son in the last couple of days. He deserves to know the truth."

The recording then changed quality, becoming even more staticky. Joshua's immediate guess was that this was a recording being played from another device, held up to the caller's phone.

"How's Joshua getting along?"

Joshua flinched and curled his lip. Even though it was faint and crackly, that was unmistakably Victor.

Then the voice that followed made his heart swell. *Darius.*

Except…Joshua's fondness quickly vanished.

"Okay, I guess. Kind of annoying, but I'm getting used to it." There was a pause. "Bellamy is a spectacular fuck. Is that what you want to hear? I pounded his sweet little arse until he cried."

Joshua's mouth dropped open as tears sprung in his eyes. *What* had Darius just said?

"I recorded that in secret yesterday," the breathy voice said. "Look, I know it's not completely awful, but that's all

I've been able to get on tape. He's said much worse. Whatever your son thinks, it's not true. Don't ask me what the endgame is, but I thought someone should have the decency to tell him he's being played."

The call went dead.

Joshua raised his hand and covered his mouth, although he could barely feel it. He'd gone completely numb and shaky, his stomach rolling over in horror.

How could his caring, patient, loving Darius have said those things?

Had Joshua been right all along with his first impression? Was Darius nothing more than a cold-hearted brute, playing the long game? Using Joshua for his looks, just like so many men before him had tried to do? But that didn't even make any sense, did it? What about all those wonderful things Darius had said to him? The ways he'd cared for Joshua when they'd been in bed?

What could possibly be the reason to lie to him like that?

"You see?" his dad said, twisting the phone in his hands. "I had to get you out of there. Victor said you weren't to leave under any circumstances or he'd rip the company apart. He wouldn't let me reply to your letters or emails or even text. He said he'd *know*. But I figured he'd have to forgive you if your old man was in a serious accident."

Joshua rubbed his damp eyes angrily. He personally doubted that. When Victor found out Joshua had left the castle, who knew what he'd do? Joshua had taken a huge risk coming here. Had it been worth it?

He wasn't sure.

"But why, Dad?" Joshua said, shaking his head. *"Why* would he pretend to seduce me? It doesn't make any sense."

His dad dropped his phone in his lap, then rubbed the back of his neck, chewing his lip. "I didn't want to upset you, but I think we're past that now. I think there's something you should know about Victor."

Joshua bristled at the mention of that asshole's name. "Okay," he said slowly, bracing himself. Could this be any worse than the puppy story?

"I've known Victor a very long time," his dad began, twisting his hands and looking out the front window at the darkening sky. "He gave me my first contract. Did you know that?" Joshua shook his head. "At the time, I thought it was my big break. I owed him everything. Turned out that was what he thought, too. Literally." His dad sighed, his eyes glistening again. "Your mum was his secretary."

Joshua gasped. "What?" he whispered. "How come I never knew that?"

"We deliberately didn't talk about it," said his dad. "It…it wasn't pleasant. Your mum and I met, and I just knew immediately she was the one. They say love at first sight is a load of old bollocks, but I know better." He laughed ruefully. "I reckon your mum felt the same. We were mad for each other, right from the get-go."

"But…" Joshua prompted.

His dad clenched his jaw. "*But* it turned out that Victor had his eye on your mum. Had done for ages. In fact, he'd been harassing her."

"Why doesn't that surprise me," Joshua grumbled darkly. "Wait – wouldn't he have been married to Maree by then?" Joshua did some maths. Darius might even have been born.

His dad's face was as dark as a thundercloud. "I don't think that mattered to Victor," he said dryly. "He certainly didn't like it when we started dating. Kept saying your mum would come to her senses, even when we got engaged and moved in together. That was when she quit her job to escape him. But Victor never gave up. Always sent her flowers on her birthday." His dad chuckled. "And your mum always took them straight up to the children's ward at the hospital."

Joshua's heart ached, thinking of the single red rose Dad had bought Mum every year. Joshua couldn't ever remember her having a fancy bouquet from anyone else as well. He was proud of her for not being wooed by Victor's wealth.

The mirth faded from Joshua's dad's eyes quickly, though, and he sniffed, rubbing his eyes. "I think he was always convinced he'd win her over eventually. But then…then there was the accident."

Joshua could feel his eyes stinging as a lump rose in his throat. God, it was a long time since he'd cried over his mum's death, but the pain was never really very far away. He got up, crouched by his dad, and held his hand between both of his. "Dad," he said sympathetically.

His dad shook his head bitterly. "Victor was furious. I was grieving and trying to take care of you, and he was ringing non-stop, telling me it was m-my fault. That if she'd married him, she'd have been driving a safer car."

"Dad, no!" Joshua cried in horror. "That's bullshit! How dare he!"

"*Victor* was the one strangling the company," his dad said savagely, sniffing and rubbing his face. "I always thought he was screwing me on the overheads, but I could never prove it. It's why we never had a bean. Then he acted like it was my fault that Claire…that she…"

Big fat tears fell down. Joshua couldn't cope with seeing his dad actually crying. He flung his arms around him and hugged him tightly. "I'm *so* sorry."

His dad shook his head and took hold of Joshua's shoulders so they were looking at each other again. "But don't you see? Him marrying you off to that brutish son of his was his final revenge. You can't trust anything either of them says!"

Joshua's heart squeezed painfully. "Yeah," he said slowly. "That explains why Victor concocted such a wild scheme. But not Darius. Dad, he's been amazing to me."

His dad's expression was one of pure pity. "But, Josh. That voicemail?"

Ice rushed through Joshua's body, like he'd fallen into that damn lake all over again.

No, he couldn't explain that.

He bit his lip, unsure what to think. Other than he wanted to speak to Darius right the hell now, but this wasn't the sort of thing he felt capable of explaining in an email. Fuck, Joshua didn't think he'd want to do it over the phone, even if he could call the damn castle. No, he needed a face-to-face discussion, and that wasn't going to happen tonight. The sun had already set, and Joshua wasn't going to be able to contact anyone to get Asher back until at least the morning.

"I understand why you were worried," he said eventually. "And that story is pretty gut-wrenching. All I can say is… well, that's not the Darius I know. I'll talk to him. Maybe there's another explanation." Joshua couldn't think what, but he had to cling to some hope.

Otherwise, he was going to start crying and never stop.

He thought he was falling in love with Darius. In fact, he could have sworn that Darius had almost said something like that just as Mrs Weatherby had interrupted them earlier.

But maybe he was wrong. Maybe Darius had been manipulating him this whole time to aid his dad in his nefarious scheme. That was what Victor liked doing by all accounts. Maybe Darius was trying to win over his father's approval finally?

Or maybe it was just a case of like father, like son. Maybe they were both sick fucks.

In any case, Joshua wasn't getting any answers tonight. So

he took a deep breath and put on his best smile for his dad. "It's nice to be home and to see you, whatever the case."

His dad finally gave him a tired smile. "Oh, give your old man a proper hug while I'm not blubbing. I've *missed* you." Joshua laughed and did as he'd been asked. "Blimey, you've thickened out a bit!"

Joshua assumed he meant his little tummy from Camille's extravagant cooking. But then his dad squeezed his bicep. "Oh, yeah," Joshua said faintly. "I've been gardening a lot. I didn't even realise I'd bulked up a bit."

He would have been pleased, but thinking of his beloved gardens made him think of Darius, and his heart hurt too much for that.

"So," he said, feigning brightness. He was still angry that his dad had manipulated and scared him like that, but then, that was the lengths Victor Legrand pushed people to. Joshua and his dad could talk about it further when their raw emotions had calmed down. "Why don't I nip up the road and get us some pie and chips. Maybe some beers?" He hadn't drunk beer in months, preferring Camille's indulgent French wines. But right then, he wanted nothing more than salty chips, a greasy steak and kidney pie, and some cheap lager with his dad.

Sure enough, his dad's face lit up like a small child who'd been told they could have sweets. "Oh, would you, son? That would be proper."

Despite how much his heart was threatening to break, Joshua firmly told himself that he didn't know anything just yet. The story about his mum hurt, but it didn't necessarily mean Darius was at fault. It just explained why Victor had wanted to punish Joshua's dad with the arranged marriage.

So Joshua should enjoy the gift he'd been given of a surprise night in with his dad, then deal with everything else in the morning. Maybe there was an explanation for why

Darius had said such vile things. Joshua smiled at his dad, swallowing his pain. Hopefully, it was all just a misunderstanding, and he and Darius would be fine.

They had to be. Joshua wasn't sure what he'd do otherwise.

19

JOSHUA

Joshua wasn't sure what had woken him, but when he realised it was still dark outside, he grumbled in annoyance. He and his dad had both been exhausted for various reasons, so they'd gone up to bed early. However, it had taken Joshua so long to fall asleep he was certain it would be at least a little light when he woke up. But when he glanced at his phone for the time, it wasn't even midnight yet.

He huffed and rubbed his eyes, wondering how long it would take him to doze off again. It was weird as hell being back in his old bedroom and his tiny single bed. It felt so soulless to him now. There were hardly any personal touches in the room, only some photos of his mum which he had on his phone anyway, and an out-of-date calendar with puppies on each month. Who the hell even *was* he before he'd moved out?

He sighed and checked his phone for messages, but of course there was nothing from Darius.

His heart was hurting in a way he couldn't have previously imagined. It wasn't like when his mum had passed. That had been the most awful day. But she had been lost in an instant, and Joshua never had any doubts that she loved him very much.

Could he say the same about Darius?

He'd driven himself crazy before falling asleep, trying to replay all the moments they'd shared, analysing them and trying to tell if they were fake. He rubbed his chest now as he stared at the ceiling. It wasn't just the sex. They hadn't even *had* full sex yet, so he was sure Darius wasn't using him for that.

Which – now that Joshua thought about it – made Darius's recorded words even more confusing. *"I fucked him until he cried."* He hadn't, and…god, Darius wouldn't do that to him, would he? He'd always been so tender. The thought that he'd *hurt* Joshua in that way was gut-wrenching.

None of it made sense. How diabolical would a person have to be to fake all those little things? The way he kissed Joshua behind his ear, the interest he showed in his gardening, the cufflinks he'd bought him.

He was his petal.

Joshua's eyes burned, and he rubbed them as he hiccuped. He didn't want this dream to end. When he was with Darius, he felt cherished beyond measure. He begged to the universe that it hadn't all been a gruesome charade.

In the silence of the house, he heard an abrupt noise. He froze. Was that what had woken him? What even was 'that'? He couldn't identify the sound, but he was sleeping in his underwear, and suddenly he felt nervous. All that talk of Victor and his malicious schemes had him on edge. It might have been overreacting, but if he was going to investigate, he didn't want to do so almost naked. So he pulled his clothes and trainers back on, then padded across the small room towards the closed door. But he stopped abruptly, jerking his head. What was that smell?

Was that smoke?

He lunged for his door, and yanked it open to a grey cloud, the sound of crackling flames making his stomach plummet.

"What the fuck!" he cried. Why hadn't the smoke alarm gone off? Had his dad forgotten to replace the batteries?

None of that mattered now. What mattered was there was a fucking *fire* in the house.

Coughing and spluttering, Joshua waved in front of his face, dashing across the landing to look over the bannister down the stairs. Jesus fucking Christ! The entrance hall was on fire! And it wasn't just there. The flames were creeping up the stairs and were probably already in the living room. Had they reached the kitchen yet? The glow was illuminating the upstairs landing.

Irrelevant! He was focusing on the wrong details. The house was ablaze, and they needed to get out, but the downstairs was already unpassable.

"Fuck!" he cried through his coughs, his eyes watering. A lightbulb exploded downstairs, making him jump. He needed to act, now! *"DAD!"* he bellowed as he dashed back into his room. He grabbed his phone, knowing he didn't even need to unlock it to call 999, and slung his backpack over his shoulders, glad he hadn't taken anything out but his phone charger.

He didn't stop to pull that from the wall, though. His phone was already close to a hundred percent, and every second counted.

"Dad! We have to get out of here!" he screamed just before the call connected. "Hello! Yes! My house is on fire!" He rattled off the address as he barged into his dad's bedroom. He was already up, wearing his pyjamas, struggling to stand with his crutches. "No time for that. Come on!" Joshua closed the emergency call after the dispatcher assured him help was on the way, then he shoved his phone into his pocket.

Now his hands were free, he helped his dad to hobble on his good foot, getting them back out onto the landing.

The flames were already higher. The ceiling was blackened from the smoke and the air was burning his lungs.

"Joshua," his dad cried in horror. "Are you okay? How did this happen?"

"I'm fine," Joshua insisted despite spluttering from the smoke inhalation. "I don't know how the fire started, but we can't stay here."

Joshua shut both their bedroom doors, not sure if it would help stall the flames, but he had to at least try. His heart was racing and they were both coughing as Joshua helped his dad into the bathroom. He shut that door as well, wetted a towel, and laid it along the crack at the bottom.

He scrambled into the tub and flung the window open, letting in some fresh air that they both gasped down.

"We have to get out," his dad protested through his coughs.

Joshua shook his head. "The fire started downstairs. I can't even see the front door." Had the old kettle sparked? Was there some faulty wiring? And why hadn't the fucking fire alarm gone off? It didn't matter now. They had to get to safety.

Joshua only knew one way how.

"Okay, Dad," he said, gripping his shoulders. "This probably isn't the best time to tell you I used to sneak out of this window in the middle of the night when I was a teenager...but...that's exactly what I did. All the time. I'm really hoping it'll save our lives now and you won't be mad."

His dad looked down at his sprained ankle, then back at the door. Despite the towel Joshua had placed down, there were still tendrils of smoke curling through.

"I'm not even mad," he said, eyebrows raised. "I'm proud. Let's get the fuck out of here. I'll hop if I have to."

Joshua squeezed his shoulder. "Okay, the hardest part is dangling down from this window. But once you drop, you're on top of the kitchen extension. Then you can climb onto the water butt and down. I'll go first and help lower you at each point. But we have to go fast." The smoke was getting worse despite the open window, and Joshua was coughing again. He took a few breaths through the sleeve of his jumper, then didn't think. He just relied on muscle memory to fling himself over and out of the window, dropping with a thud onto the kitchen roof.

Their neighbours were out in their back gardens, yelling in their dressing gowns, clearly panicking. *Fuck.* Joshua had no idea if the fire would jump to their houses. He was worried enough about their own going up in smoke. His stomach twisted at the thought of all those memories of his mum, being burned away. But he could already hear the sirens wailing in the distance. The only thing that mattered was getting his dad out. If no one got hurt, they could replace everything else.

Joshua reached up as his dad awkwardly stepped over the windowsill and began to try and lower himself. "I've got you!" Joshua said, not really meaning it. But he did at least have his ankles, then his calves, so when his dad's arms inevitably gave way, they were able to crumple in a relatively safe heap.

His dad grunted. "How did I never hear you doing this?"

"Never mind. How's your ankle?" Joshua asked as they scrambled to sit upright.

His dad made a shooing motion. "Fine, fine! Let's go!"

Joshua didn't need telling twice.

Smoke was billowing out of the house, and the roaring of the flames was pretty terrifying. More people were coming out of their houses into their back gardens, but what they were shouting, Joshua couldn't tell. He was too focused on getting his dad across the small roof, then lowering himself down onto the big green barrel that collected excess rainwater from the drains.

From there, they hobbled across the flagstones to the back gate cut into the wooden fence that ran across the end of their property. Joshua yanked back the rusty deadbolt that obviously hadn't been used in a long time, allowing them to spill into the alleyway that ran down the length of the street. A few doors down, there was another tiny alley that took them back towards the street, under a story-high alcove between two of the otherwise joined houses.

They were safe. They were out of the house, and the fire engine was on its way. Joshua stopped and hugged his dad as they both coughed.

"Our *home*," his dad whispered thickly.

Joshua rubbed his back. "I know," he agreed, trying to stay strong. "But it's just stuff. So long as we're okay."

His dad nodded, then looked up and frowned. People were still shouting. In fact, people were running towards them, causing Joshua to really look up and down the street.

He gasped when he realised how many people were out there waiting for them with open arms. Jesus, he'd never even spoken to the vast majority of these people, but there they were, most of them in pyjamas. Someone draped blankets around their shoulders. Another offered a bottle of water, which Joshua insisted his dad drink from first. As the sirens got louder, people steered Joshua and his dad to sit down on someone's front wall, while yet more neighbours guided the fire engine down the narrow road.

Joshua wanted to cry from their kindness. He tried not to think about all the photos of his mum being burned to a crisp. He had the important ones stored on his phone, and his most precious memory of her was the rose book, which was safely tucked away back at the castle, thank god.

It wasn't long before some kind soul pressed mugs of tea into Joshua's and his dad's hands. The firefighters were running from the engine with their long hoses, blasting through the windows of their house and finally smothering the flames. Joshua couldn't stop coughing as a paramedic unit also arrived, wanting to fuss over them. He was in such a daze he just did what he was told. But there was a tang in the air, and it wasn't until just before Joshua put his oxygen mask on did it finally click what it was.

Petrol.

He gasped, waving over one of the firefighters who was standing back now that that blaze was under control. The older guy jogged over, and Joshua wondered if he was a supervisor. "Can you smell that petrol?" he asked before the irritated paramedic made him breathe from the mask. Joshua had to admit he immediately felt better for it.

The supervisor nodded grimly. "I wouldn't want to speculate yet, but from the burn patterns around your door, I wonder if someone poured petrol through your letterbox and lit a match."

"No," Joshua's dad cried in horror. He tried to pull his own mask away, but the paramedic slapped his fingers. So he huffed and continued his muffled talking through the mask. "Who would do that? We could have *died!*"

Dread washed through Joshua. He couldn't say for certain, but he knew one man who would break a puppy's leg out of spite. Who had hounded a married woman and then accused her grieving widower of neglect. That had been years ago. Who knew what Victor Legrand might be capable of now?

It was pure speculation, but coupled with his dad's mysterious voicemail, Joshua couldn't help but wonder.

"Why didn't the smoke alarm go off?" Joshua asked

through his mask, raising his eyebrows at his dad. "How long since you replaced the batteries?"

"A month or so," his dad replied hotly. "I'm not an idiot."

Joshua rubbed his dad's knee, knowing he was panicking and upset, so it was no wonder he got defensive. "That's what I thought. You'd never forget that. Dad…has anyone been in the house recently?"

He could feel the firefighter watching them as Joshua's dad frowned. "Yeah, now that you mention it. A young lad came to check the gas metre yesterday. But I swear another fellow did that not long before Christmas as well."

"Fuck." Joshua felt sick, and not just from the smoke inhalation and adrenaline from fleeing the fire. He looked at the firefighter. "You reckon someone set the fire deliberately?"

The supervisor held up his hands. "We'd have to do a proper investigation," he said. "But in my professional opinion after thirty-five years of service? Yeah. I think we're dealing with an arsonist here."

"Who would do such a thing?" Joshua's dad spluttered again in horror.

"Victor Legrand," Joshua growled, rage bubbling up through him. "I bet you anything he organised that voicemail to be left on your phone so you'd get me home, and then that man from the gas company was just here to tamper with the smoke alarm."

"That's some serious accusations there, son," the firefighter said, raising his eyebrows.

"Yes, they are," Joshua said. But he was certain he could detect Victor's mucky hands all over this. Now more than ever he wanted to talk to Darius…

Who had said he was going to tell Victor that Joshua was leaving the castle grounds, specifically against the rules. That would have meant Victor would have known *exactly* when to attack. Not that Joshua expected the old man to have done this himself. But all he'd have to do was make the call and whoever it was would know to light the match.

The question was, had Darius unwittingly given his father the information he'd needed or had they been in on the plan together? If Darius was innocent and didn't know…oh, *shit*. He'd said he was going to ask Victor over.

Darius was all alone. And Victor had apparently lost his mind.

Who knew what wicked schemes he was capable of right now?

It still didn't make sense. Joshua couldn't see the big picture. But his gut instinct was screaming at him that Darius was in danger.

And that filled him with fear, more than even the house fire had done.

"Dad," he said urgently. "Is there someone you can stay with tonight?"

His dad blinked in confusion at him. "Yeah. I'll call around the boys. But what are you-"

Joshua shook his head, ignoring the protesting paramedic as he flung the oxygen mask and blanket off, and downed his last mouthful of tea.

He needed everything he could get to fortify his courage if he was right.

"Can you do that now? I want to make sure you're safe and have a bed to sleep in before I go."

His dad frowned. "Okay. But what about you? Where are you going?"

Joshua clasped his hands around his dad's, meeting his gaze. God, he'd thought his dad had looked frail when he'd arrived home earlier. That was nothing to how tired he appeared now, how bloodshot his eyes were, how pale and papery his skin was.

"I have to get back to Thorncliff. I'll call a taxi. I know, I know," he said, squeezing his dad's hands at his outraged expression. "What Darius said in that message was awful. I don't know what the truth is. But there's something really dodgy going on here."

"So you want to go *back* to that place?" his dad cried incredulously.

Joshua shook his head at his dad. "I have to get back to *Darius*. I don't know what's going on – if he meant what he said in that message. But, Dad...I love him. And I have a feeling something terrible might have happened."

His dad raised his eyebrows. "More terrible than this?" He pointed at the smouldering wreck of their house.

Joshua bit his lip. "I don't know," he whispered.

All he knew was that he had to get back to his husband. Because Darius had come for him when he'd been a selfish brat and run out into the snowstorm and fallen into the lake. It didn't matter if Darius had been playing him or said those nasty things for another reason. Joshua now knew that he, Joshua Bellamy, was the kind of person who didn't run away.

He was going back to face his fears.

All of them.

2 0

DARIUS

THE CASTLE WAS HUGE. SO HOW COULD ONE PERSON'S ABSENCE make such a difference? How could so many rooms and corridors feel so empty just because one person was no longer walking through them?

And not even for more than a few hours. It was coming up to midnight, and Joshua had left at around five o'clock. Was Darius really so pathetic that he was pining for him so quickly?

No. He scowled at himself, even though there was no one else around to see him doing it. He wasn't pathetic. He was worrying about circumstances outside his control. A perfectly natural reaction, given his upbringing.

If his father even *sensed* something was bringing Darius joy, he would seek to destroy it.

When he'd made friends at school, his father had made him change classes. When he'd been selected for the rugby team, his father insisted he take French lessons at a conflicting time so he'd been forced to quit. When he'd been gifted a puppy from his dying mother, the dog mysteriously showed up with a broken leg, forcing Darius to rehome her.

The list went on and on. The worst perhaps was when Victor had disrespected everything Darius's mother had wished for at her funeral, purely to cause Darius more pain. Where she was buried, the flowers, who was invited – Victor changed everything. It felt like in the end, Victor had hated his wife for no discernible reason, then turned that loathing full force onto their son. Only by joining the army had Darius escaped Victor's reach.

So no, Darius didn't think he was overreacting by worrying himself sick that Joshua had been taken out of his sight.

His earlier fears about Joshua choosing freedom over returning to Darius and the castle paled in comparison when he thought about what the real risks could be. Could Victor have hurt Christopher Bellamy himself? Was he deliberately trying to lure Joshua out, testing his rules? Could he have tampered with the car? Victor wouldn't care if there was someone else inside, after all.

Or was Darius taking his protectiveness over his beautiful, sweet lover too far? Was he becoming obsessed? Joshua was a grown, capable man. Darius didn't want to smother him, but honestly, as he lay there in the dark with Zeus resting on his chest, he couldn't seem to stop his mind from spiralling. He hadn't even attempted to sleep, and the thought of food had made his stomach turn, much to Camille's disdain.

Darius had almost apologised to her for wasting the dinner she'd made for Darius and Joshua, but as he'd got close to the kitchen, he heard the racket she was making and decided to leave her unfortunate, battle-hardened staff to it.

Poor Mrs Weatherby had done her best to comfort Darius, making him several cups of tea that he'd sipped to keep her happy until they got too cold. She kept assuring him that everything was *fine*. That Joshua's dad was in the *best* hands and that Joshua would be home in *no* time. Darius appreciated her efforts, but they were both aware that neither of them had any way of knowing if that was true.

Darius had left Bartholomew angrily rearranging one of the bookcases in the drawing room with a large glass of whisky, muttering darkly about what should be done with ungrateful fathers. Darius wasn't surprised that he shared his opinion that Victor almost certainly had his sticky fingers in this, one way or another. Bartholomew had been employed by him in some capacity for most of his life. Darius had a sneaking suspicion that the only reason he'd stuck around was because of Darius and his mother, for which he was very grateful. So Darius poured himself a glass of whisky too and then made sure that Bartholomew had the rest of the decanter to hand before leaving him to stew alone.

Which left Darius lying on his couch, in the dark, with the glass of whisky in his hand and Zeus lying on his chest, staring at Darius with his big, black eyes. "What do *you* think?" Darius asked the small fluffy pup. Zeus twisted his head left and right at the sound of Darius asking a question. Not having a better answer, Zeus licked the tip of Darius's chin instead.

Darius sighed. Perhaps he was just fretting over nothing. But whatever the case, he vowed to himself that if – *when* – Joshua returned, Darius was going to stop being such a fucking coward and tell him the truth.

Darius was madly in love with Joshua and would do anything to be with him.

He could only hope that Joshua felt the same way.

No matter the progress they'd made since the wedding, especially over the past week, Darius always came back to his core fear. Joshua had been forced into this marriage and into living in isolation at the castle. How could he really love Darius? Surely it was a kind of Stockholm Syndrome going on, where he was just trying to make the best of the situation with his captor.

Darius's eyes threatened to sting, so he knocked back the last of the whisky so he could burn his throat instead. He felt so empty, which was ridiculous. He knew no one should define themselves by who their partner was. He was a whole man with or without Joshua. But now that Joshua had left, Darius had to wonder who the hell he *was*. For too many years, he'd just been an angry ball of pain, mourning first his mother and then Richard, carrying his scars around like armour. Then Joshua had given him renewed energy, bringing light into Darius's sad little kingdom.

Would he still feel like that? What if Joshua didn't come back?

Darius cleared his throat and petted Zeus's curly fur. It depended on *why* Joshua didn't come back. If he decided to try and flee this antiquated arrangement and defy Victor's rules in order to reclaim his freedom, Darius would support him in that. It would break his heart, but Joshua didn't owe him his love. In that case, Darius would try his best to pick up the pieces, then find another way to bring light back into his life.

If Joshua didn't return because Darius father had intervened, or worse, done something malicious, Darius wasn't sure what he would do to Victor.

This had to end. Darius was thirty-seven. No child should still be so at the mercy of their parent at that age. But Victor had made himself so entangled in Darius's life, controlling everything he could to make him miserable, Darius wasn't sure he knew how to unravel that. He'd made a start by unlocking the inheritance his mother had left him, but he needed to take it further. Get out of the bogus position

Victor had forced him into in the company, maybe even get out of the castle.

Ironically, now that Darius was feeling the gumption to get the fuck out of Thorncliff...he didn't want to. Because this was where he and Joshua had started to build a *home.* The property was in Darius's name, after all. Just because it was given to him by Victor didn't mean it still actually belonged to his father, did it?

He grumbled to himself and drummed his nails against the empty glass tumbler. All that could wait. The only thing that mattered was that Joshua was safe. When – *if* – he came back to Darius, then they could deal with everything else. But until he did come back and Darius could get out of this uncertain limbo, there wasn't much more he could do. That did, however, sound like an excellent reason to get another whisky.

Darius knew he had another bottle stashed away somewhere in his living room, so he encouraged Zeus to hop down and help him search for it.

That was when he heard the shouts.

His army training meant he'd dropped the whisky glass and was at the door before he'd even realised his feet were moving. He flung it open and rushed out into the corridor, dashing towards the stairs with Zeus at his heels.

"No, stop that! What are you doing?" Mrs Weatherby cried out, clearly in distress. The sounds of things crashing and banging met Darius as he ran faster, and – *fuckity fuck fuck* – was that smoke he could smell?

He was sprinting by the time he reached the stairs that led down to the main entrance hall, where what he found could only be described as carnage.

Mrs Weatherby was halfway down the stairs in her dressing gown and hairnet, using a broom to shove away a thuggish-looking man who was trying to grab at her. The curtains were on fire, a display cabinet had been overturned and smashed, and papers had been scattered all over the floor from a desk somewhere. The front door had been left wide open, letting in the cold night air and the rain that had started thrashing sometime in the past few hours. Darius could hear a lot more commotion from the hallways beyond, with at least a dozen people yelling and screaming, more glass and china shattering, and the squeal of something heavy being dragged across the stone floor.

Fury made Darius's vision blaze red. He charged with an animalistic bellow at the hooligan attacking Mrs Weatherby, side-stepping her to shove the assailant back down the stairs. When he crunched at the bottom, he didn't get back up again.

Darius would waste energy caring about him later. Right now, he was far more concerned about his staff. "What's happening?" he demanded. He seized Mrs Weatherby by the shoulders to check her over and make sure she wasn't injured.

"Burglars!" she cried, rubbing her tearful face and shaking her broom at Darius. "Looters! Their mothers should be ashamed!"

Darius wasn't so sure, though. From the trashed entrance hall, he'd say these thugs were trying to cause damage, not steal the family jewels. Besides, he was sure he could smell petrol.

Some fucker was setting fire to his home.

He squeezed Mrs Weatherby's shoulders and bent down to look her in the eye. "Go. Take the car and head to the village. Find a phone and call the police and fire brigade. Then *stay* there. I don't know what's happening, but there's no telling what these fuckers might do."

Mrs Weatherby irritably smacked his hands away. "Like *hell*, I will. Those bastards are breaking things! Come on!"

She dashed down the stairs, surprisingly nimble for a woman of her age, and disappeared towards the kitchens. Darius was torn. He wanted to call the emergency services, but his need to defend his home won over, sending him down and to the right, away from Mrs Weatherby but heading closer to the loudest noise. At least a dozen staff members lived here full time, and not all of them would have broomsticks. He had to protect them.

It was like being under siege. Darius wondered again why he bothered living in a castle that didn't have a moat. They'd *never* been invaded before. The gates and security cameras had been enough to keep anyone unwanted out previously.

Well, aside from Darius's father.

Which was why Darius shouldn't have been surprised when he reached the dining room door and saw Victor inside the room, surveying the scene as several goons smashed up the furniture. As he looked at Darius, delight danced in Victor's eyes, and he curled his lip into a cruel imitation of a smile.

"Ah," Victor said pleasantly from the other side of the dining room table, as if he wasn't observing over half a dozen thugs attacking the chandelier and paintings with crowbars. "I was wondering how long it would take you to join the party."

"What the fuck are you doing?" Darius roared. He knew his father was a tyrant, but this was actual insanity. Victor always said this place was really his, not Darius's, yet now he was trashing it? *Why?*

At least, his ruffians were attempting to do maximum damage. A couple of the stable hands – including Paulo – were trying in vain to stop them.

Darius bellowed and grabbed the hoodie of the closest one, pulling him away from the painting he was slashing and throwing him into another moron who was sloshing petrol over a cutlery dresser. They both went flying, the petrol spilling everywhere. *Jesus Christ*. There were fires spreading down the corridor. He was already coughing from the smoke that was filling up the corridors. How long before the flames reached here and met the petrol?

The place was going to go up like a goddamned powder keg.

So why bother wrecking the art and furnishings? Why not just light the fires and run away to watch the place burn?

Because that wasn't his father's style. Darius knew that Victor would want to destroy Darius's home out of spite, and be here, on hand, to see Darius watch it all be destroyed. It was as if he *knew* that Darius had just started to feel true love for Thorncliff. How happy he and Joshua were here, building a home.

It *was* his father he was thinking of. It was entirely possible that he did know that, and that was why he was doing this now.

Darius didn't have time to dwell on it, though. As soon as the two thugs hit the floor, three more spun and lunged for Darius.

One of them had a knife.

Now in a blinding rage, Darius punched his way through anyone who dared to come at him, slamming the knife away from the one thug. But then another picked it up.

"Get out of here!" Darius yelled at Paulo. "Protect the stables!" What if these fuckers had lit them on fire too? What about Hephaestus? Bloody hell, it was only then that Darius realised that Zeus was still at his feet, barking and biting anyone who tried to get to Darius. "Take Zeus!"

"I don't think so," said Victor calmly.

It was so typical of him to just be standing there while all this chaos unfurled around him. A couple of the hooligans were attacking the dining table with crowbars, splintering it apart. Another of the men was smashing the windows, whilst another used a chair to swing at the paintings left on the walls. A twitchy looking young woman with wide eyes eagerly grabbed the discarded petrol can, and glugged more over the stone floor and flammable furnishings.

They'd been told to go crazy. Darius would be money on it. The point here wasn't to destroy Thorncliff.

It was to hurt Darius and everything he cared about.

Well, almost everything. Thank fucking Christ that Joshua wasn't here.

Darius was strong, but he wasn't invincible. One of the goons managed to sneak a punch in, cracking his jaw and making Darius spin around as he saw stars. A cry drew his attention as he stumbled and righted himself. The other two stable hands had been wrestled to the floor, and their hands had been bound with plastic ties. Distracted by the punch, Darius didn't turn in time as two of the bigger thugs shoved him against the wall, smashing his head against the stone with a sickening crunch. He dropped to his knees, dimly aware that Paulo had been overpowered as well.

Even though the room was spinning, Darius did his best to scramble to his feet, and landed his fist in the stomach of the next fool who tried to rush him. "Are you *insane?*" he screamed at his father. "This is family property! Why would you fuck up your own shit?"

"Exactly," said Victor. "Think of it as cleansing with fire. Starting over." His father walked around the other side of what remained of the table, his hands clasped behind his back as he smirked. "And you, dear son, are trespassing," he said simply.

Darius staggered to his feet and grabbed the first thing he could get his hands on. That turned out to be an ornamental crossbow that had been hanging from the wall. It didn't have any bolts in it, but it was still pretty good for hitting people with. It seemed most of the thugs had stopped trashing things and were coordinating attacking him, but Darius was honestly more concerned about the wide-eyed girl with the petrol can. She was giggling as she sloshed the highly flammable liquid around, skipping towards the corridor.

"This is MY home." Darius jabbed his finger at the floor. "These are MY staff you're assaulting. MY antiques you're smashing."

"Oh, Darius," said Victor with a disturbing chuckle.

This time, three of the bastards threw themselves at Darius, managing to land several punches to his head and gut. The biggest thug swiped at his leg, throwing him off balance. As Darius dropped painfully to the floor on one knee, one of them swooped in and knocked the crossbow away, shoved his wrists together, getting a fucking tie around them. The plastic bit into his skin, the idiot having obviously pulled it way too tight. Within a few thrashes, Darius could already feel the chaffing. His skin would start bleeding soon enough.

But that was kind of irrelevant if his father was going to burn half the castle down and smash up the rest of it.

Darius breathed angrily through his nose. His jaw clenched as he watched on his knees while his father approached him. But then some asshole grabbed Zeus, who was barking his head off, and held him by the scruff of his neck.

"Get OFF him!" Darius bellowed, scrambling to his feet. But the biggest thug punched him so hard across the face Darius spun on his knees, seeing stars.

"You are not in control here, son," Victor said, still infuriatingly calm. "I gave you this property, and you were always clear that I had the power to take it back. By breaking the conditions of your marriage agreement, you leave me no choice. Therefore, I am exercising my right to reclaim what is mine and evicting squatters."

Darius spat blood and glared around the room. He was kneeling by Paulo and the two other groundsmen, their backs now to the broken window where rain was lashing in, splattering what was left of the dinner table. Darius could feel the droplets on the back of his neck. The goons appeared to feel they'd done as much damage as they could in this room, so were filing out into the hall in search of more destruction. The glow of several fires flickered through the open door, and the smoke was getting thicker. Darius's throat scratched as he coughed and spluttered. At least the flames couldn't travel over stone, so they were safe for now. But the room stank of petrol. All it would take was one spark.

The two biggest thugs remained with Victor, including the one who was holding a whimpering, squirming Zeus aloft by his scruff. Darius snarled at him. "I'm going to break your fucking neck," he informed the goon.

"You *never* learned to control that temper," Victor snapped, scowling down at his son. "Honestly, you push me to such extremes, Darius. Your mother would be so ashamed of you."

"Don't you talk about her!" Darius strained against his binds, his fingers already slick with blood. "You didn't fucking deserve her. She was an angel! You're just a pathetic old man, making other people squirm for kicks. Why did you hate her so much?"

As furious as Darius was, his throat was also tight with emotion. Fear for his staff and his poor little puppy was shredding his insides, but why the hell would Victor bring up his mum right now?

To hurt him. Everything was always to hurt him.

"I didn't hate her," said Victor with a shrug and a curled

lip. "But I did resent her. The cancer was a blessing in a way. I welcomed it. Why should she have had the chance to live when others didn't? Ah, here we go. Do come in." He turned to the door as several more goons came in, shoving Mrs Weatherby, Bartholomew, and a few of the kitchen staff ahead of them. They were all bound and gagged. Mrs Weatherby was bleeding from a cut on her head.

"Leave them alone!" Darius roared. "Have you gone mad? This is assault, grievous bodily harm, kidnapping! Attempted murder!" Thank *fuck* Joshua wasn't here, but even that was worrying Darius sick. If Victor had planned this, he wouldn't strike when Joshua was away unless that was part of the plan.

So where was Joshua? Had something happened to him?

Victor just laughed. "Place them with the others, then continue with your task."

His thoughts were interrupted as he recognised one of the thugs shoving the kitchen staff to their knees. "Martin?" Darius rasped in disbelief. The man who had supposedly been in charge of installing the internet at Thorncliff. "What's going on?"

Victor laughed coldly. "You didn't think I'd honestly neglect to keep eyes on you, did you?"

Nausea rinsed through Darius. Martin had been spying on him the whole time? Actually, it wasn't really that surprising. Darius groaned, realising what a fool he'd been. *Of course* there hadn't been any progress made in connecting Thorncliff to the outside world. Martin had almost certainly been stalling and purposefully delaying installing the internet. It gave him the perfect chance to spy for Victor, but it also kept Darius and Joshua isolated.

It would also make sense that Victor had made his move only days after Joshua and Darius had progressed their relationship from friendly to romantic and intimate. What had Darius been thinking mere minutes ago?

THORN IN HIS SIDE

Victor could never stand to see Darius happy for long.

"Uh, boss," Martin said, wringing his hands. "There's some bird in the kitchen with a big fucking knife."

Fuck yes, Camille.

Victor raised his eyebrows. "And why isn't she here? You were told to round up anyone you found. Is something about that unclear?"

Martin swallowed. Darius knew he had more pressing concerns right now, but he felt a surge of spiteful triumph that the staff member he'd trusted was now feeling the pressure.

Martin and the others nodded hastily. "Sure. We'll just… uh…go get her."

As they vanished from the room into the smoke-filled hallway, Darius turned his gaze and stared daggers at his father. "You're going to jail for this," he snarled. He knew it was an empty threat. Right now, he was fucked. And he didn't want to admit it, but he was scared.

This was *exactly* what he'd been so afraid of. His father always used other people to truly hurt Darius and keep him in line, especially since he'd grown physically bigger than him in the army. Not only was Darius bound, but Victor's thugs had his staff and his puppy at his mercy.

Darius would be an idiot to think he didn't have Joshua in some way too.

Tears burned behind his eyes, but he refused to let them fall. He wouldn't let his father see just how much he was hurting. But if anything had happened to Joshua, Darius wouldn't forgive himself for as long as he lived.

"Oh, stop being such a *child*," Victor snapped, looking with disgust down at Darius. "*I* make the rules. And if I want to marry you off to Christopher Bellamy's son to torture you, *that's* what will happen. How *dare* you think you can be happy? What did you imagine? That you were falling in love?"

He dropped his head back and laughed. Darius could hear more commotion, crackling flames, and people yelling from beyond the open door, but there was nothing he could do.

"Joshua was my pawn," Victor continued with a huff. "It was a great pity Christopher and Claire never had a daughter." The smile that crawled onto his face was completely vile. "Then perhaps I could have had the marriage I always deserved." His expression turned vicious again in a flash. "I may not be a pervert, but even I could see that boy was beautiful. He was supposed to humiliate you, you lumbering brute! How I ever ended up with such a cumbersome, braindead ogre for a son, I'll never know. But it seems neither of you wanted to play by my rules, so therefore I changed the game." He laughed, the sound like nails on a chalkboard down Darius's spine. "By which I mean end the game. This was always the final ace up my sleeve. I will *not* be humiliated by any of you! Christopher, his pathetic son, and least of all not you."

Victor spat at Darius's knees.

Darius got no pleasure from discovering he was right about Victor wanting beautiful Joshua to be a form of punishment and humiliation for Darius and his ugly scars. But he was too busy being repulsed at the idea of Victor marrying himself off to a girl three times younger than him. At least there was that small miracle to be thankful for right now during the madness going on around him.

"Fuck you," Darius growled. "You're unhinged. We've called the police. They're on the way."

He knew immediately that his bluff had been called when the nauseating smile returned to Victor's face. "How?" he asked almost pleasantly. "Mobile reception is non-existent here, and I made sure via Martin that even your basic internet connection was cut off this afternoon." He leaned down so he and Darius were face-to-face. "No one is coming to rescue you."

Darius smashed his head into Victor's, making his vision explode with stars, but it was so worth it to send his old man flying. Except it earned him another punch from one of the yobs, this one finally breaking his nose, blood spurting everywhere.

Several of Darius's staff yelled against the gags that they all had now, and Darius noisily spat crimson over the stone floor he was kneeling on, his face throbbing.

"Shall I kill the dog?" the massive goon asked, almost sounding bored.

"*NO!*" Darius screamed, trying to get to his feet again.

"Oh, calm down," Victor snapped, rubbing his forehead and getting back to his feet. "I saw the credit card bill. That dog's worth a couple of grand despite coming from a shelter. The horse outside even more so. I'm going to sell them off because I know it will hurt your precious *feelings.*" He grinned savagely at Darius. "I remember how much you cried when you got rid of that mutt before. That's always been your problem, son. You care about weak little things that can be hurt to make you comply." He flicked his eyebrows and straightened up his suit. "Like that sad little Joshua Bellamy. So delicate, that one. You could tell he was a dirty queer a mile off." He shrugged. "At least you don't have to worry about him anymore."

Darius's veins turned to ice, and all the air rushed from his lungs. "What have you done to him?" he rasped.

Victor tilted his head. "It's your fault, both of you. If you'd have just made each other miserable, as planned, he would have been fine. But when I heard you were simpering around this place like fucking teenagers, I refused to stand for it." He checked his watch. "I imagine he's probably dead by now. It seems there have been a lot of unexplained fires tonight," he added in mock concern.

Darius barely heard him. By his side, Mrs Weatherby was yelling through her gag, and Paulo had tears slipping down his face. Bartholomew looked like he was devising a way to garotte Victor with a shoestring.

But Darius was too busy reeling as his whole world fell apart. "No," he uttered, aware how feeble he sounded.

Victor rolled his eyes. "Yes," he said impatiently. "Now perhaps you'll start to behave, or I'll pick a few of these to have nasty accidents too." He waved his hand at Darius's staff as he laughed hollowly. "Because it's not like you have any actual friends. Just a sad little gargoyle, hidden away from the world in his tower. And you can stop that snivelling. It's not as if that Bellamy boy ever *actually* saw anything in you. I was very clear in my letters that he do precisely what I say. He handed over that credit card you gave him to one of my loyal associates." He smiled to himself. "At least he served *some* purpose before the end."

Darius blinked. That was too much information to absorb at once.

There had been more than one letter between Victor and Joshua? Darius hadn't known that. Joshua hadn't mentioned anything after the first one. His stomach dropped in horror. *Had* Joshua been faking it? Been in cahoots with Victor, then been punished by him anyway? No, no. Darius couldn't believe that any more than he could believe his dad had finally got access to his mum's inheritance money. Darius had worked so *hard* to protect that! Joshua wouldn't betray him like that, would he?

Joshua couldn't be *dead.*

It was too much. Darius didn't know if he should be losing his shit over Joshua possibly being in danger or possibly betraying him, but Darius was losing his shit either way. The castle was burning and falling down around him, his staff had been attacked, and some fucking arsehole was still holding his puppy hostage.

"You're *insane!*" Darius yelled. "I don't believe a word of it!"

"No, I'm just tired," Victor snapped impatiently. "If people don't listen to me when I know what's best for them, it's not my fault if tragedy strikes. I did what I could, and now I will attempt to straighten out this mess *you've* caused."

He wandered to one side of the room, and inspected a ripped painting. Zeus squeaked and barked, Mrs Weatherby was still shouting through her gag, and in the distance, Darius heard more shouting and things breaking. He hoped Camille was still fending off those brutes or, better yet, had been able to flee to safety.

"This house will be declared a loss," Victor announced, letting out a fake sad sigh. "Unfortunately, you might lose a few members of staff in the blaze. That depends on how well you behave now." He grinned savagely at Darius. "Then you'll come back to live with me and take on a lesser role in the company under my supervision." He tutted and shook his head, glancing at the thug not holding Zeus. "Of course, you'll be doing so from a wheelchair."

The goon yanked one of the dining table's legs off, sending the rest of it crashing to the ground. Several people around Darius yelled and flinched, trying to shuffle on their knees away from the thug as he loomed over them, batting the wooden post against his hand. There was pure violence in his eyes.

Victor sighed again. "Spines are *such* fragile things, aren't they?"

"NO!" someone screamed from out in the hall, making everybody look. But Victor didn't turn around quick enough, as that same someone swung a gardening spade in an arch,

smashing Victor across the face with it and sending him flying across the room.

That someone then held the spade up in both hands to defend himself, pale and panting, but very much alive.

That someone was Joshua.

21

JOSHUA

THE CLOSER THEY GOT TO THE CASTLE, THE SICKER JOSHUA felt. He was either right, and Darius could be in danger, or he was wrong, and he was running back into the arms of a man who had laughed and jeered about him.

After the adrenaline rush of escaping his own burning home, he'd struggled to stay awake during the taxi ride back to Thorncliff. The driver had grumbled a bit about the long journey until Joshua had offered to pay him double. He was taking a big risk that he still had access to his credit card, but he'd deal with that later.

Except, when he checked his wallet, the credit card was gone. *Shit.* Joshua didn't say anything to the grumpy driver. He just had to hope it was either back at the castle or that Darius would pay the taxi fee.

If Darius ever wanted to see him again.

How had everything gone so wrong so fast? Joshua was exhausted and confused. His clothes stank of smoke, and he was still coughing despite all the water he was drinking. Someone – almost certainly Victor – had tried to *kill* him and his dad. Joshua's hands were still shaking, even as they passed through the village, heading up to Thorncliff castle.

He hadn't had much else to do during the journey but replay the events of the house fire and Darius's cold, sneering words from the recording. Had Darius been lying about finding Joshua's virginity a turn-on? Had he been mocking him this whole time? Joshua didn't think he could bear it if that was the truth.

Except...when the taxi pulled up to the castle gates and nothing was working, Joshua got the sinking feeling he'd been right.

Darius was in danger.

And he so wished he'd actually been wrong.

"Is this thing supposed to open for us or...what?" the driver asked impatiently as he jabbed the call button, but the thing was clearly dead.

"Yeah," said Joshua shakily. "It's supposed to. I think something's wrong. Would you mind waiting?"

The driver hissed through his teeth. "I'll give you ten minutes. Then I want to get paid and go home. Understood?"

Joshua swallowed, not caring one jot about money just then. There were strange lights flickering through the windows in the distance, and it looked like the front door might be open. "Oh, yeah," he said distractedly as he hurried out of the car into the rain that had started falling in the last hour.

He went to the gates, leaning on one to try and get a better look at the castle. But they were locked tight. Darius was inside, though, and even after hearing those terrible things, Joshua couldn't waste any time.

He took a breath, his hands trembling in the rain, and began to climb the gate.

Getting up wasn't so bad, but scaling down the other side in the dark and the storm was another matter. Joshua almost slipped and fell a couple of times. But eventually he managed to drop back on to his feet. Then he started running.

His rucksack bounced on his back as the rain soaked into his clothes. Confusion and fear outweighed his earlier sense of betrayal. Who knew why Darius had said what he'd said? Right now, something was definitely wrong in the castle.

That was fire he could see flickering through the windows.

He broke into a full sprint, his unfit legs already burning. *More fire?* Joshua didn't want to leap to conclusions, but it was very difficult to believe that fires both here and at his dad's house could be a coincidence.

It had to be Victor. What the hell was his endgame here? This was way bigger than Joshua had ever imagined. Why the hell hadn't he called the police before he'd come back here and been swallowed up by the damn signal black hole? He hadn't had any idea things would be this bad, that was why. But the front door was open, and from the illumination of the fires raging inside, Joshua could see that several windows had been smashed. There was crap blowing about in the wind, and people were shouting.

Joshua was completely and utterly in over his head. He had absolutely no idea of what was waiting for him on the other side of that door, or what he could possibly do to deal with it. How many people had broken into the castle? And to what end? Were they hoping to kill Darius like they'd undoubtedly been trying to kill Joshua and his dad? And who were 'they'?

It had to be Victor, but Joshua didn't understand how or why. He was a frail old man. He had his wits still, sure, but Joshua didn't see him running around with a lighter, setting the curtains on fire.

Joshua found himself running past the stables. He had the urge to check Hephaestus was okay, so he turned at the last second to fly into the stalls. Sure enough, Darius's faithful steed was snorting and scuffing his hooves noisily against the ground, but he appeared to be fine. No one else was around.

Joshua shrugged off his wet backpack and rubbed the horse's nose to try to calm him. "What's going on, boy?" he whispered.

Hephaestus gave an extra loud snort, curling his lip as he tossed his large head towards the house. He was clearly completely unimpressed with what was going on in there.

That was when Joshua realised Hephaestus had a window at the back of his stall that looked on to the closest wall of the castle. Joshua would be able to get a better look whilst remaining under cover.

If Hephaestus would let him.

"Heph," he said slowly and gently. Then he remembered Paulo's mint trick. Sure enough, after a quick look along the stable shelves, he found a half-finished packet of sugar-free Polos. He got one on his palm and fed it as slowly as he could bear to Hephaestus. "Okay, mate," said Joshua, rubbing his nose again. "Are you going to let me in? I have a feeling Victor is in there, causing trouble."

That was putting it mildly, but he didn't want to waste time going into the nitty-gritty.

He needn't have worried, though. At the mention of Victor's name, Hephaestus whinnied in complete outrage, stomping over to the side of his stall, his head held indignantly high.

"Yeah, I agree," said Joshua as he let himself into the stall. *"Fuck* that guy."

He gasped as he got a better view of what was happening inside the castle. Joshua could see from here into the dining room. There had to be close to a dozen people running around in there, smashing the table, the artwork, the chandelier. What the hell? This wasn't like his dad's house, where someone had just lit a fire. These people were going haywire, trashing everything!

Joshua let out a snarl as he recognised Victor, watching smugly as several huge men fought with Paulo and a couple of the other stable hands and-

Oh!

Darius!

Joshua called his name in horror, but of course Darius couldn't hear him through the glass and over the storm. Panic threatened to overwhelm Joshua. *Darius was in danger! Darius was being hurt!*

But Joshua balled up his fists. Okay. So that just meant it was Joshua's turn to save *Darius*. Of course, he had no idea how, and he wanted to vomit, collapse, and burst into tears. But the facts were clear. He was out here where no one knew, and Darius was in there, outnumbered and being overpowered despite his immense size and strength.

Joshua *had* to do something.

Hephaestus snorted and stomped his feet. Joshua looked at him.

Then he saw the spade that Paulo must have left from mucking out the stalls. It was big and heavy, and had a large, flat head. Good for smacking people away with. It also had sharp edges for doing stabby things to people if anything worse happened to Darius.

With trembling hands, Joshua reached out and picked it up. Could he really hit anyone? He'd never been in a fight in his life. Whenever there'd been a hint of trouble brewing for him growing up, he'd always run.

There was no more running.

He looked up to find Hephaestus watching him. His black eyes were narrowed. He curled his lip, then scuffed his hoof.

Like he was revving his engine.

"Okay," whispered Joshua, mustering all the courage he

possibly could. Darius needed him. There was no time to be scared. "You feel like going and fucking some shit up?"

Hephaestus tossed his head back and whinnied.

There was no going back now.

There was a tack box on the floor, so Joshua used that to stand on. After taking a deep breath, he slung his leg over Hephaestus's back. He didn't have a saddle on, just a rug to help give Joshua some purchase. For a second, he recognised how crazy this plan was. He should try and sneak in and...

Hide?

He'd been hiding his whole life. Besides, anything he'd ever learned in history class about battle and warfare was that height gave you an advantage. That was why the cavalry rode on horseback. He wasn't sure how he was going to hold on to Hephaestus and keep the spade in his hand, but the horse looked over his shoulder, waiting for Joshua's go sign.

He tapped Hephaestus in the flanks with his heels. "Let's go."

Joshua expected him to trot. But Hephaestus whinnied and reared up on his hind legs, barely giving Joshua a chance to grab onto his mane before sliding off his back. Then Hephaestus bolted out of his open stall, his hooves churning up the dry hay as they shot into the rain. Joshua just about managed to cling to the handle of the spade.

"No, Heph!" Joshua cried, trying to pull on his mane to steer him. "We need to go *into* the house." But Hephaestus apparently had other ideas, as he skirted around the barn and headed out back.

Towards Joshua's gardens.

He gasped, tears springing in his eyes as in the light flickering from the castle, he could just make out two men, trampling through the flowerbeds, slashing and crushing everything they came upon.

They were almost at Joshua's rose bushes. And they had shears.

"NO!" Joshua screamed. Not their family roses. They were his and Darius's link to their mums. He wasn't going to let some barbarians chop them up!

He didn't think. All his fear was gone. Hephaestus was still charging as the two men spun around in surprise. So Joshua brought the spade down with a yell, smacking the nearest guy clean in the face, taking him off his feet, and sending him flying several feet away.

He didn't get back up again.

Once more, Hephaestus reared on his hind legs, smashing his hooves into the second vandal, also throwing him to the muddy, rain-soaked ground. For a second, Joshua just stared at them both. Then he let out a laugh, looking down at Darius's horse.

Joshua squeaked. "Did you *see* that?"

Hephaestus nodded and brayed. Joshua assumed that meant he was impressed.

"Come on!" he cried. He tapped Hephaestus's flanks, and steered him back towards the front door. Joshua was glad he'd saved the precious roses, but that wouldn't matter if anything bad happened to Darius.

As they burst through the already open front doors, they might not have been stealthy, but they certainly had the element of surprise. One of Victor's thugs froze, his arms full of books, planning to do god knew what with them. Rage consumed Joshua. Darius *loved* his library!

Hephaestus skidded to a halt, giving Joshua the chance to swing the slippery spade handle again. But it was easier now he'd already done it once and knew how effective it could be. The thief, on the other hand, had probably not been expecting a bloke riding a horse to smack him with a shovel, making Joshua's job a whole lot easier as the goon just stood there with his mouth open until Joshua cracked him over the head and knocked him out.

There was no time for Joshua to get cocky, though. He was dripping wet, the spade was getting heavy, and his thighs were burning from clinging on to Hephaestus's sides. There was a yell as another couple of goons came running from the right, just as a wild-looking girl entered from the left. Joshua gasped, almost falling off Hephaestus as he jerked back from the assault on both sides. But the guys just kept running, making a beeline for the front door. Joshua understood why a second later when Camille came charging after them, huffing and snarling with a bleeding lip, brandishing a meat cleaver.

"And STAY out!" she screeched, waving the knife over her head. She blinked as she caught sight of Joshua. "Skinny boy! You came back! Oh. Excuse me."

The wild-looking girl twitched as both Joshua and Camille turned their attention back to her. Joshua had honestly been so perplexed by her appearance he hadn't even noticed that she was carrying a petrol can and absolutely stank of the stuff. When she realised they were looking her way, she giggled, sloshed some more liquid out, then dropped the can, and ran for the door. Camille puffed out her cheeks, then gave chase.

"I will make sure zey've all gone. Go! Find your man!"

She vanished out into the rain, leaving Joshua sat alone on the back of a horse, clutching on to a spade for dear life, whilst a number of things around him merrily burned. "Right," he said out loud, coughing as more smoke crept into his lungs. "Okay, then."

Wishing he could harness the rainwater (for both the fires and his throat), Joshua slid down from Hephaestus's back. All was quiet now from the direction of the kitchen, but there was a hell of a lot of noise coming from the left.

The dining room.

Joshua could hear the rumble of voices, but to his surprise, no one was shouting. *Fuck.* What the hell was he walking into? He expected Darius to be tearing the house down and fighting those thugs Joshua had seen wrestling him to the ground. At the very least, screaming at his father. Why was it so quiet?

Was Joshua going down there to rescue Darius...or sign his own fate as the Legrands plotted his demise together?

No. Camille obviously thought Darius wasn't to blame here or at fault. She wouldn't have told Joshua to go find him otherwise. And through the window Joshua had seen Darius fighting off those thugs, too. There was every chance they were still on the same side against Victor. Joshua didn't know why there was a mob destroying his home and setting fires, who sent that awful voicemail, or why Darius would have said such hurtful things about him, but he *did* know that he loved Darius. Whether that was foolish or not, he was probably about to find out.

So he wrapped his fingers around the damp handle of the spade and squeezed them tight. "Will you be okay out here?" he whispered to Hephaestus.

The horse tossed his mane and raised his chin.

Joshua managed a shaky grin. "I knew I could count on you. If you see anyone you don't know, kick them."

Hephaestus snorted and trotted on the spot. Joshua kind of got the feeling that he'd quite enjoy that.

Joshua counted back from five, breathing in deeply, then dashed as quietly as he could down the corridor, heading for the dining room. *Holy shit.* Anything that could burn was on fire. The paintings were slashed, the vases were smashed, and the mirrors were cracked. These arseholes had gone through deliberately trashing *everything*. Joshua wanted to cry, feeling like he'd never appreciated any of the antiques like he promised himself he would.

Then he finally heard a voice clearly enough to pick out the words.

And his blood ran cold.

"Now perhaps you'll start to behave, or I'll pick a few of these to have nasty accidents too." Victor laughed, a horrid, chilling sound. Who was he talking about? "Because it's not like you have any actual friends. Just a sad little gargoyle, hidden away from the world in his tower. And you can stop that snivelling. It's not as if that Bellamy boy ever *actually* saw anything in you. I was very clear in my letters that he do precisely what I say. He handed over that credit card you gave him to one of my loyal associates." He smiled to himself. "At least he served *some* purpose before the end."

Joshua almost tripped over his own feet at the sound of his own name. He clutched the spade to his chest. What did Victor mean by 'before the end'? And 'credit card' – the one that had gone missing from Joshua's wallet? Well, whatever he was babbling on about, one thing was for certain.

Joshua *absolutely* saw something in Darius.

He saw everything. His future, his whole life.

His love.

"You're *insane!*" Darius yelled. "I don't believe a word of it!" His voice was hoarse, but Joshua didn't care. Any voice was good. It meant Darius was still awake, still fighting.

Still alive.

There was more talking from the dining room, more bickering back and forth, but Joshua was distracted as down in the entrance hall, there was a clattering. It seemed one of Victor's goons had thought he'd try his luck back in the castle rather than out in the night. But he hadn't counted on meeting with a four-hoofed security system nor on being followed by a sleep-deprived, underappreciated French cook with a meat cleaver, who came screaming in from the rain after him.

Once Joshua was sure that Camille and Hephaestus had chased the thug off in the opposite direction, he crept closer to the dining room door.

"This house will be declared a loss," Joshua heard Victor announce in mock sadness. "Unfortunately, you might lose a few members of staff in the blaze." His tone changed to clear malice, and Joshua had to dash the last few steps and press himself up against the wall as close as he could to listen without being seen. "That depends on how well you behave now. Then you'll come back to live with me and take on a lesser role in the company under my supervision."

Joshua felt sick. Victor was going to try and burn Thorncliff down, just like he'd tried to do with Joshua's dad's house? And holy fuck, he wasn't seriously threatening to hurt or kill some of the staff in the process, was he?

Of course he was.

Joshua shook with rage. Victor was fucking with *everyone's* lives. Was this all really because all those years ago, Joshua's mum had refused to let Victor fool around with her and cheat on Darius's mum? All this destruction because Victor couldn't deal with the fact that he'd been told 'no'?

Joshua had to do something, had to stop this. But he had no idea how.

Then Victor spoke again.

"Of course, you'll be doing so from a wheelchair."

For a split second, Joshua couldn't make sense of the words, other than they sounded really, *really* bad.

Then there was an almighty crash, like something had fallen off the ceiling, and Joshua couldn't take it. He *had* to sneak a peek.

A big thug in a grey hoodie had honest to god ripped one of the legs off the dining room table, which had been smashed up pretty good. He batted it into his palm, like a cricketer would his bat, if that cricketer had turned to a life of crime and was about to commit assault.

Every muscle in Joshua's body tensed.

Victor sighed again. "Spines are *such* fragile things, aren't they?"

Joshua wasn't sure what happened next other than his feet seemed to move of their own accord, and any fear that had been holding him back morphed into pure, crazy rage. *"NO!"* he screamed, lurching into the dining room and swinging the gardening spade with all he had. It connected with Victor's face, sending a stomach-wrenching *crack* through the air, but Joshua didn't care if it broke his jaw or not. *Evil bastard.*

He stood and gripped the spade in both hands, trembling as he took a second to absorb the scene.

There were two yobs: one with the table leg, the other holding Zeus up by the scruff of his neck.

Several staff members bound, gagged, and bleeding on their knees.

Victor groaning on the floor, curling into a foetal position as he touched his smashed-up face.

And in the middle of them all, his hulking form rising and falling with every panting breath, his face covered in blood, and his beautiful blue eyes wide, was Darius.

Joshua met his gaze, feeling like his heart was going to explode in his chest at seeing him like that. He looked like a caged wild animal, punished for fighting his captors.

"You're alive," Darius croaked, his relief palatable.

Joshua didn't get a chance to reply. In the couple of seconds it had taken him to strike Victor and look at Darius, the two thugs regained their wits. The smaller one with the table leg roared, suddenly bringing it up to swing at Joshua. Joshua only just raised the spade in time to block the blow, but the same trick wouldn't work twice. Joshua scrambled backwards, aware of the fires to his back and how much the dining room stank of petrol.

The other bigger guy dropped Zeus, the poor puppy yelping as he landed back on the floor. Then the goon rushed to try and grab Joshua.

There was absolutely no way he could fend even one of them off, let alone both. Joshua tried swinging with his spade nonetheless, determined to go down fighting. But the smaller thug met his blow with the table leg, and his brute force was more than enough to send Joshua tumbling backwards, landing painfully onto his arse. The spade bounced from his grip, and the goons advanced on him too fast for him to try and pick it up again. He was left with no choice but to scramble backwards.

"Joshua!" Darius yelled, but Joshua couldn't see him between the thugs' legs and the smoke from the fires. The bigger one pulled back his fist, ready to smash Joshua in the face. So he cried out, flinging his arms up to protect himself.

It was no good, though. He was going to get a beating, and then who knew what after that.

Was Victor going to have him killed after all, right here in front of Darius?

One thought flashed crystal clear through Joshua's mind as he waited for the blow to land:

He'd never told Darius he loved him.

And now it was too late.

22

DARIUS

EVERYTHING ALL HAPPENED AT ONCE.

In the moment that Darius realised Joshua was still alive, time slowed down so it almost stopped. But then Darius had quickly grasped that just because Joshua was here and unharmed right now, it didn't mean he was going to stay that way. The roar of one of his father's goons brought time back to its rightful pace, all the sound that had dimmed rushing once more into Darius's ears, shocking him back to reality.

He gasped as the thug swung the table leg in his hand. The other thug dropped Zeus and lunged as well. Victor moaned and whimpered in the corner of the trashed room, clutching his bloody face.

Joshua had done that.

Sweet, timid Joshua had taken a fucking garden spade to Victor's sneering face, smacking his arrogance clean away.

Pride fuelled Darius as much as his rage. His precious love had come back for him, risking his own safety. Now the yobs were advancing on him, shoving him to the ground, where Joshua lost his only defence as he dropped the spade in shock and it clattered on the stone.

"Joshua!" Darius screamed. He could just see between the thugs' legs as Joshua scrambled backwards through the smoke. How bad were the fires out in the hall? How long did they have before this whole room went up like a petrol bomb?

Darius's staff were all yelling and squirming beside him, but a touch to his leg jolted Darius to look down at Zeus. He pawed at Darius's leg, whimpering with his ears flattened to the back of his head in distress.

Next to Zeus was part of a photo frame, the glass shard sticking upwards.

Not pausing one second to consider the pain, Darius moved so he could slam his hands either side of the glass, slicing through the plastic bind as well as against his left palm. But that didn't matter. All that mattered was that the bastard who had threatened Zeus had just pulled his arm back, his fist clenched, ready to punch tiny Joshua in the face. Joshua yelled, throwing his arms up to protect himself.

But he had Darius now.

His vision clouded by a red mist, Darius flung himself off the floor, seizing the larger thug before he could touch Joshua. Darius swung him around, then landed a double punch in the brute's stomach and on his face. The smaller thug obviously abandoned his assault on Joshua as he snuck in a hit against Darius's ribs. But by this point, Darius felt like his whole body was made of pain, and he barely noticed. Fury was moving Darius's limbs seemingly of their own accord as he thrashed, slamming his fists into that guy's face, then once more against the first goon.

To his surprise, the spade head came arching into view again, hitting the smaller thug over the back of his head. Joshua had scrambled back up but, instead of running, had kept on fighting.

Darius thought he might burst with love.

They weren't safe yet, though, not by a long shot. Darius was still trading blows with the larger thug, and from the sudden roar of flames out in the corridor, he was going to guess that the fire was rushing closer to them.

But he managed to grab the bigger goon and smash him into one of the walls, then throw him to the ground, where he slid several feet into the wrecked dining table. Joshua was just about managing to beat the other guy back, but when Darius turned and also landed a punch, the thug staggered backwards onto his arse, shaking his head and visibly trying to regroup. With a leap in his chest, Darius realised Mrs Weatherby had copied him with the glass. It took her longer, but eventually she freed herself from the plastic tie and gag before helping some of the others.

He almost felt a surge of hope.

Almost.

The laughter started so quietly that it took Darius a second to identify what the sound even was. "Beauty and brawn, but not a brain cell between you."

Victor continued laughing as he got shakily back to his feet, wiping his bloody face. The two thugs were also standing up again, but most of Darius's staff had freed themselves with the glass shard now. Paulo had picked up a discarded crowbar and Mrs Weatherby was ushering the rest of the staff towards the broken windows. Zeus was barking non-stop, his little tail tucked between his legs as he ran around Bartholomew's feet. Bartholomew himself straightened his tie and stood in front of the pup, picking up a chair to hold like a lion tamer.

Darius moved to stand shoulder to shoulder with Joshua. All he wanted to do was scoop him up in his arms and shield him from this horror. But that wasn't possible, so Darius raised his bloody fists instead and glared at his miserable excuse for a father, wishing he'd thought to

THORN IN HIS SIDE

knock him out before Victor's thugs had regrouped around him.

Victor pulled a handkerchief from his breast pocket to wipe his face mostly clean of blood. "Yet again, I find myself asking what you hope to achieve here? You are still outnumbered, and it won't be long before fire consumes this thoroughly uninspiring place. I told you to behave. Now you will face the consequences."

"Are you sure about that?" Joshua asked.

Darius turned to look down at him incredulously. His tone was light, and sure enough, he was grinning as he fixed Victor with a blazing stare.

Then Darius heard it.

A siren.

Victor's expression dropped immediately as the sound drifted clearly through the broken window, being carried in on the gusts of wind from the storm. It wasn't just one. Very quickly, Darius could pick out several different sirens wailing, and he shifted to try and look down the driveway. His view was mostly facing the wrong way, but more and more blue and red lights were bouncing off the rain-soaked stable outside of the dining room window.

He didn't know how, but the emergency services were almost on top of them.

"*Fuck,*" the larger goon shouted. Without a moment's hesitation, he dashed toward the broken window, and smashed more of the glass so he could throw himself out of it.

Victor spluttered. "Get *back* here!" he roared, his fists balled at his sides. But the smaller thug was already shoving his way past the remains of the dining table to do the same, following his comrade into the blustery night.

A woman's screech from the hall caught Darius's attention. He and Joshua whipped their heads to look through the doorway. The unmistakable *'whooshing'* sound of a fire extinguisher being deployed rushed to greet them, just before Camille came charging into view. She brandished the thing like a battering ram.

"Have you English *no* respect!" she bellowed in her guttural accent, even stronger than usual. "Get *out* of our 'ouse!"

Darius couldn't agree more.

He inhaled through his nostrils, turning and storming across the room towards his father. He grabbed him by the scruff of his shirt and hauled him a few inches off the floor.

"No, wait!" Victor shrieked, throwing up his hands. "Please! You don't know what you're doing! Let me *go!*"

But Darius was so fucking done being cowed by the man who had bullied and controlled him his whole life. "You will *never* set foot in this house again," Darius growled, the sound of the sirens blaring over the pouring rain. He could hear shouts down from the entrance hall, and...was that the sound of a *horse?*

It didn't matter. Whatever was going on down in the entrance hall, Darius knew one thing. It was over.

Of course, Victor wouldn't accept that. He went from cowering pensioner to rabid animal in a flash, baring his teeth at Darius and pulling at his wrists and slashing at his eyes. Darius jerked his head back impatiently.

"You just *wait* until you hear from my lawyers," Victor snarled.

Darius laughed hollowly and dropped him back on his feet again. "I can't wait," he muttered as Victor stumbled but managed to stay upright. Darius turned his back on the old man, not caring enough to see or hear his response. Instead, he marched straight back over to Joshua and flung his arms around him.

"I love you," he said before anything else could happen.

THORN IN HIS SIDE

Before the police could come and make their arrests or take their statements. Before the fire brigade could douse everything with water. Before a very long night got even longer. Darius had to make sure Joshua knew that Darius loved him.

It didn't matter that Joshua didn't say it back. There was too much going on. Darius's staff and emergency forces were shouting and starting to rush either in or out of the room. Victor looked like he considered making a run for it out of the window, but then he clasped his hands behind his back and lifted his head, no doubt preparing to negotiate with the police.

Darius wasn't concerned, not really. There were enough witnesses here to attest to what had happened. He also suspected that where possible, all Victor's cronies might have done as the two thugs here had, and made a run for it.

Victor was all alone. This was where all his plans and schemes had got him. Nowhere, with no one.

Of course, there was always a chance he could try and weasel his way out of this, but Darius wasn't going to waste energy worrying about that now.

His only concern was Joshua.

Darius wasn't going to let any harm come to him again, not that night, not ever. He was back in Darius's arms, where he belonged, each other's to protect.

At least, so he hoped.

PEOPLE WERE FLITTING AROUND like worker bees, but Darius just sat on the more or less intact armchair with Joshua across his lap, cuddled up as close as he could be, the blanket pulled tight around them both. Zeus was asleep at their feet, his heroics having tired him out.

The fires were all out. In the end, they hadn't spread too far, although the smoke damage would be substantial. The vandalism was much, *much* worse, but Darius would have time to mourn the castle's losses later. For now, all the people were okay, and everything else could be fixed or replaced.

Darius sighed. The night had been even more traumatic than he'd first appreciated. Christopher Bellamy's house had also been targeted by one of his father's arsonists, and Joshua had only just got them both out alive. When Joshua had figured out that Victor's schemes wouldn't end there, he'd jumped straight in a taxi to head back to Thorncliff. It was that driver who had called the police, making his way back to the village to find signal to report Joshua for not paying his fair, of all things. Luckily, he'd also mentioned that there seemed to be some funny business going on at the castle as well, meaning the police had sent more than just one unit and the fire brigade had followed shortly after.

Darius had personally gone out to pay the driver double what he was owed, and thanked him for saving his life. The cabbie only seemed interested in grumbling about his wasted time as he'd snatched the cash Darius offered without even saying thank you. Darius had to laugh. Some people.

He and Joshua were in the nursery where hardly any damage had taken place. Darius could see the dozens of emergency service workers racing back and forth in the hallway. The paramedics had taken their time fussing over them, which Darius appreciated, but now that the police had taken his and Joshua's statements, the first responders were busy doing other things and had no need of the two of them.

Darius had sent his staff home and told them they could take a week off, but there had been a general murmur of outrage at the suggestion. Once the police and fire brigade were done with their evidence collecting and photographs for the investigation, Mrs Weatherby informed Darius that they would all be back, as well as the day staff, ready to start tidying and repairs.

This was their home.

Darius had felt his throat get a bit tight at that. It had been tempting to blame his exhaustion, but that wasn't it. This *was* their home.

A lot of languages, including the French Darius had been forced to learn when he was younger, didn't have different words for house and home, but the difference was vast. He felt like maybe he was finally beginning to truly understand what it was like to feel home was a place not only where you laid your hat, but where your heart was.

His heart was most certainly here, with Joshua, and a lot of people he was starting to appreciate as far more than staff.

They were family.

It was so late in the night it was creeping into early morning. Joshua was heavy on his lap, possibly already asleep. Darius rested his cheek on Joshua's head. Despite the potent wafts of smoke and sweat coming from his hair and clothes, Joshua still smelled like wood and earth. He smelled like *him.*

Darius inhaled deeply.

He knew what he'd said in the chaos, but it hadn't been a result of fear or panic. That might have been why the words had been uttered, but Darius knew how he felt regardless.

He loved Joshua with his whole heart.

"Did you mean it?" Joshua asked in a small voice, almost as if he could read Darius's thoughts. Obviously, he wasn't asleep. He shuddered and gripped onto Darius's ripped and grubby jumper, his head buried against Darius's neck.

Darius's heart pounded. "Mean what?" he asked, just to be sure.

Joshua shifted on his lap and sniffed. His head was still

resting on Darius's shoulder, so Darius couldn't see his expression.

Joshua gave a shaky sigh. "My dad got a voicemail. You said I was annoying." He paused to swallow, and Darius really didn't like the way he shivered. "You said you fucked me until I cried."

Ice ran down Darius's spine. "I would never-" he began vehemently. But then he stopped. "Ah." Of course his father had been recording that delightful exchange.

Joshua lifted his head, his big brown eyes wide and full of trepidation. "Ah?" he whispered.

Darius wanted to stroke his hair and kiss his forehead to comfort him, but he needed to try and make Joshua understand first. "Do you remember when my father came to visit and I was pissed off for days?"

Joshua chewed his lip. "Yes. That's when Bartholomew and Mrs Weatherby explained about Athena."

Darius nodded and reached down to stroke Zeus's fur. He'd always suspected that one of his loyal staff had told Joshua that story and prompted him to get Zeus. "Victor asked about you that day, testing me."

"Oh," said Joshua sadly. He looked down and fiddled with a fraying thread on his sleeve. "That was before...before anything happened between...uh...us?"

Darius gently touched his chin, his heart leaping when Joshua looked back at him without Darius even moving Joshua's head. He loved that Joshua trusted him enough now to know that was what Darius wanted when he touched his chin. For them to look at one another and not hold back.

To not have any secrets.

There was no time for being coy now. Darius nodded and rubbed Joshua's side. "Before we were intimate. Yes. I already knew I loved you, even then. So I said the vilest things I could think of to throw my father off the scent. If he knew

THORN IN HIS SIDE

how dear you were – *are* – to me, I was afraid he'd hurt you."
He barely contained his sneer as he looked away, so ashamed
to be related to such a monster. "I guess I was right."

To his immense surprise, he felt Joshua touch his chin,
encouraging him to turn his head back and look at him. He
cupped the side of Darius's face. "You love me?"

Darius swallowed. Joshua still sounded sad, but Darius
was going to be nothing but honest with him from now on.
"With everything I am. I swear on my life that I didn't mean a
word of-"

Joshua's mouth crashed onto his, kissing him deeply,
desperately. Then he rested their foreheads together and
took a deep breath. "I believe you. I don't know if that makes
me a fool, but I don't care. I…I love you, too."

Tears threatened to prickle at the back of Darius's eyes.
"Yeah?" he rasped, his throat thick with emotion.

Joshua kissed him sweetly, then gazed into his eyes with
his delicate hands holding either side of Darius's face. "With
everything I am."

Darius felt a wave of shame and anger, though, spoiling
their amazing moment. "Even after what my father did?"

Victor had been quickly arrested earlier. The police
officers who had been first on the scene had been
bombarded with raised voices and pointed fingers from irate
staff. Rather than fight them, Victor had agreed to go quietly,
but Darius was sure he had a plan to contest the accusations.
Victor Legrand would never go down without a fight, but
Darius hoped that in the end, they would be triumphant.

Joshua looked sadly at him. "You're not your dad. I was so
scared when I heard that recording, but I knew deep down
you'd never hurt me."

Darius kissed him with all the strength he had left, which
wasn't much, considering all they'd been through. But it was
still a pretty damn passionate embrace. He cupped his hand

to Joshua's jaw and caressed his cheek with his thumb. *"Never,"* he rasped. "You're mine, my beautiful petal. I'll protect you until the day I die."

Joshua sniffed and hiccuped, so Darius cradled him close and allowed him to cry it out for a while. Joshua had been through so much and was beyond tired – they both were. All Darius wanted to do was take him to bed, but they had to hold on until the police had finished all their initial examinations.

So Darius was content to wait, knowing everything was in hand and his Joshua was in his arms. "Try and sleep, beautiful," he murmured when Joshua's crying eased off.

In the relative quiet, Darius was able to let his thoughts percolate and finally make sense of all the madness. There was a lot to go through.

The most remarkable part of the evening had been when Darius had discovered that Joshua had seriously ridden Hephaestus into battle, taking out several of Victor's goons with his trusty spade. Heph had then gone on to hold down the fort quite admirably, even going so far as trying to keep the police out as well. A stranger was a stranger as far as he was concerned, apparently.

Paulo had fed Heph a pound of carrots, Darius was sure, whilst Darius had rested his head against his neck and told him he was the best damn horse in the whole of the United Kingdom. Hephaestus had snorted and tossed his head back as if to say 'I know! Now can't I eat these carrots in peace?'

Darius laughed, safe in the knowledge that the stables hadn't been touched and his beloved horse was tucked in for the night, courtesy of Paulo. None of his staff had suffered anything more than minor injuries, although they were bound to be quite rattled. He would support them any way he could in easing their return to work and life at the castle.

What gave Darius the most comfort was knowing that his

father was in police custody where he should have been years ago, and Joshua was wrapped up in Darius's arms where nothing else could hurt him. Joshua had explained to Darius the story Christopher had relayed to him, and finally some of Darius's life's mysteries were starting to fall unpleasantly into place. *That* was why Victor had been so nasty about Darius's mum's illness and passing. He was still furious about losing Claire Bellamy, even though she'd never been his in the first place, and taken that out on the wife he apparently hadn't wanted.

Darius worried that would drive a wedge between him and Joshua, but Joshua had insisted that it was nothing to do with Darius. The sins of his father were not his to inherit.

Darius wasn't sure what he'd done to deserve such an incredible husband, but he was going to work hard every day from now on to prove that he was worth such kindness and understanding.

He let Joshua sleep, curled up on his lap. Even with putting a few pounds on, he still hardly weighed a thing to Darius.

It wasn't that Darius wasn't tired, but he'd learned a few tricks during his time in the army on how to stay awake. The police detectives would need to speak to him before the emergency services left, so he passed the next hour memorising the VHS film and TV collection Joshua had been watching and organising here in this room. Darius liked that Joshua had made himself comfortable in here, but Darius could do better for him, he was sure.

He began to mentally plan the refurbishment of the castle, which was more interesting than reciting film titles. Now alert and excited, Darius thought about making a proper living room with a massive telly and corner sofa for him and Joshua. He could replace the destroyed art with more modern pieces, things the two of them could pick out together. He'd never understood the expression 'house proud' before, but it was starting to make sense.

He could modernise the kitchen for Camille and give Mrs Weatherby a proper office. The staff quarters were long overdue for a refurbishment. He could even finally restore the library for Bartholomew. And himself. God, he hoped none of his books had been damaged in the ransacking.

He shook his head. None of that mattered. Everything could be replaced. And he'd enjoy doing so. Maybe this pile of old bricks would feel like a home for the first time. Now that he no longer feared his father stealing away his mother's inheritance, he felt confident on finally investing money in Thorncliff. No matter what Victor said, the property *was* in Darius's name, and he'd be in touch with lawyers in the morning to make that bulletproof.

Apparently, along with making that recording of Darius, Martin had also attempted to steal Joshua's credit card that Darius had given him. But the police had nabbed him whilst he'd been attempting to flee the scene, and he'd confessed, giving up the card and offering to dish any dirt on Victor the police wanted in exchange for leniency. Darius was pretty unimpressed by his snivelling lack of backbone, but honestly, none of that mattered. He knew Joshua wouldn't give Victor access to Darius's funds, and he never should have doubted him.

It seemed Victor had told a hell of a lot of lies to Darius and Joshua about each other. But now he was gone, and they would be free to live in peace.

Thorncliff was their home, and Darius was going to start treating it like that, starting immediately. He could modernise the technologies and sort the heating and perhaps even dig that moat he'd been grumbling about for so long.

Or at least give Joshua his pond. Darius sighed and kissed his lover's hair. Although a lot of his newly planted flowers had been stomped on, Joshua had saved their rose bushes, and the seeds under the dirt would all mostly be safe. Joshua would be able to continue with his work with only a few small setbacks.

Hopefully, he'd be tending to those gardens for many years to come.

"Excuse me, Mr Legrand?" The detective knocked softly on the door and poked his head in. "We're all done and will be getting out of your hair for now. I'll come back tomorrow afternoon, though, with a smaller team. But I thought you might like to get some sleep."

Darius tried not to be too visibly relieved. He didn't want the guy thinking Darius was ungrateful, but he was extremely eager to kick everyone out. "Thank you, yes," he said with a nod.

The detective nodded back and rubbed his stubbly chin. "I've stationed a fresh unit outside your gates. We managed to apprehend a number of the fleeing suspects in the village as well as those we caught trespassing on your premises. I hope you won't have any more trouble, but you and your husband should remain vigilant."

Darius was amazed that he didn't puff out with pride. His *husband*. To hear a grizzly man in his sixties say that without even batting an eyelid was an incredible feeling. For the first time in his adult life, he felt truly 'normal' and free of his father's disgust.

"We will," Darius promised as the detective saw himself out. With the staff either sent home or put up in a hotel for the night, it would just be Darius, Joshua, Zeus, and Hephaestus for a few hours.

Darius intended to make the most of it.

23

JOSHUA

JOSHUA SLOWLY SURFACED TO A GENTLE SQUEEZE OF HIS shoulder. "Beautiful," Darius murmured, brushing his knuckles against Joshua's cheek. His big arms were cradling Joshua to his chest.

"I fell asleep," Joshua mumbled with a frown, his tone indicating that it was an apology.

But Darius shook his head. "It's okay. I told you to, remember?"

Joshua blinked as he looked up at him. He was groggy in a way that made his bones feel like lead and his brain like porridge. He ran his tongue over his teeth and rubbed grit from his eyes. What had happened came back to him pretty quickly, so it wasn't like he was shocked. But his body was still thrumming with adrenaline and exhaustion.

"I think I need a cup of tea." He frowned and looked around the nursery where they'd been sitting. "Or red wine."

Darius chuckled and pressed his lips to Joshua's head. "Tea it is. Come on." He encouraged Joshua to get to his feet, then groaned as he stood up, stretching out his arms with a grimace.

"Was I very heavy?" Joshua fretted.

That earned him another laugh. "Light as a bird," Darius assured him with a kiss to his cheek. "Everyone's gone. It's just us and the pup. Heph is sleeping outside."

Joshua glanced down at Zeus, dead to the world on his back with his tongue lolling out. Normally they'd let him roam where he wanted during the night, but that didn't feel right now, not just because Joshua felt like keeping him close. "There's glass everywhere," Joshua said. "We shouldn't leave him alone."

Then he stopped, feeling like his brain was finally catching up. The place still smelled of smoke, unsurprisingly, and although Joshua couldn't detect petrol from where they were, it had still been splashed everywhere.

"Everyone's gone? Then why are we still here? Isn't it dangerous with all the damage and smashed windows? Darius, what if they come back?"

"Hey, shh." Darius hugged him and rubbed his back soothingly. "The police are still outside. They said it's okay to stay if we really wanted to and we stay out of the cordoned-off areas. I desperately wanted to be in our bed tonight, with you. To prove this nightmare is over. But if you want to go to a hotel-"

"No," Joshua interrupted. He squeezed his eyes shut and hugged Darius fiercely. "Oh, god. I know it was awful, but I'm so glad to be home. I thought I wouldn't…that you…" He swallowed, unable to voice his fears again. "But it's okay. Everything's okay, isn't it?"

Darius cradled his face and kissed him softly. Then he gazed at Joshua, his blue eyes wide with sympathy. "I really, really hope so. It certainly is as far as I'm concerned. We're together. The house is still standing – mostly." They both laughed ruefully, the sound odd in the eerie quiet. "I just want to fall asleep, holding you, and put this horror story behind us."

Joshua sighed. "That sounds nice," he said. He was still nervous about being in the castle after the mob attack, but Darius was right. After so many frights, he just wanted to be at *home*. They belonged in their bed, together. "Tea?"

Darius chuckled. "Tea," he agreed.

Joshua kissed Darius's chest through his tatty jumper, then crouched down and scooped up the surprisingly heavy puppy in his arms.

"I can take him," Darius protested.

Joshua scowled at him. "No, you can't," he said firmly, a wave of protectiveness washing through him so strongly that his throat clamped.

Darius blinked, then looked down at his raw wrists and the cut on his palm that the paramedics had cleaned and dressed. Luckily, Darius hadn't needed stitches, but he was still sore. Joshua's stomach flipped over at the idea that Darius was fighting his binds so hard that he'd cut through his tough skin.

So, no. It didn't matter that Zeus was heavier than he looked when he was conked out. Joshua would carry him and keep him safe.

Like Darius had kept him safe.

Earlier, Joshua had asked one of the police officers to contact his dad so he'd know that Joshua was safe. In the morning, Joshua would travel into the village because he could *do* that now. He was free, no longer a prisoner in his own home.

And with that scumbag Martin out of the picture, maybe they could finally get internet installed, truly reconnecting them to the world.

In the meantime, Joshua would go to the village tomorrow to find a signal and call his dad himself. He'd explain everything that had happened with Darius and the voicemail, to assuage his fears that Darius was a monster just like Victor. But for now, at least, Joshua could sleep easy, knowing that his dad was safe and didn't have to worry about Joshua.

Joshua refused to dwell on what might have happened, on how much worse it could have been. Because otherwise, it would paralyse him. The only thing that mattered was that they were here and they were okay.

They were more than okay.

Joshua bit his lip and felt the corner of his mouth twitch in half a smile.

He hadn't known wretchedness like when he'd been torn up worrying over that voicemail. He'd clung to the hope that Darius would have an explanation, and he had. There was a small voice in the back of his head which had tried to nag him that Darius could have still been playing him – but to what end? Joshua had seen with his own eyes the way Darius had fought to protect him from that mob. And not just Joshua. Zeus, the staff, even Hephaestus, which was kind of hilarious in the cold light of day because Hephaestus had broken the ribs of three separate hooligans and knocked another clean out whilst he'd been holding down the fort.

The point was Joshua hadn't seen anything that had really surprised him. He knew what kind of man Darius was. It just felt such a relief to have his doubts shoved so cleanly from his mind.

This was where he belonged. He was home.

They headed down to the kitchen, picking their way around the debris and devastation. It was heart-wrenching seeing everything wet from the fire brigade's hoses and broken by the mob. But Darius was right. It was *mostly* still standing. They could rebuild – and they would.

Zeus barely stirred as Joshua laid him on a clean bit of

counter in the kitchen. It felt creepy without another soul in the house as they boiled the kettle and made mugs of tea. The place was a horrible mess, to put it mildly. Joshua almost got upset, looking at the smashed-up equipment. He'd found so much comfort in this room over the past couple of months.

And he would again, he told himself sternly as he sipped his especially sugary tea. Yes, their home had been violated and Joshua was dealing with the double blow of the fire in his dad's place earlier as well, but it was all just stuff. It could be rebuilt and replaced. He breathed deeply and leaned against Darius's side, unable to fully articulate the joy he felt when Darius automatically moved his arm around and hugged him tightly.

"Thank you," Joshua said.

Darius kissed the top of his head. "For what?"

Joshua gave a one-shoulder shrug. "Everything," he said, not really able to be more specific. He sipped his tea. "Thank you for loving me," was the best he could do.

Darius placed his mug down and enveloped Joshua in his big strong arms from behind so Joshua didn't spill his tea. "That was the easy part, petal."

Joshua melted inside. How afraid had he been that he wouldn't hear Darius call him that again.

"Can we go to bed?" Joshua asked in a whisper. He didn't mean anything frisky by it. He just needed to know that he was safe and that Darius was next to him.

"Of course," Darius murmured. "But finish your tea first."

Joshua chuckled and did as he was told, feeling a renewed energy from the brew. He sighed and licked the last droplet from the rim of the mug. Despite his exhaustion, he didn't miss the lustful gaze from Darius at him using his tongue like that.

Joshua grinned and waggled his cup. "You imagining this as something else?" he asked playfully.

Darius's eyes were dark as they swept up and down Joshua's body. "Let's head upstairs, shall we?"

He guided Joshua with his hand on the small of his back. Joshua cradled Zeus to his chest, his heart panging as the small puppy twitched his paws and growled softly in his sleep. Once they were back in Darius's living room, Joshua placed the little dog in his basket, then with a sudden realisation, he gasped and ran to the bedroom.

He'd stopped sleeping with his mum's memory book under his pillow. With all the love-making, there was too much chance of it being knocked off the bed. But Joshua had put it in the drawer of his bedside cabinet. He rushed to retrieve it, and hugged it to his chest to prove that it was unscathed by the ransacking. He let out a little sob as he rubbed the spine. There were certain things that just couldn't be replaced, and although they weren't as precious as anyone's life, he was thoroughly relieved his most tangible link back to his mum was okay.

Darius came and stood beside him, stroking his back. "The first thing I did when we walked in here was check my mother's photo was okay." He laughed. "Maybe now I'll take the time to get a copy made."

Joshua nodded eagerly. "Let's make some photo albums," he said, smiling and rubbing away the few tears that had spilled in his relief. "Of both our mums. We can do it together. Then we can make sure all our favourite photos are safe in digital as well as in nice books, and it might be a nice way for us to talk to each other about them."

Darius smiled fondly at him and leaned down to kiss his forehead. "Like how you talk to them when you clip the roses?"

Joshua blushed and placed his memory book back in its drawer. "You know about that, huh?" he asked as he cuddled Darius's front. He almost hid his face in embarrassment, unsure of how Darius would feel about him talking with Maree. Did he feel it was overstepping a mark? But all Joshua's fears dissolved as Darius beamed down at him.

He nodded. "She would have loved you dearly," said Darius. "I have no doubt that wherever she is now, she and your mum are *so* proud of the man you've become."

A lump rose in Joshua's throat. "Thank you," he said thickly. "My mum would have definitely loved you, too."

Darius pulled his mouth to one side and ran his fingers through Joshua's hair. "And your dad?"

Joshua inhaled before nodding. "He doesn't know you yet. He only knows Victor, and I can't blame him for being wary of that. He'll come around."

"I hope so," said Darius sadly.

But Joshua shook his head determinedly. "You're a *catch,* Darius Legrand," he said firmly.

Darius laughed and pressed a sweet kiss to Joshua's lips. "As are you, Joshua Bellamy."

Joshua shifted on his feet. Only a few hours ago, he'd been made to question if his whole relationship with Darius had been a lie. But now he knew it wasn't, that, in fact, they had the kind of love fairy tales were made of, and he was going to stick to his promise to himself of being brave.

After all, he had nothing to be afraid of. Not with Darius.

"How about...Bellamy-Legrand. If we're going to live in a bloody castle, we might as well have a ridiculous double-barrelled name to go with it. And, um, if one day...*some*day... we wanted kids, then we'd all have the same names."

Darius's blue eyes went impossibly wide. "You'd want kids? With *me?*"

Joshua was tempted to roll his eyes and ask who else Darius thought he'd meant. But he could tell this was a landmark moment for him. He'd probably been told his whole life by his own vicious father that he'd never be a dad.

Joshua knew he'd be amazing, though. Caring came so naturally to him. If…

"If that was something you'd want?" Joshua asked. He was still young himself and hadn't been thinking of kids anytime soon. But Darius was older and might want to consider it sooner. Or not at all. Not everyone wanted children, after all.

But Joshua's heart leaped as Darius grinned, his eyes shining with unshed tears. "I'd love to think about kids. Someday. But not too far away? Once this has all calmed down. I think this place has the room for a lot more laughter and happiness."

Joshua's tummy swooped with joy. "I think so too."

Darius sighed and wrapped his arms around him, kissing him slowly, but with a heat burning behind it. For a while, they just stood together like that, the sun rising through the window. Joshua could tremble he was so happy. Darius wanted to start a family with him. They already had Zeus and Heph, but their own kids? Joshua didn't care if they went for adoption or surrogacy or what. He just knew that he and Darius could build a wonderful home for any child here.

Together.

"Let's get cleaned up," Darius said eventually, rubbing their temples together. "I need to see for myself that you're okay."

Joshua allowed him to lead him by the hand into the bathroom, Darius's thumb rubbing back and forth over his knuckles. It was a small possessive gesture that told Joshua he was going to be cared for – now and always. His heart sang. When Darius had scooped him up in his arms their first night together and growled 'Mine', that was all Joshua had wanted. It now felt so true it was like a physical thing that enveloped him.

He belonged to Darius, and Darius belonged to him. They

were each other's mind, body, and soul. And yet they were also stronger men on their own than they'd ever been before.

It was perfect.

Once Darius had closed the door, he got the hot tap running, noisily filling the copper tub. Dawn was starting to rise beyond the horizon, so they had just enough light to see by without putting any of the lamps on.

For the second time in the course of their relationship, Darius began to undress Joshua whilst the water flowed. This time, though, Darius peppered the gentle actions of his hands with little kisses against Joshua's throat, his wrists, his belly. There was no need to be nervous this time.

Darius pulled his ruby jumper over his head easily enough, but his fingers fumbled with the zip on his jeans. Joshua didn't wait for an invitation like he had the first night they'd made love. This time, he ran his fingers over the backs of Darius's hands, then eased them away to make short work of the button and fly. Once Darius kicked the last of his clothes and shoes away, Joshua turned the hot tap off. When he turned back around, Darius slipped his arms around his waist and rested his cheek on the top of Joshua's head.

They stood there in the steamy bathroom, locked in a tight embrace. Joshua would have thought them being naked would have made him feel vulnerable, but he knew he was completely safe.

"I love you so much," Darius mumbled in his hair. "If anything had happened to you-"

"But it didn't," said Joshua firmly. He looked up into Darius's glassy blue eyes and caressed the soft beard on his jaw.

"But-" Darius tried to insist. Joshua still had the last dregs of adrenaline lingering in his system, though.

"It didn't. I'm fine." He sighed and mustered up the best smile he could for his darling husband. "The house can be

repaired. The stuff we lost can be replaced. Our precious memories are safe. Even the rose bushes survived. No one got really hurt." He looked down and took one of Darius's bandaged wrists, biting his lip. "If anyone got hurt, it was you."

"I'm fine," Darius insisted gruffly, repeating Joshua's words back at him, but that wasn't going to work. He tried to pull his hand away, but Joshua wouldn't let him. He squeezed Darius's hand tightly and caught his lips in a kiss.

"No," said Joshua. "You need to let me look after you. I'm your husband, and I vowed to love you in sickness and in health." He turned Darius's hand over and kissed the palm. "Because I also love you so much," he added quietly. "Tonight scared me for a lot of reasons."

Darius hugged them chest to chest again, pressing his lips to Joshua's hair. "I'm so sorry you had to hear that. Nothing could have been further from the truth."

Joshua shook his head, though. "I know. You've got nothing to be sorry for." He smiled and kissed the twisted skin above Darius's heart. "It just…rattled me for a bit. But we don't have anyone forcing us to keep secrets now. We're going to get even better at this whole marriage thing."

Darius gave a big, shuddery sigh. "You've taught me how to be whole again."

"You've taught me how to be brave," Joshua added.

The kiss they shared was sweet and full of tenderness. Darius ran his hands up and down Joshua's back, cradling him against his chest. "Come on," he murmured.

Darius tugged Joshua's hand as he turned. Joshua watched him sink into the steamy water, leaning against the back of the copper bath. On the night of the terrible lake incident, Joshua had sat in this very bath and briefly, scandalously, wondered if Darius could have fitted in with him.

It turned out the answer was 'yes'.

Joshua hissed through his teeth as he stepped into the scalding water, but he was soon snuggled up between Darius's legs with his back pressed to his chest, Darius's large arms wrapped protectively around Joshua's torso.

"Thank you for coming back," Darius said in a low rumble. He pressed their cheeks together and breathed deeply, the lavender oil once more filling the air.

Joshua lifted his hands to cling on to Darius's forearms, the water noisily streaming off his own arms as he rubbed his fingers against Darius's coarse body hair. "Of course I came back," he said, leaning his face against Darius's. "This is my home."

Darius sighed and hugged Joshua tighter. "I think it might finally be *my* home, too."

Joshua looked over his shoulder, searching for his husband's mouth to kiss. Darius didn't disappoint. Their lips and tongues met like they were meant to belong together. Joshua couldn't imagine his mouth fitting anyone else's so perfectly.

And he never intended to find out.

Joshua gave a hum of disapproval as Darius lowered his hand into the water, tracing his fingers over Joshua's chest and stomach. "I'll replace the bandages later," Darius mumbled against his lips, caressing his fingers through the thick hair between Joshua's legs. "I need to feel you, to clean all this horror away."

Joshua sighed and leaned against Darius's burly chest, shuddering as Darius's fingers grazed over his cock. "Okay," he whispered. He wanted Darius to wash away the smell of smoke and the smears of blood on himself as well. He wanted them to start afresh, out of the chokehold of Victor Legrand.

Bloody hell. It hit him that this really was a step into the unknown. He was no longer a prisoner in his own home. But not in a terrifying way like when he'd first set foot into this cold and dark castle to be forced into marriage. He felt powerful. He and Darius were in control of their own destinies, and free to live and love how they pleased.

And Joshua had a pretty good idea of what would please him right now.

He squirmed against Darius as his husband massaged his scalp with product and kissed Joshua's neck. When their hair and skin were rinsed and the bathwater was starting to cool, Darius eased Joshua forward a little, then clambered out to fetch them fresh towels to dry off with. Joshua licked his lips, unashamedly looking at Darius's half-hard cock bouncing as he walked back towards the tub.

"Come here," Darius commanded gruffly. Joshua looked up to see his eyes blazing. Then he took the hand Darius offered out to him.

The plug pulled and the two of them as dry as they were going to get between all the kissing they were doing, Joshua followed Darius's lead and dropped his towel on the tiled floor to pick up later. Then he squeaked as Darius scooped him up in his arms.

"Your wrists," Joshua protested. Darius had pulled the soggy bandages off already, and his wrists were bright red and exposed again. But Joshua had to say they already looked better than they had been. Darius shook his head.

"Why would I care about that when I have you naked and slippery and beautiful in my arms?" He groaned and nuzzled his nose against Joshua's. "I need to make you come, *now*."

In turn, Joshua flung his arms around Darius's thick neck and grinned. "How very forward of you, *husband*," he said playfully.

Darius growled and caught Joshua's bottom lip between his teeth. "Get into my bed, *husband*."

Joshua captured Darius's mouth for a filthy kiss. "Take me there," he whispered back.

Darius went through the doorway and spread him on the mattress as the dawn light shone through the windows. Joshua was completely exposed as Darius kissed him and ran his large, calloused hand over Joshua's body.

He loved it.

"I want..." he uttered between kisses, caressing one of Darius's sensitive parts amongst his scarred flesh. The wounds on his wrists didn't seem so bad now they'd been washed, but if they also scarred, so be it. Joshua would love them as much as he loved every other inch of Darius's strong, powerful body.

"What do you want, petal?" Darius murmured.

Joshua swallowed, but he refused to be afraid. There was nothing to fear. "You." He cupped either side of Darius's face, encouraging him to look him in the eyes. "All of you. Inside me."

Darius licked his lips as his gaze trailed over Joshua's face. "Are you sure? You've been through so much tonight."

Joshua nodded. "That's *why* I want it. *Need* it. Need you." He kissed Darius's lips sweetly. "This is the start of our new life, and I want everything. I'm not afraid. You'd never hurt me."

"Never," Darius agreed emphatically. He'd slung his leg over Joshua's thighs and was rubbing his leaking cock against Joshua's hip as they kissed. "If you're sure, I'll make it so good for you, beautiful. I promise."

Joshua groaned and gripped Darius's thick hair. "Yes, yes. Darius. *Please.*"

Darius shifted so their dicks were rubbing together as he kissed along Joshua's neck, sucking at his pulse point. Joshua moaned, urging him on. "Mark me," he uttered, digging his fingers into Darius's back. He wanted to see some physical proof that he and Darius belonged to one another, no one else, so the next time he felt a wobble, he could dismiss it beyond any doubt.

Darius obliged, sucking and nipping and licking at Joshua's neck. "You're *mine*, Joshua," he growled, grabbing under Joshua's thigh and rubbing the back of his head as he kissed his lips again. "I love you *so* much. I'm never letting you go. Do you understand?"

Joshua whimpered and thrust his cock against Darius's. *"Yes,"* he moaned emphatically.

Darius gave him a firm kiss, then crawled up the bed to open one of the drawers in the bedside cabinet. He returned with a plain-looking bottle, squirting some clear liquid onto his thick fingers. He kissed Joshua's mouth again as he reached between them and began caressing Joshua's hole, probing the entrance.

A hint of panic rose in Joshua's chest, but he breathed against Darius's mouth.

"That's it," Darius rasped. "You're okay, beautiful. I've got you."

Joshua nodded and focused on relaxing his muscles as Darius pushed the first finger inside him. It wasn't as shocking as last time, and Joshua smiled as he was able to take the second digit quickly. He rocked against Darius's fingers. "Want your cock," he mumbled between kisses.

Darius laughed and rubbed their groins together again. "Yeah? How badly do you want it, darling? How much do you want me to be your first?"

Joshua let out a gasp that might even have been a sob. The idea that Darius was going to claim him like that was almost overwhelming. He screwed up his eyes, feeling the moisture collecting there. But they were happy tears. Tears of contentment and completion and from knowing he was exactly where he was supposed to be.

"You'll be my first and my last," Joshua promised, pressing their foreheads together and gripping Darius's thick biceps. "I don't want anyone else."

Darius bit Joshua's lip. "Oh, baby," he whispered. "No one else, not ever."

He removed his fingers, and Joshua watched as he slathered the lube over his red, straining cock. Taken over by a sudden urge, Joshua reached over and touched his fingertips to the shaft, feeling the cold liquid on the hot, hard skin. They didn't need to bother with a condom. Joshua hadn't had sex with anyone else, and Darius had mentioned he'd been given a full medical examination when he'd left the army. They were free to go bareback, just the way Joshua wanted it.

Darius had paused and was looking down at him when Joshua turned his eyes upwards to him. "I'm ready," he rasped.

Darius captured his lips for a tender kiss, then reached up to take one of the pillows Joshua's head wasn't on. "Here," he said, guiding it under Joshua's hips. "The angle will help."

Joshua nodded. He'd wondered what position Darius would want him in. Joshua liked the idea of being able to see Darius as they tried this for the first time. Darius gently pushed Joshua's knees up so he was holding them by his chest. Joshua loved how seriously Darius was taking his comfort. Then again, he wouldn't expect anything less.

Darius lined up the thick head of his cock, pressing the tip against Joshua's tight hole. For a second Joshua worried that it wouldn't fit after all, but then Darius was kissing him again. "Take a deep breath," he urged Joshua, breathing in tandem with him. Then as Joshua exhaled again, Darius breached him, surging inside and making Joshua's insides burn.

He cried out, dropping his knees to grab Darius's back.

"Fuck!" he gasped, tears in his eyes as he blinked rapidly. But then he took a few more breaths and did his best to relax. Darius had frozen at his outburst, but Joshua nodded and caressed the side of Darius's face before holding his knees once more. "I'm okay," he said truthfully. The burn was already fading. "You can move."

"Are you sure?" Darius asked in concern.

Joshua nodded emphatically. "It was just a shock. But it's getting better."

"Okay." Darius kissed him and grunted as he slowly sunk in deeper. "Fuck, darling. You feel so good. So perfect." He buried his face against Joshua's neck and shuddered. "I love you."

Joshua grinned, looking at the canopy of the four-poster bed before kissing Darius's neck. "I love you too, handsome."

Darius chuckled. "Thank you," he said quietly, accepting the compliment.

He felt Darius's scars against the inside of his leg and the palm of his hand. His heart leaped that Darius seemed to finally believe him when Joshua told him he was gorgeous and handsome and stunning and all the other true things.

Joshua gasped as Darius bottomed out. For a moment they just lay there, panting and clinging to one another, their skin damp with perspiration.

"Are you okay?" Darius asked, leaning back to look into Joshua's eyes.

Joshua nodded. "It's pretty big," he said, a giggle escaping from his throat. Darius laughed with him and nodded. "But it's good. I'm getting used to it."

"Take your time," Darius urged, although he was clearly straining from the effort not to move.

Joshua grinned and nipped at Darius's lip. "I'm planning on getting *very* used to you shoving that delicious thing up there, darling husband," he said huskily.

Darius raised his eyebrows in surprise, then rolled his hips. Joshua jerked at the sudden sensation, groaning loudly. It was as if Darius had stroked a bundle of electricity within him.

"F-fuck," he stammered, quivering. "What was that?"

Darius hummed and sucked his earlobe. "The good stuff. Can I move some more?"

Joshua nodded frantically. "I want everything," he whimpered.

Darius took a moment to kiss his lips passionately. "You can have it," he promised.

Slowly, Darius began to withdraw and then push back inside. Joshua bit his lip, feeling impossibly full. But as they rocked together, he became accustomed to the new experience, loving how stretched he felt from Darius's hot, throbbing cock. His own length bobbed and leaked, begging for attention, but for now, all Joshua could take was the sensation of Darius inside him, gradually gaining speed. The burn was different now, tantalising in a way Joshua wouldn't have expected. He wrapped his legs around Darius's back and clung to his shoulders, thrusting up every time Darius impaled him.

Darius's dark hair dripped with sweat, and he grimaced with concentration. He gasped and grunted as their climaxes built, kissing him and telling him how beautiful he was. "That's it, sweetheart," he rasped, digging his fingers into Joshua's flesh as his thrusts became frantic. "You're doing so well. You feel amazing."

"Come inside me," Joshua cried. He would have been amazed at his boldness if he wasn't so lost in the moment, his head dropped back into the pillows and his eyes screwed up tight as he clung to Darius like an anchor.

The bed shook as Darius rammed into him, both of them moaning and yelping. *"Joshua!"* he bellowed as he came.

Darius thrust deep inside him, pressing his whole body down on top of Joshua as he hugged him tightly. He shuddered, then released a contented sigh. "Holy fuck, baby. That was incredible."

Joshua's chest felt like it might burst with pride. All those hours he'd spent lying awake, fretting about his inexperience, and here the love of his life was telling him he'd done a good job.

"I'm glad you liked it," he said, nuzzling his nose against Darius's neck. But Darius shook his head, turning to look Joshua in the eye.

"Not 'like'. You're amazing. So sweet and gorgeous. I can't believe we get to do this whenever we want."

Joshua grinned and kissed his husband's lips. "Well, I already told you I want to have sex all the time."

Darius laughed and kissed him again, moving his hips. Joshua liked the feeling of him slowly softening inside him. Darius hummed and slowly dragged Joshua's bottom lip through his teeth. "How do you want me to make you come, beautiful?"

Joshua tingled all over, feeling so sexy and deliciously at Darius's mercy. "I want to watch you suck me off," he whispered, trying not to blush. But Darius clearly loved his sweet coyness, his eyes burning dark with lust despite already having come.

"Anything for you, petal."

He gently withdrew, then trailed kisses down Joshua's chest, sucking and grazing his teeth against Joshua's nipples, raising them into hard nubs. Joshua moaned and wriggled, relishing having Darius's full attention on him. He felt like he had a hot spotlight shining down on him, but for the first time in his life, he didn't want to shy away. He was done hiding in the shadows. He wanted Darius – and the whole world – to truly see him. Not just for his beauty but for his soul as well.

Darius stroked the insides of Joshua's legs, easing them apart as he kissed the soft flesh of his tummy. Joshua ran his fingers through Darius's thick, damp hair, crying out when he finally, mercifully, wrapped his lips over Joshua's hard length.

He thrust up, Darius encouraging him with a firm hand on his hip. The other fondled Joshua's heavy balls as he swallowed Joshua's cock again and again. It wasn't going to take him long. He was so close to the edge. They worked in perfect rhythm as Joshua let go of Darius's hair with one hand to grope at the bedsheets for purchase. "Darius!" he shouted in warning, but Darius didn't slow. He coaxed Joshua masterfully into his explosive climax, sucking even harder as Joshua arched his back and bellowed into the otherwise quiet house.

Joshua struggled for breath as he blinked, his entire body shaking. But then Darius was there, lying next to him and hugging him close. "You're okay," he rasped, kissing his forehead. "I've got you."

Joshua was confused until he realised he was crying. He was practically sobbing.

He clung to Darius and nodded. "I am okay," he insisted between hiccups. "I loved it. I love *you*. I'm sorry. I don't know what's wrong with me."

Darius laughed kindly and stroked Joshua's hair and back, pressing his lips to his temple. "It's been a long, *stressful* day. It's normal to need emotional release." He frowned. "At least, that's what my CO always told me. I never believed her, though, always bottling things in." He sighed deeply, hugging Joshua tightly. "So look at you being a responsible role model for your husband."

Joshua chuckled wetly and pawed at Darius's back, trying

to hug him even tighter. "I don't want you thinking I didn't like it. Next time I'll be better."

Darius scowled at him. "No, baby," he said with a slight growl. "You don't have to be anything other than yourself. And if you ever don't enjoy anything, you tell me right away. But I believe you that these are happy tears. I love every little bit of you." He smiled and brushed some of the wetness away. "Even the messy bits."

Joshua half-laughed, half-cried as he hugged Darius again. "We need another bath," he agreed.

But Darius shook his head. "We need to sleep. You're absolutely perfect. Just lie here in my arms with me."

How could Joshua resist such a request? He already felt miles better after a good cry, and Darius's strong arms were so safe and warm. They curled up under the duvet, breathing deeply, unbothered by the morning light streaming around the curtains or the birdsong drifting in through the closed windows. There would be plenty of time to clean up later, both themselves and their home. But for now, Joshua relaxed, feeling a kind of freedom he'd never known as sleep crept over him.

This was the start of the rest of his life, and he was going to share it with Darius.

He couldn't think of anything he wanted more.

24

DARIUS

THE SPRING SUNLIGHT BEAMED DOWN ON THE NEWLY blooming grounds of Thorncliff. Darius inhaled deeply, letting the warm, scented air fill his lungs. Away from the noisy construction work inside the house, he felt a sense of peace and calm.

This was exactly where he was meant to be.

Zeus ran excitedly around his feet as he strolled leisurely along the winding paths, following the sound of Joshua's gentle chattering to himself. Green buds were beginning to peek from the rich earth, showing the fruits of Joshua's hard labour, and overhead the trees were blossoming with a vigour Darius hadn't seen in years. The air hummed with birds and insects, the ecosystem rejuvenated and thriving. Darius felt connected and alive – a far cry from how he'd been hiding in the shadows before Joshua had burst into his life.

There was no sign out here now of the damage the mob had caused. Darius was glad Joshua no longer had to be reminded of their invasion every time he came out here. Unlike Thorncliff itself at present.

However, Darius knew that in time, the castle would not only be repaired, but it would start transforming with new life as they refurbished rooms that had been neglected for years. It was no longer a pile of bricks that he'd been forced to live in when the army couldn't keep him anymore. It was his and Joshua's home, their sanctuary. Darius couldn't wait for the builders and electricians and all the rest to be done so they could start enjoying their new and upgraded surroundings.

They already had broadband and Wi-Fi installed. That had been the very first thing Darius had organised, incensed with how easy the task had ultimately been. Yes, this was a listed building, but that didn't mean they couldn't work around that and make the damn place functional and liveable. Darius couldn't believe he hadn't realised his father had been orchestrating that delay. Bloody, traitorous Martin. Last Darius had heard, he'd got a plea bargain and fled to Spain.

Good riddance.

The castle was now bustling with life in a way Darius couldn't remember, not even when his mother had been alive, god rest her soul. She'd always had Victor's shadow looming over her, of course. Now he was safely locked away, awaiting trial on his many crimes. He was accused of not only attempted murder, grievous bodily harm, arson, and property damage, but after the police had got a hold of his company records, it transpired that he'd been ripping off contractors like Christopher for decades. All that he'd skimmed off the top was being tallied up, and it looked like there was going to be a hell of a lot of work to do to try and compensate everyone.

Darius was glad. He loathed his father's business, and this was the perfect escape he needed. The castle was completely in Darius's name, and he was now free to access his mother's inheritance, not to mention that he wanted to as well. He also had army compensation allowance and pension, meaning he didn't have to worry about work for the immediate future. He happily handed over his part in the business for the accountants to sell off in order to recoup some of the losses.

Darius breathed in deeply, tasting the sweet spring air as he stopped to admire the work Joshua had done on the pond already. It had some way to go, but the hole had been dug and the lining put in. The groundwork was there, much like the rest of the property. And for Darius's life.

For the first time since joining the army, he had taken a good long look at himself and tried to figure out what he wanted to do with his life. It had been several weeks since the mob attack and Victor's arrest, so he'd had plenty of time to think about what he wanted to do to occupy his time. He certainly didn't want to exist off his mother's inheritance. Joshua had already made noises about studying horticulture and maybe taking up gardening around the local area. Darius wanted to be useful, too.

It had been Joshua that had eventually pointed out that Darius was his best when he was caring for others, and he didn't just mean himself. Now that Darius had stopped being a recluse, he realised his favourite thing about running his household was working with the staff, and he'd excelled at nurturing the soldiers under his care when he'd been a captain.

So he was looking into what he could do in the community with youth clubs and other organisations, perhaps looking to become a guidance counsellor. But he also liked the idea of maybe getting a qualification in something outdoorsy that he could work with teenagers too. He missed the vigorous physical training he'd had in the army, and liked the idea of pushing himself again in that way.

Now that a certain someone had helped him to love his body again, he no longer looked in the mirror and saw a failure. He saw a survivor.

He saw the man Joshua loved.

His heart panged as he watched Joshua chattering away to a butterfly that had landed on a nearby branch of a rose bush. The buds were small and pale pink, but they were coming along nicely.

Just like Joshua.

He was a different person to the trembling man who had first arrived at the castle for that sham wedding. Now, he was confident and content and bursting with life. Darius woke up next to him every day, grateful that a cruel twist of fate had been just the thing they'd needed to find true love.

Darius felt an unexpected flutter of nerves. He tried telling himself he was being ridiculous, but the truth was he'd spent weeks going over this decision. He was sure he was doing the right thing, but he still wasn't quite used to wearing his heart on his sleeve. It was so much easier to lock everything away, but Joshua deserved better than that. *Darius* deserved better than that. So he looked down at Zeus, who wagged his tail supportively, and decided it was now or never.

It was a perfect Joshua moment. He was smiling and covered in dirt, bringing life where the soil had once been barren. His cheeks were pink from the spring breeze gently whipping through the grounds every now and again, and his white-blond hair was glinting in the sunlight.

How could Darius doubt he was doing the right thing? He was overwhelmed with the love he felt for this man. They had both changed so much together, blossoming into their best selves.

There was only one thing left to do.

"Hey, petal," he said as he and Zeus approached.

Joshua had been deeply focused, and he startled at Darius's voice. But then his face split into a delighted grin. "Hey, gorgeous." He pulled his garden gloves off and jumped up to give Darius a kiss. Perfect. That was exactly where Darius wanted him. "How's it going?"

Darius wrapped his arms around his waist. "Good, good. I just thought I'd come see you," Darius said, playing it as cool as he could with his heart hammering in his chest.

"Aww, slacker," Joshua teased, tickling Darius's side.

Not only had he memorised exactly where Darius's sensitive spots were amidst his scar tissue, but he had also ordered bio-oil that they'd been massaging into his skin at least once a day, and Joshua was very good at nagging Darius to do his physiotherapy. Darius hadn't felt this good in years. Even his injuries from the night of the mob attack were fading fast under Joshua's care. It was in little ways like that which Darius knew how much Joshua cared.

"I'll have you know I'm very busy and important in that castle," Darius said pompously, playing into Joshua's teasing. "I'm bossing *lots* of people around."

"Don't you mean Camille is?" Joshua asked with an arched eyebrow.

Darius snorted, nodding in defeat. "And she's *loving* it."

Joshua took Darius's hands in his and swung them back and forth, rubbing his thumbs against the almost healed red marks around his wrists. "It's okay. I don't need an excuse to see my husband."

Yeah, about that... Darius wanted to say. Instead, he cleared his throat and smiled.

"Actually, I did want to ask you something. If you've got a minute?"

Joshua stood on his tiptoes to peck a little kiss on Darius's lips. "Only if you're quick. I'm very busy and important, don't you know?"

He waggled his eyebrows and laughed, but Darius's insides flipped. Maybe this wasn't the right time? He should probably wait. He was being stupid…

"Oh, wait, hey," Joshua said, suddenly serious and tugging Darius's sleeve. "I was kidding. What's all that worry for? What's wrong?" He rubbed Darius's arm and smiled sweetly at him, his brown eyes imploring.

Some of the tension eased from Darius's chest. He was being a complete idiot. What did he have to be afraid of?

"Sorry," he said, shaking his head. "Nothing's wrong."

He didn't need to be nervous. But the butterflies were still as real in his stomach as the one on Joshua's rose bush.

Darius exhaled, trying to collect his thoughts, glancing down at Zeus. The little dog seemed to know something important was about to happen, so he was sitting quietly, wagging his tail next to Darius's feet. Joshua recaptured Darius's attention by squeezing his hands, frowning as Darius met his gaze.

"Are you okay?" Joshua asked.

Darius let out a laugh and nodded. "Yes, I'm great. I just… I love you so much."

Joshua visibly melted, tilting his head to one side as a warm smile crept over his face. "I love you too, handsome," he said sincerely. He reached up and caressed the side of Darius's face.

Darius had trimmed his beard especially neatly for the occasion, although he always tried to make himself presentable for Joshua these days. He wondered if Joshua had noticed he was wearing the same shirt and trousers as he had for that night at the opera, just without the jacket. Or the aftershave Joshua had bought him to replace the one he'd worn for years. This one was so much fresher, like the ocean, but with a hint of spice. The scent made Darius think of the two of them now, as it often mingled in with their natural musk as they made love.

His throat was tight as he turned his head to kiss Joshua's palm. "I want to do this right," he said.

Joshua frowned, clearly confused by Darius's words. But then he gasped and jerked his hands to cover his mouth, tears springing in his beautiful brown eyes.

Because Darius had just bent down on one knee.

He knew he was right to trust his instincts. The look on Joshua's face was one he would treasure for the rest of his life. Everyone deserved a real proposal. To have that moment when they knew their partner would do anything to make them happy.

"Darius, w-what are you doing?" Joshua spluttered.

Darius carefully retrieved the ring box from his trouser pocket, cracking the box open with a snap to reveal the two custom-made bands nestled within. "I'm asking you to marry me, Joshua Bellamy-Legrand."

Joshua hiccuped, looking between the rings and Darius's face, tears streaming down his face. "But we're already married?"

Darius shook his head. "That doesn't count. We didn't know each other then. It wasn't a celebration. It was a punishment. I want to show you that I intend to love you *forever*. I want to share a day of happiness with the people closest to us. I want us to both wear a ring that means something, not some cheap crap that was forced on us. I want to legally change our names, like you said."

Joshua looked at the silver band on his finger that was already tarnishing. Then he peered into the box Darius was holding up. He'd had two matching platinum bands made, each intricately decorated with roses, leaves, and thorns. Joshua gasped and glanced at the pride and joy of his garden, his rose bushes, then back to Darius.

"Are you sure?" Joshua asked.

Darius laughed and stood up, taking Joshua's hands between his own, the ring box held preciously between his finger and thumb. "More than anything. I know you've worried that we fell in love because we were forced into this marriage. I want to marry you again *because* I love you more than anyone in this whole damn world."

Joshua sniffed and nodded. "A fresh start," he whispered, standing on his tiptoes to press his lips sweetly to Darius's. "Yes, Darius. Yes, I'll marry you again. I'll marry you *properly.* And this time, I'll be married to you for the rest of our lives."

Darius finally choked out a sob, first hugging Joshua, then capturing his mouth for a passionate kiss. They were both laughing and crying as Darius removed the offending old ring from Joshua's finger and replaced it with the rose one. Then Joshua did the same for him. Zeus broke his silence and began barking, running in circles around his daddies' legs, wagging his tail furiously.

"I know we don't legally need to have another wedding," Darius said. He'd put the ring box and old bands back in his pocket, then wrapped his arms around Joshua's waist. Joshua placed his palms against Darius's chest, beaming up at him as they rocked on the spot. "But I thought we could get dressed up, say a few vows, have a bit of a party?"

"I'd love that," Joshua said with a big grin, still trembling as he wept happily. "Oh, Darius. I would never have dreamed we'd end up here, with our own, *real* happily ever after."

"Neither did I," Darius admitted. "But there's nowhere else I'd rather be in the whole world."

"Me neither." Joshua leaned up to capture Darius's mouth for a long kiss, full of promise for their lives to come.

EPILOGUE

JOSHUA – THREE MONTHS LATER

JOSHUA FELT UTTERLY RIDICULOUS, BUT HE HAD TO ADMIT HE kind of loved it. He blushed as the couple of dozen people cheered for him, waving from his vantage point.

Hephaestus, on the other hand, tossed his head back and lapped up the adoration like he'd been born to be adored. If Joshua had told himself that one day he would ride into his wedding ceremony on horseback, he would never have believed it in a million years. Yet here he was, enjoying every preposterous second.

He grinned. Darius's idea of 'a few vows' had got a little out of hand once Mrs Weatherby, Camille, and Bartholomew had started getting involved. The blooming garden was full of smiling faces of the staff, most of whom Darius and Joshua thought of as family members now rather than employees. The love and dedication Joshua and Darius had seen from them in the wake of the house invasion was nothing short of astonishing.

Joshua's dad was there, of course, as well as some old friends who used to know his mum. Joshua had also made some new mates in the local village these past months. He waved at a gaggle from the pub he and Darius frequented, as well as the ladies from his weekly keep-fit class. He blushed as they all cheered and clapped rowdily, but he refused to be embarrassed.

This was the new Joshua Bellamy-Legrand, and he didn't hide from the spotlight.

Mrs Weatherby had organised a stunning floral arch in the small courtyard where everyone was seated. Those roses were imported, leaving the ones Joshua had grown in the garden to add naturally to the beautiful scene. Camille had cooked up a feast for them later, including a three-tier wedding cake decorated with all Joshua's favourite flavours of macarons and perfect tiny roses made from sugar. Bartholomew had been in charge of transforming the newly repaired and decorated dining room into their wedding reception room. All three of them were scrubbed up in their Sunday best, waving at Joshua as Hephaestus clip-clopped down the aisle. Mrs Weatherby dabbed her eyes with a handkerchief.

Joshua had initially thought their second ceremony would be a small, private affair. But Darius had insisted he have the wedding of his dreams. Their tailor, Strutton, had been more than delighted to come back and design them perfectly fitted suits, this time making them bespoke, no expense spared.

Darius had insisted that his mother would have wanted some of her inheritance to be spent on this day. Besides, Darius was already training to be a youth counsellor and had started working with teenagers at a rock-climbing centre, so he now had a salary coming in. Joshua was just starting to take on the first clients of his own, just doing basic gardening. But one day he was going to become a landscape architect and was going to start studying for his degree in the autumn.

Having been the boy who felt despair when he thought about his options after school, Joshua was now a man with such a bright future it was almost blinding.

His heart sang as Hephaestus proudly came to a halt by Darius's side in front of the officiant who would guide them through their ceremonial vows. Legally, nothing would change. But everyone there that day knew that *this* was really Joshua and Darius's wedding, not that horrible day in the cramped, dark office with Victor sneering over them.

Darius's father had already been convicted of his many crimes, his confidence that his lawyers would be able to get him off turning out to be completely unfounded. He was the one who was hidden away now where he couldn't hurt anyone, leaving Joshua and Darius to step into the light, refusing to go back into the shadows ever again.

Strutton had outdone himself, a fact he clearly knew as he preened from the audience, applauding with the rest as Joshua took one last opportunity to smile at them from Hephaestus's back. Joshua looked down at Darius, appreciating their tailor's work for himself as his heart fluttered, and he felt a little dizzy.

His husband still did that to him, even after all this time together. But especially today.

Strutton had gone for a silvery-grey palette for them both. Joshua with a lighter tailcoat and darker waistcoat. Darius the other way around. They both had silvery top hats, black canes, and slightly different striped ties in the same colour scheme. Both their breast pockets proudly sported a fresh red rose, courtesy of Joshua's garden. Joshua was wearing the silver rose cufflinks Darius had gifted him, whilst Joshua had bought a lucky horseshoe pair for Darius.

Naturally, Darius was bulging against his suit, whilst Joshua's fit him more slimly. But they both looked the very

THORN IN HIS SIDE

best versions of themselves, obviously a pair, but celebrating their differences too.

Joshua remembered how at the opera he'd thought people must have assumed they weren't a couple, feeling they looked incongruous together. Now he proudly held his head high, knowing everyone would be under no doubt that they were meant to be together.

Darius was breathtakingly handsome as he smiled up at Joshua. He always kept his hair and beard trimmed now, no longer looking like that wild beast Joshua had first taken him to be. He offered his hand to assist Joshua in his dismount, giving Joshua a little reassuring squeeze as he did. Paulo stepped in then, looking dashing in his three-piece suit, leading Hephaestus to the side so Joshua and Darius could have some room to share their vows. The horse whinnied to a round of applause and laughter, fully milking his moment until the end.

"You look beautiful," Darius whispered.

"You too," Joshua said back.

He was finally there, standing opposite the man he loved, holding hands amidst the rose garden he'd been nurturing for months, surrounded by their friends and family. Even Zeus was with them, on his best behaviour at Mrs Weatherby's feet, wearing a little bow tie on his collar.

This was Joshua's whole world. It probably wasn't that big compared to a lot of people's, but to him, it was everything. His and Darius's rose and thorn rings glinted in the summer sunshine as they held hands between their chests. They wouldn't be exchanging rings again today, but they had written some vows to say to one another. The crowd fell into rapt silence as the officiant stepped forward.

This wasn't the same impatient man they'd had last time. Joshua and Darius had found a local council member who specialised in LGBT ceremonies. She was a lesbian in her early fifties who was all smiles as she stood before Joshua and Darius, looking between them proudly.

"We are here today to celebrate the union of Joshua and Darius Bellamy-Legrand," she said loudly and clearly, clasping her hands together. "Although their marriage is already recognised by the laws of this country, they have chosen to come together today to celebrate their love with those dearest to them."

"And so they *should!*" Mrs Weatherby gave an audible sniff, and several people chuckled.

Joshua grinned, his heart light and his eyes damp. He didn't care how informal the ceremony was. He wanted to hear people's laughter and applause. He wanted this day to be loud and joyous, just like the rest of his life would hopefully be.

"The couple are going to say their renewed vows to one another, in the presence of you all." The officiant gestured to Darius. "Darius, would you like to go first?"

Darius smiled, his blue eyes shining. Joshua was glad he wasn't the only one getting mushy. He loved it when his big, tough husband showed his vulnerable side. It proved how far they'd come since they'd met.

"Joshua Bellamy-Legrand," Darius began, rubbing his thumb against Joshua's wedding ring. "I promise to always protect you. To shelter you from the storm, in sickness and in health. You brought the light back into my life and made my heart start beating again. Fate brought us together, but love gave us a home in which to build our future. I love you, petal. I can't wait to spend the rest of my life watching you bloom."

Joshua bit his lip and shook his head with a laugh as the tears spilled from his eyes. He could hear several people blowing their noses. He didn't let go of Darius's hands, though. He just let the tears run down his cheeks as he smiled.

It was his turn.

"Darius Bellamy-Legrand," he said, his throat thick but doing his best to keep his voice steady. "My love for you started as a small, delicate seed. You kept me safe until I was strong enough to stand on my own, but our love became more and more entwined. I couldn't imagine my life without you. I promise to love you in sickness and in health, for richer or poorer. You are perfect just the way you are, and I can't wait to tell you that every day for the rest of our lives."

He felt his lip wobble as a single tear traced down Darius's cheek, so Joshua leaned over to place a quick kiss on his lips.

"Hang on, not yet," the officiant cried with a laugh, wiping her own face. It seemed like everyone in the congregation chuckled as they dabbed their eyes and sniffed. Joshua glanced shyly at them as Hephaestus snorted and scuffed his hoof. "See, even the horse is telling you to stop making everyone cry."

Joshua and Darius beamed at each other as they both brushed the other's tears away with their thumbs.

"Sorry," said Joshua with a grin.

"Nothing to be sorry for," Darius murmured, the happiness clear on his face.

"In the eyes of the law, Darius and Joshua were already married," continued the officiant loudly. "Now, in the presence of this congregation, their union has been confirmed in all our hearts. Darius, Joshua, you may *now* kiss your husband."

She arched her eyebrow with a lopsided grin. The congregation burst into applause and rose to their feet as Joshua and Darius hugged each other tightly, their kiss deep and passionate.

There would be many hours of partying to come and many months to finish all the refurbishments in the castle. But then there would be many years to spend together, their lives joined as one, their destiny to walk side by side as their family blossomed and grew with children and beloved pets.

But one thing was for sure, and that was Joshua had found his soulmate, his other half, the thorn to his rose that was so differently shaped to him and yet made him feel complete. He and Darius were a fairy tale come true, and Joshua couldn't wait to start their happily ever after.

THANK you for reading Joshua and Darius's story! If you would like to discover more of my books, including free short stories, please visit www.helenjuliet.com.

Thank you to: my invaluable beta reader, Amy; sharp-eyed editors Tanja and Meg; cover artist Cate Ashwood (who has the patience of a saint and made my favourite cover yet!); cheerleaders, Ed, Amelia, and John; loving husband; and fur babies Arya and Tyrion.

ALSO AVAILABLE

Sparkle to the Season

Aedan wants everything to be just perfect for his boyfriend of seven years, Matt, for their first Christmas in their new home. But it's Christmas Eve and he's running out of time to create an idyllic winter wonderland. To make matters worse, Matt's present hasn't arrived.

A misunderstanding means the holiday might be ruined before it even begins. But little does Aedan know, Matt has a surprise or two of his own up his Christmas sweater sleeve.

Sparkle to the Season is a short, free and steamy sequel to Glitter on the Garland, although it can be read as a standalone, so long as you enjoy happy ever afters.

Click here to get the Sparkle to the Season eBook

ABOUT THE AUTHOR

Helen Juliet is a contemporary MM romance author living in London with her husband and two balls of fluff that occasionally pretend to be cats. She began writing at an early age, later honing her craft online in the world of fanfiction on sites like Wattpad. Fifteen years and over a million words later, she sought out original MM novels to read. By the end of 2016 she had written her first book of her own, and in 2017 she achieved her lifelong dream of becoming a fulltime author.

Helen also writes contemporary American MM romance as HJ Welch.

You can contact Helen Juliet via social media:
Newsletter (with FREE original stories) – https://www. subscribepage.com/helenjuliet
Website – www.helenjuliet.com
Facebook Group – Helen's Jewels
Facebook Page – @helenjulietauthor
Instagram – @helenjwrites
Twitter – @helenjwrites

9 781916 027282